are we
having
fun
yet?

Hopscotch & Handbags: The Truth About Being a Girl

My Family and Other Disasters

The Reluctant Bride: One Woman's Journey (Kicking and Screaming) Down the Aisle

Bookworm: A Memoir of Childhood Reading

Praise for *Are We Having Fun Yet*

'Will hit home with anyone who hates the verb "to

'This r̶u̶.̶it̶ by the due date.

wincing and ̶

'You'll love this fictio̶n̶. ̶rary app.

packed with laugh-out-lou̶

'Funny and frank' *Harper's Bazaar*

'Hilarious ... will strike a chord with every parent who's ever forgotten about World Book Day' *Red*

'A work of genius, managing to be very funny, exceptionally warm and thoroughly thought-provoking all at the same time' *Scotsman*

'Utterly, utterly perfect and brilliant – I think it is, simply, a new classic, and the book every woman will be able to trust to make her happy when she picks it up. Lucy Mangan is a fucking genius. SO MUCH WISDOM IN IT. SO MUCH ANGER. SO MUCH LOVE. SO MUCH LOL. It's just exquisite' Caitlin Moran

'Such a perfectly precise rendering of life with small children, I felt like I was reading my own diary from my first years of motherhood – had I been cleverer, wittier and more intent on finding the joy and hope and humour amid all the mess of life. So deeply relatable, every parent presently in the trenches of family life should read it, to feel less alone (and all of their child-free friends, to explain why their formerly fun and capable BF is now always exhausted, late and grubby)' Meg Mason

are we having fun yet?

Lucy Mangan

SOUVENIR
PRESS

This paperback edition first published in 2022

First published in Great Britain in 2021 by
Souvenir Press
an imprint of Profile Books Ltd
29 Cloth Fair
London EC1A 7JQ

www.profilebooks.com

Copyright © Lucy Mangan, 2021

10 9 8 7 6 5 4 3 2 1

Typeset in Elena by MacGuru Ltd
Printed and bound in Great Britain by
CPI Group (UK) Ltd, Croydon, CRO 4YY

The moral right of the author has been asserted.

A CIP catalogue record for this book is available from the British Library.

ISBN 978 1 78816 107 7
eISBN 978 1 78283 471 7

For Theresa, Emily and Sally.
Great mothers. Great friends.

Wednesday, 4 January

'Get up! Get up!'

We have overslept. It's good to start the new day – and in this case a new term and a new year – with a familiar failure, I think. Eases you back into routine.

'What's for breakfast?' asks my seven-year-old ('Seven and a half and a bit,' says his voice in my head) as he slides bonelessly from his bottom bunk onto the floor for another five-minute doze.

It was going to be homemade porridge. It is now going to be 'Toast. Or bread on the walk if you don't hurry up.'

'Can I have jam?' asks Thomas's five-year-old sister as she vaults from the upper bunk and lands, like an Olympic gymnast, inches from her brother's supine form. 'Or honey? Or jam and honey?'

I inwardly calculate the time saved by them happily motoring through sugar-laden breakfast versus the time shaved off their lifespans by the Type 2 diabetes that surely beckons, and hang the morning's first bagful of compromise on my mental Peg of Weary Resignation.

'You can have jam,' I tell Evie. It's fruit, and the raspberry seeds are probably fibre or something.

Eventually the children are dressed and eating ('Over the plate! Over the plate!') round the table while I check their bags against the equipment list the school sent home before the holidays, and try to keep track of infant conversation.

'D'you think,' muses Thomas, 'it would hurt more to be hit on the head by a mallet or a hammer?'

'Uh ...' I reply, transferring one of the three trainers Evie has in her bag to the matching single one in Thomas's.

'It would depend,' says their father, suddenly sweeping downstairs. He is freshly suited and booted, ready for a day's work in chambers after his leisurely shower, and to give us the benefit of his fatherly wisdom – which apparently does not encompass having the sense to take a shorter shower at times of domestic punctuality crisis. 'It would depend on how hard you hit the head in question with each. But the respective forces being equal, the hammer would pain it more. And why?'

The children, their young minds still energetically curious, find a barrister's constant willingness to perform a deep dive on every passing conundrum exhilarating. I find it less so.

'Because metal's harder than wood!' says Thomas.

'Exactly.'

'Else how would a woodcutter cut the tree down?' says Evie, triumphantly.

I am torn between praising this impeccable piece of reasoning and protesting against the violent tone of the discussion. So I say nothing. This is always my preferred strategy, particularly before noon.

His parental responsibilities discharged, Richard turns to me. 'I'm going to work now,' he announces. 'Where's my bag, phone, travelcard, glasses, shoes, tie and documents for the thing today?'

I know where all these things are. I could lead the way to them blindfold. He turns his head from side to side as if expecting them to materialise before him in the kitchen. I say nothing, but sort of wish he was dead.

He gives up (gives in?) and goes.

'I'm full,' Thomas says, exhaling in loud satisfaction and blowing toast crumbs everywhere.

'I'm not,' says Evie, reaching for another slice, smearing it and large parts of herself with jam and pushing the whole thing into her mouth like a log into a sawmill.

'Too bad,' I say, hauling them upstairs to the bathroom. 'Teeth.'

Somehow – I presume courtesy of my jam manoeuvres – we leave in time to catch Fiona and David on the way to school.

David runs on ahead with my two while Fiona and I walk for a bit in silence. It is broken by Fiona saying morosely, 'Half past fucking eight and I'm already knackered.'

Fiona says most things morosely, which is one of the reasons she is my best friend. The others are:

a) She is, like my parents, northern. This grounds me. She and her husband Iain moved to London a couple of years ago because Iain, a university lecturer, got a job at UCL. She hates it here. But to be fair, as she points out, she hated the north too.

b) She lives just a few doors down. After children, adult friendships become predominantly geography-based. Can they pick up the kids from school in an emergency? Can you nip round whenever you fancy or do you have to carve out the time to Make a Trip? Does a playdate involve more travelling than hours freed? Can they, basically, assist you in the fight to put some slack in what you increasingly inaccurately call your system or not? Whether you genuinely like the person or not barely matters. Though I do like Fiona. Love her, actually.

c) Our first conversation was about having hated our NCT classes. We were the only people in our groups who had come for comradeship in the coming adversity rather than because we believed in natural childbirth. 'I'd have had mine sponsored by ICI if I could,' was and remains Fiona's last word on the subject.

d) Our second conversation was about the apocalypse. Like me, she is both a natural pessimist and extreme catastrophiser, and this makes us a great comfort to each other. We spend much of our time together (as indeed we do apart) planning for what we consider to be the inevitable. She's basically planning to hijack a helicopter ('You need to get *up*, Dashwood. No point going across. They'll be closing borders. There'll be

3

marauding hordes. Up. Up is where you need to go. To a hill fort, ideally. Have some sense, do') while I am concentrating more on the necessary post-apocalyptic skills: farming, first aid, filtration systems, that kind of thing. Together we will make a formidable team.

e) She will happily join me in a glass of wine at any time of day.

f) David, though he is in Thomas's class at school, gets on with both of my children. This alone would make him a pearl beyond price even without the preternaturally calm and stoic attitude with which he faces the world. His ability to spread peace through a harassed home and heart is a gift as estimable as it is bizarre. I adore him. He inherits at least part of this talent from his father Iain. Iain does not speak. No, that's not quite right – Iain does not initiate conversation. He will happily, if never lengthily, respond once someone else starts, but he will equally happily sit in silence until and unless they do. He is simply never moved, himself, to speech. Sometimes Fiona tests him by not saying anything when he comes home from work and seeing how long it takes him to kick things off. So far she has always cracked before he has even noticed anything might be remotely amiss. It drives her mad.

When it gets too much, I remind her that she would be no better off with the opposite situation. Richard's inability to have an unexpressed thought drives me insane. 'Never a moment's pause!' I tell her. 'You've got too much peace in your house? Cry me a river!' It is good to trade perspectives like this. We theorised once that we should swap furies – she could be angry with Richard on my behalf and I on hers with Iain, in a kind of psychological Freecycle – and enjoy harmony inside our homes. But, alas, the human mind is not as fungible as secondhand bikes or courgette gluts. So on we go.

4

g) She is a GP, which saves me having to go to the doctor. Apart from getting the kids vaccinated, who has time to go to the doctor?

'How was Christmas At His Mother's?' I say, as we turn the final corner before school.

'It was Christmas At His Mother's,' she says, by way of full explanation.

'Ah. And what did she give you this time?'

'A lipstick.'

The first time Fiona ever met Mrs Slater, as Iain's fiancée, the woman gave her a blouse. It was stained, the wrong size, and had a button missing. 'Thank you so much,' said Fiona the Desperately Polite Fiancée, 'but I'm afraid it won't fit.'

'It was only three pounds in Oxfam,' said her proto in-law. 'So you won't be too out of pocket.' And she held out her hand for the money. Fiona the Inwardly Convulsing Fiancée paid up. Relations have deteriorated substantially since then. The last time Mother-in-law came to visit she brought her daughter-in-law a single pleather man's glove that she had found on the floor in Boots.

'What am I supposed to do with this?' Fiona said.

'It's a perfectly good glove,' said her MIL. 'You can carry it in one hand and nobody will know you don't have the other.'

'A lipstick? That's better than usual,' I say encouragingly.

'It was one of her old ones.'

'You mean ... used?'

'Yep. She gave me a used lipstick. "I thought it would be just your colour," she said, like the absolute sociopath she is.'

'Wow.'

'Yep.'

'*Wow.*'

'*Yep.*'

Not for the first time I reflect on my good fortune in avoiding the whole in-law thing. Richard was a late, only and wholly adored child, born long after his parents had given up hope of a family, and they died when he was in his early twenties, before we'd even met. I'm sure they wouldn't have approached even the foothills of Mrs Slater's towering monstrosity, but the older I get, the more I crave simplicity and long only to stream-line my life – two things to which a partner's parents, anecdotal evidence at least tells us, rarely seem to contribute overall.

Just before we arrive at the school gates we bump into Céline who has just dropped off Romilly, ten, and Olivier, seven – Thomas and David's classmate. 'I cannot stop,' she says, stopping to kiss us both because Céline is French and, unlike the rest of us, considers there to be standards of civility and civilisation to be upheld even at eight thirty on the first Monday back at school. 'My au pair is drunk again so I must call her parents and have her taken away.'

'Like so much rubbish?' says Fiona. The ruthlessness of Céline's way of living is of perennial fascination to us.

'Well,' says Céline, rolling her perfectly made-up eyes, 'she is a rubbish au pair. She does not 'elp but 'inders.'

Though Céline definitely takes much less shit than any of us, this is not quite as cold-blooded as it sounds. Céline depends on having an au pair because her husband Philippe is a manage-ment consultant who is for ever flying off around the world to, uh, management consult? consultantly manage? Her parents are in France, Philippe's widowed mother has dementia and Céline herself is a lawyer who works all hours. (After years of being sexually harassed at work in the UK, she started special-ising in sexual-harassment cases and has worked her way up to big class-action type things and is now feared throughout the corporate world. 'I don't understand why your men are such peegs,' she once said. 'In France, of course they want to have sex with you but they are charming and if you don't want to, *bien*. Everybody shrug, find someone that does want to have sex with them and carry on with work. Here they must humiliate you. Peegs.' I hope she gets to work on legislation one day. I quite fancy watching the Enoss Wiz Zese Peegs Act work its way through Parliament.)

Anyway. Although I don't know anyone else who has one, for Céline an au pair is necessary. Apparently the problem (though I feel a bit Maggie Smith in *Downton Abbey* calling the matter of finding staff a problem) is that the bad ones are ten a penny and the good ones tend to leave after six months when they realise that looking after children is, as one lovely Danish girl put it apologetically to Céline as she packed her bags, 'really, really boring'. 'I know,' said Céline. 'This is why the advert said, 'I will pay you ten thousand a year and give you a room and meals', instead of 'Come and have a lovely treat of looking after children.' But she still left.

This one arrived about three months ago and seemed good at first – quiet, considerate, vigilant with and interested in the children. Then she seemed to realise that she was alone, unfettered by parental supervision at the age of nineteen, and if not quite in a world city then certainly somewhere with excellent transport links to one and duly went nuts for it. For the last two months she has been using Céline's house merely as somewhere to crash when she gets home after a seventy-two-hour bender, and to shower before she goes to get the morning-after pill.

'We meet on Thursday, yes?' says Céline, as she prepares to dash off. 'One of my clients has been paid off by her boss but I am not telling mine, so my week is quite easy. *À bientôt.*'

Mr Handsome, the headmaster, is waiting in his immaculate suit and tie and crisp white shirt at the school gates to welcome the children back. Thrillingly, he took over from the old – in every sense – headmaster last year and has set about with his new broom ever since. He has great academy ambitions for the school. Richard misheard me at first and brightened considerably at the thought of someone with academic ambitions in charge. I had to explain that they're not quite the same thing. We've had 136 million emails about it and it seems to be more to do with having smarter uniforms and walking quietly in corridors than learning better. But we'll see.

His name's not really Mr Handsome, of course – it's Mr Harrison – but as he's ten years younger than most of us, slim, clean cut, and we are very easily pleased, he is generally known among all but the very coolest mothers (who refer to him as John, though not to his pleasing face) by this incredibly inventive nickname.

'Good morning, Evie, Thomas, David,' he says, shaking their hands and nodding to us.

'Good morning, Mr Harrison,' they chorus, and he waves us through the gates. Evie darts off to join her gang without so much as a goodbye. Thomas's little hand creeps briefly into mine for reassurance, then he advances too.

'Well,' says David resignedly, hefting his backpack more securely onto his shoulders. 'Best be off then. Ta-ra.' He trudges towards the maelstrom of running, screaming children, contempt for the whole set-up radiating almost visibly from him.

'He seems glad to be back,' I say.

'I literally had to drag him out of bed this morning,' says Fiona. 'He kept shouting, "I've learned enough! I've learned enough!"'

Mr Handsome blows his whistle and we mothers watch the children fall into lines and be led from the playground into school, youngest class – only a year younger than Evie but already so impossibly small – first. Her first day seems so long ago but somehow I remember my own as if it were yesterday. As they skip and slouch in, as temperaments dictate, their arms as thin as spaghetti, their knees as knobbly as potatoes, into the world of safety scissors, doll-sized toilets and canteen cutlery, the thirty-odd years I have lived since collapse and vanish. All is as it was. Better security on the school doors, perhaps, which would make me feel nostalgic for gentler times if I didn't remember how many unkempt weirdoes our headmistress's secretary (very much not a head teacher's PA) had to turf out on a weekly basis, back in my day.

Just as in my day, the school is a solid Victorian effort, taking absolutely no nonsense on the outside, while its innards

8

are a riot of colour – every classroom and corridor wallpapered with the children's work. Unlike in my day, though, I see this profusion of artwork and stories now less as evidence of the children's hard graft and more as that of the teachers'. Looking at the mounting, coloured bordering, printing, pinning, trimming and arranging that goes into making an attractive display – gold out of straw, the ceaseless dedication of it – makes me want to cry and lie down for ever.

Looking at the parents – well, that always takes me back to a slightly later era. The four or five immaculately turned-out mothers who stand in scattered groups – a clutch per year – in knee-high boots, cashmere sweaters, discreetly expensive jewellery and perfectly cut jackets, each carrying a signature bag, sporting the occasional subtle tweakment, and swishing good, good hair: these are the cool girls of secondary school all grown up. They chat and laugh carefully together, constantly scanning the perimeter, always conscious of the picture they make. Do you become conscious of the picture you make if you look like that, I wonder, or do you make yourself look like that because you're conscious of the picture you make? All of a sudden, I'm fourteen again. I didn't even enjoy it the first time round, and I was thin then.

Then there's the much larger group you remember from big school: the normal ones – louder, more relaxed, more colourful. They've grown into louder, more relaxed, more colourful mothers. They're still one big gang, who go round to each other's houses endlessly and gossip – over coffee and wine now instead of orange squash and supermarket cola – and know each other inside out. Easy friendship on the outside, eternally riven with secret rivalries and hatreds within. I know this because the fourth corner of what Richard calls our 'coven square' is Nadia, and Nadia is one of those rare people – Fiona calls her The Unicorn – who is so innately lovely that everyone welcomes her. She is the bridge between all cliques, and Fiona, Céline and I mine her for info as soon as we've got enough drink down her every Thursday night when we meet.

Their normal children generally play on the scrubby bit of grass in front of the playground fence, falling over each other like a mass of puppies in racing-green sweatshirts. Evie regards them with disdain, Thomas with envy and fear. He has inherited a double dose of physical ineptitude from his parents and knows he would be killed if he joined in. I wonder if I should update the allergies and disabilities section on his emergency contact form: 'This child can fall over lying down. Please beware.'

Around the edges of the playground are my people. The nerds. The congenitally shy. The merely antisocial. For whatever reason, perennially near the group but never of it. Occasionally I make efforts to change this by holding a coffee morning or sending out a flurry of WhatsApp messages suggesting playdates while Fiona looks at me askance, but I can't sustain either the effort or the conversations in any resultant gatherings for long enough to gain traction. 'People don't change,' she periodically tells me, but I can never decide if this is reassuring or depressing.

On the way out we get caught by queen cashmere bee Savannah (works for a merchant bank, mother of three and, most importantly of *course*, Still Thin), who between braying about how glad she was that she and the family had had such an *active* Christmas skiing instead of *lounging* around 'eating chocolates and drinking!' is forcing people to sign up to the half-term fundraiser. She and her lieutenant Susannah (stay-at-home mum of another three; both smug and bitter about it because, like all of us, she knows that work is by far the more rewarding activity day to day but she enjoys people knowing she doesn't have to; beautiful boot collection; also Still Thin) haven't decided what it will be yet. 'We're thinking either a sweet little disco, a family fun night, a spelling bee, a school sleepover, a movie night, a carwash day, a balloon pop—'

'That's when you put different amounts of money in balloons, blow them up and then sell them for the chance to pop and win!' says Susannah, with a delighted smile that absolutely cannot be real.

'Or a pancake breakfast, a board-games tournament, or a movie night!' finishes Savannah. 'And, of course, all of these can be combined with fancy dress too!'

'I've learned enough,' mutters Fiona. 'Run.'

I spend the day unable to settle at work, endlessly alternating between joy and melancholy as I always do on the children's first day back at school. No sooner has joy won out than it's time to go and collect the little buggers.

'How was your day?' I ask, as we walk home with Fiona and David.

'Great!' says Evie. 'Everyone was really pleased to see me again!'

'There's new cushions in our quiet corner,' says Thomas.

'Red 'uns,' says David. 'Bit bright.'

Fish fingers, pasta and peas for tea. They ate the pasta.

Then bath, book and bed, except we ran out of time for the bath. I contemplate wetting the inside of the tub with the showerhead so that Richard doesn't find out and start helpfully listing all the ways I could have done things differently throughout the day to avoid this outcome, and decide I will just tell him to shut up instead.

He gets home, as is customary when he's working on a big case, just as the kids are falling asleep and goes in to say goodnight.

'They say they haven't had a bath,' he says, as he comes downstairs and into the sitting room.

'Shut up,' I say, handing him a glass of wine slightly smaller than my own.

'All right!' he says, clinking it against mine. 'But not for long!'

Thursday, 5 January, Twelfth Night

'Right, time to take all the Christmas decorations down!' I say.

'*Yes!*' says Evie, jumping up and immediately starting to tear down cards and strip the tree of baubles.

'*No!*' wails Thomas, his eyes filling with tears. 'I don't want Christmas to be over!'

'It *is* over!' says Evie, flinging cards at the bin. 'It's been over for ages!'

'But I still have a Christmas feeling inside me!' sobs Thomas. 'I want it to stay on the outside too!'

'Let's burn the tree!' says Evie, seconds away from lighting the match. 'It'll be great!'

Richard comes home to find me pinned to the sofa as one child cries on my lap while the other whirls round the room in a frenzy of sanctioned destruction.

'What's wrong with Thomas?' Richard mouths.

'The ineffable pain of life.'

'I see.'

'We're taking down the Christmas decorations, Daddy,' yells Evie, gleefully. 'But Thomas says it hurts him! He's a wally!'

'No, he's just a romantic,' says Richard. 'A porous-hearted being, who cannot help but privilege imagination and the emotional life above mere fact or practicality.'

'Can I punch you in the tummy?' Evie says, which is her usual response when she feels matters are getting away from her.

'Yes, not hard – well done. A romantic and a pugilist in the family. An excellent set-up, all in all.'

Thomas achieves emotional closure through the offer of sausages for tea, done with bacon round them like at Christmas.

'If I pretend I'm stupid and that I feel sad about Christmas tomorrow,' says Evie, 'can we have them again?'

Friday, 6 January

'Is Mary dead?' asks Thomas, through a mouthful of teatime savoury pancake. (Thursday is my work-from-home day after three in the office, so I managed to make batter. Friday is my 'day off' – i.e. the day I complete unpaid what I should have done over the previous four, then embark on cleaning the house until I get sidetracked by a hundred more urgent tasks that emerge as the day wears on – so I have managed to cook the actual pancakes because I have an actual half-hour to stand over the hob, frying and serving.) Evie has already bolted three and disappeared behind the kitchen sofa to put the finishing touches to her scale model of Porton Down or whatever she is building with her Lego back there, but her head pops up at this news of a possible fatality.

'What?' I say, startled. 'Mary in your class? No!' My mind starts racing. She can't be. I would have heard if there'd been an accident or if she'd fallen ill. The class WhatsApp would have gone mental. Part of my mind starts composing the message that will subtly check what's going on. The other part starts rearranging drop-off and pick-up arrangements if it turns out she's been kidnapped by a paedophile gang and the school institutes new rules until it's taken down, running through all our household items for things I might legitimately carry yet could be repurposed at a moment's notice if I needed a weapon to fight them off, and prioritising the local parks and playgrounds in order of clear sightlines and escape routes. Richard considers this part of my catastrophising temperament. My friends call it good planning.

'No.' Thomas sighs impatiently. 'Mary-the-mother-of-Jesus.'

Richard walks in as Thomas is speaking. He turns on his heel and walks straight back out again. I glare futilely at his retreating back. 'Why are you asking about this?' I say weakly. 'Christmas is over.'

'We had Christian assembly today,' explains the head above

the sofa. 'And people wanted to talk about the baby Jesus. The activity scene was still out.'

'Nativity,' I say.

'So?' demands Thomas. 'Is Mary dead?'

'Yes,' I say reluctantly. 'She is.'

'Why?'

'Because she lived a long time ago.'

'Oh. Is Jesus dead too?'

'Well,' I say, after a pause in which I wrestle briefly with a conscience that will not let me ignore several thousand years of Judeo-Christian doctrine, and think a variety of very unJudeo-Christian thoughts about the husband I can see sinking even further into the recesses of the armchair in the sitting room. 'That's sort of a tricky question.'

'Why?'

'Because … because Jesus did die, but—'

'When he was a baby?' says Evie, popping up interested again now.

'No, later on, when he was a grown-up. About thirty, I think.'

My phone pings. *33* says the text from Richard.

'Thirty-three, to be exact,' I say, through gritted teeth, as I send a one-fingered emoji back.

'Oh. Okay. So he did die, but you said "but". But what?'

'Well, the people who believe in Jesus say that then he came alive again.'

'Does that happen often?' asks Evie.

'Not often, no.'

'Why did it happen to Jesus, then?'

'Because he was … because the story says that he was the son of God. So the normal rules didn't wholly apply.'

'What's that mean?'

'It means that normally, if you're just an ordinary person, you die once' – for example, if your wife murders you for dereliction of teatime and religious-education duties – 'and that's it. But if you're a … a little bit made of God, then you can come back to life after you die. Just for a while.'

'And then what happens?'

'Uh, you tidy up a few loose ends and then you go up to Heaven to be with God.'

'That's what the story says?' asks Thomas.

'Yes.'

'Do you believe the story?' asks Thomas.

'I enjoy the story. I think it's a very good story.'

'But do you believe it?'

I am saved by Evie, who says, 'But it's Father Christmas who brings us presents, right?'

'Yes,' I say, relief driving out both hesitation and compunction over this lesser lie.

'Will *he* ever die?' Two infant faces creased with concern turn to me.

'No.'

'Why not?'

'I've got to wash up now,' I say firmly. 'Run and ask Daddy. Don't stop until you're completely happy with the answer.'

Off they go. Jesus Christ.

Monday, 9 January

A text from my sister Kate arrives as I'm binning a batch of fish fingers I've burned because half a decade of making children's teas has not yet been sufficient to teach me to catch them at the nanosecond of viability that comes in the journey from inedible frozen lumps to inedible charcoal sticks. I bung a new load under the grill and read it.

Life as a location scout takes me to New York in a few weeks, Kate says. *Do you want anything from Sephora?*

YES PLEASE! I text back excitedly. *I want anything, in the colours and finishes you think I should have and in service of my flaws in the order of priority you deem correct. THANK YOU!*

She replies with a thumbs-up emoji, a gif of Alexis Carrington in a marabou-trimmed satin robe applying blood-red lipstick at a mirrored dressing-table, and a fart noise to amuse – I presume – any children in the vicinity.

I muse on the phenomenon that is my sister who, despite being five years younger than me, has always been a repository of unfair amounts of wisdom. She knows everything about everything. From beauty products to violin-making (we once lost sight of her for a year when she vanished to Italy to learn how to make her own), art history and architecture (hence the location scouting job for ever bigger and more expensive productions) to zoology (her degree) – nothing escapes her, and once she has acquired any new knowledge, her mind closes round it like a steel trap and it will never be dislodged.

But what I find even more impressive than the fact that Kate is human Google is that all her life, since long before it was technically possible – I mean you're just not supposed to have those kind of synapses until you're an established adult, if then – she's always known herself. She is not married and has no children because she doesn't want them and never did. She wanted exactly what – as you'd expect from that kind of early knowledge and certainty – she's got. A life of complete freedom.

I force her into a deep 'n' meaningful conversation every couple of years ('I'm your big sister and it is my duty ...' I always begin, so that she can roll her eyes so far back I can see only the whites, and stage a dramatic collapse to prove how *boooooored* she is by the very idea) to find out if anything's changed. The only worry I've ever had is that she might one day feel trapped by the Bohemian image we all have of her and be unable to admit that her goals have altered – but it is slight, and it is fading.

The last time we spoke she pointed out that once you've moved past the last vestiges of teenage wanting-a-boyfriend-for-the-sake-of-it, the prospect of a relationship takes on a very different hue. 'If you're not someone who needs someone,' she said, 'if there's no emotional damage you need someone to fix, or void within that you need someone to fill, and if you don't want a baby – and I don't, I'm an aunt, I get all their best bits and you do all the rest – then all you've got left is a life of endless, needless compromise with someone who's never going to suit you entirely. Haven't you?'

I could muster neither a full nor convincing rebuttal to this, and not just because her unencumbered lifestyle makes Kate a fabulous and devoted aunt who – among many other contributions to my family's health and happiness – several times a year swoops in to put together spectacular bespoke birthday and assorted other celebrations for my children that have entered the annals of local legend. I have thought it wise not to cogitate for too long upon on my absent stock of persuasive evidence since.

I am roused from my musing by the smell of burning. I shout to the children that it will be ham and pasta instead and make a note to buy shares in Birds Eye. Might as well insure against my incompetence where we can.

Thursday, 12 January

Our shiny neighbours are back.

'I wonder where they went this time,' I sigh, as I stand on tiptoe at the sink to watch the two of them – Sofia and Amrit, very early thirties, she possibly even late twenties – tripping gaily up the weedless path of their herringbone-brick and minimal, manicured-flowerbed garden as the taxi driver unloads their luggage. They open the door, check briefly inside, then go back down the path to collect their bags. Imagine being so young and energetic you still want to do everything together, doubling instead of halving your labour whenever you can.

'God knows,' says Richard. 'Why are you sighing, anyway? You hate holidays. You hate travelling.'

'I do now,' I agree. 'But at their age? If I'd had their money? Who knows?' We don't know what they do, this quintessential young professional couple – Amrit did tell Richard once, but Richard didn't understand ('There were too many new words in his description. I couldn't make it all hang together') – but they travel a lot for work and then go away for holidays innumerable times a year on top of that. They don't tell us they're going – there's no need. They don't have a cat or a dog or – it goes without saying – children. (They do have a gardener, a cleaner and someone who comes and does the gutters and drains and touches up the paintwork every year. I don't know how they're better adults than we are, but there you go.) So they just lock the front door and leave. Off to enjoy themselves or to work for copious amounts of money. I love to watch them. I try to keep the sighing to a minimum.

Mrs Bradley, on the other side, is out too, of course. She is an elderly Scottish lady of the old school – of robust proportions and even more robust undergarments to keep them under control. The Battleaxe, Richard calls her, or Mrs Buttress, but I'm much too in awe of her to do likewise. I revere her. If the shiny pair on our right are what I wish I had been, Mrs Bradley is what I hope to be in the future. She speaks only when she deems it necessary. Direct (but polite) requests to move our car if she is having a compost delivery, perhaps, or occasionally snippets of gardening advice. ('Needs staking,' she will tell me, gesturing at one or more of the dismal patches of vegetation in our front garden. 'Campanula will fill in' was another. I googled campanula, bought one, and she was right. It has grown despite me. I love it.) And she has been known to exchange a few words with Evie, in whom I suspect she senses some kind of kindred spirit, if Evie's out by herself in the back garden when Mrs Bradley is doing her roses. She's also supremely independent – she does all her own gardening, cleaning, painting, gutter-clearing – and answerable to absolutely no one except her faithful aged hound, which she walks three times a day, come sun, rain or apocalypse. If there has ever been a husband, there isn't now. She told Evie once that she had never wanted children and made sure she never had any ('How?' said Evie. 'Bagpipes,' said Mrs Bradley). She has an unfurrowed brow, an implacable air and surveys her world as the undisputed mistress of it. I wish only that she wasn't an almost daily and, I can only infer from the steely gaze and styptic blinks, unforgiving witness to my family's various failings. But one day I shall be just like her. Proud. Unflinching. Mistress of all I survey. One day. One day.

Thursday, 19 January

The day begins with Richard announcing that the dishwasher has started making a funny noise and that 'we' need to find out what's wrong with it.

'We' on the other hand know that the dishwasher has been making that funny noise for about three weeks now and that there is nothing to be done with dishwashers that are making a funny noise except wait for things to become worse, then rapidly fatal, then order the one 'we' have picked out on johnlewis.com and hope it arrives before the very last piece of crockery has been used and piled perilously high in the sink. That is the way of dishwashers and the world.

The marital 'we' is one of the most cherished aspects of our life together. It's the opposite of the royal 'we'. The Queen's means 'I'. Richard's means 'You'. 'You need to find out what's wrong with the dishwasher'; 'You need to keep this place tidier'; 'You need to [insert any tedious, repetitive, unrewarding chore here].'

Me finds it wearing.

It's a good job today is coven-meeting night, when Fiona, Céline and I head to Nadia's house (because she not only has a seven-year-old, Leo, in Thomas and David's class but also a four-year-old plus a toddler who is not yet sleeping through the night) to drink and vent. As, I suspect, has been the main purpose of coven meetings throughout history. The only difference now is that we return home to husbands eager to tell us the heroic story of how they put the children to bed on their own instead of burning us at the stake.

Sometimes my best-friend-since-schooldays Claire joins us too, but it depends how she's feeling. She had her third unsuccessful round of IVF a few months ago – I went to visit as usual, and she just cried and cried, and there really wasn't anything I could say to make it less awful. At least I'm old enough now to know not to try. When I think of what my gauche younger self might have tried to dredge up in the name of comfort, I go weak with horror. Some things don't resolve into words, so keep schtum. Anyway, Claire may want to come out and drown her sorrows this week or she may still just want to hunker down at home. We understand, obviously, either way.

Of course, it rarely happens that even we core four can make it. Someone's always got a work/child/laundry crisis or is just feeling too bone-weary to drink anywhere other than their own sofa. All excuses are valid. But we keep aiming. The dream of a couple of hours in adult company outside the house gets us through the week.

My main contribution, as we split what turns out to be just the first bottle of wine (it's the first meet of the new year *and* we've all made it, so it feels only right to celebrate), is a diatribe about the dishwasher, the immorality of built-in obsolescence and (second bottle) modern capitalism generally and the accursed appliance's status as the emblem of all that is wrong with the division of labour in the Modern Marriage. The coven nod and slosh in understanding and give me recommendations for plumbers. I will start calling them in the morning.

Friday, 20 January

'What do you like best about going to Grandma and Grand-dad's?' asks Richard, as we set off.

'The nice food, not pasta!' says Evie, bouncing up and down in her booster seat at the thought of basic nutrition being combined with flavour.

'It's so quiet,' says Thomas, dreamily. 'Even though Grandma's noisy, it's sort of quiet underneath. And calm. Our house always feels noisy even if it is quiet on top.'

'That's because Grandma and Granddad have *systems*,' says Richard. 'We' – there's that marital 'we' again – 'will have systems one day too. And then our lives will be transformed!'

'Will there be nice food too?' asks Evie with interest.

'Could everyone be quiet and listen to their audiobooks now, please?' I say. 'We'll have enough family time later.'

The rest of the half-hour to my parents' house thus passes relatively peacefully. The trading of bickering between back-of-car siblings for improving literature (or, failing that, a collection of poo and fart jokes strung along a frail narrative thread) seems to me one of the few unquestionable gains humanity has made over the last ten years. Or is it twenty? I have no sense of time any more. Richard and I once had an actual argument about how long ago the nineties were.

I, too, am almost relaxed. First of all, I still enjoy the fact that leaving the house with the children no longer involves packing nappies, bottles, wipes, warmers, muslin squares, teething rings, soft toys so beloved that they appear to function as another vital organ, more muslin squares, squeezy pouches, breadsticks, Tupperware potfuls of puréed hours of my weeping time, more muslin squares and spares of all the above before we can even think about going anywhere. Second of all, although it is only thirty minutes away, on the fringes of Kent, spending the weekend at my parents' is like travelling to another world. They have a large, tidy house and a large, tidy garden. They have time. They have patience. And so they have us, escaping the exact opposite, at least one weekend in four. I tell them to think of it as their boomer tax: the price you pay for having lived through a time when it was possible to buy a comfortable family home without inventing a world-changing algorithm or marrying into the Russian Mafia. 'We got tax relief on our mortgages, too,' my mother once told me, as we sat drinking gin in the two spindly outdoor chairs my garden can accommodate. 'Can you imagine?'

'No,' I said. I did try, though, several times after that. I would pour myself a large glass of something and try to conjure up a world in which the government gave you money back for buying a home big enough for a family of four (and to put up a guest in the spare room) on the salaries of a part-time manager of a solicitor's office and a dentist, but it gave me nosebleeds. 'Maybe don't try any more,' said Richard, in one of his rare moments of usefulness.

My mother's job, incidentally, was meant to be full time. It had been for the man she took over from, but she got it down to three days a week within a month. So she told them they could compromise and just pay her for four ('Well, clearly I was better at the job than they deserved,' she said, when I once remarked on the boldness of this move). And they did, for the next thirty years. I try to channel this energy into my own life occasionally but somehow I never quite succeed.

We have barely braked outside my parents' house before my mother is wrenching open the car doors, gathering the children into her arms and smothering them with kisses.

'Hello, my darlings! What would you like to do today? Give me a cuddle! I thought we'd make apple crumble, then do some painting – you've lost a tooth! We'll have to tell the tooth fairy you're here tonight! We'll write a note ...' She waves vaguely at me, her firstborn, who is but an indistinct non-grandchild-shaped blur to her these days. The sound of happy chatter fades as they disappear into the house.

'When I was little,' I remark, in wonderment, to Richard, 'I sometimes used to sit with my toes clenched and she used to slap them.'

'Why?'

'To get me to relax.'

'She used to slap you to get you to relax?' says Richard, as he wrestles the suitcase out of the boot, followed by the boxes of secondhand books and toys Mum has demanded we donate to all the charity events she's involved in.

'Yes. It annoyed her that I wasn't.'

'Almost everything about you is explained.'

We go in to find Dad in his usual place – the kitchen

– somehow contriving to read the paper while chopping carrots and watching four different pans simmering on the spotless hob in preparation for a delicious meal that will be served on the dot of six without him breaking sweat, crying or suddenly panicking about a forgotten ingredient and trying to run in seven directions at once, which is what happens every time I am foolish enough to attempt such a culinary feat.

He acknowledges my entrance with a raised hand, which is a northerner's hug. 'It's slow roast pork belly,' he says, by way of greeting, because he knows where my priorities lie. 'With red cabbage, mashed potato and honey roast carrots. I've done Yorkshire puddings too, though I shouldn't. But then I thought, Why not? You're dead long enough. You can take the leftovers home in that.' He nods towards a washed ice-cream carton. 'Your mother's performed her calculations and says it'll be just the right size.'

'Then I'm sure it will be. Where have the kids gone?'

'They're helping Grandma turn the mattress,' says Dad.

This is my mother's genius. The children fit in with her day and her chores, not the other way round. Why did I not see this in time? My whole life could be different.

The three of them come galumphing down the stairs, the children both with duvets round their necks like giant capes.

'I take it,' Richard murmurs into my ear as we watch their descent, 'you would have been literally killed for this?'

'Maimed, certainly. Severely, probably.'

'I'm Queen Emperor Captain Evelyn the Best!' roars Evie.

'I'm going to make a nest and fall asleep!' cries Thomas, crumpling delightedly at the foot of the stairs and curling up.

'I'm going to finish altering Granddad's trousers,' says my mother, perching on the sofa and pulling the sewing box towards her.

'What does that mean?' says Evie.

'It means I've bought him a new pair of navy trousers from Marks & Spencer because I couldn't stand the sight of the old ones any more.'

'Gravy stains,' says Dad, sadly, wandering in from the kitchen.

'He won't wear an apron when he's cooking! He's daft!'

'I can't reach behind to do it up.'

'Then ask me!'

'You're always out or up a ladder somewhere.'

'Then you'll have to think ahead.'

'What are you doing to the trousers?' asks Evie, a child rarely deflected from her original goal.

'I'm setting three inches in at the waist and taking four inches off the legs.'

'Why?'

'Because getting clothes to fit a seventy-seven-year-old man of Irish Catholic stock, like your grandfather, is tricky.'

'It's like trying to dress a potato,' says Dad.

'Can we do apple crumble once you've finished?' says Evie.

'Of course, my darling. Have a sweet while you're waiting.'

I look at Richard to urge protest but I have lost him to the assorted actual newspapers my parents still actually buy. I turn back.

'Can I have a glass of wine, Dad?' I say.

'Of course, love,' he says. 'Or there's prosecco in the fridge?'

'Should you?' says Mum, peering up over her sewing glasses at me. 'You're driving.'

'On Sunday,' I say. 'I'm driving on Sunday.'

'Still,' she says, 'you can't be too careful. You've got my grandchildren to think of now, you know.'

I make my way to the kitchen to ensure that it's a large glass.

Mum takes the children upstairs to give them their joint bath. I hear giggling as she washes their hair. I text my sister: *You know how in hot weather we can still feel the pulse of blood in our heads along the groove Mum wore in them while shampooing our tender scalps every other night as if they had done her a recent and grievous personal wrong? It's different now.*

Times change she replies. *And the most unexpected people change with them. Drink.*

Saturday, 21 January

I come downstairs after an extravagant lie-in. Had I known before I got pregnant that sleeping in till nine or managing to complete a bowel movement without anyone interrupting me with a Lego or Nickelodeon emergency would come to seem as much of a treat as a weekend in the Maldives – I imagine – I would have thought longer about chucking the Microgynon away. I yawn my way to the kitchen, wondering exactly where the Maldives are and why I don't know, to find Dad teaching Thomas to play chess.

I know he is a man with the patience of a saint on a Thorazine drip, but even so this seems like quite an undertaking.

'He's seven, Dad,' I remind him. 'And until very recently his favourite pastime was biting balloons.'

'Be that as it may,' Dad replies.

Richard's eyes are alive with hope. 'This could be his thing!' he says. 'He could be a chess prodigy. You just don't know until they sit down with a board and ... just ... get it. He could be the Bobby Fischer of south-east London.'

'Did Bobby Fischer like to bite balloons?'

'One thing has nothing to do with the other. A child can contain multitudes.'

Thomas and Granddad sit at the kitchen table and frown over the board together. 'I love Grandma and Granddad's table,' Thomas once said in awe. 'There's never anything on it. You can always just sit down and ... *use* it.'

'That, you little scrote, is because Grandma considers any sign of human habitation in a home a moral failing and Granddad has been wholly committed over the past fifty years to the path of least resistance,' I did not say.

'And finally,' says Granddad, as I make my morning coffee,

'the castle can go forwards or sideways. Never diagonally. But the bishop can *only* move diagonally.'

'Why?'

'Because that's the way the game works.'

'Who invented the game?'

'Well, that's a very interesting question ...'

'I just want one of your short answers, Granddad.'

'People in India.'

'Can *they* move diagonally?'

'Yes. Now, the point of the game is to try to protect your king while trying to take your opponent's.'

'Which one's Yurruponents? Is it the horse?'

'No, I mean – you have to try to take the king that belongs to whoever you're playing against.'

'But the king is boring! I don't want to protect him.'

'What do you mean?'

'You said he can only move one space at a time! That's stupid. I like the queen. She can do everything! Look – zoom, zoom, zoom! All the way across the board if she likes. It's her we should keep.'

'Attaboy,' says my mother, who is kneeling in front of the ancient chest of drawers in the corner of the kitchen and, with Evie's help, sifting through a drawerful of what some would call precious family mementoes and she calls useless clutter. The light of divestment shines bright in her eyes. She makes Marie Kondo look like Steptoe.

'He clearly has an indefatigably curious and questing mind,' says Richard. 'It's a good sign.' But a little bit of the light in his own eyes has gone out.

'Why don't we let you make your first move?' says Granddad. 'Off you go!'

'I want to checkmate you.'

'You can't do it on a first go. It takes time.'

'How much time?'

The light is definitely dimming in Richard's eyes.

'It depends.'

'I'll tell you what's a much better game I've got, Granddad.'

'What's that?'

'Let's pretend all the pieces are Transformers,' offers Thomas. 'The queen is Optimus Prime, the stupid king is Chase, the horse is Blades, the castle is Boulder, and the bishop is – what's the last Transformer's name, Granddad?'

'I don't know,' says Dad, resignedly.

'Heatwave!' shouts Grandma, as she consigns a lapful of family history to the bin, held open by an eager Evie.

'And the pawns can be everyone from *PAW Patrol*! Pawn Patrol! Do you get it, Granddad?'

Thomas excitedly gathers up the pieces, jumps down from the table and starts setting out his new game on the floor.

'I suppose Bobby Fischer never had Nickelodeon to contend with,' says Richard, mournfully.

'It's game over,' I say, with a sigh. 'Checkmate.'

Sunday, 22 January

I come downstairs after another beautiful, restorative lie-in to find Granddad at the kitchen table frowning over the chessboard again. 'Has Thomas gone to the loo?' I ask. 'Or are you playing against yourself?'

'No – Evie wanted me to teach her after breakfast. She's the one in the loo. And I think,' he says, peering closer at the board, 'she's left me in checkmate.'

'In ten years' time,' says Richard, overhearing, 'she'll be in prison or ruling over London as an independent state. I await with eager interest to see which.'

Monday, 23 January

Bloody Mondays.

Tuesday, 24 January

Bloody Tuesdays.

Highlight of the day was getting my contraception renewed without fainting at the idea of rods being pulled out and pushed under my skin. Worth it, of course. Three years more of blessed, unthinking safety. Thank you, medical science, the NHS, Marie Stopes, and however many activists and reformers I owe control of my reproductive system to. I really, really do appreciate it. Almost as much as I appreciate Rachel, mother of two girls – one of whom is in Evie's class and has the physical and mental fortitude to be her friend – who agreed to pick up both children from school so they could have a playdate and tea while I ensured I don't ever have to start this cycle again

The dishwasher is still playing up. No plumber has yet appeared. I'm thinking of trying a summoning spell instead of leaving voicemails. Richard is still baffled by my apparent dilatoriness. I still might kill him.

He gets home just as I am putting the tea on.

'What are all these big lumps of fur doing everywhere?' he asks, delicately stepping round a ginger tuft and over another.

'They're Henry's,' I say. 'You could pick them up rather than stepping over them.'

'My huge and roving natural intelligence, honed thereafter by years of legal training and arguments, whetted by the daily grind through multiple sources of evidence, evaluating and qualifying them as they go did enable me to deduce that they belonged to the cat,' says Richard, stooping reluctantly to pick them up, his expression as he hands them to me ('No, put them in the bin') suggesting that he has been asked to handle radioactive waste dipped in stoat entrails rather than a bit of feline fluff. 'My query, *au fond* – though not formulated quite as precisely as it could have been, for which I apologise – was: why has Henry suddenly taken to denuding himself in so spectacular a manner?'

'I don't know,' I say. 'He's been tearing it out from the base of his tail for the last few days.'

'You should take him to the vet,' says Evie, looking up from her tea. 'I thought you loved him. That's why we can't give him away and get a dog.'

'I do,' I say, though 'love' barely begins to describe the engulfing joy I feel whenever the gigantic, complacent, absurd, endlessly beautiful ball of orange fur I raised from kittenhood heaves into view. His magnificent indifference to human feeling is balm to my soul. Cats don't care about you at all. They care only that you have opposable thumbs with which to tear open a pouch of Brand Name Overpriced Stinking Meat Bits in Jelly twice a day and keep their sleeping area of choice free of your contemptible human detritus. They will let you stroke them, if they feel like it – though Henry never does, considering himself more a piece of living sculpture to be admired from a distance than a domestic pet to be handled – but they still don't *care*. They don't need you. Dogs, though – they need walking and emotional investment, both of which are increasingly beyond my capabilities. I need an animal that disdains both: I need a beautiful, sinuous, sun-warmed reflection of the indolence, self-indulgence and assorted other desires buried too deep in my heart for easy excavation, upon which I can gaze with the profound primeval hope that one day – one day – it will be my turn to sleep for twenty-three hours a day while people tiptoe in tremulous awe around me. Cats are pure id, neither loving nor needing to be loved, like a poor, loyal, hapless canine. You don't open your heart to a cat. They'd eat it.

'I will take him to the vet,' I say. 'I'll ring them today.'

'If he's got a deadly disease,' says Evie, brightening, 'can we get 101 dalmatians like in the film?'

'No.'

'You're a mean mummy,' she says, without rancour, just adding it to the mental tally of examples she keeps until bedtime, when she allocates everyone in the family their 'points' for the day, via stickers in a large, carefully curated scrapbook. I'm always impressed by the discipline she brings to the project while slightly fearful of the sociopathic tendencies it surely suggests.

'Don't worry,' Richard assured me, when I first voiced my concern. 'I used to do exactly the same thing at her age!' I find this ever less reassuring as time goes on.

Wednesday, 25 January

Forgot to ring the vet.

Thursday, 26 January

Or chase the plumbers.

This is a crap time of year. There's no Halloween. There's no Bonfire Night. There is, above all, no Christmas. It's cold. It's dark. There's another four weeks of bleakness by the name of February bearing down on us all.

'I'm *boooooooooooooored*!' is all I hear. All any of us hear, from offspring across the land. I curse our pagan and Christian forebears for not inventing something to break up the remainder of the dead season. Somehow I didn't fancy my chances of getting Evie or Thomas interested in Burns Night. ('On January the twenty-fifth, you'll have the chance to eat haggis! No, it's not very like pasta with tomato sauce but you *will* get to recite poetry in an auld Scottish dialect! Come back here!')

When I were a lass, children were expected either to turn the television on (all four channels of it), make their own entertainment or to be bored. I read, mostly. Or made pompoms. Yeah, made a lot of pompoms in my time. I don't know why. Never made them into anything. What *can* you make pompoms into? They just lie there gathering dust, intimations of mortality, spherical testaments to the futility of life in coloured wool. I cannot, in good conscience, offer their manufacture as a quality experience to my own offspring. Also, I've no wool.

As Modern Engaged Parents, of course, turning on the television is anathema. As a child of the eighties, largely raised on *The Flumps*, *Cheggers Plays Pop* and *Why Don't You?*, I didn't really understand this until I was screen-shamed by a set of crunchy mums from Thomas's nursery. You know the crunchy mums – they're the ones who let their sons' hair grow in artful tangles to their shoulders, only eat organic, go for healthful walks, make their own hummus and are for ever toasting trayfuls of seeds in the oven, though to what end I am never entirely sure. They look like gravel and cannot be edible. Sprinkle them on your drives, not your salads, FFS. Anyway. I accidentally got swept up in the entourage one morning and ended up ensconced among them in the artfully draped home of their queen bee – or would she be more of an avocado wasp? – sipping crap coffee from some wholefood shop's Joyless Vegan range and making polite conversation. I was gamely exclaiming with delight over some homemade gluten-, egg- and dairy-free cake ('Wow! This doesn't taste like the weeping void that lives inside us at all!'). I was not reacting when they talked about disposing of the mini-packet of Haribo recently brought home in someone's party bag as if it was a diseased syringe from the local shooting gallery. I thought I knew the rules, but I did not. Thus, at some point, I made a joke about *PAW Patrol*.

Six heads, wearing expressions of careful confusion, turned slowly towards me.

'What,' said Granola, sweetly, 'is … *PAW Patrol*?'

Ah. I realised. Nicely played. 'It's a cartoon,' I said. 'On television.'

Spiralisa's brow furrowed delicately. 'Did you let Thomas watch it as a Christmas treat?'

'No,' I replied. 'He watches it every day.'

It was as if I'd told them I tied him to a post in the garden every night so that I could go clubbing. There was a collective intake of breath. One moved her unbleached cotton tote slightly away from me. And, lo, the floodgates opened, and the tide of judgement did rush in upon me.

How could I do that to my child?

Very easily.

Did I not know about the studies showing that television and iPad use blunts skills, inhibits frontal-lobe development?

Ignorance is bliss.

Was I aware that for every minute of screentime a child has before the age of seven, the chances of him becoming a cat-killer double?

I will warn Henry.

They sat back, staring at me with the patented mix of pity and glee that is the hallmark of mean girls everywhere, and waited for my response. 'Hmm,' I said. 'Interesting. And as fully bollocks as all your clean-eating, non-dairy, Calpol-eschewing nonsense is, a handful of *PAW Patrol*s a day isn't going to kill him. I will, though, if I don't get half an hour to cook tea, put a wash on and shout down the phone at whatever service provider is currently not providing us with service, without the children getting under my feet.'

No, I didn't. I should have. I should also have pointed out that, unlike most of them, I had (then) a full-time job – flexible, but full-time – and my husband had an unpredictable (and, when in court, violently inflexible) one. By the time we all got home from a full day of work/nursery, we were all bone-weary. We're allowed to give ourselves a bit of a break. I could have told them that when Thomas gets home, he has a bath, *PAW Patrol* (or *Tree Fu Tom* or, if we're feeling highbrow, *Scooby-Doo*) and then his tea, over which we chat, laugh and, often, consider the relative merits of Marshall, Rubble, Chase, Rocky, Zuma and Skye, and why we abjure Robo-Dog ('Not real!'), and then is put to bed with a story, further chat, long goodnights to all his soft toys before he drifts comfortably off to sleep on the sea of love, care and attention upon which he has floated, continues to float and will float all his life.

Instead, I simply said, 'Well, it's clear we're never going to agree on this, any more than we're going to agree that this cake is not a valid foodstuff, so I'll see myself out. Bye!'

No, I didn't do that either. I came home and burst into hot tears of humiliation. But then I watched some *Scooby-Doo* with Thomas and it cheered me right up. Television never lets you down.

Saturday, 28 January

'Fiona's got a costs meeting after work and can't do Tuesday pick-up,' I tell Richard. 'Mum can't do Tuesdays because she's got speed yoga. Can you do Tuesday?'

'Isn't speed yoga corrupting an ancient art and spiritual heritage?'

'I haven't enquired. Can you do Tuesday?'

'Maybe it's a normal yoga class and she just whizzes through it in double time like she does everything else. No, I can't do Tuesday. I'm definitely *hors de combat* until Thursday. There is currently a sixty-five per cent chance of me being available on Friday.'

'When will we know definitely about Friday?'

'Friday.'

'Okay.'

I remember when Saturday nights used to be the best night of the week. They used to be for getting dressed up, putting on makeup and hurling yourself out with a gang of friends into a world pregnant with sexual possibility and excitement. Now, at least for the vast swathe of us who constitute households with two working parents but not with jobs that bring in serious – i.e. nanny – money, it is the night when we all sit down with our respective partners, phones balanced on sofa arms with various WhatsApp groups on standby, trying to cobble together the week's childcare arrangements. The maths goes: money + long hours = buy in help. Short hours + no money = do it yourself. Money + short hours = hahahahahahaha.

Long hours + no money = does not compute. Average hours + average pay = interesting times. You'd better hope you have and get on with siblings, two full sets of living grandparents, and the fellow mums at the school gate, and that they all live within a twenty-minute walk of your home and school and have no jobs or interests of their own. 'Au for an au pair!' Richard – who dismisses Céline's experiences as a run of simple bad luck – cries every time, labouring as he does under the profound misapprehension that the law of diminishing returns does not apply to his jokes.

We don't have it too badly.

Theoretically, I work in the office three days a week and from home for a fourth – persuading rich bastards to part with small crumbs of their corporate or individual fortunes to furnish children who have nothing with the materials that will enable them to master the rudiments of learning in a way that doesn't sap what little energy impoverished life has left them for such a feat (or 'Fundraising for a literacy charity!' if you ask me at a party). Mum and Fiona equally theoretically do those three pick-ups and keep them occupied (Mum here, Fiona at hers) until I get home. On Thursday and Friday I pick up my two and David, and look after them here until Fiona gets home. (Richard does not enter into the basic equation because, as with any barrister, his hours aren't dependable. He does what he (says he?) can when he can. Which is better than nothing, but not much. At least he is always happy to do it. If he was one of those men who refer to looking after their own children as 'babysitting', I would have to throw him in a canal.)

In practice, Mum's, Fiona's and my tripartite 3:2 split has worked as it's supposed to approximately once in the last three years. As with the coven meeting, any one of a million things can happen to throw this ramshackle, puttering jalopy of an arrangement off course. See Fiona's costs meeting above. Plus we're all adding Céline's two to whatever pick-ups we are doing, because Stephen's away and she hasn't found anyone to replace nineteen-year-old Drunky McDrunkface yet.

The best thing about working for the charity sector is that, although the money's crap, client misery is great and the sense of futility is often overwhelming, it is basically run by middle-aged women and you rarely have to deal with shitty bosses who don't understand if you have to leave early or arrive late because of childcare problems or assorted other breakdowns in domestic arrangements, or who don't trust you to make up the hours later. We are all on the same page. We know shit's just gotta get done, and that it will, even if it kills us. And we know that it can't always be within the neat confines of a nine-to-five day, much as we might wish otherwise. This has a value beyond measure. I would go insane otherwise.

Still, it takes this weekly brainstorming session to ensure we've done our best. The first port of call comprises the coven, of course. After that we will open it up to the class group, then on to Mum and Dad, various other friends, and after that we'll just go out and start accosting non-predatory-looking strangers in the street and asking if they can spare two hours any day after 3 p.m.

'We could ask Nadia to do Tuesday,' I say, 'because we took the boys' rabbit to the vet for her last week after he tore his ear ...'

'Nadia would do it anyway,' says Richard.

'Yes, but that's exactly why we can't ever use her unless we've actually done something for her,' I say. 'People take advantage of her all the time. We're not going to be one of them. Or two of them. Whatever we count as.'

I message Nadia and check the family WhatsApp while I'm there.

'Ooh, hang on – Mum wants to collect them on Thursday because she's got a coupon for the pizza place that runs out on Friday! Result!'

'Is that instead of her other day or as well as?'

'Damn! Doesn't say. Hang on.'

I text back.

My notifications ping.

'That was quick – no, wait, it's Nadia. She can't do Tuesday because the wee one's being vaccinated. But she can do Friday.'

'Sign her up quickly. Then you can swap your Tuesday with your Friday and do Tuesday pick-up.'

'Can I? Does that work? I've lost track.'

'Yes. I think so. Where are the war papers?' He drags the notebook in which we try to schedule our lives towards him.

'I've got Mum Monday, you now Tuesday, Fiona Wednesday, Mum Thursday-brackets-pizza, Nadia Friday.'

'Not if Mum means pizza instead of Monday.'

'Hey, let's play chess while we do this – it'll make it even more fun! Blindfolded!'

A ping. We dive for the phone.

'Mum means as well as not instead of,' I say with relief.

'It's a rollercoaster ride, is it not?' says Richard. 'Or is it more like bathing in a rough sea? I can never decide.'

'Wait,' I say, paling. 'Mum can't cope with Céline's two as well as ours and David on Thursday. We need to start again.'

'Ooh,' groans Richard. 'Au for an au pair!'

We work long into the night. At one point Richard suggests having my implant removed. 'We'll just have another baby,' he says. 'And you'll get maternity leave. It'll be simpler in the end.'

It's sorted now. I think. And without recourse to the shameful begging of favours via the class WhatsApp group. We'll know by how many children we have left at the end of the week how well we did.

My phone pings at midnight and my heart fills with dread. But it's Kate, sending me a picture of the haul she has amassed for me in Sephora, New freaking York. *Got you an exfoliant that would plane a doorframe*, the accompanying text reads. *Plus heavy-duty tweezers and a shitload of lipsticks. Half in your preferred shades of Not Visible to the Naked Eye For Fear of I Know Not What and the other half in shades you should be wearing.*

I have a vague feeling that I should feel at least slightly insulted but in fact am suffused by the warm glow of knowing that thousands of miles away someone is thinking of me and trying to make my life a little bit better and more colourful. Resolve to wear all the lipsticks in rotation, come what chromatically may.

Sunday, 29 January

'Why *don't* we get an au pair?' says Richard, when we have been sitting in companionable silence for what he clearly considers too long this evening.

'We've discussed this before,' I say. 'Many times.'

'Let's discuss it again!'

'Okay – we can't afford it. End of discussion.'

'We could afford something, though?'

'Only technically.'

'What does that mean?'

I sigh. It means two things. One – that we could afford, say, a cleaner, and indeed have done in the past. But I was brought up to believe that if there is one thing you must do in this life, it is clear up your own shit. The stress caused by having someone else do it was far more draining than doing it myself. Especially as I used to do it all myself before she came round, so that I wasn't humiliated. Two – we can't afford anything above cleaner-tier because I need to keep money in the bank. Richard comes from a class that doesn't quite understand that savings – that's the money we manage not to spend each month out of the two income streams that are our salaries, as I have oft been required to restate – are all we have. He and his friends come from a world in which there is always more money. Somehow. I don't even know how. But their actual monthly wages are just a part of the pool of cash in which they splash about. I suppose it can't be cash, really. It's investments, shares, reinvested dividends, estate-planned gifts from parents, inheritances from yet another distant relative, the rent from a couple of flats they didn't have to sell when they moved in together ... Yes, we were insanely lucky that Richard's parents left him a bit and he hadn't entirely blown through it by the time it came to put down a mortgage deposit together, and we are a billion times better off than most, but we need to live within our two finite monthly means. And, for my peace of mind, well within those means. I want as big a financial cushion between us and the unforgiving vicissitudes of life as possible. Richard, in essence, doesn't believe that there are any vicissitudes of life and certainly none that won't forgive him. 'Money is meant to make you happy!' he cries, whenever he ventures the spending of it on a new car or an extension or branded biscuits. But being financially secure makes me happy. So the cushion stays, and is plumped up whenever we can manage it. That's how I can sleep at night. And Sainsbury's own digestives are delicious.

But I'm too tired to go through all this again tonight.

'You know what it means,' I say. 'And nothing's changed since my last explanation.'

'I thought maybe you might have had a small stroke since then,' he says hopefully. 'One of those harmless ones that everyone misses but which slightly alters your personality nevertheless. Ah, well. You're young yet. I'm sure the time will come!'

No vicissitudes, you see. Just a life of endless golden opportunities.

Tuesday, 31 January

Fiona and I are preparing to start our New Year resolutions. We decided a couple of Christmases ago that it was ridiculous to expect us to revamp our lives while the glow and goodwill of the season still hung about the house ('How often do you feel happy any more?' Fiona pointed out. 'We should make the most of it') – there was still chocolate everywhere, and the children weren't yet back at school. 'I'm not playing Guess Who? and putting Ninjago Lego together all frigging day without a glass of wine at the end of it,' she added furiously. 'You can forget it.

Let's do it in February. February's fucking bleak anyway. Let's just lean into it. It's like penance and self-improvement at the same time.'

Did I mention we both come from Catholic families? For those of you who haven't had the pleasure, this basically means that the best we ever feel is bad that we don't feel worse.

Our profound wisdom in the matter of New Year resolutions has since spread, as profound wisdom will do. And so it has become traditional for the coven to assemble on 31 January to eat and drink as many of the calories we have left in our respective houses as possible and embark on our new regimes the next day. 'Or whenever your hangover wears off,' says Fiona. None of us can throw them off like we used to. It seems particularly cruel of the body to stop metabolising effectively just at an age when the need to drink is becoming ever more acute, but here we are. And this year on a Tuesday too. We discussed postponing it till the weekend but Céline put her foot down: we have compromised enough, she said, and new traditions must be followed assiduously lest life become a travesty entire. Something like that. She was quite exercised.

Claire is coming and I'm hosting because Kate is paying a flying visit on her way to look at oast houses in Kent for some docuseries that needs oast houses in Kent, and Nadia has such a houseful of relatives staying that there are enough willing hands on deck to deal with any number of wakeful children for the evening. As we work our way through the lake of prosecco and mountain of leftover cheese, cold meats, puddings and chocolate people have brought, we decide on our goals for the year.

'I'm going to clean up our shithole of a house,' says Nadia. 'I'm worried we're going to lose the children.'

'Social services aren't going to take them away because you've got a messy house,' says Fiona. 'Your mother might, but not social services.'

'No, I mean I'm worried we're actually going to lose them. When they disappear into the maze of laundry piles and bags of stuff waiting for the charity shop. Or when the mould from John's forgotten coffee cups finally joins up and seals them off behind a penicillin wall.'

'Get one of those decluttering people in,' I say.

'Can you pay them extra not to judge you?' Nadia asks.

'I shouldn't think so,' says Fiona. 'That's probably the bit they enjoy most.'

'Fuck it, then,' says Nadia. 'Here's to a year of fucking tidying. Or at least reading Marie Kondo. I've got her book. Somewhere. Now, you,' she says, leaning over to refill my glass, 'what's your plan?'

'The usual boring basics,' I say. 'Lose a bit of weight. Get fitter. Stop procrastinating. Stay on top of the washing. God, kill me now. Kate, cheer us up and tell us your glamorous alternatives.'

'I'm going to spend the year testing a theory,' she says. 'I'm going to go back to all my really bad and really good shags and have sex with them again to see if there's ever room for improvement in the former, and whether the latter are ever reproducible.'

'Oh, God,' I say, and clap my hands over my ears. It's almost as bad as hearing about your parents' sex life. No blood relations should talk about such things in front of any other blood relations. She carries on regardless, adding, 'Or is it always just a one-off matter of the right penis at the right time with the right amount of alcohol beforehand?'

'Why, though? Why not just carry on having new sex?' asks Claire, cramming another handful of crisps into her mouth.

'I'm just interested. And I think I should be using my vagina for good. Adding to the sum of human knowledge.'

'You're very noble,' says Fiona. 'Here, have some more wine. And chocolate. You need to keep your energy levels up.'

'I want cheese,' says Kate, reaching for the board and knife. 'Hardworking vaginas need dairy.'

'They're about the only bit of us that doesn't need cheese, actually,' says Fiona, popping a Mars Celebration into her mouth. 'Nobody's sending calcium down there. You can't get osteoporosis of the vagina. It has no bones. Just boners paying the occasional visit. Listen to me, I'm a doctor.'

'Claire's turn,' says Kate, as she secures the last piece of Brie on a cracker.

'Just to keep trying to have a goddamn baby,' says Claire, lifting her glass of Shloer in a gesture of dedication, 'without losing my mind.' We raise our glasses too in solidarity. 'Céline? What about you?'

'Me, I am going to read more novels.'

There is a pause before Claire says, 'That's the most French thing I've ever heard.'

Céline raises her hands in mock despair. 'What can I do? I am slim enough. I'm not giving up wine. I am *fantastique* at my job. *Les enfants* are happy enough. And I need to read more novels. *Ça suffit.*'

'"*Ça suffit*" should be our joint resolution,' says Fiona. 'Good enough is good enough sort of thing.'

We are going to get it put on T-shirts.

Friday, 3 February

My hangover has gone. In accordance with what I vaguely remember of my resolutions, I have eaten an apple and gone to bed early. This is the last I am going to speak of it because I am – what's a polite way of putting 'bored shitless'? – already. The dishwasher has gone from knocking to knocking-and-grinding. The Day of Judgement is surely at hand. Though a plumber is, as yet, not.

Tuesday, 7 February

Richard's case has been unexpectedly adjourned – 'So the other side can find its arse with both hands' – so he took the children to school and I had a leisurely bath before work. Just kidding. I swept the floor, tidied the kids' room, half changed the bed, split the next laundry load into lights and darks and was about to head for the train when Richard returned.

'Can you finish changing the bed and put the dark wash on, please?' I say.

'Are the washing-machine instructions on one of my cards?' he says, this man who handles with ease criminal fraud cases that cross continents.

'Yes,' I say, nodding towards the drawer where we keep the bundle of cards that have accrued over the years on which are handwritten notes about washing programmes, simple meals, children's violin and homework timetables. I both bless them, and curse their necessity – I mean, WTAF? – at the same time.

'Savannah was undressing me with her eyes again,' he says, as he opens the drawer and starts leafing through the stack.

I pause in my hunt for a lip balm to put in my bag and look at him. Shirt frayed at the collar, ancient cords, tweed jacket inherited from his grandfather, shoes that are best not spoken of – none of which he will let me throw away ('They're just a bit battered! Not rotting!').

'Yes,' I say. 'But only to re-dress you immediately in something more seemly.'

'That reminds me – Evie said her shoes were too tight on the way to school.'

Oh, Jesus, no. I all but cross myself.

'They can't be,' I say fiercely. 'I asked her how they were at the end of the holidays and she said they were fine.'

'I dunno what to tell ya, sweetcheeks,' says Richard. 'Children grow outside specified hours. It's kinda their deal.'

Shoe-shopping with Evie – even within the narrow parameters of school apparel – is hellish. When did children get so many opinions? And when did they start expecting them to be listened to? In my day, shoe-shopping involved being dragged to the local Clarks, having your feet X-rayed by some carcinogenic machine or jammed into a pincer for an approximate measurement, then the saleswoman and your mother agreeing over your head which pair you'd get, three sizes larger than your actual foot to allow her to get her money's worth, and you'd go home to spend the next six months tripping over yourself until you grew into them.

Now, somehow, it's turned into the Rodeo Drive scene from *Pretty Woman*. Also, it takes half a day with travel – when are we going to find time for that before her toes start bleeding?

I cannot worry about this now. I find a lip balm and head out the door. 'Darks,' I remind Richard. 'Not lights.'

'Ah!' he says, and starts pulling the washing he has just loaded back out. 'The monochromatic scale defeats me once again!'

I pass my shiny neighbour on the way out. She looks well. I tell her so. She smiles, thanks me, and hesitates. I carry on past her without breaking step.

Wednesday, 8 February

6 a.m. Dragged to the surface of sleep by the sound of a chainsaw being started. Which is to say, Richard has rolled onto his back and started snoring, like every other pissing morning. I kick him savagely onto his side, which reduces the noise to that of a belt-sander and lie there trying to doze off again rather than mentally calculate how many precious, precious hours of sleep I have lost to this inescapable (we've tried every frigging thing) morning ritual.

6.45–8.35 a.m. Get up, get dressed, get breakfast, get children fed, abluted, into uniform and into school before bastard husband has even got his socks on, like every other bastard day.

8.35–9.50 a.m. Late for bastard work because cocking train was bastard late. Emit a few sobs of frustration in privacy of lift up to office.

9.50 a.m.–1 p.m. Tear through: 800 emails mostly from people too stupid to live, Mars Bar, applications and proposals that all deserve to be accepted and none of which can be, meeting with potential donor that makes me want to smash my own and his face in, another Mars Bar, fifty more emails that arrived during meeting.

1 p.m. Go out for sandwich. Go mad and try new one. It's fucking horrible. Eat Mars Bar instead, followed by Crunchie for pudding. Scroll through news headlines. Cry in loo at state of world.

1.30–5 p.m. Work. Colleague on maternity leave sends picture of three-day-old baby. Cry at beauty of new life and state of the world into which poor scrap of innocence has been born.

5 p.m. Hurtle out of door, join heaving mass of idiots who have also picked this moment to go home. Every single person in London apparently hell bent on crossing my path, elbowing me in the head, or knocking me off course with their stupid fucking rucksacks the size of dead fucking bodies on their backs. Every baby-boomer woman who only comes to the city once a month to have lunch somewhere *nayce* with boomer fucking friends and forgets to ready her travelcard before approaching the turnstiles is ahead of me. One turns to me with a helpless 'Aren't I a one!' smile that fades rapidly as I say, 'May I?', take the stupid card out of her stupid hand, turn it the right way and strip my lips back from my teeth in a ghastly simulacrum of a smile as I say, 'Black stripe DOWN,' and shove it and her through the machine.

6 p.m. Pick kids up from Fiona, who waves away my apologies for lateness like the saint she is. 'Are you all right?' she asks.

'Yes, apart from life's shit and everyone who isn't us should die in a fire.'

She nods. 'I've given them their tea,' she says, as Evie and Thomas pull their coats on, yelling their goodbyes and thank-yous. I thank her too, almost on my knees.

6–7 p.m. Tell the kids to tidy their room (I don't care if they do, I just want them out of my sight), put a wash on, gather shit from around the house, swear at shit, put shit in its correct place, check bread bin and fridge for staple foodstuffs, text Richard to buy various missing staple fucking foodstuffs on his way back from work. He texts back that A Thing has come up so he won't be back till nine if he has to go to the supermarket. I tap out *I don't care what fucking time you come back as you're missing shit o'clock* [a.k.a. bedtime] *anyway. I care only that you bring sodding milk and bastard bread with you as some minor pissant contribution to the smooth running of this household.* Delete it and send *Get it. Doesn't matter if late. Need for morning.* Swear wildly under breath and press send.

7–8 p.m. Get children undressed, abluted, into pyjamas and bed. Read *Harry Potter and the Interminably Detailed But Still Astonishingly Unconvincing Adventure* through the vision of a large gin and tonic that is dancing before my eyes. Put light out. Kiss children ('That almost hurt, Mummy!') and retreat.

8.01 p.m. Make gin and tonic vision a reality.

8.12 p.m. And again.

8.30 p.m. A voice through the monitor: 'Mummy?'

'You little ... scrote,' I whisper viciously before pressing the button and saying in carefully neutral tones, 'Yes, darling?'

'I need a wee.' Thomas has recently conceived a fear of crossing the landing in the dark and can't find the light switch by himself. And we can't leave the landing light on because Evie needs tomblike darkness before she will power down for the night.

I count to five. 'I'm coming up!' The cheeriness of my voice has an undeniably demented edge to it.

'I'm sorry,' he says, looking up at me with big, anxious eyes as he hoicks his little dinkle out of his pyjamas and fires a jet of urine at the back of the bowl. 'I know you're cross already. But I had to go.'

My heart breaks and my eyes fill with tears. I lean and nuzzle the back of his warm little neck so he can't see. 'I'm not cross, darling, of course I'm not. Or, if I am, it's not with you. It was with the silly people who were on the train home with me. Sorry.'

I lift him up and cuddle-carry him back and his sleepy, warm little body melting trustingly into mine almost undoes me. I lay him down, give him a kiss – and one to Evie, who thrusts an arm up into the air to let me know that even at the edge of sleep she remains alert to any possible sign of favouritism – and head downstairs again to have a good cry.

I have just finished this and started on my third gin (realising halfway through and caring not that I haven't had a thing to eat today except Mars Bars) when I hear Richard's key in the lock.

He takes in the scene. 'Not ... a good day?' he says cautiously.

'Terrible,' I say. 'Everything's been shit. I've done nothing but rage, cry and eat chocolate for fifteen hours. I don't know what's wrong with me.'

'Do you not?' he says even more cautiously.

'What did I just say?! No – I. Don't. Know. What's. Wrong. With. Me. GOD.'

'I think ... I think you'll find another instance of uterine sabotage is under way.'

'Do you mean my period?'

'I do.'

'Fuck my life. No, it's not.'

'It is.'

'It's not.'

'You do this every month. We have this conversation every month. Or, at least, every four to seven weeks. You haven't been entirely regular since Evie. And then you forget. We have been together fourteen years – glorious, *glorious* years – and I have watched the advent of this frequent visitor come as a complete surprise to you every time. You're like the person in a supermarket queue who stands there watching her shopping being added up, then starts patting her pockets in a panic and searching for her purse only when the girl on the till actually says she has to pay for it.'

'This is rubbish, what you talk.'

'It's not though, is it?'

'No.'

I go to bed. Fuck my life. Even my fucking period's not my own.

Thursday, 9 February

My period has arrived. Mental anguish replaced by the blessed tangibility of physical pain. Decide not to linger on why these should be my only options one week in every four. Four to seven. Take ibuprofen instead.

I have lost count of how many plumbers I have rung, conversations I have had, assurances I have received and voicemails I have left but I do know that no one has yet actually turned up to look at the dishwasher. I remember as a student having a friend, Amy, who was trying to break into acting. She would insist brightly as she did the rounds of auditions that for every fifteen noes you were bound to get a yes. Maybe plumbers are the same.

Amy is now an accountant.

Friday, 10 February

Richard came into the kitchen limping ostentatiously this morning as I was wrangling the children into their coats and rucksacks (when did children start taking so much to school? They look like they're about to join Shackleton on expedition).

'Why,' I asked, with all due sense of anticipatory fatigue and dread, 'are you limping?' Not for Richard is the philosophy of Seneca – 'Scorn pain – either it will go away or you will.' His philosophy is more 'Writhe in agony and deliver a running commentary on every twinge as if it were a biblical mortifying of the flesh.'

'I have a sore toe,' he says, lifting his foot out of his slipper and proffering it to me as if it were some delectable sweetmeat or trinket instead of a man's foot, which, as everyone knows, is one of the worst things in the world. I don't even want to see Hugh Grant's feet.

I glance, as briefly as possible, at it. It is a bit red around the nail. 'You've got a sore toe,' I say.

'What should I do?'

'I'd have a full body amputation if I were you,' I reply.

'No, really.'

'Really? Nothing. See if it goes away. Like I do with my aches and pains. Like I do with much of life.' I think for a moment about all the aches and pains I have – my body has enjoyed finding a new way to disappoint me pretty much every day since I turned thirty-five – and ignore on the grounds that (a) if I didn't, the entire household would grind to a halt, (b) I'm not dying, and (c) I'd be embarrassed to demand attention even if I was.

'Shall I wash it?'

'Why not? Go nuts, put a bit of Savlon on it afterwards, see if that helps.'

'Will it?'

I feel I have devoted enough of my precious resources to this subject already, and so turn my attention back to the

48

children. I get them out of the house, off to school, walk back via the shops with Fiona to get milk because the children drank an extra pint between them this morning (David, she tells me, will only drink semi-skimmed. 'I think he takes after me,' she says. 'There's a general feeling that you'd better not get too used to the richer, creamier things in life. Then you'll be that much better off when it all turns to shite'), pick up some dry-cleaning, fielding various work emails and texts from my mother about when she's next seeing her grandchildren as I go.

When I get back, Richard is still sitting contemplating his toe.

'Haven't you got things to do?' I ask.

'I've got a sore toe,' he replies.

Another advantage to having a pet, by the way, is that if and when you are ever driven past the point of silent endurance by an activity, say, or the behaviour of a nearby party and find yourself muttering, 'Dick!' in so heartfelt a manner that you're overheard by said party, you can pretend you were annoyed with the animal (a large ginger cat, for example, can always be lying where it shouldn't or be about to trip you up) and both of you, if you've any sense left at all, will pretend that this is so. Tacit mutual deceit is a vital part of marriage and don't let anyone tell you otherwise.

At least his misfortune reminds me that Evie still needs new shoes. She's had a special dispensation from the teacher to wear trainers until the weekend but after that I think I get detention. At pick-up Fiona and I are caught again by Savannah. The half-term event, it has been decided, is to be a junior disco and we are to be heavily involved. 'Half-term disco?' spits Fiona later. 'Not a thing! Not a thing!' But everything is a thing nowadays. Otherwise there would be no money for books and … things.

As my Irish grandmother was wont to say, I'm *agin* discos. Especially of the pre-pubescent variety. Why anticipate the adolescent day? Why emulate painful forthcoming rites? The readiness of adults to coo and 'Aww!' and insist that little girls and little boys being friendly was them being 'boyfriends' and 'girlfriends' baffled me even before I had my own, and its persistence in the face of what now amounts to a semi-official movement against the sexualisation of children is officially *mental*, as well as making my teeth itch. I explain all this passionately yet cogently to Savannah, who thanks me profusely, says she's never thought of it like that and will come up with something else instead.

No, of course I didn't. She barely broke step and I couldn't get a word out in time about anything. We were simply given to understand that our specific duties will be assigned at a later date along with, I presume, our uniforms and dog tags. Urrrgh.

The bitterest irony is that if she had attempted to strong-arm me into this forty-eight hours ago I would have torn her throat out and walked away smiling and free. Bloody PMT is never around when you need it. Oh, well. At least this way Fiona has company.

Saturday, 11 February

'What are we going to do for Valentine's Day?' demands Richard, over what is once again a ready meal on our laps in front of the telly instead of the casual yet delicious chicken supper with sides of leafy greens from a properly laid table, as I always presume everyone else our age is managing to do.

A proper answer to this question recedes further from our grasp every year.

I never let him buy flowers because the irony and insanity of growing flowers in an environmentally unfriendly way so that they can be shipped round the world in bunches makes me cry more than all the other ironic, insane, environmentally unsound things we do.

We never could face the hordes out for an overpriced evening meal but we used to drop the kids off for an over-nighter at Grandma and Granddad's on the nearest Saturday and do something together. But we can't go round any more stately homes or historic monuments because I cannot face another of his rants about the diabolism of the National Trust. (Don't ask. I haven't listened for years. Something about nationalisation killing off the country house, I think ... an unwarranted extension of the government in private charitable form, maybe. This is what happens when you marry slightly up the social ladder. Instead of getting furious about the state of the NHS they use up all their energy raging against the dilapidations of baronial seats. This is one of the many reasons I don't recommend it.)

'Let's go for a walk in the countryside,' he says. This is another posh thing. Fresh air.

'I thought you had a sore toe?'

'I will push through the agony in a manner so stoic it will make Captain Oates look like Niles Crane.'

'It's too cold,' I say.

'You always say that.'

'Because I'm always too cold. I don't like to go outside until summer. Which is defined as the two weeks in August when it's warm enough just to wear a cardigan under my big cardigan.'

'Let's go to the theatre,' he suggests.

I roll my eyes.

'I was, essentially, joking,' he says. 'Nobody wants to go to the theatre. We'll go and see a film. There's not so much acting.'

'A good film, or one of the ones you like, with subtitles and "lighting" and "cinematography"?'

'Well, Sorrentino's *The Great Beauty* is on at the Prince of Wales cinema—'

'No.'

'All right.' He sighs. 'Have it your way. We'll go and see a "good" film. One that's been written by a thousand monkeys on a thousand typewriters and stars at least one Chris, Ryan or Tom. Or that one who looks like a clay otter.'

'His name,' I say, with dignity, 'is Benedict Cumberbatch, and he is a god. A *god*.'

'Clay otter who got lucky,' Richard says firmly.

I am too excited by the idea of my basic needs being met for an evening to object further.

'But we're going to a cinema in town,' Richard adds. 'One in London town.'

'No,' I say.

'Hang on – let me check my scrotum. Yes, they're still there, and so – I insist.'

'Do you know how much it costs to get into town and then into the cinema?' I cry. 'That's sixty quid gone before we even buy sweets! Just to see a film! That we might not even like! We can't take that kind of risk!'

My trouble is that I was brought up not only on far less money than Richard but also on parental tales of endless Saturday mornings spent sucking equally endless gobstoppers at the Ritz, Gaumont and Picturedrome while the adventures of Tex Ritter, Hopalong Cassidy and Flash Gordon unspooled before their rapt audience. These formative accounts instilled in me an entirely outdated but deep-seated sense of just how much entertainment I am owed for a sixpenny outlay and nothing violates it more obscenely than the price of a London ticket for anything.

Eventually we decide to do the only thing we can do. We're giving the kids to my parents and staying in. I will cook Richard his favourite meal – Batchelors Mild Curry Super Noodles, cut-up hot dogs and the special secret ingredient, spousal tears – and he will gift me a day of silence. He will not speak, he promises, from 8 a.m. till 8 p.m. He thinks – and I wholeheartedly agree – that this will best be accomplished by him staying out of the house from 7.59 a.m. to 8.01 p.m.

Compromise, you see. That's the thing.

'Why have we ended up with all the shit jobs?' Fiona murmurs to me, as we look at the list of work allocations for the volunteers at the upcoming junior disco. She and I are setters-up and wipers-down of the tables, floors, faces and fronts that will be drenched in squash long before the first number – played on a state-of-the-art sound system lent by Savannah – has finished.

'You know why,' I murmur back, nodding towards the head of the committee.

'Oh, yes,' says Fiona, remembering. 'Leigh-Anne doesn't leigh-ike you.'

I blotted my copybook with Leigh-Anne very early on. It wasn't my fault. We were at the very first PTA coffee morning, a few weeks after Thomas started school. Non-attendance, even – nay, especially – by those who had been working very hard for the first few weeks to keep things on a nod-and-wordless-smile basis while scurrying in and out for drop-offs and pick-ups was not an option. All reception-class parents were extremely firmly invited to what turned out to be essentially a recruiting session carried out with marginally less subtlety than Scientologists at a Cruise family barbecue. The committee members fanned out around the room and sniffed at us like police dogs picking up new trails. Does this one smell of money or free time? Hmm … a top note of neediness here – could be useful. A definite wave of hostility coming off that one – best left till the autumn fete call-up.

I don't know what they got from my corner. Nothing pleasant, I'm sure, given that I hadn't actually managed to have a shower before I left the house, despite the very best intentions. Bewilderment and BO was probably my signature scent.

Anyway. We were all sitting at long tables in the school dinner hall and opposite me was the mother of the triplets. I didn't know her name but, like everyone else, I had seen her three little dark-haired boys going in and out of school, all so completely alike that it made your eyes go funny as they trotted past. She had showered, I was interested to note. And dressed nicely and put on makeup. It was like looking at a different order of being. If anyone had ever extracted three babies at once from me, I would still be curled up in a bed somewhere demanding comfits and fine wine and very much considering my work in life done.

This was Leigh-Anne. I read her name upside down on her form. We were all filling them in with our names, contact details and so on, so that someone with an administrative capacity and work ethic stronger than my own could compile a list and circulate it round the whole reception year to facilitate the making of playdates among offspring and, unless we were very careful, nights out among parents. There was a box to tick if you were interested in becoming a class rep. Leigh-Anne, whose three boys were split across two classes, wondered aloud which one she should rep for. 'Oh,' I said, smiling – I was even smiling as I said it! In what I still and will for ever contend was a genuinely friendly manner! – 'Just pick your favourite and do his.'

Now *look*. I am NOT a mother of triplets. I would be in an *asylum* somewhere if I were. BUT. I do still know that such mothers do not have favourites. I do. I mean, you might slightly prefer the quieter one, or the one who sleeps through the night most often, or the one who learns to make the best martini, sure, but it would be first among equals.

'Pick your favourite' was, in short, a joke. Clearly.

Or so I thought. But Leigh-Anne totally froze, fixed me with a stare that went some way beyond hate and replied icily, 'I don't *have* a favourite.' And, like lightning, the expressions on the faces of the other mothers down the length of the table – who had been preparing to smile, at least as much as my small piece of nonsense was worth – followed suit and turned to stone.

This is the problem with motherhood. You think you're in a gang – you think that the experience of creating and successfully expelling via whatever means possible an actual new human life from within would form some kind of universal unbreakable bond between you – and then, too late, you realise you're not. The early days, when you clung to each other for survival during the breastfeeding, bottles and broken nights, misled you. What you are five years later is a loose coalition of powers at best, most of whom are constantly seeking competitive advantage and ultimately the crown. It's *Game of Thrones* without the bloodshed.

Leigh-Anne, of course, was made Thomas's class rep. He had no playdates with any of the triplets that year, nor any other year since. I remain very definitely not her favourite.

When I eventually get home, I remind Richard of his pledged Valentine's Day gift to me of a day of silence/absence. He presses his lips together, then mimes locking them and throwing away the key.

Tuesday, 14 February

It's been great.

On her way back from taking the kids to school (earlier than I do, even though she lives a half-hour drive rather than a five-minute walk away), Mum dropped off the cards the children had made for me yesterday evening. 'Happy Ballentins day mummy I love you very very much love Thomas xxxxxxx' reads one. 'Wat he seyd,' reads the other. 'A romantic boy and a practical girl!' says Mum fondly. 'Much the best way round to have it!'

I look forward to my own grandmotherly years, when all of life is suffused with such a roseate glow that neither doubt nor truth can penetrate it. A beautiful belated recompense for the childrearing years and the apparently endless days spent being internally shredded by uncertainty and guilt. I. Cannot. Wait.

Wednesday, 15 February

Amrit and Sofia are back from what I presume was a Valentine's Day minibreak. They are glowing. I am happy for them.

Thursday, 16 February

A plumber came round today. He looked at the dishwasher and went away again. I don't know what he thought or if he's coming back. I did ask. He just didn't say. I will ring him later, see if he's more forthcoming after a chance to reflect.

Céline is having similar difficulties trying to find an au pair. There's a dearth of them at the moment because everybody signed them up for the new year. She did find one, but when she collected her from the airport the girl just sat there in silence picking her nose and eating it. So Céline put her on a flight back the next day. 'She might have been very good with the kids,' I protested feebly when she told us.

'*Non*,' said Céline. And that, very much, was that.

Friday, 17 February

The junior disco was glitter-and-squash-strewn carnage. Everybody, adult and child, was enraged and exhausted by the end. An excellent start to half-term.

Saturday, 18 February

Took Evie shoe-shopping this morning. She now has plain black sensible shoes and a Lego set from their Blatant Bribery range. I have PTSD and the shades of several generations of better mothers shouting at me for my lack of moral fibre.

Mrs Bradley was weeding her front garden when we got back. 'Got new shoes!' Evie yelled at her.

'I hope you were good for your mother,' Mrs Bradley replied.

'I was not,' said Evie.

'Then she should skelp your bum,' said Mrs Bradley, returning to her weeding. Feel oddly supported by this.

Sunday, 19 February

The dishwasher noise is getting worse. The plumber has not returned my calls. Tomorrow I will WhatsApp more widely.

Monday, 20 February

Rachel's husband Alex came home from work last night and told her he was leaving. Because 'It's just not fun any more.'

'Did you have any idea it was coming?' I ask, when we all converge on her house after school (as requested, with children, so they can all play in the garden together and distract hers from the simmering horrors of a situation they don't yet know about. She's told them he's on a work trip).

Rachel is sitting on the edge of the sofa, hands clenched between her knees to stop them shaking. 'I didn't even think we were going through a bad patch,' she says.

She is the latest in an epidemic of divorces and separations in Thomas's year. We are, after all, entering a dangerous age. We're all a decade-ish married (or together), two-ish kids into it. We're all staring down the barrel of middle age. Spreading. Softening. Looking at a future that is for the first time shorter than the past. And, no, a lot of it – childcare, marriage, work, the daily grind, the traffic, the sex that, even if it still satisfies, is too much a known quantity to thrill – is not fun.

'And who the fuck,' says Fiona, as she adds whisky to Rachel's coffee, 'ever said it was going to be? Who ever thought it was going to be? Who ever considered that a lifetime of fun was an option? Really?'

Nobody round this table, for sure. If you're lucky, you get one period of pure fun in your life. Mine was at university, when I escaped the endless bullying that had made my entire school life a misery. It was university, too, that spelled the first freedom for Fiona, who spent her childhood helping her mum look after her dad after he had a stroke when she was eight. Nadia had an idyllic childhood but lost her twenties to an eating disorder after she was nearly raped on the way home from a nightclub at nineteen. Céline had a grand time throughout but now spends her spare time on the phone or on the Eurostar home to try to care – or arrange care – for her ageing parents, and that's one that's going to come to the rest of us too, soon enough. On it goes. It looks bad all clumped together like this, but it's all perfectly well within the parameters of normal experience – or normal female experience, which I suppose is what I mean.

Even in the absence of any specific traumatic events, you just grow up with a more realistic sense of life as a thing rarely arranged around your best interests, don't you? More chores fall to daughters than sons. As soon as you look remotely pubescent your body becomes public property. Newspapers and whispered stories at family gatherings are full of tales of violent men and the women no one and everyone knew they were hurting. In any context, anywhere, people look to the nearest woman to solve their problem, to help their world run smoothly, while we don't even get the courtesy of seatbelts that fit round boobs properly or car boots you can close without straining a ligament. Plus you get pressed into childcare service – babysitting, helping out with family babies – as soon as you can be trusted to support an infant head. I'd changed more nappies by the time I was eighteen than Richard has after two children.

You can't not know, is what I'm saying, that life can be hard and that children make it harder (better, overall, if you're lucky, but harder day to day), and that if you manage to have some fun along the way – well, my friend, that's a bonus, not a right.

But men don't seem to think of it like that. Some do, of course, but because of the exodus so many of them are currently performing it's hard just now to keep the faith that they're in the majority. It feels like they've never had to grow up, and now that they've had their nice illusions about life shattered, they have, like overgrown kids, chosen to run away from their responsibilities and start anew.

'I almost understand how he could do it to me,' says Rachel, starting to shake again despite the whisky, and I put my arm round her. 'But how can he leave the children?'

There is no answer to this. I never understand it. I can understand falling out of love with your partner. I can understand not falling out of love with your partner but falling in mad, delirious lust with someone else, making a massive temporary mistake and hopefully recovering from both. But I cannot understand being able to walk away from your children – *because it's not fun any more.*

'How am I going to tell them?' says Rachel, helplessly. 'How am I going to tell them he's just … changed his mind?'

We stay with Rachel as long as possible, making the kids a massive communal tea, and when her son asks if David can stay overnight, Fiona (after an eager nod from Rach) says she'll stay over too. So that's the first night covered. For the rest of the week we'll all have the children round at ours as much as possible. At the weekend, they're all going to her mum's. What happens after that, alas, will depend on Alex.

Long after I'm in bed I lie in the dark as Richard snores gently beside me and wonder about my own marriage. Would Richard ever leave me? I don't think so, but how can I know? Rachel didn't even think she and Alex were going through a bad patch. Does the fact that I don't know mean he's more likely to or less? I think back to when we met, and to the children being born. He says he knew when he first saw me that he wanted to marry me, which may or may not be true (it wasn't for me – I can still get paralysed by the need to choose between BOGOF offers in Sainsbury's; I was never going to be in the market for a *coup de foudre*), but I saw his face when the nurse put his babies into his arms as soon as their cords were cut. It was the face of a man being instantly reprogrammed, head to toe, with a new kind of love.

But that can hardly be unique. And Rachel doesn't have tales of Alex looking down with cursory interest, then dropping either of their babies back into the hospital cot and wandering off in search of a telly. And yet every morning at the school gates there are more tearful children, more bewildered and betrayed partners, and more spaces left by men who walk away to find more fun things to do.

Wednesday, 22 February

Alex has told Rachel he doesn't want to see the girls until the flat is fully furnished and he is properly settled in. 'He just wants to cut all ties,' she says, bewildered as ever and almost visibly aching as she hunches over a mug of cooling tea at her kitchen table. 'I don't understand,' she continues, as I boil another kettle. 'I don't understand. And I feel like my whole life with him was a lie. I never thought he could do this. I never thought anyone I knew could do this. Who could do this?'

At home when I recount the latest body blow dealt to Rachel, Richard says feebly, 'Maybe it's Alex's way of avoiding admitting to himself what he's done. He can't face his kids, so he's said – that.' I look at him. 'But he's a dick,' Richard adds hurriedly. 'And none of that makes him any less of a dick. He's a complete, unbounded dick. I want to make that very clear. Very clear indeed.'

He puts the kids to bed, possibly as a gesture of unsolidarity with Alex. I listen on the monitor as he reads them a story and then has a chat that, as is the custom when he rather than I covers bedtime, is not limited to confirmation of the emptiness of bladders and a reiteration of what special equipment is required for the next school day, but ranges far and wide. Tonight they cover what would have happened if the Germans had won the war, why 'sheep' is both singular and plural, why hair doesn't feel pain. Eventually Richard prepares to leave.

'You can ask one more question before I go,' he says.

'Why not two?' says Evie.

'Is that the question?' he says.

'No.'

'Well, what is the question?'

'Why?' she says. 'And that's it.'

Bet he's feeling a bit more solidarity with Alex now.

Friday, 3 March

I have been ill for a week. This, of course, is not possible. You can't as a working person or a mother, let alone a working mother, be ill for a week. The world simply does not accept it. So I have been dragging my aching joints, swollen throat and periodically pounding head around most of my usual tours of duty, and becoming increasingly hacked off.

Maybe some people get pleasure out of watching their household fall apart without them working at full stretch to maintain it; a testimony to their prowess, delivering a twisted sense of pride in one's indispensability. I am not one of those people. I would very much like proof that I am not the pivot upon which three other people's worlds turn as well as my own.

Being ill only makes me realise how many more of life's tasks I need to delegate, so that next time I need some energy to fight my viral load, I have it to spare. In the meantime, my path to recovery is strewn with shit. A single example will suffice. I have not strength for more.

RICHARD: Evie says it's World Book Day on Thursday.
ME: Is it full costume or accessories only?
RICHARD: I don't know.

If I had my health and strength this would be a Teaching Moment. I would explain that he needs to look on the school newsletter that is emailed to each of us every week and contains this and many other pieces of vital information, available at a moment's notice to all with a smartphone and a search facility. Why TF I need to explain this to someone who has been receiving them for several years would be a question for yet another time.

As I do not have my health and strength and my throat is too sore either to explain or rage, I just look it up myself.

ME: It's accessories.

RICHARD: So what do we do?

ME: *You* look in the dressing-up box. There's a fox mask in there somewhere.

RICHARD: What's that got to do with World Book Day?

ME: *Fantastic Mr Fox.*

RICHARD: Thomas says he's got to go as his favourite character.

ME: Tell him his favourite character is Fantastic Mr Fox.

At least he doesn't ask what Evie will go as. Evie's antipathy towards any form of dressing up is deep, real and legendary. If he had missed her many expressions of disfavour towards the practice over the years, I really would have had to consult a medical practitioner for signs of frontal-lobe damage. Her objections have not been discreet, they have not been short, and they have not admitted of any ambiguity in the matter. From her earliest days Halloween has been greeted by a full-on, arched-back meltdown at the idea of donning so much as a plastic mask. The first birthday party that said guests should come as fairies or wizards had its invitation ripped to shreds by furious four-year-old hands. Last year, news of National Costume Day (why do schools make extra work for themselves and us in this way? Why? Why? I mean, I understand that we need to celebrate the students' diversity and try to inoculate their open, innocent young minds against infection by the foetid forces of darkness gathering within and without our national gates, but on the other hand – do I really have to cobble together another bloody costume for the child? Or, more likely, add to the mountain of online-sourced polyester-robe landfill it must surely generate every year?), broken over the breakfast table, was greeted with a stony expression and glacial silence. Eventually she gave a slow, deliberate blink, and said, as if she were picking the words out from between her teeth with a screwdriver: 'I. Won't.'

'But why?' asked Richard.

Body unmoving, Evie's head swivelled Chuckyesquely towards him. 'I. Am. Me,' she said. 'I wear my own clothes.'

'But this is about showing what country you come from, not about pretending to be someone else,' Richard said.

'Raarrrrrghh!' said Evie, and just about put her fist through a wall. So that was the end of that.

RICHARD: Okay. Where is the dressing-up box?

ME (as my sore throat further tightens with tears): It's the box in their bedroom marked 'Dressing-up box'. And [performing rapid calculation about whether strain on throat of issuing further instruction is worth avoiding the potential fatigue and rage that will ensue re the clearing-up required if it is not delivered, and deciding to proceed] be careful of the lid because one of the hinges is coming off, and look properly because the mask might be near the bottom because he hasn't used it for ages, and put everything back in if you have to take it out.

Adds silently: *I hate you beyond the telling of it for not knowing all this in your bones like I do. Why don't you? Why don't you?*

I sat on the sofa to take another handful of painkillers so that I could unball the socks, turn them the right way out, punch the correct programme into the machine, add the powder and do all the other preparatory work that would allow Richard to 'do the laundry' tomorrow morning when I tried again for a lie-in.

I listened as the inevitable unfolded. Richard told Thomas he was going to be Fantastic Mr Fox for World Book Day. Didn't suggest it, nudge him towards it or try to sell him on the idea in any way – just told him. Thomas – a generally amenable child, but just then post-violin lesson and as frazzled as everyone else by my general incapacitation – objected. Voices rose. Hostilities escalated. Evie got involved. I levered my aching carcass off the sofa and went to intervene.

On the way upstairs my inner monologue unspooled furiously. 'Do you know what dealing with a child requires? Self-control. It actually requires you to dig quite deeply into yourself and not get cross. To stay your tongue. To set aside your own feelings and consider that the person you are dealing with does not have an adult's comprehension, appreciation of the need to compromise or any of a thousand other things you would like him to have. And go from there.' You can imagine how well I managed to follow my own strictures by the time I got up there. It was a mess.

This is just one example. It occupied twenty minutes of the day. There have been a lot of twenty minutes in the last seven days. The race to replace my resources faster than they are depleted feels even less winnable than usual. I may never be well again.

Saturday, 4 March

Not that I should be complaining, really, I suppose. Messages keep arriving from Rachel with new instances of Alex's abdication from duties. Failure to turn up at children's football matches, cancellation of planned pizzas after school, and so on. And he's asked to be 'let off' paying his share of the household bills until he's got the new flat sorted. It's becoming increasingly hard to know what to say. He is literally leaving us speechless. Although I believe Céline found some choice legally freighted words that she put in a letter about the bills. She had no idea what she was talking about – it's not her area of law at all – but she put it on the firm's headed paper and the money arrived in Rachel's account two days later, so it seems to have worked. Now if we could just find a solicitor pal for the thousands upon thousands who don't have one to call on, we might actually start to get somewhere.

Sunday, 5 March

Richard takes the children to the Science Museum on Saturday and then for an overnight stay to Mum and Dad's till Sunday so that I can convalesce. I do a week's professional and domestic tasks in forty-eight hours and feel worse than ever. But I'm back in the office tomorrow, so that will be a relief.

Monday, 6 March

'It's my birthday on Friday,' says Richard.

'That it is,' I say.

'We should go out.'

'It'll be the final episode of this,' I say, pointing to the television, upon which we have just watched a thriller starring either Philip Glenister or David Morrissey, if indeed they are different people. 'It's running every night for the week.'

'You could watch it later on iPlayer,' he says.

'That goes against the entire principle of the exercise,' I say.

He looks at me. I eye him back. He keeps looking at me. I crack.

'If you – YOU – can find a babysitter,' I say, 'we can go out. But YOU.'

'Okay.' He sighs. I relax. We do not have a great history with babysitters.

The first handful we tried after Thomas was born were no good and that was my fault. I just couldn't leave him with anyone. Nothing personal, all you legions of friends, family, hired professionals who turned up at the appointed hour for another attempt at me leaving the house to have a glass of wine in the pub round the corner. (Crazy post-partum times, dudes! Crazy post-partum times!) I'm sure you were all sane, non-murderous, non-baby-trafficking types really, and I'm sorry about all those muttered imprecations as you tried to heave me out of the front door, but I just wasn't ready. Maybe we should have started smaller. I could perhaps have begun with a carton of juice on a stool at the bottom of the garden and worked up from there.

Ah, well. Part of the problem at least was solved by Evie coming along. Honestly, once you've got a spare, everything changes. A tiny blemish on the precious firstborn's skin sees you booking a private appointment with a dermatologist at two o'clock in the morning. Rip-roaring chickenpox on the second, and you're just spooning in Calpol and hoping for the best. Precious firstborn gets puréed organic everything, second gets whatever's in the fridge (you call it baby-led weaning; it's actually called leftovers). If I had a third, it would probably be dressing its own wounds and foraging in bins for scraps.

And you're happy to go out. Desperate, in fact. Even if, like me, going out was never your thing, the presence of two under-threes in the house will have you scrambling for the door every night possible.

Unfortunately, by that point, all our sources had dried up. Family had moved, friends had all had new babies of their own and professionals seemed to have raised their prices to such a level that Richard suggested we just hire a solicitor to babysit and work on our car-insurance claim at the same time and save ourselves a fortune.

Then the woman who runs the local café overheard me on

my phone trying to find someone and offered her daughter, Leila. 'She's a good girl,' she assured me. 'Hardly any trouble.' This was not entirely reassuring but this was a woman who had many times in the early days of motherhood let me drink my decaff while breastfeeding and pay her days later when I next remembered to bring my purse with me, so I owe her much (apart from the cost of the Americanos. That debt's all cleared).

Leila turned up in tears.

'Oh, my goodness!' Richard said, as she stumbled up the garden path. 'What's happened?'

'Geffen broke up with me!' she wailed, as she collapsed in a sobbing heap at the kitchen table.

'Oh,' said Richard, turning an agonised face towards me. I said nothing. We were clearly not going out. I would have to get my entertainment here. 'Well,' he said, turning resignedly back to her and patting her awkwardly on the shoulder, 'what kind of name is "Geffen" anyway?'

'It – it – it was *his* name!' cried Leila.

'Ah, yes, I see,' said Richard, turning to look at me more agonisedly. I said nothing. 'Well, affairs of the heart are – uh – always tricky, Leila, especially at your age. What are you – twenty-eight, twenty-nine?'

'Sixteen!'

'Well, there you go. Bound to be bumps in the road then. Did he – um – give you any idea of why he wished to sunder the relationship?'

'I wouldn't let him finger me before the AS mock!' she said. 'I wanted to concentrate!'

A pause.

'Which AS mock?' said Richard, valiantly, before I took pity. I spent the rest of the evening feeding her tea, biscuits and a lot of lies about how it would all get easier in time. Richard watched *The Great Beauty* ('to cleanse my mind') until I'd satisfied myself about the state of both her emotions and her contraceptive knowledge and let her go home.

Babysitter number two was the daughter of the woman who ran Evie's Rhythm 'n' Rhyme! class (exclamation mark not optional), who was so intimidating that I could never say no even when she made me be the bunny who hop, hop, hops to be funny, so I could hardly refuse when she requested work for her daughter Lisa who was saving up to – I don't know, do something pointless in a foreign country after her GCSEs.

Lisa turned up with a rucksackful of wine and vodka. We could hear her clanking as she came up the path. 'Makes a change from sobbing, I suppose,' Richard said. A quick perusal of her Facebook page showed she was planning quite a night of it. She was both baffled and hurt by our refusal to let her stay. She was going to buy the new Urban Decay palette with her childcare proceeds, apparently, and now her life was ruined.

To be honest, I found it quite refreshing to be faced with a tantrumming youngster and not feel the slightest twinge of guilt about it. Not, perhaps, as refreshing as a night out but by that stage I was learning to take what I could get.

And number three, a friend of a friend of a friend's daughter, didn't turn up at all. 'Just didn't fancy it,' she – is the word 'explained'? – when I bumped into her on the street a few days later.

By that time, fortunately, I no longer cared. Life with two children had eroded my desires. By then I craved small domestic delights, not big nights out. A bath. A book. An uninterrupted bowel movement. Bed before nine. Preferably in that order. So things have remained since.

Richard, alas, remains infuriatingly eager for a social life. 'So, go!' I tell him, every time. 'Do something! Have fun somewhere!'

'But I want to be with you!' he says, as baffled by my inability to grasp this as I am by his inability to understand that I dream of being home alone, staring out of the window at an empty landscape, holding a cup of coffee that is magically refilled for ever without anyone coming near me.

Does that mean we really are in need of a night out together, to reconnect or something? Or is it a sign that we really, really aren't?

'Fourth time lucky,' says Richard, buoyantly, as he scrolls through his phone looking for possible contacts that will lead him to babysitter number four. He alas comes up with the excellent idea of messaging Céline to ask if she has a new au pair yet with whom she's happy and if so, can she ask if we can hire her for the next evening she's free? *Oui* and *oui*, Céline replies, before I can get to my phone and instruct her otherwise. *She is free a fortnight today. Contact details follow.* Richard breaks the good news to me. 'But never mind!' he says encouragingly, as he hugs me. 'A fortnight's a long time! You may be dead by then!'

Wednesday, 8 March

In order to try to persuade him to stick to the plan, Rachel sent a video to Alex of the children saying how much they were looking forward to seeing him after school tomorrow. He has been bombarding her with messages about her 'cruel emotional manipulation' ever since. She's asked us not to act any differently towards him when we see him but Christ, he's making it hard.

Friday, 10 March

Richard's birthday. I let him have sex with me last night and the children gave him homemade cards this morning. '"Hapee burthday Daddy",' Richard read aloud. 'Thank you, Thomas. And "Happy berthdy fat man." Thank you, Evie. I shall have a spring in my step all day.'

It's my day off so I run errands for six hours, before doing pick-up, dropping David home, then bundling my own offspring through the front door with an enthusiastic 'Right – everybody into the kitchen to help me make Daddy's birthday cake!'

Their faces drain of hope and colour.

'No,' says Evie, executing a smart about-turn and disappearing into the sitting room.

'I will if you really need me, Mummy,' says Thomas, backing slowly away, 'But ...'

'But what? I thought you'd both want to! Baking cakes is fun!'

'It's not,' shouts Evie, from the sitting room.

'It is!' I shout back.

'It's not,' says Thomas.

'Why not?'

'You get so cross.'

'Really cross,' says Evie, appearing at the doorway.

'Like, really, really cross,' agrees her brother. 'And you sort of cry under your breath.'

I think back to the gingerbread men baked for Christmas, so inedibly hard we ended up using them as stencils for paper chains. To the summer-fete cupcakes so full of my tears of frustration that we had to bill them as salted caramel. To the flapjacks instantly christened 'flopjacks'. To the traybakes that wouldn't leave the trays. To ...

'I'll make it on my own,' I say, and watch their tiny faces fill with relief.

'Right, you fuckers,' I say as I eye the ingredients laid out on the kitchen table, 'let's do this.'

When the timer goes off, the children come to witness the results of my labours being taken out of the oven.

I place the tin on the table.

The children regard it wordlessly for a moment.

'It's very ... thin,' says Thomas, eventually.

'Shallow,' I correct him. 'It's very shallow. Shallower, actually, than when it went in.'

We return to our wordless contemplation. Evie is next to break the silence. 'We were talking about *Bake Off* once and Mrs Fisher said the best cakes are made with love.'

'That's maybe where I went wrong.' I nod.

'We'll ice it for you,' says Thomas, kindly. 'That'll maybe hide it a bit.'

I mix them, at the insistence of Evie, who has recently learned about primary colours, three batches of icing in red, blue and yellow and take myself off for a shower and further swearing in private.

When Richard gets home we present him after tea with what looks like a Frisbee covered in shit.

'I forgot that all the primary colours mixed together make brown,' says Evie, thoughtfully.

'It won't taste like poo, though,' says Thomas, brightly.

'We don't know that,' I point out. 'All bets are off since it came out shallower than it went in. That isn't technically possible but it happened.'

'Then,' Richard beams as he picks up a knife, 'you have technically baked – and iced! – a miracle! Thank you very much, clever family.' He cuts a piece for each of us, the sweat of exertion beading his brow by the third slice.

I congratulate him later, as I slide the rest of the debacle into the bin, for manfully finishing his slice after the rest of us abandoned ours. 'I thought it was a Frisbee covered in shit!' he says cheerfully. 'Biting into it and finding it was actually made of food was a nice surprise.'

Just then the doorbell rings. We stare at each other, alarmed. 'Who can that be?' says Richard. 'Everyone we know is here.'

It is Mrs Bradley. We are even more dumbfounded. She is holding a cake, a beautiful Dundee cake. 'I made this for his birthday,' she says, handing it to me and nodding in Richard's direction. I am dumbfoundeder. 'Th-thank you so much,' I manage. 'But how … how did y—'

'Evie came out into the garden and told me what was going on,' she says. 'Not that I couldn't smell most of it. So,' she turns back down the path, 'there you go.'

'Please stay,' I shout, at her retreating back. It's like shouting at a galleon in full sail. 'And have a slice, won't you?'

'No,' she says. 'I've a quiet evening planned.'

I. Revere. Her.

Sunday, 12 March

I actually don't know what we did this weekend. I know the children didn't do anything stimulating or holistically educational. They look clean, so they must have been bathed. I know I'm exhausted and the washing's done. I know Richard was in and out. It just – went. Bloody hell.

Wednesday, 15 March

Claire is pregnant! On her fourth and final round of IVF! We both cried down the phone.

'That's tremendous work,' says Richard, when I tell him the news. And it is. Now all it's got to do is stick. God, I wish I believed in God. You really do need something to pray to at times like these.

Realise later that the children took advantage of my dizzied distraction to extort new, improved homework terms. Thomas did most of the talking, while Evie stood behind him meditatively tapping a pencil, like a piece of lead piping, on her palm. They now get fifteen minutes of television for every ten minutes of *uninterrupted* homework they do. They are very pleased with themselves. But little do they realise it is a hollow victory! Evie cannot yet tell the time, much to her frustration, Thomas doesn't think to look, and I set the timer on my phone. The amount of telly they actually watch depends entirely on how knackered I am and amounts to far more than they're entitled to. I just nominally link it to homework because it's the only way we can get the bastard stuff done.

Actually, I am not sure who is the victor here.

I FaceTime Rachel in the evening to see how she is. She

has just learned that the flat Alex is proposing to rent is a one-bedroom.

'One bedroom! I said, "Do you not want the kids to come and stay?"' she tells me, sotto voce because the children are up and down all night since he left. '"Oh," he says. "I didn't think of that." He says he'll look for a two-bed now but ...' She shakes her head wordlessly.

So do I. I can think of literally nothing to say about a man who rents a home too small for his children to stay in, at least while there is a chance those children could overhear me. Except – 'I'm sorry,' I say quietly. 'I'm so sorry.'

Thursday, 16 March

Evie barrels into the sitting room, bawling her head off.

'What's wrong, darling?' I say, setting aside my attempts to get Netflix working again. Five years of one or other of them appearing in this state, yet the faint dread that this time – this time! – it will be something serious, unfixable, fatal to emotional health if not physical, the shattering blow none can mend still curls round my heart, ready to take on solid form and grip it with a fatal force when the terrible news comes.

'Thomas – Thomas said ...'

'What?' I say, as the grip tightens.

'He said – that I'm made of plastic!' She throws herself into my arms and gives herself wholly up to the weeping moment.

My heart lives to fight another day.

Let joy be unconfined, but quietly – Richard's birthday meal is off! We've lost Élise as our babysitter. Céline came home unexpectedly early from work the other day and found her and the children sitting at the kitchen table painting peg dolls. She was initially delighted to find such an explosion of artistic activity in the heart of the home, but upon closer inspection it turned out that they were painting dozens and dozens of peg dolls and that the children looked quite weary. Enquiry ensued and the findings were that Élise had formed the children into a painting production line in order to expand her business selling the dolls – made to look like various pop stars, famous superheroes and TV celebs – online. Romilly and Olivier painted the base layers and she added the distinguishing clothes and features thereafter. Élise had been keen to explain that theirs was a win-win situation. The children were being paid for their work but the nearly threefold increase in saleable items meant there was still only a benefit to her bottom line. 'She showed me her spreadsheets,' said Céline, when she rang. 'I was actually very impressed. But the children were tired and I suppose on the whole it is not good that she makes them work like this. But then I thought – what good discipline! It is better than watching television, *non*? But, no. It is not right. So she has gone.'

Thus she's back to the au pair drawing board. Which reminds me, I must find a new plumber. And chase all the old ones. I have some time back now. The job of tracking down another babysitter remains with Richard, so I can cross 'shaving my legs, finding unladdered tights, defrosting ready meals for children and person of unknown origin and dietary require-ments' off my list for at least another month and re-dedicate myself to dilatory home appliances.

Friday, 17 March

In the evening I am not-watching some rubbish on telly when 'You've got a thousand-yard stare on,' says Richard, as he plonks himself down on the sofa, pushes a mound of stuff off the coffee-table onto the floor – 'We must be tidier,' he adds – and puts his feet up on it. 'What are you thinking about?'

'I'm totting up the week's accounts,' I say.

'Don't we have bank statements and, possibly, apps and things to do that?'

'Not money. All the other things.'

'There are no other things. There is only money.'

'There's "Number of times I have been to the gym/hit daily steps quota/gone for long, healthy walk this week".'

'Which is … ?'

'Zero.'

'I see. What else?'

'There's "Number of times I have not had chocolate this week" which is minus one, because I ate a packet of Jaffa Cakes *and* a KitKat on Wednesday.'

'Why did you do that?'

'Because I really, really wanted a packet of Jaffa Cakes and a KitKat on Wednesday.'

(This is why I had to come off Facebook, I realise. So many judgements – from others obviously, both overt and exquisitely covert, but the internal self-flagellation it triggered was worse and, I figured out just in time, completely unsustainable and incompatible with any kind of truly happy or healthy life. The moment I deleted my account I felt an actual weight lift from my shoulders. And in subsequent weeks, it was as if a giant, soul-sucking parasite was gradually and inexorably withdrawing the tentacles it had wrapped round my organs so stealthily I hadn't noticed, and was no longer feeding off them or pumping its toxic excreta back into my unwitting and weakening system. Now, with only me poisoning me, I am far more robust. Result!)

'Continue,' says Richard.

'"Number of times I have failed my friends". This is potentially infinite, because obviously they're not going to tell you most of the time, so what I generally do is just give myself a daily figure that sort of feels like what it would be if you averaged the failures over a lifetime, you know?'

'I do not and hope I never shall.'

'Well, this week is twenty plus a definite one because I still haven't found a way of repaying Mrs Bradley for the cake.'

'She doesn't—'

I hold up a silencing finger. For once it works.

'"Number of times I have failed my children in a way that matters". So, publicly, one – gym shoes, Thomas's, the forgetting of; nutritionally, seven; physically, zero (the only injuries acquired were at school – not my watch); emotionally/morally/spiritually, don't know. Their therapist can send me a list in twenty years' time. But! The number of times I have not had wine in the evening is three!'

'Really?' Richard says, impressed. 'When was that?'

'Monday I was good, Wednesday I fell asleep on the sofa, and tonight!'

'You've got a half-drunk glass in front of you now,' Richard observes.

'Oh,' I say, looking at the half-drunk glass of Pinot Grigio that, it turns out, is indeed in front of me. 'I must have poured it without realising. And drunk it on autopilot. That's probably not a great sign, is it?'

'Friday is not the time for reflection,' Richard assures me. 'It is a time for automatic wine. I'll go and get some more so you can enjoy it consciously this time.'

'I'm a very good husband,' he says, on his return. I comment that if he was an even better husband, I possibly wouldn't be so desperate for a drink by the end of every day that I was capable of throwing it back as naturally and unnoticingly as breathing.

'But isn't that what marriage is?' he replies, as he returns to kick more stuff off the coffee-table so he can rest his feet at a slightly more comfortable angle. 'Helping the other person undo the problems you yourself have created?'

I think about this. I have many thoughts about this. But, in the end, 'You're right,' I say, after a long sip of wine. 'Friday is not the time for reflection.'

Saturday, 18 March

I am listening on the monitor to Richard tucking the kids in for the night. They are discussing poo. Apparently Evie did one at school that left no trace when she wiped her bottom.

'Ah,' says their father, with a level of gravitas I would more usually associate with the citing of vital case law, 'that is what is known as a "ghost poo".'

'Really?' says Thomas.

'Makes sense,' says Evie, and I can practically see her nodding sturdily as she always does when she finds something adding satisfactorily to her world view.

'Yes,' says Richard. 'And sometimes you can do poos that just disappear round the loo bend and it looks like you've flushed already.'

'If you do one of those,' says Evie, slowly, 'and it's a ghost poo too, does it actually count as doing a poo?'

'That,' says Richard, proudly, 'is an *excellent* question. I shall leave you both to ponder that fascinating proposition into the night. You can deliver your responses to me in the morning.'

Some people go to church on Sunday mornings, I think dispassionately. Still. It takes all sorts to make a world, does it not?

Sunday, 19 March

The family consensus is that you did still do a poo because your bottom is empty and a new poo has room to start building up. Internal signs count as much as external, and an important lesson in weighing evidence has been learned, apparently.

My own consensus is that I should start turning the monitor on only after Daddy chat time is over. And maybe start going to church. A strange yearning for grace is upon me.

Monday, 20 March

Rachel's children came back from their first weekend alone with Alex at his interim flat, where they'd camped on the living room floor in sleeping bags. High as kites from the novelty, still smiling and chattering as he left, beaming himself at the success of it all. At bedtime they crashed, of course, and Rachel was up until the early hours comforting one or the other as they cried, woke from nightmares, or just woke to ask questions she couldn't answer. Questions to which there are no answers.

'I couldn't stop thinking about him fast asleep half a mile away,' she tells me, when I pop round to see how she's bearing up. 'Undisturbed. By anything at all.'

Wednesday, 22 March

Richard comes into the kitchen half dressed as I am making breakfast. 'Get more clothes on!' I say. 'Mrs B's scarifying the lawn out there!'

'Feel this,' he says.

'No.'

'It's cancer. Feel it.'

'It's unhygienic while I'm cooking.'

'Feel it!'

I feel it. 'It's not cancer.'

'Why not?'

The things they don't teach you in marriage school. 'Because you can't get cancer of a spot, and that's a spot. How exactly you managed to get a spot there, let alone notice that you'd got a spot there, is a question for another time. Now flip this pancake while I wash my hands.'

'My toe's getting worse!' he shouts, as I turn the tap on.

'No, it isn't,' I say, and even Richard can tell from my tone that I consider the subject closed. He'll start another case soon, I hope.

Thursday, 23 March

'What do you want for Mother's Day?' asks Richard.

There are many answers to this question. The first is the one Fiona texted back to Iain when he asked her last year: *A world in which we are not expected to fall with slavish gratitude on the one day a year when our fathomless and ceaseless contribution to the smooth running of the world, the production, survival and civilisation of the next generation and the cleaning of shit stains off the toilet bowl is recognised with a bad card and worse bouquet, but instead one in which our constant social, professional and domestic industry, avoidance and/or mitigation of disasters and toil at the cliff face of child- and every other sort of care is spoken of with the same reverence down the ages as the Labours of Hercules and in which we are treated every day with the unswerving respect and quiet awe that is our due.*

And if I can't bring this about by Sunday? he replied.

Something from Aromatherapy Associates would be good. Link below.

I decide to try for the middle ground. 'Another day of peace and quiet, like on Valentine's Day, would be nice,' I say.

'Consider it done!' he says, with a dramatic flourish of his hand that knocks two mugs off the draining board and sends them hurtling to the floor. 'Now bring me a dustpan and brush! And pretend I was never here!' They were my two favourite mugs. At least since the last two he broke.

Saturday, 25 March

I turn forty in May and this morning I made the mistake of looking at my face full on – I usually squint or just take in bits – in the bathroom mirror.

It doesn't exactly make me mourn my lost youth – more the fact that I never used it while I had it. ('Mourning your doubly lost youth, then?' Richard offered helpfully when I foolishly mentioned this thought to him.)

And now – on a bad day, an especially tired day, or on a day when the news headlines paint an even more vivid picture of a world on the brink of destruction than usual – I feel so old.

'I should have partied more when I had the chance,' I say to Richard, as we lie in bed that night.

'But you didn't want to party,' he reminds me. 'From everything you have ever told me, all you wanted to do was stay at home and read. And it was all you did do.'

It's true. My mother and I once had a fight – an actual fight – about a disco at the local youth club. She was adamant that I was going. I was as adamant that I was not. 'You're going,' she snarled, grabbing my wrist and pulling me to the front door, 'if I have to drag you there myself!' She bundled me into the car like a kidnap victim, threw me out ten minutes later and watched until I had plodded through the doorway into the church hall, which was already full of the smell of Lynx, teenage hormones and spilled Mad Dog 20/20.

'What are *you* doing here?' said Tracy S, a question born of confusion rather than malice (she was one of the nicer cool girls from school).

'My mum made me come,' I said.

Tracy shook her head at this disturbance to the natural order of things. 'That's not right,' she said. 'That's not right.'

We stood awkwardly for a few seconds. 'Do you want ...' she said hesitantly, '... do you want me to, like, try and show you what to d— I mean, show you around?'

'No, honestly,' I said. 'I'll be all right.'

She frowned. It was obvious to both of us that I wouldn't be, and it was clear that she didn't feel she could go off and leave me without protection. Then her brow cleared. 'I'll get Terry to walk you home!' Terry was her boyfriend. My protestations went unheard as she shouted him over and explained his duties. He nodded. Terry never spoke much. He was too handsome.

'Take her!' said Tracy, cheerily, waving us off. 'Get some cider on the way back, T.'

He nodded.

'Thanks, Tracy,' I said, the relief of going home outweighing by a considerable margin the humiliation of everything else.

'No problem,' she said. 'See you Monday!' and she sashayed off, beautiful, confident and queen of her domain, into the heaving mass of humanity that so terrified me.

Terry walked me home in silence. At my door, I thanked him too and apologised for taking him away from the fun. 'It's just,' I said, gesturing helplessly in the direction we had just come from, 'not my sort of thing, you know?'

He grinned suddenly. 'Not mine either, really. It's Tracy's, though, so just gotta be done. You have a nice night now.' He loped off into the darkness, towards the off-licence.

They were together for ages – in teenage terms at least – and I was quite upset when they split up. The idea that the only two – it seemed to me then – kind people in the year had found each other and found something in each other seemed to promise that the moral arc of the romantic universe could and would eventually bend towards justice for us all. I hope they're both with other lovely people now. I'd get on Facebook and find out but – what are the odds? I'd rather keep the dream alive.

'You were – and remain – so antisocial,' says Richard, breaking into my reverie, 'that you are technically a mineral. You couldn't ever have changed your nature, so you haven't really lost anything. And minerals age brilliantly. Problem solved. By me!' He turns over happily and goes to sleep.

I lie awake a little longer, and resolve to see what moving up a price point in moisturiser can do.

Sunday, 26 March, Mother's Day

My card from Thomas reads: 'Hapy mothers day Mummy. I love you so mutch.' Evie's reads: 'Happy motheres day mummy hav a goode tim I nid a new bakpac.'

I ring my mother. 'There's no need,' she says, as she picks up the phone. 'Your sister's already rung.'

'Well,' I say, 'I'd already booked this call with the postmistress so let's make the most of it anyway. Happy Mother's Day!'

She sighs. 'It's "Mothering Sunday", and it's all nonsense. Cards, phone calls and whatnot!'

'I know,' I say. 'These outpourings of human emotion have got to stop.'

'Anyway,' she says, 'I'll see you after school tomorrow with the children. I'm taking them via the park so we can see if the secret daffodils are up.'

'Great,' I say. 'Thanks. And hey, Mum ...'

'What?' she says warily.

'THANKS FOR EVERYTHING!' I yell. 'I REALLY DO APPRECIATE EVERYTHING YOU'VE DONE AND DO FOR ME!'

'Oh, for God's sake!' she says. 'I'm putting the phone down now!'

'You'll hear me say I LOVE YOU before you do!' I shout. 'Yeah, baby! You did! You heard!' I hear her laughing and huffing before the line goes dead. That was fun. I shall do it again next year.

Fiona's Mother's Day – sorry, Mothering Sunday – is less fun. Her mother-in-law demands the full works: picked up at noon, driven to a fancy restaurant for overpriced lunch while she criticises Iain's income, Fiona's outfit and David's table manners, driven back, kept company for another hour to extract further obeisance, and setting her prisoners free just in time to drive the ninety minutes home before bedtime. Of course Fiona floats the notion of breaking with this desperately inconvenient tradition in the service of a certified witch every year, and every year Iain goes chalk-white at the idea of confronting his hag-mother in any way.

'How was it this time?' I say, when we FaceTime in the evening.

'She spent most of it venting her outrage about the fact that yesterday there was not only a homeless man sitting outside her favourite café but that when the woman in front of her offered to buy him a cup of coffee "the villain asked for a latte"!'

'I don't understand,' I say.

'I think the feeling was that if you're homeless – or "a beggar", as she puts it – you don't get to specify a drink. You don't get to like one thing or another, you just accept what you're given and be grateful. Or she did at one point say, "What's he doing knowing about lattes anyway?" So possibly you just shouldn't know about milky drinks full stop. Who the fuck knows?'

'She ... she does know that he's a person, right?'

'She doesn't believe anyone truly exists outside herself. She's not going to start with a homeless man, is she?'

'She is the worst. It's fabulous, in a way.'

'I'm glad you think so. You can take her next time.'

Tuesday, 28 March

Am reading a book on the sofa when Richard wanders through, gazing at his phone. 'Debra Messing,' he announces, 'says that fifty is the new forty.'

'So?' I ask.

'Nothing,' he says. 'Just ...' he gestures vaguely around him '... let that free you.'

Thursday, 30 March

Rachel and I go for a coffee after drop-off. The children, she says, are settling. Rachel herself is settling. Alex seems a bit less settled than he thought he'd be. He'd hung around when he'd dropped the girls back last time, as if he was hoping to be asked in.

'And did you ask him in?' I say.

'I had to,' she says. 'If the children look up at me with their bloody begging saucer-eyes, wanting him to stay for tea and an evening of everything looking right. What can I do?'

'Nothing,' I say. It is an impossible situation.

'He's looking more tired and woebegone when he brings them back too,' she says. 'That helps.'

'Because you feel sorry for him?'

'God, no.'

Get home to find Mrs Bradley out inspecting her daffodils ('Good morning!' 'Hmm') and a card from a plumber saying he called while I was out. I ring the number. It has been disconnected.

Friday, 31 March

Have checked again with Richard – he still hasn't found a baby-sitter. We have officially agreed to roll the birthday dinner into whatever sorry excuse for my birthday celebration we come up with. 'Kill two birds with one stone,' says Richard. 'In fact,' he brightens, 'do you remember in the old house when we had that actual dead pigeon on the lawn? And you couldn't clean it up because you were massively pregnant and before I got round to it, next door's dog jumped over the fence and ate it?'

'Yes.'

'This is like that. Efficiency arising out of inefficiency! I think it may be my superpower!'

The dog got very ill, I recall. We had to go halves with the neighbours on the vet bill. But uprooting Richard's ability to rewrite history in his favour goes beyond the energies I can muster today.

'Maybe,' I say. 'Maybe.'

Saturday, 1 April

Rachel – or, rather, Rachel's brother's sister-in-law – has discovered Alex on Tinder.

'Well,' says Fiona, when I tell her, 'weren't we all just fucking waiting for this?'

We may have been. Rachel wasn't. She comes to spend the evening with me after dropping the children off – at the block's front door, waiting till she sees Alex come down from the flat and let them in before driving off immediately thereafter – because who wants to be alone when they've just found out their husband is advertising his penis as ready for business ten minutes after he's left? Fiona's joined us for moral support.

'I basically just start crying the minute I get home from drop-off to the minute I have to leave for work or pick them up again,' says Rachel, wiping her eyes and blowing her nose. 'I barely even notice I'm doing it any more. Sorry.'

'No apology required, I assure you,' I say, bringing her more tissues and wine. 'I'm so sorry. About it all.'

'It's just another ... I don't know.' She sighs exhaustedly. 'You run scenarios in your head, don't you? What if he came crawling back? What if he apologised, couldn't believe what a mistake he'd made, if he declared undying love for me, blamed a moment of madness ... And when he started looking tired and – what the fuck did I say? Woebegone? *Woebegone* – I ran them more. Because I *did* start to feel sorry for him. I did start to feel a – a weird sort of hopeful. And all the time he was ... And that's why he was tired! And that's what it's all been about. Just wanting to shag someone new. All the possibilities I've entertained, all the scenarios – and it's been that obvious, the most basic, basic, ordinary, stupid thing all along.'

What can we say? 'No, there'll be more to it than that'? 'Yes – the desire to put his penis in a new vagina trumped, absolutely, the love and life you'd built together'? Neither is exactly useful. So instead the three of us draw up a list of playdates, pick-ups and so on, so that Rachel can expend her energies on trying to hold herself and what remains of family life together. So the children are protected as best they can be, and so Alex can continue his sampling of new delights unconcerned. It's the way it's always gone and the way it always goes.

Monday, 3 April

'Get a move on, get a move on, hurry up, you can, you're nearly eight years old that's why, what's the matter, just ignore him, why don't you try thinking for a moment, do I have to do everything myself, how many times have I told you, do, don't, turn it round the other way, no, the other way, for God's sake, get a move on, use some common sense, it will be where you last left it, I don't know, you should know, what are you playing at, you're nearly eight years old that's why not, put that down, pick that up, don't just leave it, put it away, when I was your age I always, switch that off, slow down, where did you last see it, why don't you try looking properly, I can only do one thing at once, I only have one pair of hands, because in this family we help each other, get a move on, hurry up, we're going to be late, when I was your age I never, don't be rude, don't be cheeky, be polite, stop that, you've got it inside out, don't do that you'll break it, well I warned you, and what do you think I can do about it, because you're five years old that's why, I don't know, it doesn't matter why, just do it, just don't do it, we are not made of money and this place is not a hotel, because I say so that's why, it is a reason, get a move on, hurry up, we're going to be *late*, indoor voice please, am I talking to myself, take it off, not like that, like this, if I've told you once I've told you a million times, you're five years old that's why not, don't ask why just do it, I don't care why not, just go and play, no, you can't, get a move on, we're going to miss the thing, where's your, why's it there, don't talk back to me, don't say that about people, it doesn't matter what Daddy and I do, get a move on, get a move on, hurry up, it's getting *so late*, get undressed, get a move on, get your teeth done, get into bed, get a move on, stop talking, give me a kiss, *goodnight*.'

So passes another day.

Mrs Bradley has been mostly in the garden reading a book, with the dog asleep at her feet.

Friday, 7 April

That evening as Richard and I undress before bed a vestigial memory twitches, of the days when this was an inescapably erotic act instead of just another hurdle that separates me from an already insufficient night's sleep, and I have to ask. 'Dingus?' I say.

'Yes, light of my life,' he says, peaceably turning another page of his book. (Somehow he is always in bed before me. Probably because I still, after thirty years, cannot undo my bra in one swift or easy motion.)

'Have you ever had the urge to run off and pork someone new?'

He sighs and puts his book aside. 'I have been waiting for this,' he says. 'So listen to me very carefully. No, I have not.'

'Really?' I say doubtfully.

He sighs again, holds up a hand and starts enumerating on his fingers. 'I have seen comely women during my passage through life since I met you and recognised that they are comely. I assume you have done likewise on the vanishingly rare occasions on which you come across men marginally more handsome than I.

'I have – occasionally – wondered what it would be like to have sex with them or someone new, as yet unmet.

'I have never had anything remotely approaching "an urge" to do anything, anything at all, about it. I have never had to dissuade myself from doing anything. I cannot imagine the circumstances – or the woman – that would induce such a necessity. You alone mean too much to me, never mind the children. I love you, and porking you, and you and the porking of you only.'

'So why has Alex … ?'

'I cannot speak for other men,' he says. 'And you must not ask it of me. To speculate on another's innermost desires, thoughts and motivations is beyond both my abilities and inclination. And so, please, now, may I return to my book?'

'You may,' I say. 'And thank you.'

'What for?'

'For your frank and full answer,' I say. 'And for only wanting to pork me, still.'

'You are very welcome,' he says. 'I don't suppose I could do it now, could I?'

'I'm really tired.'

'As you wish, my pet. As you wish.'

Saturday, 8 April

In penance for everything we've ever done wrong in this or any previous life, we spend the morning at Tate Modern with the children. Thomas stands in front of each piece for a dutiful ten seconds and moves on, the thought of the milkshake we have promised each of them at lunchtime trammelling any recidivist urges nicely. Thank God the forces of bribery are invisible to passers-by, who glance fondly at my perfect little boy.

Evie, meanwhile, marches round pointing aggressively at each exhibit in turn and growling, 'Not art! Not art!' as her finger jabs the air ever more fiercely. I am mortified but Richard is proud.

'She's right!' he says happily. 'It's not art – it's rubbish! Like everything after 1959. I didn't tell her that – she realised it herself!'

They enjoy the milkshakes.

In the afternoon, we park them guilt-free in front of the television and get on with chores. Richard takes the bins out and then comes upstairs to tell me all about it. He finds me sobbing on the bedroom floor. He is not unduly perturbed. This happens about twice a month on average – once because of my period (I realise, as ever, later), once because of … y'know … life.

'What is it this time?' he asks, not unkindly.

I gesture wordlessly at the piles of tiny clothes around me.

'You are … decluttering?' he says carefully.

I nod.

'And these are' – he nudges through a pile with his foot – 'Thomas's clothes?'

I nod again. He nods back, sits down next to me and puts his arm around me.

'It's just the fact that – look! – these are so small! And he's so big now.' And at the same time still so small. In my head, he still fits into these clothes. In my head, he will fit into these clothes for ever. 'And then there's all the rest,' I say, properly crying now and burying my face in Richard's side so the children won't hear me. He hugs me tighter.

It's the fact that they bring back such bad memories that should be so happy. I had a terrible time giving birth to Thomas ('It was like the second day of the Somme,' Richard once told a friend many years later when I would allow him to speak of it. 'You know – once their optimism had worn off') and postnatal depression infused everything for the first eighteen months of his little life. I took no pride or delight in dressing him or bathing him or changing him. I left it all to Richard, and to my mother, who basically came and lived with us for the first three months while my body, at least, healed. They took him out and showed him off to the world. I stayed at home and worked and tried to pretend life hadn't changed.

There's a tiny, tiny hand-knitted cardigan and cap that a family friend called Michael sent me a few days after Thomas was born, which his own mother had made for him sixty years before. It was the kindest, sweetest, most unexpected gift I've ever had, and although Richard dressed Thomas in them when the day finally came for us to leave the hospital, I couldn't write and thank Michael because my mind was broken.

The bigger clothes – the three-year-old's dungarees, the four-year-old's jumpers, worn by him and passed down to Evie – make me compare the happiness of Evie's birth (a straight-forward, elective Caesarean) to his and mourn again the waste of that precious first year and a half. You could say I've missed nearly a third of his life. That proportion will go down, obviously, and I'll feel better. Just not, perhaps, today as I sit in the middle of this island of tangible reminders of the worst of times.

On the other hand, I reason, as I wipe my face on Richard's sleeve and try to pull myself together, at least I *am* sitting. Couldn't do that seven years ago with a shredded whatnot and a busted coccyx! And I'm totally fine about being more than eight feet away from the loo. Practically insouciant, really. Things do get better.

My mind is mended too. It's in a slightly different shape – a bit like my whatnot, really – and I do think it has weak spots that weren't there before (again, a bit like my whatnot, which is why I went for the Caesarean). But day to day it works fine (a bit like – well, you get the idea). At least as long as I don't try to streamline my wardrobes, drawers or memories too often.

'You can keep it all, you know,' says Richard. 'Let's just put everything back, and keep it all.'

'Can you do it?' I snuffle. 'I've got a thank-you letter I must write.'

Sunday, 9 April

The lock on the loo door that has been hanging half off for six months finally gave up the ghost today when Evie cannoned in – I haven't had a quiet wee in nearly a decade – to ask me whether cows drink milk. I will add the fixing of it to Richard's list of things to do, I think. It is a short list and I keep it for laughs. Dry, hollow laughs.

Wednesday, 12 April

7.20 a.m. On loo having a wee: interrupted by Thomas informing me that he and Henry have knocked over the Honey Nut Clusters. Can he eat the ones on the floor that the cat hasn't licked?

4.40 p.m. In loo changing tampon: Evie disobeys explicit instructions and barges in to show me a drawing of – well, I can't remember. I was too busy leaking clotted blood everywhere while I tried to find the disposal bags, which were not where they should be, and trying to hide evidence of what Richard has taken to calling 'your time of womanly suffering' ('You say that as if womanly suffering were limited to a few days a month,' I snarled last time. 'It's not'), lest her fragile five-year-old sensibility be traumatised.

'Those,' she said matter-of-factly, pointing at the box I'd got down from the cupboard, 'are pompoms.'

'Are they?' I said. 'How do you know?'

'Tasha brought one in and showed us in the playground once,' she said. 'They're for stopping nosebleeds in your bum.'

'That's good to know,' I said. 'But I did say not to come in here, didn't I?'

'Yes,' she said, leaning casually against the doorframe. 'Hey, I've got eczema, look.' She lifts up her knee to show me. 'What is it?' she says.

'It's eczema,' I say.

'I thought so.' She nods. 'Thanks.'

'No problem.'

Off she goes.

5.45 p.m. Take advantage of the kids eating their tea in relative tranquillity to slip to the loo and do a poo.

5.48 p.m. Both children barge in, panicked and wailing.

'We didn't know where you were!'

'We thought you'd gone for ever!'

'Why didn't you tell us where you were going?!'

'Because I'm eight feet away, in this toilet under the stairs and I thought you would assume that is where I had gone.'

'We're not sidekick!' says Evie, furiously.

'What?'

'She means psychic,' explains Thomas.

'Oh, I see. Well, I'm sorry for my oversight. Now, could you get out, please?'

'It smells funny in here,' says Evie.

'That's because I'm about to do a poo. Could you. Get out. Please.'

'Really?' says Evie, interest piqued. 'I didn't think grown-ups did poos.'

'Of course they do,' says Thomas. 'Anything that eats does poos.'

'Is that right?' says Evie to me.

'I – I think so,' I say, automatically starting to run basic biological processes through my head. 'Yes, it must— Hang on. GET OUT. I am a thing that eats and I want to do this poo in peace. GET OUT.'

'All right, all right,' grumbles Evie. 'You only had to say.'

8.40 p.m. Children in bed, I'm in the bath and making one of my biannual efforts to shave my legs. In walks Richard. 'Why, my hobbitty little half-woman!' he cries, when he sees what I'm up to. 'However shall I recognise thee hereafter?'

'Get out,' I whisper. 'Get out.'

'Of course,' he says, undoing his flies and stepping over to the lavatory. 'Just let me have a wee first. If it turns into a poo I'll go downstairs, don't worry.'

'You're a god amongst men,' I say.

Oh, a new plumber came. He was twenty-two, drank three cups of tea while describing his daily workout routine to me and said the dishwasher needs a new spdffusdkjfdyurb.

He didn't have a spdffusdkjfdyurb in the van for our model because he's only seen one that old in his nan's house, but he will be back in a few days with one.

Mrs Bradley was out weeding so she watched him return to his van and drive away. 'Number five, was that?' She sniffed.

'They're plumbers,' I replied, without thinking. 'Not lovers.'

Most unexpectedly, she chuckled. 'Ah, well,' she said. 'Maybe next time.' She nodded in a decidedly friendly manner and went indoors. When the shock had worn off, I realised that, given the choice, I would rather have a decent plumber than a decent lover. Spdffusdkjfdyurb.

Thursday, 13 April

Today Fiona WhatsApped me a picture of Amelia Earhart's letter to her fiancé: 'Please don't let us interfere with the other's work or play ... In this connection I may have to keep some place where I can go to be myself, now and then, for I cannot guarantee to endure at all times the confinement of even an attractive cage.'

Fired by her example, I have ordered a new lock for the loo door.

Good Friday, 14 April

Before we leave for Grandma and Granddad's, where we are to spend the long Easter weekend, I grab the children by their necks, shove a chocolate egg into Thomas's hands and a packet of seeds into Evie's and march them over to Mrs Bradley's door. My Easter gift to myself is getting that Dundee cake off my conscience.

I knock. Evie demurs. 'She doesn't like people!'

'Nobody in their right mind likes people,' I say. 'But they still have to see them occasionally. Smile.'

Mrs Bradley opens the door. A flicker of surprise crosses her face.

'These are for you!' says Thomas, handing her the egg and nudging Evie into handing over the seeds. 'Because you like gardening and because everyone likes chocolate.'

'Not everyone,' says Evie. 'And if you don't, you can give it back.'

'It's just to say happy Easter,' I say hurriedly, while mentally treading firmly on Evie's throat. 'And thank you again for the lovely cake.'

'It really was nice,' says Thomas. 'I ate loads. I ate more than Mummy even knows.'

'I'm glad you enjoyed it,' says Mrs Bradley. She looks at the seeds. 'Platycodon.'

'I just had to go by what looked pretty and wasn't too late to plant,' I say anxiously.

'They're right,' she says.

'Great,' I say.

'Would you like to come in?' she says reluctantly.

'Would *you* like us to come in?' says Evie, and I tread on her throat again.

Mrs Bradley considers. 'Not really,' she says.

'We won't, then,' says Evie, cheerily. 'Goodbye.'

'Goodbye,' says Thomas, equally cheerily.

'We do have to get to my parents',' I say weakly, uselessly.

Mrs Bradley nods. 'Thank you very much for the seeds and the chocolate,' she says. 'And drive safely.' She shuts the door.

My reverence for her increases every time we meet.

Easter Sunday, 16 April

The adults are all sucking down strong gin and tonics as we watch the children hunt for Easter eggs in the grandparental garden. Well, Thomas is hunting. Evie is just following him and picking up the eggs that fall from his basket every time he leans over to collect a new one and putting them in her own.

'She's so clever, isn't she?' Grandma says fondly. 'And he's so wonderfully unacquisitive!'

'He's a fool and she's a sociopath,' says Richard, refilling everyone's glasses. 'But they're *our* fool and sociopath.'

Easter is the perfect holiday. PERFECT. Why have I never noticed this before? I think it's because for the first few years of having the children we still automatically, unthinkingly used to up sticks for ten days and try to manage a 'proper' break in the countryside or by the sea. God, the stupid things you do when you're young.

If you stay put, you fully appreciate all that Easter has going for it. The length, for a start. Two weeks. Not three. Not six. Two. And half of that is bank holiday. Thank you, Jesus, for dying and being resurrected on separate days and to whatever confluence of socio-culturo-econo-historical forces rolled one over into Monday. I'm having the full four days, Richard's managing three, plus the quiet run-down and gentle re-immersion that bookends the official time off. There's something about the time of year that militates against full-throttledom at every turn. We're coming up on a full seventy-two hours of being like a real family, the kind you see in books and on telly. Three generations tumbling about the grandparental home, chatting, playing, laughing together, and drinking, age-appropriately. And – thanks to Granddad – eating delicious and nutritious meals around a kitchen table two or three times a day. It's amazing.

Then there's the weather. Bright, but not hot. You can go outdoors without a coat yet not burn. Your child needs a cardigan, not hourly applications of noxious suncream. You can give guiltlessly in to demands for chocolate because it's Easter and the world is temporarily made of chocolate and it would be absurd not to eat it.

There is just enough excitement. There is neither the boredom and frustration of half-term (which, like my hair, is just too short and unmanageable to do anything interesting with) nor the frenzy of Christmas, which leaves everyone in tears of exhaustion by the end. A holiday that starts with daffodils, ends with walks in the park, hoping to see ducklings, and has a chocolate egg hunt in the middle is a holiday that all ages can enjoy.

And there is so much stuff laid on by everyone! Bunny trails everywhere, quizzes, readings of Easter-y things in bookshops and libraries, your local churches going nuts, of course, and trying their hardest to make the Crucifixion family-friendly. I feel for trendy vicars at Easter, I really do. There are some things that are so ... irreducible, you know? Evie has managed to glean the basics, supplementing the few details I was forced to provide a few months ago, and become consumed with the unfairness of it. As it relates to her, I mean, not the unfairness of the blameless son of God being nailed to a cross for our sins. She unfortunately took her concerns to Granddad, who – honourable man that he is – instead of conjuring up imaginary ducklings or stuffing her mouth with gold-foiled eggs tried to engage with them instead.

'Why can we not all come alive again if Jesus could? Just because he's the son of God, it's not fair.'

'It is quite fair. Being the son of God – it's like a job, not just like being an ordinary son of an ordinary person. So he's the only one who can come alive again. If you believe in him, of course.'

'So,' said Evie, slowly, 'if I don't believe in Jesus I *could* come alive again?'

'Er ... no, sorry ... I meant ...' stammered this poor, misfortunate man who had only ever meant to dispel some gauzy mists of ignorance from his beloved granddaughter's world '... actually, it's more sort of the opposite really, because Christians believe in Heaven and ...' This was the point at which I noticed something was amiss. Whenever Evie literally leans into a conversation, it means her attention has been well and truly seized, and this rarely bodes well. I started legging it up the garden towards them, but I had to get out of the sun-lounger first and gone are the days when that was an unthinking manoeuvre.

I reached the two of them just in time to hear her say, 'Whaddya mean "roll up like a scroll"? What does the Last Trump sound like? Will I come back even if I've broken the Swingball? Because I have.'

Never mind. Occasional awkward theological conversations are the only downside to the season.

The world expands. Spring is in the air. The garden – even if our scrubby patch cannot compete with the grandparental Kentish acres* – becomes usable once more and effectively adds a whole new room to your house. Children can come over and play outside while you and their mothers drink coffee and watch them through the window, a level of involvement that suits everyone.

And then suddenly the fortnight's up and they're all back at school. Before you've had time to get sick of them or they of you. You are both left wanting more of this lovely time instead of longing for it to end. If motherhood could be like this more than once a year I could really begin to see the point of it. Ah, well. Roll on next April. Long may the ducklings cast their spell.

Easter Monday, 17 April

'We need to talk about your fortieth,' says Richard, as we finish dinner. (Spaghetti bolognese, not even made in accordance with any Nigella/Nigel/Yotam-sanctioned recipe. Just mince

---

* My parents' garden is seventy feet long but with my mother's customary efficiency she has packed more delights into it than Euclid would have deemed possible. A wooden swing from the apple tree. A climbing frame screened by a clematis-clad trellis so we don't see them endangering their lives. Nesting boxes buried along ivy-covered walls. A little wooden house – no adults allowed. Enormous paddling pool in the summer. And a Swingball, of course. None of this was there in my day, I hardly need point out. We were allowed to play down at the bottom as long as we didn't go near the flowers, picked up all the fallen apples in autumn ('Ignore the wasps! They can only sting you!') and rearranged the grass after we'd trodden on it.

and whatever was red, liquid and to hand in the cupboard. An achievement of its own in this day and age.)

I sigh and grimace.

'It's that or have sex,' he says.

I sigh and grimace again. 'Okay,' I say. 'Let's have sex.'

He looks startled. 'What? Really?'

'Yes.'

'I was not expecting that. I am not prepared.'

'Well, get prepared. I'm going upstairs.'

He looks quite flummoxed as I leave. Not flummoxed enough to stop him following me up very shortly thereafter, but never mind.

Tuesday, 18 April

I have fitted the new loo lock. Amelia Earhart lives!

My high was brought crashing low by the words 'We still need to talk about your fortieth birthday party' uttered by Richard as we sat down to bowls of reheated spag bol – because we know how to live – in front of the TV once we'd flung the children into bed.

'Oh, yes, let's!' I say. 'I'm not having one!'

'You are,' he says.

'I'm not, though,' I say.

'Why not, though?' he says.

'Because,' I say, holding up my hands and enumerating *most* clearly with my fingers, in order to leave no room for manoeuvre, 'one – I'll be forty. Not only will I be one year closer to the grave, which is a weird thing to celebrate anyway and largely why birthdays shouldn't be acknowledged past the age of twelve, but at the indisputable halfway mark through life. From now on there is officially less road left in front than there is behind. This is something I'm happier not confronting. Two – it's a party and I hate parties. You hate parties. We didn't even enjoy our wedding. Three – everyone we know hates parties.

Even if they liked them when they were younger, they hate them now. That is the only benefit to getting older. People come round to your way of thinking and no longer to your house. Four – it's nothing but hard work, cleaning beforehand, cleaning afterwards, having a hangover. Five – just no.'

'Hang on,' says Richard. 'I enjoyed our wedding. Did you not enjoy our wedding?'

Ah. Well. Hmm. Ah. No, I did not enjoy our wedding. I did not realise until it was far too late that I had unconsciously bought into the myth of the Special Day – specifically the transformative aspect of it. I was thirty and should have known better – should certainly have known myself better – but it turns out those myths get in early and they get in deep. I never even questioned whether I would enjoy walking down the aisle in a Proper Frock with a hundred faces turned towards me. I just assumed I would. Even though I don't like dresses. Even though I don't like crowds. Even though being somehow the centre of attention has been the centre of most of my anxiety dreams since I was old enough to have anxiety dreams. I believed somewhere deeper and more powerful than rational thought that my entire personality would set itself aside and I would just be A Bride. Radiant, empty of everything but joy, and revelling in the glory of the big day.

What a tit. Of course, I remained me. To have thought it would be otherwise is as risible as to have thought I would suddenly be five foot six and gazelle-slim (which actually, I realise now, I also did. This, too, should have been a warning that my expectations were awry). The aisle, the ceremony in front of everyone and the faces endlessly pressing in around me all afternoon were all awful. I had to escape to the loo every twenty minutes to cope. Thank God I was wearing a corset and could blame dizzy spells.

I disgorge something of this to a frowning Richard.

'You didn't enjoy our wedding?' he repeats, as I reach a bumbling close.

'Well, no. Not much. But that was my fault. I should have

known I'd prefer a ten-minute register office do in the middle of the night and chips afterwards, but so what? It's just a day. I've been unhappy lots of days.'

'You were *unhappy*?'

'Let's refocus. The point is – it was an important party I'm glad I went to even if I didn't have as much of a blast as I thought I would. It doesn't have any bearing on anything else.'

'So you enjoy being married? You are happy in our marriage?'

'Yes, I do,' I say firmly. 'Yes, I am.' The poor man has had enough nuance for one night. On the plus side, I feel I may have got out of having a fortieth.

Wednesday, 19 April

Thomas bursts into our bedroom early – early, early – this morning. 'Look!' he says joyfully. 'I've invented a spy wave!' He covers his eyes and waves.

'That's – very good,' says Richard. 'Very inventive.'

'Well done!' I say. He rushes out. As he leaves, we notice Evie leaning against the doorway, her striped pyjamas rather adding to than detracting from her air of 'unimpressed thirties gangster'. She fixes us with a lengthy look that goes some way beyond contempt – I can't be sure she doesn't start paring her nails with a flick knife – before walking silently away.

'We'll sleep in shifts tonight,' says Richard.

Thursday, 20 April

Rachel and Alex have gone out for a meal to try to discuss things on neutral territory. I am babysitting.

She comes through the door white and shaking. She asked him about Tinder and he said his friend Sean had put him on there 'for a laugh'. Then he added, 'I only had sex with two women from it. And they didn't mean anything. That's, you know, kind of the point.'

'He mansplained Tinder to me,' says Rachel, pulling a bottle from the fridge, sloppily pouring two large glasses of wine and handing one to me. 'And then' – she starts to laugh at a high pitch – 'he said – he said … "I think I'm ready to come home now."' She drinks. My glass's journey to my mouth halts midway.

'What?' I say.

'He said. I think. I'm ready. To come home. Now. As if – as if everything – as if he'd – as if I was –' Hysteria keeps overtaking her. In the end, I start laughing too. Why not?

'I'm going to rename the house,' she says, through gasps and tears, 'so that the next time he drops the girls off it's to Casa What The Actual Fuck.'

When I get home and tell Richard, he asks if she wants him to put her in touch with a divorce lawyer.

'She hasn't actually mentioned divorce, or lawyers,' I say, considering. 'It's all still happening, if you see what I mean. There's been no time to take stock, really, let alone think ahead.'

'She needs to think about it,' he says. 'Ahead of Alex.'

'He wants to come back,' I say.

'But she said no?'

'Well, she told him she couldn't think about anything yet,' I say.

'He'll hear that as a no, feel defensive and wronged, and then get a lawyer,' Richard says.

'Would you?'

'No, but again – I don't know why I have to keep making this point to you – I am not as other men,' says Richard, placing a hand reverently across his breast. 'Yet I am sufficiently affiliated with the breed that I may speak with some certainty as to the likely thought processes of one of my kind under duress. He will return to his baser instincts – if indeed he ever departed from them. They are of self-preservation. They are of entrenchment. They are of – however inappropriately – revenge, at least getting one's retaliation in first. So tell her. Lawyer up, or take him back.'

'That's some choice,' I say.

'It's no choice at all,' he agrees. 'But we are where we are. Tell her.'

Friday, 21 April

I finally managed to make a vet appointment. Richard helps me wrestle Henry into the cat carrier and put him in the car ('How can one cat weigh this much? He must be denser than the sun') before he heads off to court.

I sit in the waiting room, Henry staring at me with baleful eyes through the hatch of his prison. 'I'm sorry,' I whisper. 'I'll make it up to you when we get home, I promise.'

The vet listens to my beloved's heart, prods at his gums and examines his balding tail. 'Basically,' he announces, 'he's depressed.'

'I'm sorry, what?'

'He's depressed. And anxious. Have there been any big changes at home? A new baby, anything like that?'

'No. I've been thinking of getting a new sofa, but that won't happen for a couple of years yet.'

'New pet?'

'No – oh, wait. The people over the road have a new cat. Could that be it?'

'Probably. Old cat like this doesn't like dealing with new arrivals, doesn't like change full stop.'

I knew there was a reason I loved Henry. We are clearly destined to march in lockstep till the end. My soulmate. I grill him some fish when we get in and he curls up on my lap afterwards, which is literally the best thing that has happened to me all week.

'What are you up to?' says Richard, later that evening, when he finds me squatting by the sitting-room door and swearing quietly.

'I'm trying to get the cat's anti-depressants into this socket,' I say.

He cogitates upon this for a moment. 'No,' he says. 'I'm sorry. I'm going to require a little more in the way of explanation.'

'Henry's been tearing his fur out because he's depressed by the new cat moving in over the road,' I say. 'This' – I hold up what looks like an ink bottle filled with clear liquid – 'is his medicine and it's supposed to attach to this pluggy thing, heat up and gently diffuse into the room he spends most time in, so he can breathe it in.'

'It's a mood-enhancing Glade air freshener for cats. Is that what you're telling me?'

'Yes.'

'And is it okay for us to breathe in too? For the children?'

There is a moment's pause.

'I didn't ask,' I say.

'I see.'

He googles the brand name. 'Safe for use in a family home. I suppose we will have to accept this. But if we all die of tumours overnight, I'm suing them and you. Now, is there anything in this house for a hungry man to eat?'

'I made you some salmon,' I say.

'That's a bit exciting for a Friday night,' he says, looking pleased. 'Or else … No. You cooked it for Henry's tea, didn't you?'

'I cooked enough for both of you,' I say.

'Who came first? Of whom was the thought that lit the piscatory fuse?'

'Let's just be pleased that it ended with a delicious omega-something-rich supper for you,' I say, getting up and heading towards the kitchen. 'And not,' I add, kicking the bowl from which Henry is licking the last pink shreds of his meal under the counter, 'dwell on details.'

Saturday, 22 April

I don't really know what to do about Rachel now. It feels like I would be backing her into a corner by telling her what Richard said about lawyering up. But on the other hand, if he's right – and it all sounds terrifyingly plausible – then I have a duty to arm her as fully and as quickly as possible, don't I?

I sigh and pick up my phone. I ring. I tell her. A slightly softened, hedged version, making it clear these are Richard's thoughts on the matter – only Richard's, only thoughts – and she thanks me. Says she'll think about it. I put the phone down. I sigh.

Sunday, 23 April

I took Thomas, David, Evie and Evie's friend Yinka to Pizza Express for Thomas's eighth birthday. Yes, that's all he wanted. No, he didn't want to bring another friend ('Can I, then?' said Evie, when we made the astonishingly painless arrangements last week, after seven dogged years of mass celebration that Thomas endured as stoically as he had all the dreadful parties we were repaying. 'I need to make up to Yinka for … things'). David had a meat feast, Evie and Yinka shared an adult's pizza. 'With everything on it,' they instructed the waiter, with unblinking stares. '*Everything*.' And Thomas had a Margherita, though we did insist that he joined with everyone else in having a milkshake too. 'It's your birthday,' David reminded him.

'He's friendless,' says Richard, later that night, in bed. 'Ambitionless. Unimaginative. Forgetful to the point of imbecility.'

I sigh. Richard often frets about the ease of raising Thomas, instead of simply revelling in it as I do.

'He prefers meaningful relationships,' I counterpoint. 'And simple food. He is happy in the moment. And he is eight. He is also kind, generous, thoughtful and – above all – quiet and a good sleeper. So be grateful.'

'I'll try.'

'Now stop worrying and go to—'

A gentle snore emanates from the immobile body to my right. I lie awake till two fretting that my boy is indeed too gentle for this world and is doomed to become its endless victim. Happy birthday.

Thursday, 27 April

The plumber has returned! He has fitted the new sfherh-feisfhdksfoik. The dishwasher is no longer making a noise. He relieved me of £195 and bade me good day. Mrs Bradley watched dispassionately as I waved him off with a hanky from the door, straining valiantly to contain the surging emotions in my breast.

Friday, 28 April

The dishwasher has started making a worse noise.

Fiona's MIL keeps asking her when they're going to have a second child. Or rather 'another grandchild for me'.

David's status as an only child is fixed. A couple of years ago, Fiona and Iain were standing in the kitchen discussing in lowered voices the possibility of trying for another (generally, I mean, not there and then) when David popped up from behind a counter and said, 'Why would you bother? I'm a lot of work.'

'You're not too bad,' said Iain.

'I thought you were upstairs playing Octonauts?' said Fiona.

'You thought wrong,' said David, simply. 'I was seeing if I could fit in a cupboard.'

'Why were you seeing if you could fit in a cupboard?'

'Why not?'

'Wouldn't you like a baby brother or sister?' said Iain.

'I would not,' said David.

'Why not?'

'Everyone at school's got one,' said David. 'They get no peace. We get one – I *will* have to live in a cupboard.'

He left them staring at each other as he, a supremely, unerringly methodical child, ducked down to put the dishes back into his test-cabinet and then went upstairs to – presumably – play Octonauts.

'He's got a point,' said Iain, into the sudden silence.

'And that,' said Fiona, as she finished telling me the story, 'was that. With all three of us not that keen, it didn't really seem like much of a runner. Plus, I'd have had to have so much sex.'

'People never warn you about that,' I agree.

Fiona and I both took the better part of two years to become pregnant (not that we knew each other then – it would have been great if we had: all my friends were ridiculously fecund and dropping babies by the dozen, each more beautiful, smiley and sweeter-smelling than the last. I could have done with Fiona by my side to snarl viciously at life). It's an extra bond between us, those shared memories of sex gradually being drained of spontaneity and joy by the keeping of ovulation diaries, staring at mucus in your knickers and insisting on being banged on schedule and only on schedule. 'I always thought being used for sex would feel markedly better than this,' Richard said once, as he lay post-coitally next to me as I drew my knees to my chest, the better to tip my pelvis and send his – carefully recorded in another diary – delivery to its destination. 'I feel like a thing. Which is ironic, because I can no longer feel my thing.' We were coming up to the end of another strenuous mid-month session during which I'd basically demanded a seeing-to every eight hours. I could feel my thing only too well. At that point, chafing was the most painful experience my vagina had ever undergone. We laugh about it all now. Occasionally.

Saturday, 29 April

'So what do you want for your birthday?' asks Richard. 'Present-wise, I mean.'

I pause in my pulling-on of a pair of latex gloves, preparatory to venturing out into the garden to pick up a week's worth of Henry's poos. The anti-depressants have stopped him destroying his tail but seem to have disturbed his psycho-digestive balance. He now disdains the litter tray and deposits his work under the forsythia instead. It's a good job I love him.

I realise that what I really want is completely impossible to achieve, but on the other hand I am about to spend half an hour foraging through hedges for animal shit so I feel like I am entitled to dream a little. 'What I really want,' I reply, 'is to spend the day curled up in bed with Thomas and Evie, reading them stories while I cuddle them and they burrow into me and pat my face, like they used to do when they were younger. Occasionally they will gently interrupt me to tell me how much they love me and will never leave me.

'You will bring us food to eat, drinks to drink, fully charged iPads for the two of them to play with while I nap gently in between, and we will not leave the room. Because I will have checked beforehand that the ceiling and floor are in good repair, that the smoke and burglar alarms are working, and all doors and windows are locked – you will have to stay inside too, sorry, because I can't absolutely trust you to re-lock behind you. I will know that they are completely safe and cannot be harmed in any way and thus I will be granted for twenty-four hours my only remaining true hope and ambition in life: relief from the otherwise constant and corrosive anxiety that I am entirely sure will bring about my early death, which is a whole other worry that I won't get into here, lest I choke hopelessly on my own fear, but remember that everything you need in practical terms is in the orange filing cabinet in the sitting room in an overstuffed and undivided file marked "Insurance, bills and stuff like that".'

'You cannot spend twenty-four hours locked in a room recreating the womb with our children.'

'I think I can.'

'I think you cannot, should not and will not be allowed to.'

'All right. Then I would like a night in a hotel.'

'God, that's a good idea. We haven't been away for a night in for ever. I'll call your mother – do you think she'll want to stay here for the night or have them round at hers?'

'No. I want a night in a hotel. On my own.'

'On your own?'

'Yes!' I say excitedly. 'I'll get there in the early evening, go to the gym if it's got a gym – I'll make sure I book one that doesn't have a gym – then a couple of drinks in the bar, then up to my room to watch crap TV while in sole charge of the remote, order room service that will bring me food I haven't cooked myself – can you just shove that chair over, I'm getting a bit giddy, need to sit down – then go to bed whenever I want! Just clean my teeth and go to bed! It'll take five minutes! No feeding the cat, tidying the kitchen, locking up, unplugging chargers—'

'I keep telling you, you don't need to unplug chargers. They're not dangerous. When something's connected to an outlet but not drawing power—'

'No arguments about whether it's necessary or neurotic to unplug chargers, no finding sports kits, no signing homework diaries! You'll be doing all that! Miles away! At home! And then – listen, listen to this! – I'll sleep! And I'll sleep until I wake up. No alarm, nobody snoring, nobody pulling the covers off me because they still haven't learned how to move under bedclothes without disturbing them even though it's a skill that can be learned so early that I personally cannot remember a time before I mastered it, nobody calling for a drink of water or asking if it's morning or wanting me to explain eclipses when they wake with the stray thought at midnight. I'll sleep until I just ... wake up!'

The light of quasi-religious fervour shines in my eyes. A

tremor of near-sexual arousal (if memory serves) runs through me.

There is a short silence.

'So, what you're saying,' replies Richard, slowly, 'is that for your birthday you would, for twenty-four hours, either like to put your children back into your womb or to forget that you are a mother – and a wife, but we'll maybe come back to that another time – entirely? Does that not seem a little odd to you? Irrational? Inconsistent? Contradictory in the extreme?'

'Mm?' I say distractedly. I've already stripped off my gloves and am rapidly googling hotels and typing numbers into my phone. 'Hello? Is that the Garden House Hotel? Tell me, do you have a gym? ... No? Great.'

Monday, 1 May

'Why is this infernal machine still making a noise?' says Richard, glaring at the dishwasher. 'No. Why is this infernal machine making an even worse noise than usual? I thought we were sorting it.'

'We have had other things on our mind,' I say. 'We arranged callouts with various plumbers and we waited in at various times and we were never visited. Or we had to go out to collect we's children and the plumber turned up at that non-specified time so we missed we's chance. Then we briefly believed it had been fixed. But we was wrong. So we has had to start all over again.'

'That's ridiculous,' he says. 'You're clearly not being assertive enough.'

'Am I not?'

'No.'

'Okay, you take over.'

'I shall!'

'All right. From this moment, you are now in charge of dealing with the dishwasher. Brilliant. I'll cross it off my list.'

He stands there. 'What?' he says uncertainly.

'Tell you what,' I say, marching to the fridge and taking a sheaf of papers from under the sturdiest of our magnets, 'I'll even be generous and provide the documentation so far. These are numbers I've called and never heard back from, these are the disconnected, these are the ones who never turned up, these are the ones who turned up while I was out, these are the ones who tried to charge a three-figure callout fee, these are the ones who couldn't find anything wrong, this is the one that made things worse, these are the ones I have yet to try at all because I'm trying to keep hope alive and enough hours in the day to run this household.'

He gazes down at the variety of scribbled-on flyers, sheets of notepaper and dog-eared cards I have accumulated over the past three months. 'I think I'll just call in the navy,' he says.

'Exactly,' I say, gathering them all back and shoving them savagely under the fridge magnet again. Exactly.

Friday, 5 May

My birthday plans are expanding. When Fiona and Céline heard about them, they wanted in too. 'Who wouldn't?' said Fiona.

'Good mothers?' I wondered.

'We *are* good mothers,' said Fiona, firmly. 'That's why we need a break from it. Doing it properly is fucking hard work.'

With that, the last vestiges of guilt suddenly left us. And with *that*, it became not merely a plan but a mandate.

So I've cancelled the Garden House Hotel ('It is three stars,' said Céline. 'So – *non*') and we've set up a WhatsApp for pooling ideas, research, dreams and dates. Céline is translating it all to a spreadsheet and will send a collated update round once a week. 'Half of any *joie*,' she says, and she is so right, 'is in the anticipation.' Claire – now closing in on the magical twelve-week mark – is starting to relax a bit about it but says she still wants to stay near home ('Just till the baby's eighteen'), but Nadia's in if her mum and dad can come down and help cover her absence.

Richard has pointed out that even if I booked a five-star hotel and drank the bar dry it would still be cheaper than holding a party somewhere big and central enough to contain and be convenient for all the friends and family we'd have to invite, and has promised 'to work extra hours down t'pit' if it will encourage me to set aside my natural caution and try to have a good time in pleasant surroundings.

It will take a while, of course, to sort out everyone's arrangements – this may be the longest and most *joie*fully anticipated event in recent history – but we are going. Of this we are certain. We are going to have a weekend away together soon. Or, if not soon, later. But definitely, and before we die. Definitely.

Saturday, 6 May

Am watching *Outlander* (Tobias Menzies – would; Jamie Thing – wouldn't, in case you were wondering) when Richard walks in.

'Can I just say something?' he asks, more or less rhetorically.

I sigh, pause the TV and look at him expectantly.

'Now that I've looked into the matter, Katie Holmes was too good for Tom Cruise.'

A moment's pause. It appears I am required to say something back. 'I'm glad you're enjoying the internet,' I say.

He nods and leaves.

Yes, I think, unpausing *Outlander*. Definitely Tobias Menzies. Definitely would.

Sunday, 7 May

'I have news,' announces Richard, over the meal I am calling 'danger brunch', comprising as it does an eclectic assortment of foodstuffs that I culled from the fridge this morning on the grounds that nobody has started or finished them before their sell-, use-by or best-before dates. Especially the dates, which I bought before Christmas, stuck in the salad drawer and forgot about.

'What is it?' says Thomas, dipping a wizened tomato into some once-live, now either dead or rather too alive Greek yoghurt.

'It's not going to be interesting,' says Evie, gnawing on a lump of what was, after I cut a thick horny outside layer off, revealed as cheese.

'Maybe not to you,' says Richard. 'But to the most important person in this room – namely, your mother –' The children's heads swivel towards me. Evie in particular seems to regard me anew, as if seeing me as a separate person – or possibly just a person rather than a simple dispenser of goods and services – for the first time.

'– it will be of deep significance and possibly even greater joy!'

'Is it about money?' says Thomas.

'Is it about *more* money?' corrects Evie.

'An excellent guess, *mes* mercenary *enfants*, but no. As an early birthday present to my beloved I am going away.'

'For ever?' asks Evie.

'No,' says Richard. 'To give a talk at a conference. Which, including travel, will occasion my absence for ...'

I clasp my hands in anticipation. My vision narrows to a pinprick.

'... five days!'

My vision flares and fireworks burst around its edges. The greatest gift of all. Peace. My mind starts racing.

Fiona and Nadia and Céline – now that she's found an au pair who doesn't seem wholly indifferent to the children drinking bleach in front of her – will help. Fiona and Céline because they know how rare these gifts are, Nadia because she will feel sorry for me struggling and the children yearning for their absent parent. If the worst comes to the worst, I still have thirty-five years' worth of friendship chips to cash in with Claire, pregnancy be damned. And my parents will definitely have the children for a sleepover. Maybe even from after school Friday to Sunday lunchtime. I will have the house completely to myself for at least forty-eight hours, maybe seventy-two. Wait – did he say he'd be gone for the weekend?

'Yes,' says Richard, reading my mind and nodding. 'Enjoy *all* the feet off your neck!'

If it's seventy-two I could sleep in twice and *still* do the kitchen cupboards.

'Thank you,' I say, flinging my arms around him. 'Thank you!'

'You're weird,' says Evie, and she and Thomas slip down from the table preparatory to returning to their cartoons on Godrotyou TV.

'You'll understand one day!' I shout after her. 'Unless you're very careful indeed!'

Later I WhatsApp the coven and tell them the good news. Fiona responds with balloon emoticons and smiley faces, Céline with *Très bien*, and Nadia is, as predicted, horrified. *I don't understand*, she writes. *Why are you happy?*

Sweet child, replies Céline.

So young, writes Fiona. *So soft, so uncankered of heart. Bless you.*

Remember what Dolly Parton used to say whenever someone asked her how she and Carl Dean have managed to remain married for so long? I add. *'I stay gone!' It's that.*

The endless wisdom of Dolly, says Fiona.

That makes me sad, comes Nadia's reply.

There is a pause.

I think we should kick you out of the group, writes Fiona. *I feel like we're corrupting an innocent.*

Kicking a puppy, agrees Céline.

No, no! cries Nadia, in an emoji-stuffed message. *I need to toughen up! You have to help me!*

Go to bed, child, replies Fiona. *We'll brutalise you more in the morning.*

Five days, though. Five days!

Monday, 8 May

A number of us get an email from Rachel.

> Too exhausted to talk to anyone, sorry – just to let you
> know, A and I have spent the last fortnight hammering
> things out. TL:DR version – I'm taking him back and we'll
> see how things go. The kids miss him so much. I miss what
> we had and I'll feel worse if I don't see if we can try and get
> it back – for me, but mostly for them, obvs. Fuck knows if
> this is the right decision. But it's the only one I can make
> right now. Thank you, so much, everyone, for all your help.
> I feel sort of guilty for doing this. I hope you don't feel I've
> let you down by trying again.

Céline is predictably – but privately, on the coven-only
WAG – incensed. But I email back with multiple reassurances.
Because I barely know what's right for me and my family. How
on earth am I supposed to preach to others? I don't know if
those who do are possessed of greater wisdom or just greater
egos than me but it doesn't matter. I can only do as I see fit.
Which in this case is keep my fingers crossed and hope. Everything's fundamentally un-bloody-knowable, isn't it? People
themselves, their relationships, everything. Only Rachel can
really say how things stand for her and weigh how much she's
suffered against the likelihood of a workable future with Alex
and how much it's worth to her. She's the one best placed to
know what's best for her children. She still may not be right,
but she is the best placed. She'd just better give the rest of us
time to recover before we have to see him again, that's all.

Wednesday, 10 May

Today I found Henry curled up on the pile of clean washing (good) in the kitchen that I had failed to put away in time (bad). He looked so beautiful and comfortable that I couldn't bear to disturb him. I'll just wash the top layer again when he moves. I wonder, later, if this is all in some kind of vague supplication, an offering to unknown gods who will encourage someone, somewhere one day to perform a similar kindness for me.

Henry's only his official name, by the way, not his real one. In my heart and when I am alone in the house he is known as Floof de la Boof. 'And why?' I heard myself crooning as I was allowed a rare stroking of his magnificence as he lay there ruining my washing. 'Because you fill my heart with floofs, that's why!' I am burning this diary now.

Thursday, 11 May

We have been invited to dinner by people we met years ago on holiday when we were happy and our defences were down.

'I'm not going,' says Richard. 'I will brook no riposte.'

'We have to,' I say. 'We've got out of it twice. Mum's already got the kids that night so she can take them to some jamboree for a new underfunded disease she's discovered. We can't swerve them again without rupture.'

'Would that matter?' says Richard. 'What do Sam and Calendar really add to our lives?'

'Calandra,' I say patiently.

'Whatever,' he says. 'The point stands. You couldn't give me three things.'

'I'm not going to codify friendship like that,' I say, because you don't live with a barrister for fourteen years without learning an evasive trick or two yourself. 'They're nice people,' I say.

'But they're *vegans*,' he wails. 'I can't eat with people who think avocados are problematic.'

'You can't drink either,' I point out.

'Why not?'

'Because then you'll say things. Mainly about growing up in the countryside and seeing animals killed every day.'

'I *did* grow up in the countryside and see animals killed every day!'

'I know, but—'

'That's *why* the animals were there!'

'I know, but—'

'If we didn't kill and eat animals, there wouldn't be any animals! Is that what they want? For there to be no animals?'

'I don't know. I think, maybe … yes? If they're going to be killed. Or milked.'

'I'm going to ask them.'

'No, *don't.*'

'Almond milk! What's that? You can't milk a nut! It doesn't have udders. For the very good reason that it's a nut!'

'I think—'

'I mean, vegetarians are bad enough but who doesn't eat eggs? Hens lay eggs! They just do! That's just what they *do!*'

'I think you're misunderstanding a complicated—'

'No! I'm not! They're idiots! And her name's Calendar!'

'Calandra.'

'Is that supposed to be better?'

We pause.

'Are you done?' I say.

'Yes,' he says, after a moment. 'I think so.'

'So I can email back and say we're coming?'

'As long as I'm allowed to drink three glasses of wine. The wine we bring, not their organic, moon-harvested Château de Craven Bullshit, and we can get a takeaway on the way home.'

'Done,' I say, my feeling of triumph lasting until I've sent the email and realisation dawns that we're now going to a poxy vegan dinner party next Friday with the world's worst food and the world's nicest fucking people instead of … Well, instead of doing, eating or being with anything or anyone else at all.

'Yes,' Richard says, nodding, as he sees my face fall. 'My point exactly. But it's too late now.'

Saturday, 13 May

Tonight is the weekend horse-trading session regarding the children's pre- and post-school supervision and welfare for next week. All is going well till we get to Wednesday, when a perfect storm of doctors' appointments, violin lessons, work deadlines and other machinations of the devil stymie us. 'Maybe we can send them to school in the morning with extra packed lunches and they can just stay there till Friday,' Richard suggests. I laugh, but do find myself googling 'modern boarding schools' later that evening. Not seriously, of course. Just idly. Idly. Idly, idly. Idly.

Sunday, 14 May

I decide to make the children try on last year's summer clothes to see what still fits and what can go to the charity shop.

'You're *sooooo booooooooooring!*' Evie cries, three minutes into the project.

'Don't be rude,' I say, as I yank my favourite skirt (stiff gingham cotton, like in a book) over her gorgeous little bum – what *is* it about children's bums? – and see with delight that it still does up. She remains steadfast in her refusal to wear it anywhere, but you never know.

'I thought you liked truthfulism?' she says.

'In surprisingly small doses and within strictly demarcated contexts and boundaries,' I reply.

'Why are you talking like Daddy?'

'Occupational hazard of marriage. My natural voice has been subsumed by the larger, more dominant personality.'

'Stop it! And take this skirt off. It's scratchy and looking at it makes my eyes go funny. And it's boring.' A moment's pause. 'Like you!' she adds, delighted by the verbal flourish rather than the insult itself. Or so I choose to believe.

Tuesday, 16 May

I have PMT. People say it makes you angry. The hormones play havoc with your emotions and it sends you crackers for a few days. Not true. What it does – and fucking listen up at the back there – is erode your ability to repress your emotions. You with PMT is not an altered state, it is the natural one. It's the rest of the month that's an artifice. Most of life, ergo, is a lie. 'Inwardly mutinous, outwardly mute' should have been the motto of women throughout history. You're welcome.

I give up on a week of appointments and deadlines from hell and go for a walk. I bump into Nadia and go for a coffee – the first spontaneous thing I've done since 850BC and all the more restorative for that.

Thursday, 18 May

On the other hand, I long for a life as well regulated as Mrs Bradley's. Mrs Bradley has two friends. One comes on Tuesday mornings, one comes on Thursday afternoon (and duly arrived today). They greet each other unsmilingly and yet somehow fondly. Occasionally they both come on a Saturday morning and then they drive out to the garden centre after lunch and come back laden with plants. They distribute Mrs Bradley's share round her borders then head off, presumably to repeat the process with the rest at their own homes. Mrs Bradley plants them out, waters them in, then goes indoors as the light fades. As my mother always used to say, 'It's a grand life, if you don't weaken.' I never knew quite what it meant as I was growing up (I also thought it was a self-minted motto, but Richard has since informed me that it's from some wartime popular song) and I'm not sure I do now. And yet still somehow it makes more and more sense every day.

Talking of plant-life: tomorrow is dinner at Sam and Calendar's. *Calandra's*. I have been telling Richard for the past two weeks that it's too late to cancel but he just intensifies his pleas. I mustn't weaken.

Friday, 19 May

It was fine. We drank our wine, gamely choked down something made of chickpeas, avoided each other's eye throughout, and got a Chinese – 'Extra MSG,' ordered Richard – on the way home. 'I do understand they're going to be the ones who save the planet,' he said, as we flung our empty rice and noodle boxes into the bin later. 'But what's the point when everyone on it would rather be dead than eat another sprouted sprout en activated-charcoal croute?'

I see both sides, I must say. I see both sides.

Saturday, 20 May

Richard left for his conference in a flurry of papers, kisses and instructions for me on how to run the house and raise the children while he's gone. 'And send me a picture of an arse and an elbow as soon as you're back on Wi-Fi!' I yelled at him down the drive. 'I don't want to get confused between them! Twat!' I didn't say 'twat'. The kids were there.

Sunday, 21 May

'Isn't it quiet?' Thomas says, looking up from my phone, on which he is reading *Harry Potter* over breakfast.

I look up from my Marian Keyes. 'It is,' I agree.

'Daddy coughs a lot,' says Evie, without looking up from the potion she is making at the kitchen counter from water and whatever petals from the garden and dry goods she has found to be within her reach in the larder.

'He does,' I say.

'And sort of snorts in between as well,' she says.

'He has a lot of phlegm,' I say.

'Why?'

'Because I did something wrong in a former life and God is punishing me.'

'And Daddy is always moving things around,' says Thomas.

'He is.'

'And he breaks things quite a lot.'

'By accident,' says Evie, fairly.

'And he gets annoyed,' says Thomas.

'Yes,' I say.

'And he sighs a lot.'

'That's him.' I sigh.

'You just always know he's around,' says Evie, and I reflect, not for the first time, on the under-acknowledged perspicacity of the young.

'Totally,' I say. And we return peaceably to our books/ dandelion-toilet paper-talcum powder-bulgur wheat mush.

Tuesday, 23 May

The deeper peace comes as the week rolls on. My mother does a couple more pick-ups and stays for an hour afterwards, but that's pretty much all the cover I need. I stand down the rest of my valiant troops. The extra time I gain from not having to explain my decisions to anyone, or consult on alternatives, more than offsets Richard's missing domestic input. My mother simply accepts, as any normal person would, that by the time I say something, I have already completed the necessary thought processes and determined that the strategy I have chosen is the one that will best serve us all. We both know – and she occasionally articulates this, lest she burst – that the system itself is in need of root and branch reform. But – and here's the thing – we also both know that this would take the better part of five years and so, day to day, we stand together, united and steadfast in the knowledge that, within this imperfect but presently inalterable world, I and I alone am best placed to command the scene. It is like slipping into a warm bath, compared to fighting an endlessly raging sea.

I try not to dwell on this fact. It can help no one. I try just to enjoy the moment. All the moments, with no one to interfere with my timetable or put a spoke in the wheels of my plans. Just me. A single unbroken line of authority.

'Good, isn't it?' says Fiona, when she drops round some clothes for Thomas that David has grown out of. 'I remember when Iain went on his first work trip abroad. I thought it was going to be so hard. But it was so much easier.'

'It's amazing,' I say in wonder. 'I just give the children an array of options that suit me and Mum, they choose between them and we go smoothly on from there. Or the other morning I let Thomas read *Harry Potter* on my phone without having to fend off cries that I was turning his eyes and brain to glue for twenty minutes. We just read and had breakfast. It was easy. It was simple. Streamlined. Life is elegant and it is beautiful.'

'No one second-guessing you, lobbing a curve ball in – Iain quite often suggests going to soft play just before tea and I have to claw them down from the walls when I say no – and I'm including Iain here.'

'Exactly,' I say. 'But I'm trying not to dwell on it.'

'It can help no one,' she says.

Wednesday, 24 May

I'm not dwelling, really I'm not, but, oh, the joy of not having to cook without onions because Richard won't eat them. (Do you know what an onion-free culinary existence is like? I haven't experienced depth of flavour since 2008. If I ever have an affair, it will be because someone came at me with a braised beef casserole in his hands, not lust in his eyes.)

I don't have to make sure I'm fully asleep before the snoring starts. (See previous entry on phlegm. If asked my marital status, I have to fight the urge to reply, 'Mucosal.')

And, above all, I do not have to listen to all the ways in which people in the office, on public transport, or in the news have deprecated upon Richard's – possibly all men's – vision of a world that bends entirely to his will.

I feel like I am living the dream.

The dream ends a few hours later, with swearing at the front door, a furious jangling of keys and the crash of it being flung open hard enough to dent the wall again.

'I'm back!' cries Richard. 'Did you miss me?'

'Of course!' I say.

Evie looks at me questioningly. I frown back at her. This is not the time for more perspicacity from the young. Silence, for a few fleeting minutes more, is what we need.

Thursday, 25 May

Richard, who has been working from home all day, comes out of his study to greet us when we arrive back from school. 'Hello!' he says cheerfully, then mouths quickly to me with a fearful look on his face, 'What. Did. She. Get?'

I say nothing but draw out the tearstained Evie from behind me.

'What happened, darling?' he says, crouching down to her.

'I got' – her lower lip trembles – 's-s-seven out of ten!' She dissolves into paroxysms of tears again and it's all I can do not to follow her lead.

Her class has just started having weekly spelling tests. A new list of ten words comes home every Friday to be tested the next Thursday. Our happiness as a family now lives or dies every week by the resultant score. Never has anything more thoroughly proved the point that parenting is 90 per cent repressing/inverting your child's natural inclinations and proclivities than these bloody spelling lists. When Thomas, a constitutionally – 'pathologically', Richard once declared – sanguine child started bringing them home, we had to spend half an hour every night cajoling and bribing him even to look at them. And we certainly couldn't get him to care. Good marks or bad, they effected barely a ripple of delight or concern in him. At best, he seemed happy for us if we were pleased with a nine or ten out of ten and sorry that we took anything under five so badly. But his own mood remained imperturbable. 'So clever,' said his grandma (before whom I was throughout my childhood required to explain any mark under a B+ while she sat – in my memory at least – on a burnished Throne of Judgement before she brought down the Staff of Maternal Disgust across my soul). 'He already sees how pointless tests are at his age! He sees right through the teachers!'

Now, because Evie is an entirely different child, we have found ourselves reverse-ferreting at speed.

'Seven out of ten is *very* good!' says Richard, lifting the tiny sobbing body up with one arm as he stands. 'Very good indeed!'

'But it's not ten out of ten! I got three whole ones wrong! And I didn't get a sticker on my flower!'

Only full marks get a sticker to fill in a petal on the outline of a flower they all have in the backs of their spelling books. It's meant to be an incentive. For Evie it just crystallises her 'failure'. Nothing we do can persuade her that less than full marks is not a disaster. She is just not built that way.

It is bringing out the worst in everyone. The ruthlessly

competitive mothers now have something tangible to latch on to – you can't fudge test results like you can reading ability or (back in the day) block-stacking – and they post their eights-and-above on the class WhatsApp group with captions like 'Practice makes perfect!' or 'Didn't practise this week – looks like we didn't need to ☺!' depending on whose hackles they want to raise or shame-glands they want to activate.

All this amuses me on a good day and infuriates me on a bad one (it merely baffles Richard – 'You'd think they'd passed the civil service exams!' he said in wonderment, when he read the first crop of posts). But it's a side issue to the main event, which is to teach our battered little five-year-old not to fall apart in the face of 'failure'.

Which first means teaching myself not to fall apart.

'Did we overreact when she came home that first week with ten out of ten?' I asked Richard, after her meltdown over a nine the next week. 'Praise her too much? Make her feel like only that would do? Does she think our love's conditional on good marks? On anything? How have we made her so insecure?'

'Our daughter calls me "Fat Dad",' said Richard. 'She's the least insecure child I've ever met.'

'So we overreacted to the good mark?'

'We did not. She had done well. We were pleased. We told her we were pleased. We told her she could have an ice pop for pudding as a reward. The fact that she always gets an ice pop for pudding did not seem to occur to her.'

'What do we do when she gets a low mark? A properly low mark, I mean, not seven.'

'We say, "That's a pity! We'll have to practise more next week, won't we? Would you like an ice pop for pudding as consolation?"'

'I think, just so she's clear, I'm going to tell her she could murder someone and it wouldn't make us love her any less,' I said.

'Good idea,' said Richard. 'No overreaction, that's the key to any success.'

Evie moves out of the initial stage of grief and into fury. 'It's not fair!' she rages. 'Everyone knows how to say "book"! You don't have to put two Os in *every* time! And having kicking cuhs and curly cuhs is just STUPID!'

As ever, I want to tuck the child under my arm and rush to an extreme. I could banish all possibility of tears, disappointment and trembling lower lips by either homeschooling her for ever or by making her practise for eight hours a day until she can spell 'hook, look, book, took, crook' in her sleep. And, as ever, I must restrain myself and fight to keep to the middle way. But the middle way is hard. How do you teach someone so young that tests only test one thing? That some people are better at spelling than others and that she will – probably – be better at other things in her turn. ('Military strategy,' suggests Richard, when he hears me attempt to explain this to her later. 'You could be the next Rommel. Girl power!') How do you impress upon them firmly enough that doing your best is different from and better than getting full marks? Evie looks at me in a way that goes comfortably beyond contempt when I try. 'It's not, you know,' she says. How do you teach them that results can sometimes be important for things but not, in any real way, to Mummy and Daddy?

'Why don't you give her an ice pop?' says Thomas, as Evie's roars of injustice continue to split the air.

Evie brightens. 'That would calm me down,' she says.

Richard heads to the freezer. I feel like I've just been through some sort of test myself, though whether I have passed or failed I have absolutely no idea.

Later that night, Richard muses aloud about whether, instead of trying to suppress children's natural inclinations and encourage them in the attitudes and activities that come less easily in order to usher forth that elusive creature, the well-rounded individual, anyone has ever tried the opposite. 'Just reinforce all their strengths and hope that compensates for all the things that – let's face it, however much effort you put in – they're still basically going to be crap at. Much easier, and how do we know it's not better unless we try it?'

'I'm afraid I'm not willing to undertake this kind of long-term experiment,' I say. The spellings are enough.

Friday, 26 May

I am forty. It is midnight. I have been working since the children went to bed. I ate my supper at my laptop and it is a new day and I am forty.

Forty.

Forty.

I am writing it down because I cannot say it out loud. I know we're all supposed to be ecstatic about ageing nowadays because of Madonna, and Michelle Obama's arms, and basic intelligence that tells you it's much better than being dead, but I'm not. It doesn't make sense. Your body is, objectively, getting worse. Outwardly, of course, as crow's feet and strange brown patches of skin start appearing among the proliferating wiry hairs that require removal with secateurs (I came across a photo of me at twenty the other day and I looked like a peach in human form. A peach), but inwardly too. My knees start to hurt if I go up too many stairs. WTF is that about? I get heartburn if I eat too much. Everything's ever so slightly slowing down and stiffening up. How are we supposed to celebrate – anything, really – once our own bodies have started intimating their mortality?

I'm going to bed. Maybe things will look better in the morning. And I've been promised a lie-in.

Saturday, 27 May, my birthday

I have woken early, of course. But at least that gives me extra time to contemplate the infinite while squeezing various handfuls of my somehow plump-yet-sagging flesh in weary resignation. Still, I think, trying to raise myself to a better frame of mind, at least I've never had any looks to lose! Now that really must be depressing!

Low expectations, my mother always taught me, are the key to happiness.

Richard turns over and realises, sleepily, that I am awake. He pulls me to him so that I can feel his erection against my thigh. 'Don't worry,' he murmurs into my neck. 'I'm not going to make you do anything. It's your birthday, not mine. I just thought you'd like to know I still fancy you.' This makes me like him so much that I do almost want to have sex. Fortunately we both fall back to sleep before we have to bother.

I am gently coaxed out of slumber to re-greet the dawn by the sound of Richard smashing the lavatory seat down as if it has done him a grievous personal wrong. Just as the adrenalin spike begins to plateau and my heart rate is returning to normal the children burst in to wish me a happy birthday, waving homemade cards and a balloon on which they have drawn—

'Your face, look!' says Evie. 'We put your glasses and your funny tooth and your hairy mole so everyone knows it's you!'

'Terrific,' I say. 'Did Daddy mention anything to you about me having a lie-in today? He did sort of promise me last night ...'

'Yes, but he said we could come in and then you could go back to sleep.'

Do not swear in front of the children. Do not unpack the seventeen things wrong with that sentence and do not swear in front of the children.

Mother- and wifehood, I note, are largely a matter of editing. Very little of what I actually utter is a first draft.

'Ah, yes, good idea. Well, thank you for all of this. Give me a kiss – don't screw your face up like that, Evie, you know it just makes me kiss you more – and go and have your breakfast with Daddy and never tell me what it is.'

'It's jammy toast with hot chocolate and marshmallows!' says Thomas, over his shoulder, as they barrel out of the room.

Fantastic. Tell Daddy the insulin is in the fridge.

'What a lovely, very rare treat only for really special occasions,' I shout. 'Enjoy.'

I do not, of course, manage to go back to sleep but I do manage to resist the temptation to get out of bed and go downstairs to untangle the various snarl-ups and head off various disasters I deduce are occurring from the sounds and exclamations emerging from downstairs. I lie with my arms rigid by my sides, fists clenched until the front door bangs – no, wait, leave it ten minutes because I didn't hear anyone confirm they had both Zip cards, yes, here they come, back again. Thomas's is missing. It'll be in his school coat pocket because we came home on the bus from his last playdate. Will anyone realise … ? Yes, that's the sound of coats falling to the floor as he knocks them off in the search. 'Got it!' Hurrah – they've gone. Again. Ten minutes more and I judge it safe to get up.

I spend the first hour of my birthday clearing up my family's breakfast detritus. I get a text from Richard halfway through. *Sorry we left a mess. I thought you would rather we got out of the house ASAP and before the noise woke you up.*

I contemplate sending one back that reads, *Actually, I would rather you were capable, as I am and any sentient adult should be, of feeding three people without leaving a kitchen looking like Ground Zero of a cereal-based terror attack*, but I resist.

The next text I don't send reads: *You are so sweet! I have just found the drops of tea you've spattered across seven cupboard doors and various small appliances, which I presume spell out 'Happy birthday, darling wife!' in English Breakfast Morse code, because the alternative would be to assume that you are a 44-year-old man incapable of transporting a teabag cleanly across the three feet separating the kettle from the bin.* Editing, you see. Editing is key.

I manage to have a bath, and am curled up on the sofa with my book when they get back.

'Presents now!' says Evie. 'Mine first!'

She tears the paper off it herself and hands the gift to me. It is a chicken and avocado Pret a Manger sandwich.

'I got Daddy to buy it. I know it's your favourite,' she says proudly.

'It is!' I say, and I am touched. 'How did you manage to hide it from me?'

'I made him put it in the salad drawer in the fridge,' she says. 'Nobody ever looks in there.'

'Moving on,' says Richard, nodding encouragement at Thomas to come forward with his parcel.

I take it from him and unwrap it. It is a packet of wine-bottle stoppers. Thomas beams.

'He saw them in the supermarket when we were doing the big shop last week,' says Richard, 'and thought they would be ideal.'

'Because you're always saying that you have to finish off a whole bottle when you open one otherwise it will be ruined,' says Thomas.

'As he explained to the cashier,' says Richard. 'Very loudly. The whole queue was very entertained. Concerned and entertained.'

'These are lovely presents,' I say firmly. 'Thank you both very much indeed. More birthday kisses now, please.' Thomas burrows into me for a good yumming; Evie rolls her eyes and lets me kiss the top of her head before slithering off the sofa to start trying on my shoes.

'I'm a big lady,' I hear her muttering, as she starts clomping around in my trainers. 'And you do as I say or I'm gonna stomp on your head. Even soft shoes feel hard then.'

I decide not to dwell on this until after my birthday, and start opening Richard's envelope instead. Inside is a membership card and a brochure.

'What's this?' I say, because it can't be what it looks like.

'It's a year-long gym membership!' he says, looking unfathomably pleased with himself until he sees my expression. Then he starts hurrying to explain himself. 'Not for the gym bit, though – for the swimming pool. You used to go swimming all the time before.' He gestures in such a way as to take in the children, family and professional responsibilities, and the proliferating chaos of life generally. 'And you're always going on ab— I mean, saying you'd like to get more exercise, so I thought ...' He tails off into uncertainty. This is rare for Richard, but then it's rare that he sees my face after he's given me a year-long gym membership for my fortieth birthday.

'Thank you,' I say politely, as I put the card and the brochure back in the envelope with exaggerated care. 'I shall certainly think of you every time I use it.'

'I'm sorry,' he says.

'Not at all,' I say. 'Not at all.' I notice it has two guest passes included in the fee. I will use one to take him with me, and I will drown him.

Wednesday, 31 May

Fiona and I are going round to Claire's tomorrow. She's safely on the far side of the first trimester and beginning, cautiously, to relax.

I am going to control myself, obviously but, oh, the urge to give advice to a pregnant woman – or new mother – is a fierce one. Even if it's just some random person you see in the street. Much worse when it's one of your best friends. For the last three months I've had to stop myself texting Claire every five minutes with a new pearl of wisdom.

I didn't understand it until I had Thomas. The number of women who came up to me in cafés or on my commute when I was pregnant with him and offered me various pieces of intelligence, stories, instruction and recommendations was astonishing. I didn't find it offensive, or overwhelming (though I see how you might if you hadn't happened to come from a large Catholic family in which anyone under twenty-five, over sixty or up the duff is considered common property and therefore had long been used to your peace, quiet and privacy being invaded on a daily basis) but I was baffled. Why were they bothering? How could I, a stranger to these ersatz counsellors, prompt so much attention and elicit so much effort from others?

And where had they been in the early nineties when surely someone, with a well-placed word or two, could have stopped me wearing a burgundy velvet scrunchie every-bloody-where?

Well, I know now. From the moment I expelled Thomas from my protesting nethers, I've had to fight the compulsion to glom onto every preggo I see and download everything I know into her unwilling but captive ears (you can't run when you're pregnant! And your pelvic floor will see that you never run again afterwards either! This is one of many facts I wish to share) before letting her resume her daily business. You want to tell them because you know, now, how huge a thing it is that they're about to undergo. You want one person at least to benefit from your hard-won, heavily stitched, bleeding-nippled wisdom (or possibly, if you have a good birth story, to tell her how wonderful it can be, in order to counteract the horror stories the likes of me are telling her).

Plus, I so rarely in my life get to offer advice. I've been a late starter in everything from riding a bike (thirteen), to sex (don't ask) to having babies, so can act as a trailblazer for virtually no one. The chance at last to distil my wisdom – so painfully earned! – and hand it down to a neophyte from on high is hard to pass up.

Pregnancy is such a fantastically strange thing. It still boggles my mind. Collectively, it's the commonest thing in the world. Almost every woman does it and we've been doing it since the very dawn of time. We're all basically just one long vagina linked through time and space. But, individually, it's one of the rarest experiences you'll ever have. Most of us do it once, twice, three times in our lives. But the magnitude of the upheaval to those lives is so entirely out of proportion to its frequency that the urge to tell your story and try to balance things out – spread the news! Spread the load! – is strong.

Sometimes I want to apologise to the women I've button-holed, but on the other hand they'll all have given birth by now and will know exactly what I was up to. Another link in the vagina chain is forged.

Worthy of a boggle, I really do believe.

Thursday, 1 June

'How do you feel?'

'Pregnant! I feel pregnant!' Claire beams at us both as she takes our coats. We beam back. This baby has been five years in the making.

'Has your morning sickness stopped yet?' I ask. Claire started puking from more or less the moment the thing took root. It's how she knew that this time it had worked. You've never seen anyone happier to be in and out of the bog all day.

'Not quite!' she says delightedly.

'You are actually managing to glow,' Fiona says. 'I thought that was just a myth. Maybe you'll have one of those easy labours I hear so much about too.'

'That's just because I'm not working,' says Claire. (She was a social worker who stuck it out longer than most manage under the daily double cosh of people's overwhelming misery and no money with which to help them, but had to give it up after her third failed implantation because it was all too much to bear. So. They are *brassic* but they are *pregnant*.)

She piles plates high with biscuits as the kettle boils. 'I'm not eating sugar,' she says. 'So you have to eat it for me. I'll just watch you like the pre-diabetic pervert I am.'

'Are you eating everything else?' I ask.

'I was already decaff anyway, but I've given up soft cheese and sushi,' she says. 'Even though I know it's mostly balls. French women practically mainline listeria, and Japanese people just carry straight on with their raw fish, but, you know ...'

'It's a votive offering,' says Fiona. 'You give something up to placate the gods. Makes you feel better. Until you need a drink. Or caffeine. I managed three months without coffee, six without booze and then I reckoned most of the work was done – they just get bigger, basically, for the last three months, don't they? And it was Christmas. Nearly.'

I am finding it very difficult to sit still. It's so great that she's pregnant. For her, sure, but even more so for me because

I get to have a baby around again without actually having to have a baby. It's amazing how fun it is to push an infant around in a pram, sing daft songs to it as you wander round patting its back and waiting for it to gift you its sick over your shoulder, bath it, even change its nappies when you know you're going home in a couple of hours.

But I'm also fidgeting because of all the advice I have inside me, bursting to get out. And then, just as my vision is going slightly fuzzy, Claire leans forward and says, 'So, O Wise Women of the Hills, any advice for a first-timer? Nobody's dared mention anything about the subject to me for the last five years. I'm assuming there haven't been any major developments in anatomy, though I'd be delighted if there were, but any insights, idiosyncratic details you think I might benefit from – let rip.'

'Well, number one,' says Fiona darkly. 'Don't say "let rip" to anyone who's ever given birth or who is going to be involved in you doing so.'

'Totally,' I say, nodding profound agreement. 'There have indeed been no welcome developments over the last five years. The baby is still planning to come out of your vagina and this is exactly as appalling as it sounds. If you wish to make alternative, humane, Caesarean arrangements you will need to start making loud noises of distress and anxiety in front of all medical personnel from NOW. Don't wait until you go into labour. It's too late then.'

'Word,' says Fiona. 'You're like a beast in a field then. You won't be able to say things, and people won't listen when you do.' I see Claire blanch slightly, and I kick Fiona under the coffee-table to remind her of the pact between all post-partums: you work with the newbies in only broad-brush terms at first, filling in the details as the months wear on and they are starting to intuit the worst.

I turn to lighter but still vital matters of concern.

'Number two, Buy Topshop maternity jeans. Because they will still look good when you're still wearing them to take the child to nursery three years later because you haven't had time to shop since your waters broke. Don't buy Marks & Spencer jeans. You're a mum. You're not your mum. Or indeed her mum.

'Three. Take five minutes every day to sit back and think, Look at *me*, going about my life, doing my work – or, you know, whatever, seeing my friends, altogether takin' care of business – while all the while *knitting together an entire new person inside myself*. I am impossibly amazing. I congratulate myself whole-heartedly. Stock up on this feeling. Draw on it during the late-night feeds to come, when you feel you're not amazing at all. Because you were, are and – especially to the newly knitted child – always will be.'

'That's what you have them for, after all,' says Fiona. 'It's kind of a build-your-own-acolytes deal, at least till they hit their teens.'

'Four. Stock up on adjectives too,' I say. 'You'll need them to describe to your partner/mother/GP/friend the variety of discharges you will experience over the coming months. Let the record show that I will answer any questions about them or the state of your vulva but I will not look at anything.'

'Five,' says Fiona. 'Write a detailed birth plan. Imagine God laughing. Tear it up.'

'Six. Always do a spare wee before you leave anywhere. Always. Because that child is always growing and by the time you get home you will have even less space in your bladder than you did when you set off.'

'Oh, yes,' says Fiona, nodding vigorously. 'Spare wees. Always. Spare wees are the thing.'

'Seven. Men tend to freak out when you show them the baby moving under the skin. Try not to despise them for it. It's one of those things that's more unsettling to see when it's happening to someone else than when it's happening to you. Like blackhead-popping.'

'Eight,' says Fiona. 'If you can face doing perineal massage for the next six months, go for it. You're a better woman than I.'

Claire, who had been looking perkier, blanches again. 'If perineal massage is what I think it is ...' she says.

'And it is,' says Fiona.

'... then you can forget it,' says Claire. 'Those are two words that should never be used in conjunction. Like "carpet" and "tiles" or "carrot" and "cake".'

The intuition is already strong in this one. She's going to be fine.

I'm going to go for a bloody swim tomorrow, as it's already bought and bloody paid for. I vaguely reason that if Claire can give birth, I can do this. Or something.

Friday, 2 June

I walk into the sitting room after the children are in bed – if not, judging by the racket, asleep – to stand four-square in front of Richard. He looks at me with trepidation as his hand crab-crawls to the remote and presses pause on *War Documentaries for Ageing Farts* Volume VIIXXVII. I take a deep breath. 'I have something to tell you.'

Trepidation turns to naked fear. 'Are *you* pregnant?' he whispers.

'What? No! How? *No.* I need to tell you that I was wrong to be so arsey about my birthday present. It's brilliant. I went today and it's the best thing anyone has ever bought anyone in the history of the world, ever. So – thank you. Really, this time. Thank you.'

'That is delightful news,' he says, with relief. 'And you are very, very welcome. But – and without wishing to suggest that I was ever visited by even the most momentary doubts about the eventual success of my plan – what precisely is it that has brought about this radical change of heart?'

So I tell him. I tell him about what swimming has, even on its best days, unavoidably meant to me. The leisure centre. Filthy changing rooms either freezing cold or claustrophobically hot.

Perverts. All for a few happy minutes in the water before the hairs and plasters tangling round me make me moribund. Queues for mouldy showers and asthmatic hair dryers. A bleakly punitive atmosphere mixed with a last-days-of-Communism vibe and the faint but constant smell of piss.

'It is the odour of municipality,' he says.

'This place you signed me up with is different,' I say.

'It is private,' he says. 'It is a commercial venture, run for profit, guided by market forces that know most people prefer happiness to sorrow and will pay to secure it.'

'It's like a wonderland.'

'Go on.'

I tell him how warm and calm and clean it is everywhere – from changing rooms to shining showers and everything in between. There are no raised voices. In fact, people barely speak. They nod and smile acknowledgement at each other as they move from – warm, calm, clean – space to space, but the mood is serene, contemplative, not sociable. It does not allow children. It is basically as I would wish my home to be, but with better water pressure and hair-drying facilities.

'I may not be back here very much from now on,' I tell Richard.

Because on top of everything else, in the rest of the – equally warm, calm, clean – complex there is free Wi-Fi, a restaurant ('Selling proper food!' I say excitedly. 'Not just quinoa and aubergine shite! There's chips! But posh chips!'), a café with good coffee, sofas, peace, quiet and SPACE.

'And did I tell you they don't allow children?' I say. 'Because they don't. Not anywhere.'

So – I can have a swim (or take an exercise class or have a little run on a treadmill to show willing), then come out, have a coffee and do some work without ever leaving the building. And unlike my home, the whole place seems designed to help rather than hinder me in this endeavour. No one interrupts me, unless it's to ask if I'd like another coffee (yes, please – and a cinnamon bun: I showed willing on the treadmill today), nor does technology conspire against me. 'The Wi-Fi never drops out,' I say, in an awed whisper. 'I think they beam it straight from the Wi-Fi factory. And did I mention how clean the place is? It's really clean. Without me having to do anything. It's like having an au pair or concierge service or something, but much, much cheaper and you get fit too. I commend it to all working women – mothers or not, but truly only mothers will be able to extract full value from spending time in a child-free zone.'

I fall back on the sofa after delivering my paean of praise and into a reverie about the delights that have been and that will come again. Richard breaks in after a minute or two with the question: 'And how was the actual swimming?'

'Oh, the swimming!' I say, leaning eagerly forward once more. 'It's wonderful! The pool is so warm, it's like getting into a bath. Everyone's just doing lengths. There's no splashing. No playing. No divebombing. No hairs, no plasters. No piss. It's unbelievable.'

'It's capitalism,' explains Richard. 'You're getting what you pay for.'

'Well,' I say, 'we should pay for things more often. Life as a rich lady *rules*.'

I lie awake in bed feeling bad that I can afford things when others cannot. I am abandoning my municipal roots. I drag the iPad into bed and increase my charity direct debits. 'Come on in, hypocrite,' I murmur. 'The water's lovely.'

Saturday, 3 June

The direct debits have absolved me. I went guiltless swimming again today. It's like being newly in love. I want to be there all the time and I can't stop thinking about it when I'm not, or talking about it to whoever will listen.

It's the perfect thing, I find myself WhatsApping to the coven from the café. *It's just complicated enough to drive all the normal, boring, anxious thoughts out of your head and then, once you're about* ten lengths into the swing of things, new ones come in. I guess because you're doing a new thing? Your brain is all 'Look at this! We're moving through a whole different medium! The feet aren't even on the bottom! I'M SHOOK!' and gets out of its rut.

I swear, if you have a novel in you, you will plot it while swimming. If you have always longed for a farmhouse and five-acre garden, you will find it in your mind and furnish and plant it before you've breaststroked half a mile. Whatever your imaginary world is – personally, I'm a lone crofter on a deserted Hebridean island to which I shipped all my books before beginning my new life of small-scale arable farming by day and reading by night – it will be more real to you by the end of an hour in the pool than whatever awaits you when you have left the watery womb for home.

Saturday, 10 June

'Can we rate *Transformers* on Netflix?' asks Thomas. He, David (who is round here for the morning while Fiona readies the house for a visit from her mother-in-law – 'Grinding up the glass to put in her food, the Valium for mine, that sort of thing') – and Evie have just watched six straight episodes. ('I don't care,' says Fiona, when I ring her later to apologise. 'What does it matter? They're all going to die fighting over water anyway.')

'What do you mean?' I say, distracted by trying to pair up the 800 slightly different-sized black socks yielded by the three washloads I let accumulate during the week so that I would have something fun to do at the weekend.

'You can rate programmes – see? That's what the little stars at the top there are about. Viewers' ratings.'

'I see. Um – no.'

'Why not?' says Evie, looking up from the seven-dimensional marble run she is building on the floor.

'Because ...' Vague fragments of thought and half-formed

sentences about privacy and data and not giving anything away online if you can help it float through my mind. Richard would probably have a three-page speech for them ending with 'And remember – if you're not paying for the product, you are the product!' to explain it. I can only think of Facebook paedophiles and Skynet, neither of which I particularly want to get into on a quiet Saturday morning.

'All right, then,' I say. 'And well done for asking. Remember, we always ask before doing anything on the internet.'

'We know, we know,' says Evie. 'Chicken Clicking tells us at school.'

'Aye,' says David, examining the marble run with his hands behind his back and the air of a master surveyor. 'Lotta foxes about.'

'There are,' I say, relieved that I am not the only one involved in the fight to keep our children safe from new, unseen and unfathomable dangers. At least until they are old enough to die fighting over water.

Sunday, 11 June

I have upset Richard. I was evangelising again about the pool this morning, and he said, 'You know what? You've convinced me. I think I'll join too.'

And I said, 'No.' Except I didn't say it so much as scream it. A sort of quiet, strangulated scream because my throat was constricting in horror at the same time as the rest of my body was trying to express it, but a scream nevertheless.

'That was heartfelt,' he said.

'I'm sorry,' I said, quickly composing myself. 'It's just that most of what I've been saying is about how lovely it is to have an hour's peace and quiet, isn't it?'

'I'm not going to disturb you while you're swimming. I'm not even suggesting we habitually go together.'

'Even so ...'

'You need the whole pool – the whole gym complex – to yourself?'

'It's more ... it's more that I need the whole idea of the whole pool and gym complex to myself.'

'I require further and deeper explanation.'

I tried, but everything I said just made things worse. Things like the words 'bolthole', 'escape' and 'sanctuary'. 'Genuine freedom', I seem to remember, was a phrase with which he particularly took issue.

Later, lying in bed, there is still a certain *froideur* between us.

'I'm sorry,' I say eventually. 'Would you like to have sex?'

'No, thank you,' he replies. 'I wouldn't want to crowd you.'

I sigh.

'I'm sorry,' I say again. 'It's just that I get so little time to myself. Really to myself, I mean.'

'But,' he says, turning round to look at me at last, 'you have two days a week home alone, when the kids and I are gone from nine till nearly four. You have about three evenings a week when I'm late home, at least an hour after the kids have gone to bed. And I take them out most Saturday mornings.'

I mentally assemble my response. It runs something along the lines of 'Areyoufuckingkiddingme? Working from home is not "time to myself". The hour between bedtime and you coming home is spent tidying while cooking our supper. And you take them out one Saturday morning in seven, with at least ninety minutes' prep by me beforehand so that you can survive alone with the two of them till noon.' I delete it in its entirety.

Out loud I say, 'Not much of that is actually what I call time to myself. I really need to be away from you all. Because whatever I'm doing, you're on my mind. I literally think about you all the time. If I'm awake, some part of my brain – large or small or medium, it varies, but always part of my brain – is thinking about this family. Being away, physically away, doing something wholly unconnected with any of you, away from the chance of you bursting through the door with some new problem, or situation, or interest is the closest I come to having my brain to myself. For one hour.'

'Really?' he says, with interest, propping himself up on his elbow, the better to examine the oddity he suddenly finds himself in bed with. 'You think about us all the time?'

'Of course I do.'

'That's so weird,' he says. 'I don't.'

I know, I think. I know. You prove in a hundred different ways every day that anything that does not occur right before your eyes at a time when your full attention can be engaged by it simply does not happen. I sometimes think you believe that when you shut the front door behind you, the children and I simply lock into position, like a film on pause, only unfreezing and returning to our business when you walk back in. It's why you know nothing about homework, playground friendships, crazes, which toy is currently cherished/banished, why the threads of life never seem to weave together into a whole for you as they do for me.

'I know,' I say. 'You can compartmentalise. When you work, you work, and that gives you a rest from home. When you're home, you're home and that gives you a rest from work.'

'Unless I'm working at home,' he says. 'Then I'm getting a rest from home while I'm at home. Which is quite a talent to have, really.' The *froideur* has lifted. He is pleased with life and with himself once again.

'You are amazing,' I say. 'Truly, quite amazing. I mean it.'

'Thank you,' he says. 'I'll try to teach you how to do it, if you like. Though it comes so naturally to me that I don't know if I can really put it into words.'

'Don't worry,' I say. 'It's too late for me. It's all far too late for me.'

Monday, 12 June

Texts from Claire are now arriving every few days with various queries about preglife. Today's is: *Had dream last night that Tom did something mean and horrible to me. Can't remember what it was but have been in bad mood with him all day because I feel he must be doing something wrong to cause dream. Is this normal?*

I text back. *Yes.*

Wednesday, 14 June

This morning I walked into Evie and Thomas's room to hear the dread words: 'Mummy, I don't feel well.' So faint and weakened is the voice that I have to turn on the light before I can identify which child it actually belongs to. Thomas is still fast asleep. Evie, eyes wide and tearful, looks up at me.

'All right, my darling,' I say, hurrying forward to cuddle her while my mind starts to race. 'Mummy's here.'

Nothing's covered in sick. If she does puke and misses the bowl that I'm about to bring her, she can go in Thomas's bed till I have time to change hers. If she's sick in there – still got two sides of the marital bed to go.

'Let's see how hot you are.'

I push a hand under her fringe while also performing the covert Meningitis Rundown: no stiff neck, not bothered by the light; peer down nightdress for rash. Okay. She's not wheezing. She's just a bit hot and pale at the same time, thus ruling out diphtheria, cholera, typhoid, overnight-onset TB, mumps, plague, sleeping sickness, scarlet fever, swamp fever and every other disease I've ever seen or heard mentioned in baby books, pamphlets, on the internet, among friends, in travel guides or historical novels. Clearly the nightly supplication that runs unbidden through my head when I look down on their sweet, sleeping faces before I go to bed – the naked innocence, the tiny lips, the translucent skin of their eyelids with their ethereal tracery of pinks and purples making it seem impossible that they will ever get through life unharmed – is still working. (It is wordless prayer to a God I don't believe in, but were I to write it down it would probably run something like this: 'Please, please, don't let them ever get cancer, be in a car accident, be kidnapped or die in any way. Take anything, take everything from me, kill everything else I love a thousand times but not that, amen.') The current malady is, simply, A Bug.

Except, of course, there's nothing simple about it. The Bug protocol must be activated, but even with that in place, it's going to be an unavoidable shitshow for a week.

Protocol Step 1. I wake Thomas, tell him his sister's ill and that he must now get dressed, on his own and without my help. Otherwise, my tone and wild-eyed stare unmistakably convey, punishments will rain down upon his head the like of which he lacks the ability even to imagine. He slithers out of bed and starts pulling pyjamas off and pants on without further ado. If I had time, I would stop and goggle at this miracle. But from here on out, I have no time.

Step 2. Repeat Step 1, this time with Richard.

Step 3. Return to patient, gather symptoms and requests: 'I feel yucky and please can I have my bendy pen and water?' Children always get so polite when they're ill. I suppose it's in unconscious service of eliciting better care, but it pulverises the heart nevertheless.

Step 4. Assemble breakfast while calculating possibility of working from home today and availability of babysitters. Send email to boss, texts to everyone, call Mum. Wish I had one of those mock battleground maps with miniature troops and little croupier-pusher things you see generals use to work out military tactics. Mum is definitely free. She will stand by phone and await further instructions.

Step 5. Settle Thomas in front of breakfast, officially pass responsibility for loo, handwashing, teeth and depositing at school to his father – no, wait, Fiona has texted saying she is out all day but can do drop-off and pick-up, God love her. Issue the amended instructions to Richard, emphasising that it is now imperative, however, that Thomas be ready by the time Fiona calls at eight twenty-five. He salutes. I would like to have him court-martialled for insubordination.

Step 6. Gather water, bendy pen, thermometer, Calpol, measuring spoon, muslin square to catch dripped Calpol (best case) or projectile post-Calpol vomiting (worst case) and notepad and return to Evie.

Step 7. Administer liquid, medicine and thermometer. Temperature 38.9, whatever the fuck that is in real money. Google tells me it means Proper Ill and definitely requiring a day off work and school so at least that decision is taken out of my hands and the creeping guilt forced back by the hand of righteous maternal concern. Log temperature and time Calpol was taken in notebook because long experience has taught me this is the only way to keep track.

Step 8. Say hello and thank you to Fiona and goodbye to Thomas, then to Richard ('I'll be back as soon as I can. Keep me updated on life in the plague house'). Check email. New temporary boss – a stripling of a thing who knows nothing and is covering for real boss who is on three-month sabbatical because they found out she hadn't been on holiday for seven years – is allowing home working till child better but is clearly narked. Ring Mum back to find out when she can get here and how long for so I can hopefully email boss back to grovel and promise earth. Dad answers the phone. 'She's already on her way,' he says. 'She's been up since seven and had already finished the day's chores so she didn't see the point in hanging about. She's just got to drop off a casserole at Joy's because her oven's broken but she's still got the microwave, and some laundry at Marion's because her washing-machine's on the blink. Things aren't built to last these days. Except your mother, fortunately.'

'Amen to that,' I agree, and put the phone down, practically weeping with gratitude. If she left soon after my phone call, then she should be here about—

The doorbell rings. My mother is on the doorstep clutching

a huge handful of weeds. 'I just gathered these as I came up the path,' she says, thrusting them at me as she strides in, eyeing the breakfast dishes sternly on her way to Evie's room. I swear they jump into the dishwasher of their own accord as she passes. 'Put them in the compost while I go and see this poor child. I can stay till three,' she calls over her shoulder. 'Then I've got to take your father for his feet.' She disappears before I can ask what this means, which, on reflection, is probably a good thing.

Thanks to Grandma, the day passes relatively easily. I am able to do enough work to keep my boss happy (in fact, at one point she sends me an email saying, *Gosh, already! We shall have to have you work from home more often!*, which I take as a passive-aggressive dig at my office productivity in revenge for not being there today. It's capable of a more generous interpretation, I know, but only if you've never met her). And all while still being able to look in on my poor, wan child who doesn't even want to watch television, dispense cuddles, and generally appear to be doing some parenting while Grandma in fact shoulders the burden. She ferries water in favourite cups back and forth, bananas cut lengthways according to instruction ('It's funnier than chunks,' says Evie. 'My ill needs to laugh') and reads endless, endless stories. When she needs a break, she says so briskly to Evie (who nods in perfect acquiescence), puts on an audiobook, comes out, makes a coffee and drinks it while tidying the house.

'Please, please, have a proper break,' I beg her.

'I am!' she says, baffled.

This is probably true. She cannot stay still. We estimate that she hasn't remained static since going into labour with my sister thirty-five years ago and that, to hear her tell it, only took ten minutes. 'Nothing to it in those days!' she once said, as if vaginas had really gone downhill in the last forty years.

The main impediment to the smooth running of the day is Richard. His texts arrive at roughly seven-minute intervals.

What's her temperature?

38.9.

What's that in real money?

High.

Should we get a new thermometer?

You want a second opinion on her temperature?

Why not?

Don't be insane.

What's wrong with her?

A bug.

What kind of bug?

A bug bug.

Should we call the doctor out?

No.

Why not?

Because we're not in an episode of Dr Finlay's Casebook.

Keep her hydrated and nourished.

Are you actually telling me to remember to give our child food and drink?

Yes, I think so.

Go away.

Thursday, 15 June

More of the same.

Friday, 16 June

Another morning, another set of limpid, tear-filled eyes looking up at me – Thomas now has the Bug too. 'It's okay, you little angel,' I almost say to him. 'It's Friday. I don't work on Fridays. You can be ill any time you like, as long as it's Friday.' Milk, toast (after a nuclear war it will be just cockroaches and Thomas's appetite left standing) and Calpol are administered to them both. They have a little sleep and then I make up a joint bed on the sofa and move them downstairs. We assemble the necessary on the coffee-table: books, water, curly straws, grapes, cherry tomatoes (in case anyone is weak enough to bend to my will in the matter of vitamins), Teddy, Lion and Bear ('I don't want them in with me, they make me too hot. But I need to be able to see them'), medicine, thermometer, remote control, iPad.

I go into the kitchen, where Richard is cramming his mouth with toast and pacing around looking for something that I don't doubt is in plain sight within a five-foot radius of where he started, and fretting that my provisions are both too much ('We shouldn't let them watch television! Or have all those soft toys!' 'Why not?' 'I don't know!') and not enough ('We should have an air purifier! Or humidifier!' 'Do you know what either of those things is and what effect they might have on juvenile health?' 'Not in the least!' 'Go to work'). He finds his keys – it was keys, and they were on the corner of the table ('I was looking in the middle! That's where I left them!') and eventually leaves us in peace.

It is an oddly blissful day. The Calpol relieves most of their symptoms, leaving them just quiet, tired and happy to watch Disney without leaping all over the room or bickering. I break the screenhold every now and again by lying down with them – head at Thomas's end first, we decide, because he's iller, then Evie's – and reading stories aloud. Then they watch some more crap while I power through chores uninterrupted yet guilt-free because illness suspends all the normal rules. I even manage to make a giant lasagne and extra bolognese sauce, which are then divided into portions, put in labelled containers and plastic bags and bunged in the freezer against one of the many days I am no more in a position to make a meal from scratch than I am to have a holistic massage or a perfumed bath. Then I go back to my babies on the sofa and get all the cuddles there never seems to be (my) time or (their) inclination for on an ordinary day. We chat. We nap. We read more stories. The world goes away, just for today.

Saturday, 17 June

Evie recovers suddenly and completely, as five-year-olds will. I send her out with her father. 'Where shall we go?' he says.

'Anywhere that allows you to pee, eat and stay out of here for a minimum of four hours,' I say.

They go to Hampton Court. Evie returns thrilled to the marrow with how many wives Henry VIII had. 'I'm going to have six husbands and chop all their heads off too!'

'No, no, no,' says Richard. 'I told you – it's divorced, beheaded, died, divorced, beheaded, survived. Two out of six.'

'Chop, chop, chop!' roars Evie. 'Chop, chop, chop! I'm going to build a glottin!'

'Guillotine!' Richard says, as they disappear into her room together. 'And that was later on, remember? Anne Boleyn and Catherine Howard were decapitated with an axe or sword.'

'Gonna build one anyway!' shouts Evie, the bloodlust upon her.

'Then we're going to need some string ...' is the last I hear from Richard, as I decide that this is overall a feminist rather than sociopathic endeavour, return to reading *King Zebra* to Thomas on the sofa and leave them to it.

Sunday, 18 June

Thomas is recovering but will still need Monday off. My teenage boss has been emailed. I am too tired to worry about her response. His sister, however, is bouncing off the walls. Richard offers to look after Thomas while he catches up with work. I can see a number of flaws in this plan and also have a number of objections to the terms in which it was couched, but Evie has already printed out an itinerary of activities, flung her coat on and is jingling the car keys impatiently at the door, so I have to content myself with reminding Richard that his offspring is due another dose of Calpol and Calprofen ('Why can't I just give him two lots of the one?' 'Because you'll kill him') and reiterating that, however pressing the work is, he needs to leave his study whenever called – and at least every half-hour – to provide company and reassurance to his sick eight-year-old son.

This day is not peaceful. But tomorrow is Monday, and chambers, and school for Evie and so normalish service can resume, thank Christ.

11.30 p.m. Richard has just come to bed. 'I don't feel well,' he says. This is the point at which my heart truly fills with dread. My husband is not a good patient. Tomorrow is going to be a long day.

Monday, 19 June

So it proves. He moans. He groans. He contorts himself and clutches portions of his body in a manner better suited to a recent multiple-gunshot victim than a forty-four-year-old man with a mild temperature. And yet still, somehow, he sees no irony in the fact that he has the strength to text me endless detailed instructions on how best to restore him to health (tablets – *lozenge-shaped, not round*; tea – *not too hot; four minutes' brewing*; books – *nothing too heavy, in both senses. I cannot manage a hardback, my arms are too weak*; a cheese sandwich he thinks he could manage, all to be brought on a tray *for stability, because a bed is soft*) and to run me through the tasks for the day he thinks I will overlook if he is at home but not actually there to supervise.

I don't follow these instructions, of course, because I am (a) busy and (b) not insane enough to enable yet further help-lessness in my technically equal partner in life, love and child-rearing. But I am interested to note this has no effect on the number that issue forth. It's as if it is enough just to make his presence felt. To feel that he has made shift to improve the world and can relax without the need to see these things executed. Which only makes it more annoying. What happened to the generations of men you read about in books, or hear about in stories from your grandma, who actually went out, worked hard, did things, occasionally lost limbs in accidents and wars without batting an eyelid, came home, fixed things, ate their dinners, all in silence before dying, equally quietly, in their fireside armchairs after forty peaceful years?

When I do go up to the bedroom to chuck a sandwich at him and replenish the jug of water beside his (cruelly circular) paracetamol, I am greeted with an update on his symptoms. 'It's like there's a cold fire burning inside me,' he says at one point, in the hollow whisper he has adopted for the duration.

'I know the feeling,' I say, as I stand at the foot of the bed remembering the story of how when David was six months old, Iain went away on a rock-climbing weekend and the baby and Fiona both got gastric flu. She had to lay plastic sheeting from the garage over the bed, with towels over it for the two of them to lie on, and she put the oilcloth from the kitchen table down in the bathroom. She finally called someone to help her after she puked in the bathroom with David lying beside her and felt her bare heels becoming warm from the gush of diarrhoea that was pouring out of the other end of her, and her toes from that pouring from the baby at the same time. I walk away as Richard embarks on a minutely detailed description of what he calls – without shame, without embarrassment, this is the part I least understand – 'leaden periods interspersed with peripatetic shivering' to visit the second room of the sanatorium, where my little boy lies quietly awaiting my return. 'What would you like, my darling?' I say, lying down next to him, stroking his head and promising myself I will start a campaign to fund research in how to siphon children's viruses into willing mother-host bodies to save infant suffering.

'Nothing, thank you,' he whispers, closing his eyes and pushing his face into my shoulder.

'What about some milk? Would you like some milk?'

'Yes, please,' says his muffled voice.

'Hot or cold?'

'I don't mind. But don't go.'

'Okay. Would you like a story?'

'Yes, please.'

'Which one?'

'I don't mind. Just stay.'

We read *Wizarding for Beginners* until a desperate cry from the next room disturbs us. I've left my phone downstairs and don't want to shout – especially given the things I want to shout – with Thomas right next to me, so I grit my teeth, roll off the bed and go in to investigate.

'I need more tissues!' gasps Richard. 'Not the ordinary ones. The balsam ones.'

So, I murdered him. Then I went downstairs and got some hot milk for Thomas and brought it up to him. He drank it while we finished *Wizarding for Beginners*. No jury in the land will convict me. And if they do, at least I'll get some peace.

Tuesday, 20 June

Thomas is back at school and in time to take part in building what according to him is a full-size replica of the Pyramids of Giza in the playground as part of their ongoing quest to capture the reality of life in Ancient Egypt.

I am back at work. My twelve-year-old boss is not missing a chance to note my every perceived professional failing (she recently graduated from business school, majoring in Entitled Bullshit, and is planning to overhaul the entire charity sector by the time she's old enough to vote). But I'm so glad to be out of the plague house that I don't even want to say, 'I've been doing this job longer than you've been alive, so off you fuck, poppet'. I simply grin ecstatically at her instead. This discomfits her so much that she soon retreats in confusion. It feels incredible to start the day with an inadvertent win.

Wednesday, 21 June

Richard is convalescing – not actually wearing a silk wrapper, and we don't have a chaise longue, but he is certainly capturing the mood. His gradual return to health is an even more exhausting process – for me – than his illness because his powers of speech are fully restored and mostly devoted to a reconstruction of his malady, despite the fact that it signally failed to thrill even in its original form. 'Lulled into a false sense of security at one point by a cessation of symptoms that, placing too much stock in the robust and rebarbative nature of my immune system, I mistook for full recovery rather than temporary remission of suffering, I got out of bed. I became – a new sensation for a man of my vigour and temperament – dizzy and disoriented, much as I imagine young people feel when they take their drugs and go dancing. I did not enjoy it, and returned summarily to bed.'

He literally follows me round the house to deliver further instalments. He won't go to the supermarket ('There's a scything wind!') so I give him a list of gentle chores to do around the house. With plenty of rest in between ('I'm so frail still') and a nap in the afternoon, he manages to complete most of them. He goes to bed early.

No jury in the land, I'm telling you. No jury in the land.

Thursday, 22 June

I deem him fully recovered, leave him in charge of the children and bedtime, and take myself off for a swim. Find myself amazed by simple buoyancy. The water actually holds me up! Supports me! Helps me on my journey up and down the pool. Realise I am feeling grateful to the forces of physics. Do not know what to do about that.

Get home and listen to the bedtime conversation through the monitor.

EVIE: (over the sound of pillows being plumped) I'm more related to Mummy than I am to you.

RICHARD: How so?

EVIE: She gave birth to me! From her tummy!
(Ruminative pause.)
What does the man do to help anyway?

RICHARD: He catches the baby when it comes out, so it doesn't get all mucky on the floor.

Monday, 26 June

Sofia was leaving for work at the same time as the children were pelting down the path to school. She watched them, her eyes round - in, I presume, horror at the noise they were making and the state their hair, shoes and uniforms were somehow already in - all the way to the corner.

'Monday blues,' I say, jokingly. She smiles politely and carries on her civilised way.

Wednesday, 28 June

Thomas comes home saying that Andrew in his class is annoying him. Keeps calling him 'Tommymas' and pushing him.

'Have you told him to stop?' I say. 'Told him you don't like being called that?'

'Yes,' says Thomas, adding without rancour, 'Obviously. He doesn't care. Obviously.'

I am on hold at the bank, trying to order a new bank card because mine has stopped working since Evie took it out of my handbag and used it to try to jimmy open a door as she had seen on a TV programme I didn't know she'd watched.

'Well, hopefully he'll get bored soon and—'

'Bite him,' Evie advises.

'Evie! No!'

'Yes,' she says. 'Bite him.'

'I don't want to bite him,' says Thomas. 'I think it would feel horrible.'

'I'll bite him for you, then,' says Evie.

'No,' I say. 'Nobody's biting any— Oh, hello, yes, sorry, I need a new card ...'

'I bite people all the time,' says Evie. 'It feels great.'

'I'm sorry,' I say to the nice man on the other end of the line, 'I'm going to have to go. Evie – what?'

'In my mind, I mean,' she says, rolling her eyes. 'I tested it on myself, on my arm, look' – she sinks her teeth into her forearm – 'so I'd know how it would feel in my mouth. And now I can imagine biting other people when they do wrong things to me.'

'Don't,' I say.

'Why not?'

'Because you shouldn't,' I say feebly.

'Why not?'

'Because it's not good to imagine doing bad things.'

'It's fine,' says Evie, with assurance. 'Because then you're not doing them.'

'I—'

'Goodbye,' she says, slipping off the kitchen stool and disappearing up the stairs, leaving me and Thomas together in the kitchen.

'Don't bite anyone,' I say.

'I won't,' he says. And that, I suppose, will have to do.

Friday, 30 June

Fiona and I have signed up to help with the summer fete. 'It's this or Christmas,' she said. 'And by Christmas we may have developed the strength of character to say no.' I do not even have the strength of character to resist Fiona, so we dragged our weary arses along to the committee meeting and offered to man a stall. Everyone else wanted the lucky dip, human fruit machine or the tombola, something with a bit of glamour. Fiona and I volunteered for jumble. 'What TF do I care?' said Fiona. 'I quite like jumble. Jumble speaks to me. I am jumble.'

'Plus,' I point out, 'getting ready for jumble means emptying sixteen binbags full of crap onto a portable picnic table ten minutes before the doors open on the day.'

We high-fived each other. Then nemesis came a-calling. The old hands on the committee, it turned out, were of course well aware of the light preparatory duties required by jumble and had lists of supplemental tasks to hand.

So here we both are, sitting in Savannah's house for the third evening this week cutting out circlets of checked paper and using coloured ribbon to tie them over the lids of 150 jam jars filled with sweets, and tiny plastic toys whose journey towards landfill sites we are but briefly interrupting. 'Just tiny vessels full of child labour and diabetes, when you think about it,' I say, holding one up to the light.

'Best not to think about it, then,' says Fiona. We pick our oakum alongside two of Savannah's most devoted wingwomen and a couple of mothers from the two other classes whom we don't know very well but seem nice enough. 'What are you in for?' whispered Fiona to them on the first evening, when Savannah and her team were in the kitchen admiring a new soft-closing something.

'We're all going to be away on the day of the fete,' one whispered back. 'Salayha's visiting her cousin' – Salayha rolled her eyes and kept cutting – 'and Maria's away for her wedding anniversary. Which one, Maria?

'Tears,' replied Maria, throwing a handful of frayed ribbon ends into the bin, 'and Melanie's dog's having an operation. Savannah misheard and thought Mel was having one herself at first, but the idiot went and corrected her.'

'It wouldn't have made any difference anyway,' said Melanie. 'I'd still have been able to do jam jars now.'

No booze was forthcoming on the previous two evenings, so this time Fiona and I brought two bottles of wine each and started pouring them for everybody. After a few nervous glances flicked in Savannah's direction, all but the wingwomen accepted. The circlets are getting less circular and tying the buggers on is going to become a bit of a problem sooner or later, but at least we're happy.

Savannah comes dancing through, trailing more ribbons and rolls of paper which she dumps on the coffee-table in front of us with an encouraging smile. She tends to cut very few gingham circlets herself on these evenings. She sees herself more as workhouse overseer than fellow worker.

'Good news!' she trills. 'Carole has taken a stall for her homemade beauty products and candles!'

Sounds of celebration are conspicuous by their absence. This is because Carole's beauty products and candles all smell like dogshit. Seriously. If you don't have a dog but want your house and face to smell like dogshit, buy some of Carole's stuff. You won't look back.

(In case you're wondering, nobody has told Carole her stuff smells like dogshit because Carole cares day and night for her aged parents as well as her two children and has no life at all, except for turning inoffensive basic emollients and waxes into something that will strip your nasal membranes raw. Instead, we buy them in secret sympathy, keep one for display in case she ever pops round and throw the rest away. Or, in Fiona's case, give them to satanic mothers-in-law as acts of passive-aggressive but still pleasing minor revenge.)

She glides away again. Her minions follow.

'How many jam jars have we done so far?' asks Fiona. 'I'm guessing nine hundred.'

I count. 'Twenty-eight.'

'Okay. I've got an idea. Let's smash the rest and feed the shards to Savannah.'

We all clink glasses. Sumer is icumen in.

Sunday, 2 July

So tired. Cannot wait for our girls' birthday/Mother's Day/Just Because weekend away. Twelve days to go. That's it. That's all. So tired. Cannot wait. Twelve days.

Monday, 3 July

Trying to clear up email inbox and notice that Child Boss refers to my working-from-home days as 'your "working-from-home" days'. Does ... does she not believe me? Or does she just not understand punctuation? I close my eyes and let the wave of rage (either way) pass through me, and re-count the days till my weekend escape. Cannot make it fewer than eleven.

Tuesday, 4 July

Mrs Bradley brings over half a dozen platycodon plants she has grown from seed, with detailed instructions on how to plant them out. 'You might want to give one to the little madam,' she says, looking at Evie, who hears this as she runs naked up the stairs on the way to the bath and raises a hand in gracious acknowledgement. 'For indoors. See if she can keep it alive. Bit of responsibility, be good for her. But the boy,' she says approvingly, 'is an old soul.'

I tell Evie. 'Course I can keep it alive!' she snorts.

'You have to remember to water it every other day,' I say.

'Leave it to me,' she says.

I resolve that I will. I will not save this plant for her if she forgets. Responsibility, the teaching of. That is what Mrs Bradley wants, and with her ultimate authority exercised, that is what she will have.

Wednesday, 5 July

Evie watered her plant today, with a withering eye on me at all times.

Of course, there is always a price to pay for anticipated happiness. Between me and my weekend of freedom and non-debauchery lie two parents' evenings. Thomas's today, Evie's – her first, God help us – next week.

They are always stressful – less because of our children (though Evie's turning into a bit of a wild card and I can feel a certain amount of apprehension building) than because of Richard. Our first time with Thomas still haunts me.

'I just want to know if he's a moron or not,' Richard had said, as we set off towards the school. 'Isn't that all that matters? Why can she not just tell us that?'

'Because they're not allowed to any more,' I explained.

'Why not?'

'I think maybe casual cruelty's fallen out of fashion.'

'But it's all people want to know!' he insisted, as we took our seats in the queue for Miss Milligan's class.

He's not right, there. I could have pointed to at least seventeen mothers who were wanting only to be told that their child was a genius. 'Above average' won't do. 'Not-moron' certainly won't do. 'Moron' itself would kill most of them. The rest would turn violent and kill Miss Milligan.

Snatches of conversation drifted over to us from the parents who came and went from the teacher's table before us.

'Adam is doing Lego for seven-to-twelve-year-olds at home!' we heard one fond parent trill proudly.

Richard and I avoided each other's eyes. The first – and last – time we gave Thomas Lego he gave it back to us, the pieces still in their sealed bags twenty minutes later. 'What's this?' asked Richard.

'It's a present for you!' Thomas beamed. 'It's a ship you can build yourself!' (We gave it to Evie a few years later. She gave it back to us after twenty minutes fully finished, with a

Meccano laser shield added, and a demand for more.)

Dylan's and Ethan's parents, each pair louder than the other, were before us. Ethan spent his days writing stories at home, apparently. Thomas did too, to be fair. He scribbled all over pages of paper and called it 'ant language'.

'What are the ants saying?'

'Oh, you know, Mummy,' he would say cheerily. 'Ant things.'

And Dylan was already a voracious reader of chapter books, according to his devoted mama. About three days away from tackling Proust, by the sound of things. We were still attempting to breathe life into the Alphablocks who help F-I-X the V-A-N in a J-A-M. Richard was suffering violent fantasies about the Alphablocks – twenty-six elaborate murders with appropriately initialled weapons were permanently under mental construction.

At last it was our turn. We sat in front of Miss Milligan. 'How is he doing?' said Richard.

'He's coming along really nicely,' said Miss Milligan.

'What does that mean?' he replied. I shot him a warning look.

'He's very articulate, very helpful in class. He's a lovely boy to have around.'

'But what about the real things? Reading, writing, maths?'

'We really don't like to worry about those too much at this stage.'

'But when should we start worrying about them?' asked Richard, despite my continued warning looks and the addition of a warning hand on his thigh, near his scrotum, which we early in our marriage agreed I was allowed to pinch if it looked like he was about to ruin any important social, familial or economic relationship for us. 'Should it not be now? I think it should be now. If there is anything to worry about. Is there anything to worry about?'

'He's coming along very nicely.'

'But – but – but—'

'I think what my husband's trying to say is – is there

anything in particular we should be doing with Thomas to help him? What would you say he needs more practice in at home?'

'He's fine,' said Miss Milligan, with a smile so wide I knew Richard could see his son's future disappearing into it. 'We don't like to see them pressured. He's coming along very nicely.'

The timer buzzed. Our ten minutes were up. In the corridor we mopped up the blood coming from Richard's ears ('I want to go back! Let me speak to her again!' 'NO'), then made our way home.

'How was it?' asked my mother, who had been babysitting and, through whatever the witchcraft is that she has always had at her disposal, got both of them undressed, bathed and into bed by the time we got back.

'I think he must be a moron,' I said. 'Miss Milligan just doesn't want to be the one to tell us.'

My mother morphed instantly into Devoted Grandma Preparing to Smite All Anti-Grandchild Comers.

'He's a *genius*. Look!' she said, holding up a piece of ink-spattered paper. 'Ant language! Because he can't be bothered to write! And a Lego ship that you can build yourself! Because he's no more interested in stupid bloody Lego than you were! He's not a moron!' she cried triumphantly. 'He's lazy!'

'We'll take it,' said Richard, after a pause.

This time, when we arrive at school, Fiona, Iain and David (they had no one to leave him with because everyone's at parents' evening, they refuse to 'impose' on my mother unless in extremis, and you could no more get Iain's to babysit than you could get a scar to blush) are just leaving.

'Greetings, Slaters all!' says Richard, rubbing David's head. 'Are you returning from the Front? Or still to go over the top?'

'Been,' says Iain. 'Done.'

'We're on our way home,' says Fiona.

'How was it?' I say.

'Awreet,' says David, before Fiona can answer. 'You can't

really object to me. I'm not one thing or the other. Just middle of t'road.'

I look questioningly at Fiona. She shrugs. 'That's about the size of it,' she says. 'Though' – turning to David – 'she did ask me why your accent was still so strong.'

'What did you say?' asks David.

'I said I thought it was because you still miss the countryside a bit and are maybe trying to keep the memory going of living there.'

'I think I'm just stubborn,' says David, considering. 'Tell her not to worry.'

I look at Fiona. She shrugs again. 'He is. I will. And hopefully she won't.'

We sit and wait to be called. We're quite early in the list and nobody seems to have overrun their ten-minute slot (though I'll bet Savannah's had a damn good try) and we find ourselves seated before Miss Anderson, who looks about five years older than her charges, promptly at six twenty.

She professes herself entirely happy with his schoolwork. 'But,' she says, and my bowels turn instantly to water, 'I'm just a little bit concerned about his interpersonal skillset.'

'His what skill-what?' says Richard and I edge my hand scrotumwards in warning.

'I've noticed,' Miss Anderson says carefully, 'that Thomas doesn't play very well with others.'

'What do you mean?' asks my husband, with interest, while my mind is instantly colonised by visions of Thomas as an eight-year-old Flashman, bullying everyone in sight and torturing the class pets. Not that they have any class pets. And not that Thomas has ever shown the slightest scintilla of a whisper of a hint of an inclination to impose himself in any way upon anyone. Nevertheless, by the time Miss Anderson replies, I have him being expelled from school and him – a brutal, scarred figure in tiny fatigues – blowing it up behind him as he leaves.

'I mean,' she says, as I inwardly convulse, 'he likes to play on his own a lot, or with David or just a few boys and girls.'

'So,' my husband says judiciously, 'he doesn't play badly with others. He just doesn't play with them very much?'

'Yes.'

'Are they ignoring him? Is he ignoring them? Andrew was teasing him at one point, and I did tell him to—'

'No,' she says. 'No, it's just that he doesn't always seem to want to play with everybody.'

There is silence. My husband and I look at each other. I signal, by the fractional movement of my eyeballs to which he has learned over the long years of marriage to respond without question, that this is his field.

'Then,' he says delicately, 'I'm not sure I see the problem.'

Miss Anderson looks worried. 'He doesn't always want to play with other children,' she says.

We nod. We have understood. We still do not see the problem.

'Children should,' she says.

'I don't think that's true,' says my husband.

'The thing is,' I say quickly, 'is that Thomas – well, he's like us. Unsurprisingly. He doesn't really like big groups of people. He likes one or two, on playdates, that kind of thing, and of course he's very close friends with David, but I can imagine that being in the playground with everyone doesn't really bring out the best in him. It didn't in me.' God, those hours spent standing in the middle of a tarmacked wasteland while yelling, laughing children ran and skipped and whirled round me, all apparently effortlessly finding a kind of fun in the playground and in themselves that I couldn't even begin to locate.

'I'm better than her now, with adults,' says Richard. 'But as a child I used to refuse to go out. They soon gave up trying to prise my fingers off the doorframe and let me stay in and read the *Children's Britannica*.'

'At least Thomas isn't doing that!' I say brightly to Miss Anderson, whose look of bafflement is deepening to a kind of concerned panic, or possibly panicked concern. I reflect again on how young she is. I probably have cans of soup in the larder that are older than Miss Anderson.

We sit in silence for a bit longer as she tries to assimilate this view of life.

'He's just an introvert, like us,' Richard tries again, seeking – I think – to reassure. 'Do you know what the clinical definition of an introvert is? It's someone who is drained by being with lots of people. Extroverts are energised by it.'

I can see by Miss Anderson's expression that none of this is helping.

'Most people are extroverts,' he continues. 'You too, probably. So introverts seem weird. But we're not! Or, at least, you seem just as weird to us!'

'We'll tell him to try to run around a bit more,' I say.

'And maybe he'll bump into people he likes!' says Richard, delighted to have found a compromise.

'All right,' says Miss Anderson, uncertainly.

I don't want to say anything more in front of Richard in case it plunges him into full barrister mode and we're there till we die, but I try to convey through a kindly yet knowing yet unpatronising final glance at Miss Anderson as we leave that I will bring it up with Thomas next time we are on our own. Because when I think about it, acquiring 'an interpersonal skillset' earlier in life would have smoothed my passage somewhat. I first learned to fake interest in people – which is what I presume Miss Anderson means *au fond* – in my early twenties. I dutifully exercised this untalent for about a decade before deciding, as I think most of us do in our thirties, that it was one of the many games in life that wasn't worth the candle. The skill is now stored in some neglected oubliette of my mind, to be dusted down and dragged out now and again for a work do of Richard's or something, but other than that, I get by with a pleasant expression, ambiguous half-smile and occasional 'Mm-hmm!' while I plan the next day's tasks or replay favourite *Brooklyn Nine-Nine* episodes in my head.

As we head back down the corridor Richard is in a jaunty mood. 'I got a bit worried there at first, but it all went rather well in the end, didn't it? No clear signs of moronicity – except perhaps in Miss Anderson, but she's young yet – which is about all we can hope for at this age, don't you think? Yes, not too bad at all, overall!'

'Mm-hmm,' I say. 'Mm-hmm.'

Thursday, 6 July

It was my turn to pick David and Thomas up from their joint violin class today. There is nothing I rue more than giving in last year to a momentary vision I had of nurturing a musical prodigy. A leaflet came home from school advertising a cheap deal made even cheaper if children went paired, and extolling the creative and disciplinary virtues of learning an instrument. In that weak moment, I persuaded Fiona to sign David up with Thomas. It's been unremitting agony. Neither of them has the least aptitude. ('Yehudi?' said Richard, when he first heard Thomas. 'Yehudon't.' Even Grandma flinched at their first 'showcase performance' and has declined to attend since.) But at least David applies his usual stolid workmanlike attitude to the task and has some vague idea about what he's supposed to be doing and what the end goal is supposed to be. Thomas approaches every note as if it were a charming novelty each time. I once, after we had been through it eighteen times on the trot, sang 'Au clair de la lune' to him to try to give him some sense of the rhythm and phrasing. 'That's nice,' he said, with interest. 'What is it?'

'We started a new tune today!' says Thomas, as he throws his instrument into the boot. David takes it out, then gently but firmly wedges the two of them in together so they can't rattle about, and gives me a thumbs-up.

'Oh, really?' I say, giving David a thumbs-up back as we all climb into the car and strap in. 'What's that?'

'"Ode to Joy",' says Thomas.

'It's nowt of t'kind, though,' says David. 'We sound terrible.'

Friday, 7 July

Evie watered her plant again today. 'This is *so boring*,' she snarled. I catch her so many times after school eyeing it meditatively that my worry becomes not whether she will be able to keep the thing alive but whether she will refrain from bringing it to an untimely end.

Saturday, 8 July

The summer fete.

'*Vaya con dios!*' shouts Richard, spraying milk and cereal over every surface and child within a ten-foot radius – a.k.a. 'doing breakfast' – as I head out the door. I mutter something unprintable under my breath, and join Fiona, who is waiting for me at the gate looking as fed up as I feel. We creep like snails – old, tired, resentful snails – unwillingly to school to embark on our jumble duties.

Actually, I muse later from the safety of the sofa and beginning to enjoy the anaesthetising effects of a bucket of wine, it wasn't too bad. Someone got his head stuck in the tombola barrel and had to be eased out with some of Carole's moisturiser, then taken home for a Silkwood scrubdown. Three fingers were broken at the splat-a-rat stall, one better than the previous year. The jam jars went like hot cakes. So did the cakes. Fetes should just be cakes, really. However old and (more) canker-hearted I become, the sight of other people's home baking will never fail to cheer me. Though fair play too to all those who donated shop-bought Bakewell slices and apple pies. You know I feel you.

Jumble was … jumble. We weeded out the actively pestilent

donations the night before, sold about ten per cent of the remainder, had another five per cent stolen by pensioners, and have dumped the rest in Fiona's garage to sort for recycling before we bin the rest.

And fair play to Savannah, there were, amid the comfortingly reactionary stuff like raffles, books and homemade jewellery by and for people you don't like very much, some great innovations. Pupils walked around selling popcorn and sweets from usherette-type trays, or ran individual stalls offering henna tattoos, manicures, hair braiding and chalking, hand massages and help to gamers seeking to unlock new levels of whatever it is gamers play. It all bespoke the kind of entrepreneurial spirit that I suspect will culminate soon in a management buyout of the PTA.

I availed myself of a manicure after my jumble shift. A tiny ten-year-old girl hunched over my fingernails with such care and concentration that it near broke my heart, despite the profoundly unprepossessing results. 'You should ask for your money back,' said Evie, appearing at my shoulder as the girl moved a tiny electric fan over my nails to dry them.

'Shush,' I said. 'I think they look very nice.'

'They look absolutely terrible,' she said unrepentantly. 'Give us the pound back,' she ordered the girl.

I readied for ructions but there was no need.

'No,' said the salonista, with admirable simplicity. 'Go away.' So we did. I can't work out whether I'd like to meet her mother, and if so, whether it would be to praise or warn her.

I take Evie to find the rest of the family. They are at the tombola, where Richard is trying to acclimatise his son – who at the moment is being very much my son – to the concept of risk as fun. 'Don't spend any more, Daddy,' I hear him begging as we approach.

'But we won a box of orange Matchmakers last time!' Richard says.

'But this time we might win nothing!' says Thomas. 'Or something we don't like!'

'We might win something better,' says Richard, which is why he has none of the online passwords to our accounts. 'And look!' he says, opening his wallet and showing Thomas its contents. 'There's still one, two, three, *four* pounds left in there. When you're dealing with these kinds of sums, kid, you basically can't lose. You have to speculate to accumulate.' He hands over another two pounds. Thomas and I quail, Evie and Richard quiver with the thrill of it all. The children take it in turns to dip their hands into the bag and pull out a ticket. Nine pass without reward. The tension is unbearable.

Evie's hand goes in for the last one. 'Forty-five,' she says. The man in charge scans the trestle table upon which the family's happiness and financial stability now depend. He reaches to the far end and hands her a hand-knitted teddy bear in red dungarees. 'Number forty-five,' he says. Evie roars in triumph. Richard punches the air.

Thomas and I lean against the table, emotionally spent. 'Can we go home now?' says my boy.

'Don't you want to have another go? See if you can win something for yourself?' says Richard.

'No,' says Thomas. 'It makes me feel sick. Can I have a Matchmaker instead?'

'Yes,' I say, taking them from Richard and thrusting them into his shaking hands. 'You can have the whole box.' My poor child. I'm so sorry for all the things I have genetically done to you. We share the same taste in chocolate too, though, so I consider the Matchmakers handover a sufficient sacrifice on the altar of maternal guilt for today.

Speaking of maternal guilt – our girls' weekend away fast approaches. I hope we don't all end up consumed by it. Fiona reckons we'll be fine if we just drink steadily throughout and occasionally lay our hands on Céline to absorb some of her … Célineness to boost our reserves.

Sunday, 9 July

The golden couple were out sunbathing in the garden today. The garden right next to ours. So near and yet so far. I sort of wanted to lay my hands on them too, and absorb some of their lean-flanked, flat-bellied youth. When the envy became too overwhelming, I sent Evie and Thomas out to play and drive them inside. Instead, they ended up playing volleyball over the fence with them. Because as well as firm flesh they have energy and an appetite for life. I forgot about that.

I come downstairs after changing the beds and putting laundry away this afternoon to find that Evie has constructed an irrigation system for her plant. She has put a bucket of water on the kitchen table, the plant on the floor, one end of my dressing-gown cord in the former and pressed the other into the soil of the latter. The water, apparently, will gradually work its way down the cord, thereby delivering a constant, refreshing supply to the plant.

'What?' I say. 'How did you ... Where did you get this idea from?'

'Dunno.' She shrugs. 'Saw something like it in a book at school once, I think. Or maybe David's? Can't remember. It was years ago.' She wanders off. I am left in her wake, feeling proud and troubled at the same time. It is a sensation I am getting used to.

Monday, 10 July

With the indefatigable enthusiasm and idiocy that defines the young, Infant Temp Boss has commanded us all to submit updated work biogs for 'a new dataset' she is putting together, which must include two recent achievements and the key roles we hold outside the organisation. Emails have been flying among staff ever since. 'I haven't achieved anything since my cycling proficiency test. Too busy trying to earn a fucking living,' says one, representing the essential tone of all. 'Key role outside the organisation? What does that mean? Key roles don't *exist* outside an organisation.'

'I was here from eight till eight yesterday,' someone replied. 'I'm not sure *I* exist outside this organisation.'

But we'll scratch something together, of course, each of us. Wasting valuable time and limited energy, because it's still better than trying to explain the futility of this kind of thing to someone who doesn't have the life experience that proves it.

Tuesday, 11 July

It is Evie's parents' evening.

'Another one?' groans Richard, as he rushes through the door, dumps his briefcase, kisses the children and heads back out with me. 'How many children have we *got*?'

Fifteen minutes later we sit down to hear what Miss Brio has to say about our second-born. Miss Brio looks even younger than Thomas's teacher. Richard calls her Miss Embryo in private – and, there is every chance tonight, to her face too.

'She's very confident!' says Miss Brio.

'She is,' I agree.

'She calls me "Fat Dad",' says Richard.

'She certainly knows her own mind,' says Miss Brio.

'She's an absolute tyrant,' says Richard. 'You must try to break her anew each day. We do.'

'Apart from her spelling, where we're still trying to persuade her that consistency is better than invention, her schoolwork is exceptionally good,' says the teacher. 'But she doesn't seem to want to accept any praise for it.'

'We scorn that which comes too easily,' says Richard. 'Give her some trigonometry to do or *Anna Karenina* to read. Or spell. That'd put a spoke in her wheels. Hey,' he says suddenly, a new light in his eyes. 'How's her interpersonal skillset? Apparently that's a thing now, you know. They've all got to have one.'

'She gets on with everyone,' says Miss Brio.

'That's because you never know who might come in useful when you're putting your coup together,' says Richard, sagely.

'And she seems very popular. Forceful presences often are.'

'Are you saying you think she rules through fear?' asks Richard, with interest.

'No,' says Miss Brio, who now has the distinct air of someone being battered by a rough sea. 'I just think it will be good for her when she meets someone who can go toe to toe with her instead of letting her dominate. She'll enjoy it.'

'She won't,' says Richard, cheerily. 'It'll be a bloodbath.'

The buzzer, mercifully, goes off. I drag him away. 'Thank you, Miss Embryo!' he calls cheerily over his shoulder. I don't know about our children but he still has much to learn.

Wednesday, 12 July

Goddammit. Or godammit, or goddamit or however you fucking well spell it – Savannah's forced a playdate upon us all. I have to take Evie and Thomas round there. Poor buggers. Savannah works her way round the class with these invites because no one ever volunteers to get involved with her vile children. She always does it face to face because she knows WhatsApp and text messages can be ignored. It used to be alphabetically until we got wise and started avoiding school when we knew she was getting close. Now it's done according to no pattern we can discern, though we keep trying, in order to shield our blameless offspring from after-school purgatory with Oenone (yes) and Olivad (we think she made it up), who poke and preen and stop bickering only to unite against any visitor wanting to play with their newest toys, of which there is always a tempting array. And I will be required to submit to at least twenty minutes of small-talk at pick-up before she'll let them go. And when I say small-talk, I mean standing there while she blows conversational poison darts at me and watches me flinch.

And then, of course, I'll have to have them on a playdate in return. FML.

Why the bollocks did you say yes? replies Fiona, when I WhatsApp the coven my woes.

Bcs she did what she always does. Waited till I was distracted by a minor crisis – E had decided she was scared of Velcro that morning so I had to tighten her shoes for her before she went in – and asked. I wasn't prepared.

Well, writes Céline, *you know my way. Follow it.*

U know I can't, I tap.

None of us can, adds Fiona.

I French-eyeroll you all, Céline replies.

Céline's way is to display complete and utter disinterest. This is made easier by the fact that she *is* completely and utterly disinterested. Céline has the inestimable advantage in life of genuinely not caring what anyone – beyond a few close personal friends (possibly including me, I cannot tell) – thinks of her, her house, her job, her husband, her children, the way she's raising them, and any and all points in between. She is a marvel and I hope to be just like her when I grow up. Until then …

You only have to do it once, her next message says.

The first and only time Céline was invited round to Savannah's was a total success – for Céline. Savannah probably rages about it still.

'I sat down,' she told us when we all met for a drink the next night, 'and she started. What had I done to my hair? "Washed it," I said, as if she was simple. Had I heard of the new Pilates class, tried the new local restaurant, so on and so on. I just looked very, very bored – because I was very, very bored – and said, "No." She looked a bit *déconcertée* and started listing all the new stuff she had – car, handbag, kitchen floor, maybe pelvic floor, I was not really listening – and I just said nothing.'

'Nothing?' said Fiona.

'Nothing,' she confirmed.

'How can you not say *anything*?' I said, trying to imagine stopping myself making even the small noises of acknowledgement that come as naturally as breathing to my well-trained, hidebound self.

'Why *would* I say anything? It was so boring. I didn't even nod. And she just sort of stopped. Trailed away. Then we sat there in silence. I wasn't going to break it. She lasted three minutes, then called for the kids and we *disparu* into the night. Never to return.'

We have all tried to emulate her ever since, but we have never come close to this majesty.

Thursday, 13 July

I arrive at Savannah's to pick up the children. Despite having bribed them with the promise of extra time playing games on Daddy's phone if they make the best of the situation and don't appear too eager to leave when I get there, they zoom like road-runners to my side as soon as I step over the threshold. The two upturned faces silently beseech/threaten me but before I can begin our extraction manoeuvres, Savannah laughs. It sounds like a steel door clanging shut. 'There's no need to stop playing yet!' she exclaims. 'I'm going to make Mummy a coffee so we can have a lovely chat before you go!' Her two goblins lead my unfortunate offspring gleefully back to the playroom, land of no parental supervision. Thomas marches stoically towards his doom. Evie casts a look back at me, contempt now mixing with her darkening fury. I shall be paying off this moral debt for years.

'So,' says Savannah, brightly, somehow contriving to take my handbag and tuck it neatly in a corner while thrusting a coffee at me and forcing me onto the sofa (Loaf) where I become marooned among too many cushions (eclectic). She knows no one ever chooses to stay. 'How *are* you?' She sits down next to me, curling her socked (by Toast) feet cosily under her and cocking her head to one side, like a bird – a terribly, terribly innocently concerned bird.

'I'm fine, thank you,' I say warily, curling my own socked

feet under me, though less cosily because my own footwear is by the Bedroom Floor In Semi-Darkness This Morning and does not quite match but does quite possibly smell.

'You've been looking a bit washed out,' she says, porcelain forehead furrowing slightly above perfect eyebrows.

'Have I?' I say.

'We've been worried about you!' she trills.

'Have you?'

'Of course. You're always pale – English rose! – but recently you've been looking almost grey!'

'Have I?'

'Shall I whizz you up a juice instead of a coffee?' she says, holding out a hand to take my cup back. It sounds solicitous but is in fact a test. If I take the juice, I am accepting her judgement of me, of Savannah as my superior in life – or at least lifestyle – and professing a willingness to do better. If I keep the coffee, on the other hand, I won't be asserting my superiority. I will be a tragically rebellious teenager, *and* I'll become the subject of delighted, faux-anxious conversations between her and her gang about how I'm not even trying any more. The next conversation will have her pretending to be worried about me being depressed ('I'm not – I just like big cardigans!' I will howl uselessly into the void) and – uuurrrgh.

'Ooh, I'd love a juice, please. Thank you!' I hear myself say like a GIANT TIT.

Fifteen minutes of faffing in the kitchen ensue. Fifteen minutes! I could have been home and punching a wall by now. She returns eventually, with a glassful of something that looks like she's blown it out of her own nose. 'It's broccoli, kale, just a smoosh of avocado, Greek yoghurt and a lime!' she says gaily. This is not a combination that should exist, I roar inwardly, as I take the glass with a rictus grin of gratitude plastered onto my stupid face. You might as well say it's cherries, kangaroo liver and a bag of sorrows, it would make as much gustatory sense.

'Full of iron,' she explains, 'and the lime shrinks fat cells.' Ah, you splendid bitch.

I drink it down. I think back to my early years of sexual misadventure, learning not to gag during various practices, and apply that hard-won knowledge once more. O tempora and your increasingly miserable mores.

'Delicious,' I say, banging the empty glass down on the coffee-table, like Marion finishing her shots in *Indiana Jones*. 'But now I really must go.' I really must. I want to get round the corner before I throw up.

You should at least have spilled the juice on the sofa, comments Fiona, when we cyberconvene once again that evening.

I French-eyeroll you all again, writes Céline.

Your way next time, C, I text back. *Vraiment.*

Friday, 14 July

The great day arrives. Our weekend – *the* weekend – starts here. As my battered suitcase and I trundle down the path after teatime and goodbyes, Sofia and Amrit are arriving home and *I* get to wave goodbye to *them*. It is thrilling.

The coven congregates at the station and we compare end-of-week fatigue on the train. We are equal. We arrive, dump our bags in our beautiful, spotless rooms and head for the restaurant. We eat. We drink cocktails and two bottles of nice wine. We go out onto the patio and call our respective homes ('Pretend we've got – I dunno – evening meditation class or something in five minutes,' instructs Fiona. 'Don't get dragged into anything. Say your goodnights and get out') while Nadia has an illicit fag. We have another bottle of wine, then repair – carefully – to our rooms. I have a bath. In a clean bath. I dry myself on a large, clean, dry, white towel. It is like wrapping myself in Heaven. I get into bed, read my book for half an hour and fall asleep, all by half past nine.

Saturday, 15 July

I wake up twelve hours later feeling weird. Realise it is the feeling of having slept for twelve hours.

I get dressed. Go downstairs with my book. Have a leisurely coffee that someone brings me without my asking and then keeps refilling at perfect intervals while I alternate between reading and looking out over the beautiful gardens as I wait for the other three to emerge. Fiona comes down first. 'I feel like I'm floating,' she says in wonderment.

'I wonder how early we can go to bed tonight,' I say eagerly.

'First sitting in the restaurant is at six,' says Fiona. 'We can be done and dusted by eight, easy, I reckon.'

'Imagine,' I say, sitting back in my chair and sighing with anticipatory satisfaction. 'Imagine.'

Then Nadia arrives. 'Sorry I'm late!' she says. 'I woke up and just lay there in silence for twenty minutes because I could.'

I hold up a gently admonitory hand. 'You're not late,' I say. 'There is no "late" here. There is no anything here, except coffee – here, have some, it's a new pot, they just keep bringing them – and the opportunity, should you wish, to move lightly from delight to new delight, like a butterfly amid a meadowful of flowers.'

'You're right!' says Nadia, her face taking on a look of ecstasy. 'Time has no meaning. What shall we not do?'

'Let's not go into the village,' says Fiona, who has been idly paging through the brochure about nearby attractions and facilities. 'And not go shopping.'

'Excellent. And let's not call home.'

'Let's not get any painful treatments. I was going to be waxed, but now I'm just going to have a massage.'

'Let's not move from here until we've finished this coffee and need a wee.'

'Let's not indeed.'

And we do not.

The afternoon passes in a beautiful haze. We are sober and drug-free but the joy of being together – yet at any moment free to be alone! – and unshackled from domestic cares and woes, basically puts us in a blissed-out state unsurpassable by any chemical ingestion. With only ourselves to please, the day seems to go on for ever. I want to frame each golden moment and line the walls of my home with them so that I can relive it whenever I need to.

Eventually, after about eight hours of wandering in the gardens, having another sit-down, reading books, eating cakes, scrolling through our phones and comparing throws and rugs on our favourite throws and rugs sites, it is dinner time. We float to the restaurant to eat, uninterrupted, delicious food that we haven't cooked ourselves and upon which no washing-up is attendant.

Conversation during this idyllic meal – upon which, by way of delightful contrast, wine is most definitely attendant – wouldn't pass the Bechdel test and we occasionally make the effort to address issues more abstract and philosophical than the various ways life would be improved with different-to-no-husbands and/or boarding schools with full time nannies and chefs in the holidays, but cannot think of any. We try world affairs, too, but that's very quickly very sad and even more intractable than the husbands/childcare thing, so we give up. 'And anyway,' says Céline, 'we need to talk about our lives as they are lived. Get our therapy where we can. We are essentially at war. All the time.'

'Harsh,' says Fiona, lifting her glass in salute. 'But fair.'

'It's maybe more like just working a huge shift at a factory,' I offer, in uncharacteristically cheery mood. 'You clock in at five fingers dilated, join the assembly line and try to keep up with the conveyor-belt that runs all the bits of ... of everything past you just too fast for you ever to succeed, and then clock off thirty years later.'

'I want my statutory tea and lunch breaks,' says Nadia.

'You're not getting them,' says Fiona. 'This,' she says,

gesturing widely to take in the restaurant, the hotel, the weekend, 'is more like a false fire alarm going off and all of us gladly rushing outside to stand in the cold for twenty minutes before we're forced back inside.'

The talk turns to all the ways we have found to carve out a little time to ourselves. Fiona fakes paperwork and stays at the surgery for an extra couple of hours every few weeks and reads a book. Nadia manages by snatching a few minutes at a time throughout the day by doing extra wees and playing AlphaBetty while she's on the loo. I just let my house go to shit. Céline's, as ever, is simplest and most effective – she takes a Valium. 'Early Friday or Saturday evening,' she recommends. 'So that by the time the children are fed, your edge is off for putting them to bed and then you can enjoy sitting in front of the television with a soft, quiet mind and later go to sleep with no problems of your own. They are far away.' It's basically a way of cramming twelve hours' relaxation into four. Once again, I am gifted another insight into the Way of Ruthless Efficiency.

Other points of interest raised over the course of the evening:

- No one's having the right amount of sex. But we're all averaging about once a fortnight.
- There was no chorus of disagreement when one of us announced that she was monogamous through fatigue and lack of opportunity, not choice.
- We do not understand how men rule the world when they see so little of what needs doing, cannot complete an entire job in one go and have a nervous breakdown if anything doesn't go according to plan.
- We all want dogs.
- We could mostly weep for our younger selves.
- When the last of us turns fifty, we will start drawing up plans for the enormous mansion house we will share once we are all safely widowed.

- We will start playing the lottery now so that we can afford the enormous mansion house and the necessary re-landscaping of the UK so that it can be in the centre of a Georgian town, the Scottish Highlands, on the coast and in London at the same time to suit all tastes.
- All our periods are due yet there isn't a whisper of PMT to be heard, thus proving my theory absolutely. I knew it wasn't us. It's them, always.
- We were lying about sex earlier. It's more like once every three or four weeks and we'd like to be having more. Just not with our husbands.
- But nobody's contemplating an affair.
- Yet.
- All men believe in the Toilet Fairy. How else would the skid marks they leave behind disappear? No human could possibly demean themselves by actually ducking inside a toilet and removing them, could they? *Res ipsa loquitur*, Céline advises us. It's a legal term, meaning 'the thing speaks for itself'.
- We all, at our advanced ages, know exactly when to stop drinking to avoid a hangover and it is now.
- We should have just one more.

Sunday, 16 July

Everyone is very pleased to see me home, albeit in a slightly fragile state. Evie even went so far as to kiss me voluntarily. And it was lovely to see them again too. Less lovely to see all the things undone, or not done as I would do them, around the house, but the children are clean-ish, fed-ish and the building is still standing, though there's piss on the lavatory seat and shit stains on the bowl and I choose not to dwell on why this seems like an entirely reasonable thing to come home to and automatically clean up. Nor do I dwell on what a lot of things there are in my life that I have to choose not to dwell on.

All that is left for us to do is get through the summer holidays. Six weeks of purgatory begin in seven days' time.

Monday, 17 July

'Love you!' called Richard on his way out the door and down the drive to work this morning. 'Wouldn't want anyone other than you! Unless Gemma Arterton has any genuinely new insights into the Battle of Thermopylae! Then we've got a problem!'

The delightful quiet when he leaves is broken only by the sound of a text arriving from Claire: *I could hump every man that comes within a twenty-foot radius of me. Is this normal?*

Yes.

Wednesday, 19 July

We have just passed the six-month anniversary of the dishwasher starting its funny noise. I feel I should throw a party. Maybe invite all the plumbers.

I stumble across Evie playing Snakes and Ladders in the corner of the bedroom by herself as I'm putting away some washing.

'Didn't Thomas want to play with you?' I say conversationally, as I open his underwear-and-random-plastic-bits drawer.

'Didn't ask him,' she says, moving a counter determinedly down a snake and throwing again.

'Why not?'

She shrugs. ''S a game of chance,' she says. 'Doesn't matter who plays. And this way I always win.'

I drop in the last pair of socks, close the drawer and back quietly away.

'Which do you think is the more troubling part?' I ask Richard, when I finish telling him about it later in bed. 'The ruthless penetration of the smokescreen of pleasure, or the gimlet-eyed focus on victory?'

'How old is she again?' he says.

'Five.'

'I think *that's* the most troubling part. But let's not worry too much until she actually starts killing pets, shall we? Sufficient unto the day and all that.'

'But the troubles of the day contain the seeds of all the troubles to come,' I say. 'And, by the way, you've still got all the ripples of the troubles that came before.'

'That's an interesting way of looking at it,' he says thoughtfully. 'So, in a way, you're saying we are always in the midst of every trouble – past, present and future?'

'Yes.'

'What an extraordinary way to live!' he says cheerfully, punching his pillow into shape before he lies down properly. 'I'm surprised you sleep at all! *Do* you sleep at all?' he adds, turning over onto his back and letting out a fart as he undulates up and down on the mattress, dragging the duvet half off me as he makes sure he's absolutely comfortable.

'Not much,' I say. 'Hey, could you let me have some of the duvet back?'

A light snore answers me. It has taken him literally three seconds to fall asleep. What an extraordinary way to live.

Text from Claire: *I never want to have sex again. The very idea! Is this normal?*

Yes.

Thursday, 20 July

I knew, obviously, that there would be no avoiding the reciprocal playdate with Savannah's children. That is the point of playdates. But does it have to be today? The day before they break up from school? The day they are all at their most wired, frantic and awful? Well, yes, it does. And why? Because Savannah 'desperately' needs time to pack so that they can head straight to Tuscany after school tomorrow. Because if she doesn't get some 'proper sun' soon, she will 'simply go quite, quite mad!'

So I inform the kids that the time has come. A chorus of pleas (Thomas) and threats of violence and severe property damage (Evie) ensues, but it is no good. 'Everybody,' I announce, 'is just going to have to suck it up.'

Savannah's children – Leopold and Loeb, Richard calls them, and not just because he can never remember their ridiculous names – arrive bickering and Chinese burning each other and it goes downhill from there. They snark at the children's toys, break a few of them, pick at their tea but eat the entire plate of mini rolls for pudding between them while my back is turned and before Thomas and Evie get a look-in.

I do what I can – Evie is under orders not to retaliate on pain of death – to curb the worst of it. But you can't unpick a lifetime's parental indulgence in an afternoon, and if you try (Fiona in particular has many tales to tell, because she cannot and will not bite her tongue like I do), the little scrotes will just spin it into a tale of adult bullying when they get home and then you will find yourself trying to explain exactly what did happen to coolly enraged parents on your doorstep, without explicitly saying, 'You, because of your own innate selfishness that leads you to grant your children unfettered licence in all things because it's so much easier for you while you pretend it's in the cause of raising free, independent thinkers, have raised – as stupid, selfish parents like you always raise – monsters.' Or something.

Savannah is, of course, forty minutes late. 'So sorry!' she trills. 'I was trying things on before packing and I've lost so much weight since last year, it took *aaages* to find three weeks' worth of things that still *work*.' But eventually they are gone, leaving Thomas white with anxiety and Evie puce with rage. I bring out a plate of proper-size chocolate rolls and say, 'These are for you. Eat as many as you like for being such nice, good, lovely children, whom I can actually take anywhere and not fear – too much – the outcome.' Just occasionally, I think, you should put aside hedging and overthinking and complicated parsing of the potential ramifications for your children's moral characters and just reward them in unambiguous terms for a good job well done. And yourself too. There are more chocolate rolls in the cupboard left for me.

Friday, 21 July

End of term. 'End of days,' Fiona says, as we stand in the park letting the children let off somewhere between a day and ten weeks' worth of steam. Even David is moved by the occasion. He stands in the middle of the roundabout as Thomas pushes and Evie tries to do a headstand on the seat, bellowing like a Viking.

'What's all this?' says Richard, when he returns from work late this evening to find me sitting on the sofa, head in hands, with sheets of A4 covered in scribble scattered across the floor.

'Thomas came home with a note in his schoolbag saying that next year they're doing a project about The Future in history.'

'They're doing a project about the future in history? Has no one pointed out the logical fallacy here?'

'I think logical fallacies are Year Five. You'll have to wait. Can I continue?'

'Do.'

'As they are doing a project about The Future next term, could parents write a letter to their children about what they see their son or daughter doing then?'

'And?'

'Well, my first line was "You're all going to die fighting over water." It's something Fiona said and I haven't been able to get it out of my mind since.'

'I see.'

'And things went downhill from there.'

'I see,' he says again, picking up a random sheet from the floor and starting to read aloud. '"I'm really sorry but when I agreed to get pregnant the world was a better place. Things have fallen apart really quickly. Nobody had any idea how fragile everything was, and nobody really knows what to do about it now. You can stop reading Twitter and things but that's not the long-term macroeconomic, socio-political solution that's needed …"'

'That's page two,' I say. 'There's much more, but beyond page seven you can't really read much through the tear stains.'

He picks up another sheet. '"I'm reading a book called *The Knowledge: How to Rebuild Our World from Scratch*. It's all the basic chemistry you'll need for making fuel and soap and metal and things, but it's a bit short on actual survival skills. I'll get another book for that, don't worry. I'm also looking into how best to leave you money. Of course, fiat currencies will be worthless, but it's trickier to lay your hands on gold than you'd think. All my jewellery is crap, but my engagement ring might get you a couple of hens or something. It's platinum, not silver, so maybe even a piglet."'

Richard puts down the page carefully. 'Are you really reading this book?'

'Yes. It's called "being prepared". It's part of good parenting.'

'It's called "being a prepper".'

'What's in a name? Anyway, it's the only thing that calms me. And you'll be pleased to know that actually I've found out since that you can buy gold coins on the internet. They're called Britannias. They have a face value of a hundred pounds but they're actually worth a thousand. Not sure how that works, but I'll find out and we'll buy some once I've worked out the best place to hide them. At the moment I'm thinking of hollowing out a book. Maybe *Gone With the Wind* because then I'll remember it as Gold in the Wind. Though this isn't really the time to be making jokes.'

Richard blinks and picks up another sheet. 'This is damp,' he says, frowning.

'As previously noted, I was crying quite heavily from page seven onwards,' I say.

He starts to read aloud again. '"... Whatever happens, just remember that we love you with all our hearts and we are so sorry for everything. We wished only happiness and good things for you, and I stopped using aerosols back in 1991, but there's nothing I could do about the people who wouldn't, or the ones who kept using pointless antibiotics and increasing mass resistance, or about Trump or Brexit or Amazon or the robots and so it was end times before you turned thirty. My greatest hope is that we all get to die together. North Korea is supposedly testing nuclear missiles as we speak, so chin up! There's every chance!"'

'My tenses got very mixed up,' I note thoughtfully.

'Even the greatest copyeditors have been known to crack in the face of imminent apocalypse,' Richard assures me. 'But tell me – do you feel better for having got all this down on paper?'

'Marginally, yes.'

'Good,' he says. 'Now hand me the pad and the pen.'

I do so. He flicks to a dry page and starts to write in a firm, legible hand.

Dear Thomas – In the future, we think you will be tall like me and blond like Mummy, but maybe a bit darker than you are now! You will still like television but maybe different programmes from the ones you enjoy at the moment! When you are very big, if there is a subject you like a lot at school you can go to university and study it and make lots of friends who like that subject too! Mummy and I look forward to seeing everything you and Evie do.

I make him take out the exclamation marks. Let us lie to our children, let the apocalypse come, but let us not make things worse with extravagant punctuation.

He rewrites it gladly, relieved that sanity seems to be reasserting itself once more.

When he goes upstairs to change, I look into Britannias. And water purification tablets. And herbal medicines. Just in case. It is called being prepared.

Saturday, 22 July

Claire texts: *Just stood in a lift for five minutes wondering what the buttons were for. Is this normal?*

Yes.

Monday, 24 July

It's the summer holidays.

Tuesday, 25 July

Still the summer holidays.

Wednesday, 26 July

Dear God, is it STILL the summer holidays?

Thursday, 27 July

Somehow, it is still the goddamn summer holidays.

At least the wheels haven't come off yet. The grind is relentless but better than a derailment catastrophe. The systems everyone put in place (because of course it's not just your own you depend on, but the smooth working of all the others with whom you intersect via reciprocal playdates and other favours), by drafting all available bodies into service, are holding. Supplemented by whatever classes, courses, camps, improving and non-improving activity days we can afford and to which we can ferry our overexcited broods without a net loss of time (not money: in summer most of us work at a loss, just to keep our jobs open), we might just make it. Though every time you drop a child off you find yourself hoping against hope that none of them is run by a shell company for Paedophiles R Us. Jesus, if I could just go one day being able to do things without at some point having to stop and stare into the blackest abyss of the human condition I'd be a happy woman.

Anyway. Onward.

Friday, 28 July

Summer holidays.

Saturday, 29 July

Summer holidays.

Sunday, 30 July

Questions I have not been able to answer today:

1. 'Where is the bit of red Lego I need?' No further details supplied.
2. 'What would you do if you could breathe underwater? You have webbed feet, gills, swim fast but no actual special powers? And you're not allowed to sleep, because that's what you always say.'
3. 'How big is yellow?'

4. 'What is an orgy?' Thomas pronounced it with a hard *g* so it took me a moment to work out what was going on. Apparently it is a word used in the Asterix books. I told him I had never read Asterix and that he should ask Daddy, who's a big fan.
5. 'What if the Germans had won the war?' I sent that to Daddy too.
6. 'What is the average heat?' What exactly did she mean by that? 'Just what I say.'

Claire's was easier: *Am hungry all the time. I start dreaming of my next meal before I've finished the one I'm on. Is this normal?*
Yes. For some of us, even when we're not pregnant.

Monday, 31 July

Time has no meaning. Summer holidays.

Tuesday, 1 August

On my third time of coming out into the garden to break up a dispute between my two rotten children within an hour of Grandma going home, Mrs Bradley beckons me over to the fence. 'When I was wee,' she says, 'my mother let us dig a hole.'

I look at her blankly.

'In the garden,' she says. 'She said, "You can dig a hole. As big as you like." We didn't have a nice garden, but neither do you, and it kept us busy for days. Turned it into a den. Got some other children round. Dug out some more. We loved it.'

'I'm not sure ...' I say doubtfully.

'Kids are daft,' she says, with certainty. 'Try it.'

Another row breaks out behind me. I turn round. 'Stop that,' I say. 'And dig a hole.'

Their eyes widen. Their faces begin to shine. I furnish them with trowels, spoons, holiday buckets and spades, the grown-up shovel from the shed, and they get to work with a will.

'Daft as brushes,' says Mrs Bradley, as silence descends.

They sleep like logs that night too. She is an unremitting genius.

Wednesday, 2 August

David joins them. Another day of industrious earth-moving ensues. The combination of creativity and destruction of Making a Hole seems to hold them in thrall. Glorious, silent thrall.

Thursday, 3 August

A war artist could paint us. Swap men staring glassily into their pints for women staring bleakly at glasses of prosecco, caption it *Before the Fight* and we are indistinguishable from any group of old friends having a last drink before heading off to bloody conflict and an unknown fate.

We are mothers in the pub who are all due to go on holiday with our families in the next few days. We all, honestly, know how lucky we are to be able to do so but—

'What are you dreading most?' asks Nadia, draining her glass and motioning to the frightened twenty-year-old lad serving us for another bottle.

'The packing,' I say instantly. 'Enough shit for a fortnight for four people plus emergencies does not fit into any suitcase or any car I've ever known.'

'Plus enough for finding out that the washing-machine in the place you've rented doesn't work,' says Fiona.

'And allowing for complaints that this T-shirt's too small, those shorts are too big, that jumper's too scratchy. I might just take twenty yards of burlap sacking this year and tell them to make the best of it.'

'The beds are always too small,' says Céline. 'I have a super kingsize at home. Philippe and I basically sleep in different postcodes. But on holiday – he is right there. And he thinks this is *fantastique. Mais ce n'est pas.*'

'And it encourages them to want sex,' says Fiona, darkly. 'You either have to give in or spend half the night slapping it away from you. Either way, your night's ruined.'

'I don't mind having sex,' says Nadia. We nod. She's five years younger than us, and we've seen her husband. As Fiona once said, now we know what the next-generation folk mean when they say 'keeping it tight'. 'But the days are terrible. You've got to do stuff.'

There is a collective groan of despairing agreement.

'Iain thinks every minute has to be spent frantically having New Experiences. I used to wonder where he got the energy from and halfway through last summer I realised – he gets it from never lifting a fucking finger at home. That really improved my mood.'

'I just don't get why I'm supposed to enjoy going somewhere I still have to do everything I normally do but with kids who are as high as kites because they can see the sea and smell chips all the time,' I say.

'You should start going abroad,' says Fiona. 'Take them to Florence or somewhere, where all they can see is art and culture. That'll knock the spirit out of them.'

'And add a furious, futile search for passports to the annual horror?' I say. 'No, thanks.'

'We just need to stop thinking of it as a holiday,' says Nadia, philosophically. 'You know, like how brown rice is terrible if you think of it as rice, but fine if you think of it as just another food entirely. Think of it as a work trip and we might find it quite relaxing. It's only when you measure it against the pre-kids version of the thing that it fails.'

'Like most things,' agrees Fiona.

I am very committed to drinking, so I say nothing. But it does strike me – increasingly often, actually – that if you were to put our husbands together in a group in the pub on this very same day, they would not be having this conversation. An upcoming holiday would not be dominating their thoughts because they would be looking forward, in an uncomplicated fashion, to a nice break, or not really thinking about it at all.

I don't quite know how or why – I have some theories, but I don't *know* – things always fall out this way, but they do. I am moved to speech. It is not clear speech but my listeners catch the gist: start sharing the burden. Delegate. Assign tasks to all. Spread the load.

There is a silence.

'It never works, though, does it?' says Fiona, motioning Prosecco Lad over again. 'You wake up every day with the resolution to stop taking all the shit on, but ...'

'It takes too long,' says Céline. 'It's like training someone new at work. It's not a help, it's a hindrance for months and months until they're up and running. You've got to tell them what to do, how and why, how it fits into the whole company set-up so that they can learn to do it and to think for themselves and not have to come to you for every little thing for ever more. You don't get a return on your investment for months, if not years. You can't come home and do it all over again. There's no time. Plus, the only thing stopping you killing the idiot intern at work is that you're being paid to train them. Nothing would be stopping you at home.'

We sit contemplating our glasses bleakly again. The new bottle of prosecco, lobbed from an increasingly safe distance at us by the boy, provides – as bottles of prosecco often do – the solution. Or at least a solution.

'We'll all go on holiday together,' says Fiona. 'Like the weekend, but longer. Much longer. Twelve ... is it twelve? ... years from now, when the youngest of our kids has turned eighteen, we'll all go somewhere hot and just lie around and do sweet FA. That's what we'll call ourselves. The Sweet Fanny Adamses. We'll get gang tattoos. On our arses.'

We raise our glasses. I'm looking forward to it already.

Friday, 4 August

I am supervising four loads of holiday packing. My own, of course – a relatively simple affair, requiring the folding of anything that can pass muster as (a) clean and (b) summery. This amounts to two pairs of chinos apparently approved by the International Institute of Sexlessness, four long-sleeved and three (if you stretch the word 'clean' to its absolute limit) short-sleeved T-shirts, one dress that makes me cry when I think of how it would look on someone else/me ten years ago, and a pair of sandals. I will wear my jeans and trainers for the journey and doubtless for the entire fortnight thereafter. I pack books (ha!) and headache tablets into all the remaining spaces in my suitcase and I'm done.

Thomas has to be persuaded that he cannot take everything he owns. Much of our discussion centres round the difference between 'need' and 'want'. As in, you need underwear, you want Transformers. As in, you need wellingtons, you want a cubic-foot boxful of soft toys As in, you need to understand what I'm saying to you, I want to kill everyone.

Evie needs to be persuaded to actually pack in the first place. She prefers to stand at the front door bellowing 'Come on!' up the stairs at the rest of us, despite the fact that we are not leaving for another twenty-three hours.

Richard just needs to have his imagination trammelled. Every year he seems to think that going on holiday – even though we go to the same cottage in the same seaside town on the same stretch of East Anglian coast every time – will transform us. Specifically into Jay Gatsby and Daisy Buchanan. Left to his own devices, he will pack four suits, full black tie, eighteen dress shirts, a large array of cufflinks and the smoking jacket his grandfather left him. I know this, because once I left him to his own devices and this was what greeted me when I opened his suitcase in the distinctly casual environs of North Norfolk in high summer. Fortunately we had no children then and I was able to find it funny.

Saturday, 5 August

I realised too late in my own personal development that you should never marry for love. For true contentment you should pair up with someone on the basis that you agree what constitutes a reasonable volume for a TV and temperature for a bedroom, and that they bring to the relationship a set of skills entirely opposite to your own. So, I should have found someone who enjoyed cooking, was good at computers and – crucially – had a sense of direction.

We have been coming to Wells-next-the-Sea for twelve years now and never yet succeeded in finding it first time. This year is no different. We have been in the car for four hours for a three-hour journey. Thomas has been sick once ('I'm okay!'), Evie twice ('Just keep driving!' she gasped between spews. Troupers, the pair of them, especially when a miniature train down to the seaside is in the offing). We have heard Miriam Margolyes read *Matilda* two and a half times. She's a talented woman, but – enough.

'I think I can see Norwich,' I say to Richard. We're generally okay once we've got through Norwich.

'You're always seeing Norwich,' he says. 'Sometimes ahead of us. Sometimes in the rear-view mirror. Sometimes reflected in the softly rebuking eyes of a cow when we get stuck behind a tractor and have to take in the scenery. It is – ironically, given the famed flatness of our current surroundings – like John Winthrop's shining city on the hill for you.'

Another hour passes.

'Look!' says Richard, exuberantly. 'There's a sign for Stiff ... Well, it must be for Stiffkey. Scratching out the K is probably a rite of passage for juvenile vandals in Norfolk.'

'Why are you driving so slowly?' says Evie. 'I need a wee. And you usually drive too fast.'

'And too close to the car in front,' says Thomas.

He also hugs the kerb as if it were a departing lover, and—

'Because,' says Richard, 'we are now behind a convoy of three cars whose occupants are, I can only presume, on their way to a canasta evening in Sheringham and do not wish to arrive overstimulated by having approached double figures on the speedometer. Or perhaps they are lingering Diana cultists roaming the countryside looking for somewhere to mourn. Or they may be aware, as I am not, that the red-triangle-with-a-wiggly-line-in-the-middle actually means "Advance at a rate not immediately discernible to the naked eye".'

'Wait – can I see Norwich again?'

'That is not Norwich. That is a cloud in the shape of Norwich. Also, we don't want to see Norwich. If we see Norwich at this point, it will mean that we are once again going in the wrong direction and I will have to stop the car in order to beat you with something heavy and unyielding. Like one of your cakes.'

'Don't start.'

'I love Grandma's cakes,' says Thomas. 'I wish I had some now. I'm so hungry.'

'I know, darling,' I say, turning round to pat his and Evie's knees as their wan little faces gaze back at me. 'But we have to give your stomachs a break after you've been sick, don't we? But we'll be at the cottage soon, and then – you know the holiday rule! First day there, you can eat anything you like whenever you like.' This is a great rule. Constant grazing means we can just unpack, wander round the town and beach till bedtime and nobody has to get back and cook a damn thing. 'Wait – why are we pulling over?'

'That's St Stephen's Church of the Intercrural Baptists over there, which has a roof with two tiers of purlins and crenulated tie-beams on pierced arched braces and an ashlar-faced clerestory. We have to see it.'

'Do we, though?'

'You can stay here. Partly because you do not understand a word I have just said and partly because your secular liberalism pollutes any church you enter.'

'Well, if it hasn't got a lierne vault then I'm not interested anyway.'

'If I thought for a moment you actually knew what a lierne

vault is rather than having just caught sight of the phrase when I opened a Pevsner and salted it away for future attempts to wrongfoot me, I might almost begin to believe we have a future together.'

'I want to see it!' cries Evie, throwing off her seatbelt as we pull into the graveyard. She does, in fact, enjoy a spot of church-hunting with her father. I have my suspicions as to whether her motivation is the same – it's possible that an appreciation for the wonders of medieval ecclesiastical architecture and the honouring of the sublime and ineffable through physical labour and tangible creation are overwhelmed by her unflagging desire to possess all knowledge in the world and smash all those who would challenge her intellectual superiority into dust – but either way I guess it's something that should be encouraged now and then, possibly, tempered at a later date. On this occasion, her enthusiasm is heightened by the needs of her bladder. Before we can stop her, she pulls down her jeans and knickers and pees behind a gravestone. Then she disappears inside with Richard. Thomas and I stay outside counting butterflies and dead people. We stay in the oldest sections where, as Thomas puts it, 'It's history, not sad.'

Twenty minutes later, Richard and Evie declare themselves purlinned out so we pile back into the car. 'Onward!' I shout. 'To Norwich! Or somewhere! And eventually Wells!'

Sunday, 6 August

Am lying lazily in bed with the sun streaming through the window while the children work their way delightedly through the ancient cartoon DVDs that have been in the cottage ever since we started coming here. This viewing is now a Glorious Tradition. Feel vague sense of guilt. Glorious Traditions should surely involve early-morning walks, streams and hedgerows? Do I mean hedgerows? Are they different from hedges? I don't think I've ever been within touching distance of a hedgerow if so.

I don't know why I feel I'm failing my Generation Whatever suburban children by not reproducing the kind of early-fifties rural childhood I used to read about in my own. And which, for all I actually know, might have been as much an idyllic fantasy then as it was to me reading about it thirty-odd years later.

But then there's no legislating for maternal guilt. It's like water damage in an old house – insidious, unstoppable, and unpredictable. You can try to damp-proof your psyche all you want, but the guiltwater always finds a point of ingress somewhere. Then it creeps quietly, stealthily along invisible faultlines until the damage shows up miles from where you expected and you're completely unprepared for it.

My phone pings. It is Fiona. My phone is pinging a lot and it is always Fiona, because Fiona has been forced – by Iain and David's unfathomable enthusiasm for the activity – on a camping holiday.

Her texts to me so far have run thus:

It's insanity is what it is.

Thousands of years mankind spent improving his condition. Protecting himself from the elements, developing a way of life that amounts to more than a constant search for food, warmth and a decent place to crap. And what does Iain do? Frogmarches us out of a fully plumbed, weatherproof brick dwelling to live under nylon in a Dorset field.

Everything you do while camping is just a longer, more compli-cated, less efficient or more tiring version of what it would be at home. It took us three hours to cook and eat tea last night. WHAT'S THE EFFING POINT?

Her latest reads: *FML.*

Is David enjoying himself at least? I tap back.

He's found an older boy with 'survival skills', she replies. *Currently being shown how to chip flints or tan hides or something. Couldn't be happier.*

Well, that's something, I reply encouragingly. *And he'll be more useful come the apocalypse.*

Hiking to oldest working windmill in UK now, comes the reply. *FML.*

I fall back on my pillow – consciously acknowledging it as the marker of true civilisation that it is – and, wonder of wonders, fall back to sleep and stay that way while Richard gets up, dresses and takes the children out for a cooked breakfast at the café we love on the little high street. I walk down to join them just as they're finishing, after a hot shower, hot coffee and a read of my book over my cornflakes. I feel like I'm full of sunlight.

'I feel like I'm full of sunlight,' I tell them, as I pull up a chair and finish off the delicious bits of bacon, black pudding and egg yolks left on various plates.

'Why?' says Evie.

'It's too hard to explain,' I say.

'Try,' she says.

'No,' I say cheerily, because I am rested and strong.

'Okay,' she says, regarding me with an appraising eye. 'Okay.'

The first day of holiday is always my favourite because of another tradition: devoting it to pottering. We have our big set-pieces planned for the coming fortnight – a day at Dinosaur Adventure, another at Hunstanton for its SeaLife and its funfair, Cromer for the most seasidey possible day at the seaside – but we have learned to try to do as little as possible in between. Children's appetites are insatiable if you unleash them, so we don't.

So we always spend the first day pottering. We work our way slowly round the little town, with plenty of stops for tea, cake, ice cream, cockles, wees, and rests on quayside walls, checking that all the important things are as we left them last year and noting what small changes have taken place in our absence. The children dart off in various directions without causing us heart-stopping anxiety because there's no traffic and even I can't believe they'll be abducted by one of the early retirees in sunhats and sensible shoes who make up the bulk of the adult August population. I know Savannah and her ilk probably despise us for the smallness of our needs and ambitions and our willingness to repeat ourselves, but neither

Richard nor I could face the stress of going somewhere new every year. Maybe it's different if you can afford to jet off for a month at a time to somewhere luxurious and fully catered, but by the time you've spent a few days bedding in and getting the measure of a place, it's almost time to start preparing to come home. Of all the forms of competitive parenting you're supposed to take part in, competitive holidaymaking is surely the stupidest and most ruinous. Maybe there is an argument for exposing your children as early as possible to other countries and other cultures, but there's surely plenty of time for that when they're older and aren't sucking quite so much energy out of you each and every day? Anyway, it's impossible, as I sit and watch Thomas and Evie fill with joy when they see the soldier statue outside the rock shop is still there, to feel we're depriving them in any significant way. Our holidays feel like they fit the small-scale needs of childhood.

When I was a child, we used to go and stay with my grandma, Mum's mum, in Lancashire. My happiest memories are of playing with my cousins (all my mum and dad's siblings had stayed up north) in the park, being asked for stories about That London and pleasing everyone by saying how much I hated it and wished I lived near them, and of walking along Blackpool and Morecambe beaches with Dad, eating chips out of newspaper (they were still doing that then, because I am 108) in companionable silence, while my mother and sister did something noisy and active together elsewhere. (Improving sea defences, joining in naval exercises or something.)

And that's what you take your children on holiday for, really, isn't it? Happy memories.

We go gillying and gasp in wonder at the sight of real live crabs in our bucket before pouring them back and gasping at our power and munificence, and to the park to check that the pirate ship is still ship-shape and whether Thomas has become brave enough to follow his sister up to the crow's nest. He has not. 'Maybe next year!' cries Evie, encouragingly, from her vantage point eighteen feet above the ground.

He looks up cheerily. 'Who knows?' he replies, and runs off to the roundabout to let several smaller children push him round. At home I would worry about the utter lack of ambition that lies within my firstborn's breast, but I am on holiday so decide to see it as praiseworthy lack of ego and sign of innate resistance to the outside pressures of toxic masculinity. Or something.

We have fish and chips as either a very late lunch or early tea. Another text arrives from Fiona: *You cannot sit comfortably on the ground for long enough to eat a meal past the age of twenty-five. It's just not possible. That's why picnics are so fucking stupid. The chair is the greatest invention ever, after Solid Walls and the Tiled Roof.*

I text her back about all the happy memories of eating sandwiches and sausages under an open sky that David will be storing away for ever.

FML, she replies.

We go home, watch a bit of telly and the kids are – wonder of wonders – so tired they go uncomplainingly to bed and fall asleep as soon as their wind-tousled heads hit the pillow. Richard and I stay up just long enough to sink a bottle of wine between us and then follow suit.

'Do you want to have sex?' I ask, as we climb into bed.

'It's okay,' he says. 'We've got a whole fortnight to get to that.'

I sigh in contentment. Slipping under a freshly laundered duvet whose cover had already been wrestled on before we got here is joy enough for one night.

Tuesday, 8 August

Had sex last night. Now I can truly relax and enjoy myself.

Thursday, 10 August

Another charmed day.

Fiona texts from a field a long, lovingly detailed list of all the chairs in her house *all ready for use at a moment's notice – hitherto unsung heroes all. I will never take them for granted again. Ditto Netflix, Kettle Chips, duvets and windows.*

Saturday, 12 August

Another lovely day. I'm getting nervous now. It'll be a relief when the other shoe drops, to be honest. God, I hate myself.

Fiona has walked for forty-five minutes through a flower meadow and some woods to get to a pub for lunch. *There are two pubs within five minutes of our house, both reached via paved, easily traversed roads. So the fuck what if there are no purple hairstreak butterflies on the way? But at least the pub had seats.*

At least you're going home soon, I reply.

Forty-eight hours, she says. *And then I'm never, ever leaving again. For the rest of my life I cannot be indoors enough.*

Tuesday, 15 August

Richard comes downstairs in the middle of putting the kids to bed. He is ashen-faced. 'I think …' he whispers, 'I think … Thomas has got worms coming out of his bum.'

The relief that the spell has broken lasts for a brief but glorious second before the practical difficulties rush in. 'Oh, God,' I reply, thinking how far we are from the nearest open chemist and how very like us to have our first episode of threadworms so far from all the conveniences of home.

'I know,' he says. 'What should we do? Call the doctor? An ambulance?'

'Why?' I say. 'Did you break your leg coming down the stairs?'

'Didn't you hear me? I said Thomas has got worms – actual worms, little waving worms – coming out of his little actual arse.'

'Yes. They're threadworms.'

'And that's a thing?'

'Yes.'

'Worms coming out of a child's bumhole is a thing? I think I should have been told about this. I think before you got pregnant you should have alerted me to the possibility that worms coming out of a child's bum could be a thing I one day saw.'

'I'm sorry. I didn't really think about it at that stage.'

'Well,' he says, collapsing into a chair and wiping beads of cold sweat off his forehead, 'you really, really should have, okay?'

'Okay.'

'Okay.' He draws a deep breath. 'So, if not an ambulance, what do we do?'

'Well, when my sister and I got them in our youth, we used to lie on the bed with our legs back over our heads and my mum used to dig them out with a cotton bud.'

'I'm sorry?' he says. 'Did you just say that your mother used to dig them out? With a cotton bud?'

'Yes. I remember it well, for reasons that should not need explaining.'

He leans forward and puts his head between his knees.

'She put Savlon on the tip to help it go in easier,' I offer.

'Stop saying all the worst things I have ever heard.'

'Okay. But it stopped the itching quicker than the medicine. And I've got cotton buds and Savlon here.'

'You're not doing it. I'm using one of my three vetoes per paternal lifetime for this. You're not doing it.'

I'm willing to be persuaded. I am not as dexterous as my mother, and I lack the almost pathological levels of self-confidence required, it turns out, when actually faced with the prospect, to undertake what suddenly strikes me as a quasi-medical procedure.

'All right. But you'll have to drive to a chemist to get medicine now.'

'Anything. I will do anything for the child who has invertebrates crawling out of his anus. I cannot emphasise enough how great my willingness is to do what is required in this regard.'

Off he goes.

Thomas comes downstairs. Evie follows, her curiosity fully aroused. I explain the situation and the life cycle of the threadworm and take them to wash their hands while I lecture them about the importance of doing so every time they go to the loo and as often as possible in between times too. 'But. Mummy,' Thomas groans, 'it's so *booooring!*'

'Trust me,' I say, eyeing the cotton buds on the shelf. 'The alternative is worse.'

Wednesday, 16 August

A quiet morning. Richard's still in shock. It would be even quieter if Evie wasn't alternating between hysterical laughter at the thought of Thomas's bum as a worm-incubator and demanding, in the spirit of scientific endeavour, that he take his pants off and show her in case she can see any of them dying from the medicine we all took last night. 'Just let me show her,' he says wearily, when I tell her to shush for the eighteenth time. 'Then maybe she'll stop.' So I do. I should have a look myself, I reason, check there's nothing happening down there I ought to know about. Thomas whips his pants off, assumes the position and – as Richard flees to the sanctity of the kitchen – Evie and I peer in. Nothing.

'I want to take a photo,' Evie says. I take the phone from her hand. 'Come on!' she shouts. 'I never get to see his bumhole!' I deny her request. 'Fine,' she says, stomping off. 'I'll draw a picture instead.'

Text Fiona the highlights of yesterday's drama. *Bloody hell,* she texts back. *FYL. BTW*, she adds, *I'm home and I now see the point of camping. Like shiatsu massage or sex, it's lovely when it stops.*

By lunchtime we have recovered enough to draw up plans. Sea Life, at Hunstanton, figures largely. Then Richard suggests that if I brought my swimming costume I could indulge my new-found love of the aquatic by swimming in the relatively warm waters of the Wash. 'I'll take them to the fish house,' he says ('Sea Life!' bawls Evie, somehow overhearing him from the loo upstairs), 'and you can meet us at the funfair afterwards.' I am seventeen types of discommoded by this offer.

'In the sea?' I say.

'Yes,' he says. 'It's a large body of water, which many people, throughout history, have found remarkably conducive to the process of swimming.'

'But it's outside!'

'But – it's still water. A little less controlled, a little colder, a lot saltier but still water. Not still-still, obviously – one of the sea's USPs is that it has waves. I mean, of course, that it remains water.'

'On my own?'

'Yes. I believe this is a thing you like.'

'While you do the fish house?'

('SEA LIFE!')

'Yes. Which I believe is a thing you hate.'

'I couldn't!'

'Why not? Do you think you'll drown?'

'No. Maybe.'

'Do you think I'll lose and/or kill the children?'

'No. Maybe.'

'Get your costume. You'll have the thirty-minute drive to get used to the idea. That's usually enough.'

Thursday, 17 August

Cor! That's all I can say. Cor! to swimming in the sea. I shall add it to my list of things – sex, drugs, Brie – to regret being too scared to try when I was young. It was brilliant, soul-cleansing, clarity-bringing, ineffable-cosmic-forces-connecting-through-your-body stuff. My new ambition is to live by the sea and swim for eight hours a day. I have a new vision of myself as a sinewy centenarian carving my unstoppable daily way through the waves, a local legend and, eventually, an immortal spirit whispering into the ears of middle-aged women shivering on the shores of possibility – 'Yes, you can!'

Until then, duty calls. It's afternoon. We are wandering down one of our favourite high streets – all higgledy-piggledy Georgian buildings and butcher-baker-candlestick-makerish shops, plus an abundance of cafés. After long, detailed discussion among themselves, Richard, Evie and Thomas choose one to grace with their presence so that I can do an hour's shopping among the lovely, civilised, tasteful things that abound in this lovely, civilised, tasteful place. The first thing I see that I want, however, is a hot Belgian waffle with honey advertised in a café a few doors down, so I go in and order that (and a peppermint tea) instead. I feel vaguely guilty but reason that my shopping hour is really intended as an unencumbered hour of peace, and if waffles and honey fulfil that brief better than stroking beautiful storage jars in old-fashioned department stores and imagining having a kitchen that deserves them, then my conscience is clear. Or at least temporarily, but still restoratively, silenced.

I wonder when having an hour to myself began requiring these complicated inner manoeuvres, but I do not linger long on this. The waffle is too good.

I have taken two and a half bites when I get a call from Richard saying – I paraphrase, but only slightly – that things have gone tits up at work, he needs to make seventeen hundred phone calls to different people starting, like, NOW, so could I get back here and look after the children please?

I swear quietly and violently. Leaving my waffle feels like parting from a lover too soon. Our relationship has barely begun. On a flash of inspiration I ask the waitress if I can have it as a takeaway. She says, 'Sure.' I feel vaguely guilty that I have asked for help and been helped, banish this thought too to be studied later, and leave with my food in a box and a lid on my tea.

I have some distant hopes that I will be able to eat some on the way and that I will get to the café to find the children have finished their cake and are ready to go. Then we can find a bench somewhere and consume the rest before it goes completely cold.

None of these hopes is realised, which is why I generally try to avoid having them. I storm in to find Thomas and Evie still nibbling at their Victoria sponge ('We're having a compe-tition to see who can make theirs last longest!') and Richard swiftly disappears, already shouting into the phone about what I tell a very interested Evie was actually 'a royal muck-up'.

'What does that mean?'

'I don't know, darling. It must be a legal term.'

Seconds after Richard goes, a waiter descends. 'You have things that were not bought here,' he says.

'I know,' I say. 'I'm very sorry. I'd just ordered these in another café when my husband called me back because he's got a work emergency. Look, there's the tea and scone he bought for himself. My children are still eating theirs. Possibly for ever.'

'You can't have that in here.'

'I'm not eating mine. I'm going to have the tea and scone. I'm not even supposed to be here. I'm just – emergency cover. I'm really sorry, I'm totally embarrassed, but could you just … maybe … let it go this once?'

This is the bravest I have been since labour. In both cases, I note with detached interest, I feel like I could crap myself at any moment.

The waiter looks at me with an expression that goes well beyond hate, and leaves.

My bowels cease their uproar and I relax enough to be able to tell the children without snapping to end their competition and hurry up.

A few minutes later they are slurping down the last of their milk, when a woman in managerial uniform arrives.

'One of my staff says you've come in with food from elsewhere,' she says.

'I did. We talked about it. I thought we were okay.'

'Well, the thing is, you can't do that.'

It's not that a red mist descended. It's more like the giant abacus in my head that tots up over the days, weeks, months and years – without conscious effort from me – all the slights I tolerate from strangers, the accommodations I silently make with friends, all the rules constructed for other people's and companies' convenience that I bow to, and all the general shit I swallow especially within the confines of my own home to make others' lives easier, starts tilting slowly but inexorably to one side, until all the beads fall over to the 'Strike the board and cry, "No more!"' side. I think in some strange way its bolts were loosened by yesterday's swim. Someone who was commanding the oceans mere hours ago can surely find the strength to …

I stand up. I explain the situation again. Emergency cover. Children and husband food buyers. I brought mine here. But me not eating mine. Me picked at husband's while waiting for kids to finish interminable cake. Very sorry, I say. But firmly.

She does not budge. 'What you've done is not allowed,' she says. Repeatedly.

The abacus falls apart. Beads roll everywhere.

'I understand,' I say, after a moment's adjustment, 'that I have not obeyed the spirit of café law. But I would never have done this under ordinary circumstances. I am not someone who pushes her luck. Ever. My whole life is about not pushing my luck. Ever.'

She looks increasingly furious. So I go on.

'But at the same time – and without wishing to diminish the validity of your policy, or your emotional pain, or whatever's going on here – I cannot feel that this is the crime of the century. It would be very, very nice if you – if someone, anyone at all – could cut me, just this once, just this tiny, tiny, tiny bit of slack.'

I would prefer it if my voice weren't cracking on every third word, but never mind. She leaves. I ram the rest of the scone down my throat in some kind of attempt at a last gesture of defiance and haul our asses out of there.

Then I rush back in and gather up my forgotten waffle and tea.

By the time we get to the car, where Richard is waiting for us, I am crying my eyes out. The children explain the gist of the situation to him instead. He, a man who views arguments as a dog does a meaty bone – 'It's the stuff of life to me! Lemme at it!' – is delighted with me. 'You should be proud!'

'I am, sort of,' I wail, as we pack ourselves into the car. 'Or I will be once I've recovered. It was so *teeerrible*!' And I collapse into sobs again.

'You can build on this!' Richard says enthusiastically, as we drive back to the cottage. 'And next time, you can cut all the nonsense and just tell them to feck off!'

'Daddy said "feck"!' crows Evie delightedly from the back. 'And, Mummy, you *should* have said it too. They were fecking horrible.'

This is enough to make us laugh and snap back into parental mode in order to deliver swearing admonishments, attenuated to allow for the special circumstances.

I estimate it will take me about three days to stop shaking, and Holt, the holiday and possibly the whole of Norfolk has obviously been ruined for me for ever – but out of their ashes a new woman shall arise. Next time I confront someone, my voice won't crack.

The time after that, maybe I will manage a 'Just feck off.' Who can say what the future holds once the abacus has come unmoored?

Friday, 18 August

All our woes – and parasites – are forgotten in the glory of today, for it is our favourite family day of the year: the Holkham country fair. 'Show,' says Richard. 'They're country shows. Basically, middle-class pride rallies. Call them fairs and you'll be shut in the serfs' enclosure. Serfs' enclosure! That's a very good joke, if you only knew your agrarian and feudal history.'

The Holkham country *show* has something for everyone. There's always a military band (for Richard), loads of things with horses and a funfair (funshow?) for Evie and Thomas, and so many stalls dedicated to canine health and comfort that it is clear the fine British rural tradition of preferring dogs to children remains as healthy as a local labrador's coat. After spending most of the year in the overheated bubble of modern urban parenting, this restores my equilibrium at a level I can barely comprehend.

Plus, country shows keep you alert. They always have a bit of an edge to them. A robust approach to health and safety means that chainsaw carving competitions (grizzled farmers take chainsaws to the largest bits of tree trunk they've come across that season and try to carve it into a recognisable thing or person) spray splintered wood over a quarter of an acre of unprotected bystanders. ('Stop blubbing, Wiveton! You've got another eye!') Target shooting is done with real crossbows instead of plasticky airguns and there's no prize to take home, except a nod of approval from the silent man in charge, who is often bleeding freely but nonchalantly from the wayward bolts of beginners. And there's always a hog roast. I actually staggered backwards when I saw my first spitted Old Spot. 'That's a whole pig!' I said, to my country-born husband. 'Like in medieval times!' He sighed and Looked at me. I was Looked at a lot in those first few Norfolk-holidaying years together. When I laughed immoderately at the news that the cobblestone-and-cement mixture that most of the county's cottages are made out of is called 'clunch'. When I became – I felt, charmingly

– overexcited by the sight of very basic forms of wildlife running over fields (fields!), across gardens or along verges. 'Pheasants look just like their pictures! Or is that partridges? Wait, what's a grouse? And we saw a hare! Not a rabbit – a hare! But I still haven't seen a plover. Is a plover a bird? It might be a sort of pastry. I would like to see one, either way.'

But I have learned a lot since then. And I have become hardened. By twelve years of country shows, by marriage, by parenthood and by life. Now I only get excited by real country stuff. Like the knife stall, where is laid out every size of penknife, hunting weapons galore, delicate but lethal-looking filleting blades, mini-machetes, curved sickle-type things and butcher's hatchets. My eye was caught and instantly developed a covetous gleam. 'They could come in useful,' I say to Richard.

'What could?'

'Any of them. The bigger ones.'

'What for?'

'For ... you know.'

'Is this,' he sighs, 'about the apocalypse again?'

'Of course,' I say. 'Why do you think I took the crossbow shooting so seriously this year? And you'll be grateful one day. Sooner than you think.'

'I've told you before, you overanxious, godless mass of fevered insecurities fast dissolving in your own unreflective panics, we are not living in the end times.'

'Yet.'

'You're not going to buy a knife.'

'I am. A big one.'

'You're not.'

'Then I'm going to buy a crossbow.'

'You're not.'

'I am. It's quieter than a gun and I reckon you'll be able to carry them openly sooner than you would a firearm once social breakdown begins. Also, I'll get more time to escape if someone wrests it from my feeble grasp to use against me in a desperate battle for the last bottle of antibiotics in a looted chemist.'

'You have thought too much about this.'

'I believe I have not yet thought about this enough.'

'You couldn't kill anything anyway.'

'I'm not a good enough shot yet, but I'd practise.'

'No, I mean you couldn't kill anything for moral and/or squeamish reasons.'

'I'm not squeamish. It's you who can't deal with worms. Or cat sick.'

'That's not the same.'

'Anyway, I totally could kill something. That's sort of the bit I'm most looking forward to, actually. Remember when I stopped being depressed after Thomas and I loved him so much that I used to lie in bed wishing I could prove it by knocking a burglar unconscious to protect him? And then when he was lying on the floor, I'd bash him again just to make sure, and if he died, he died? Too bad for him. Don't come for my baby.'

'You never told me that.'

'Well, that's what I feel like all the time now, but with more rage. Because I've got two of them. And you can't even deal with cat sick.'

'I'll tell you what,' says Richard, after a pause. 'We'll go home and talk about this some more. But in the meantime – let's not arm you quite yet.'

'Okay,' I say, striding on to the hog roast. 'But you'll need to soon. Sooner than you think.'

Saturday, 19 August

Going-home day. The children are making the most of their last hour in the glorious unspoiled countryside in their preferred ways. Evie is playing Inappropriate Violence IV on the iPad and Thomas is gazing at the view from the highest window, trying to imprint his beloved countryside on his memory before we insist on tearing him away and restoring him to the barren grey vistas of suburbia. Richard is marching round the cottage, checking things off The List. I am sitting reading on the sofa, knowing that everything on The List can be checked off because while he was at the beach and amusement arcades with the kids yesterday I did everything on The List. (That's not a pass-agg comment, for once, by the way. I would much rather be working my way through The List in an empty cottage while I catch up on podcasts I would very much like to become a regular listener to than go to the beach – so sandy! So windy! So much like hard work! – with the kids. Plus I would now be constantly resentful about supervising paddling rather than throwing myself in the sea and striking out for Scandinavia.)

'I AM LOOKING UNDER ALL THE BEDS,' he bellows.

'Good, good,' I murmur, turning another page of my book.

'I AM CHECKING "LOOK UNDER ALL THE BEDS" OFF THE LIST.'

'Mm-hmm.'

'I AM CHECKING THE WARDROBES AND WASTEPAPER BASKETS.'

'Tremendous,' I say to myself.

'I AM CHECKING "CHECK THE WARDROBES AND WASTEPAPER BASKETS" OFF THE LIST. NOW I AM CHECKING NOTHING IS LEFT IN THE SHOWER. NOTHING IS LEFT IN THE SHOWER. NOW I AM COMING DOWN.'

'Do,' I say politely.

'Okay,' he says. 'Wastepaper baskets and kitchen bin down here – done. Appliances left on or off according to cottage owner's instruction booklet – done. Dishwasher empty – yes. Right, to the car, family!'

'Okay, final end-of-holiday checklist,' he says, once we're in the car. 'Satnav – yes. Working badly enough to impart a spicy sense of mystery and peril to the journey home? Surely. Children in car seats?'

'Yes,' I say, turning round to check they have strapped themselves in properly.

'Our children?'

'Almost certainly.'

'Have I eaten my own bodyweight in locally sourced bacon?'

'You have.'

'Have you bought several basic items of homeware tricked out in Farrow & Ball paints for six times their innate value?'

'Fifteen-pound ball of string on a stick in West Highland White Terrier, and a twenty-six pound random box in Random Box!' I cry happily.

'Children convinced either of enduring superiority of urban living – Evie?'

'Yes!' she yells, thrashing about in her seat in her eagerness to set off.

'Or mourning our departure from the pastoral idyll representative of the prelapsarian innocence in which we all once dwelled – Thomas?'

'Do you mean I don't want to go home?'

'Yes.'

'Then, yes,' he says miserably, turning tear-filled eyes to the window to catch a last glimpse of his beloved countryside. I squeeze his knee. 'Can't we stay longer?' he begs.

'I'm sorry, Thomas, we can't.'

'We are broken on the wheel of term dates, my dear child, like every other breeder, unfortunately,' says Richard. 'It's a bugger but we have to go home.'

We do. It is a bugger, though.

Tuesday, 22 August

I feel like I'm crawling over broken glass towards the finish line, Fiona messages our special summer FuckThisForAGameOfSoldiers WhatsApp group.

On my knees here, agrees Nadia.

Ah, the doggest days of August, when the air fills with the sound of grinding teeth, soft weeping and occasional screams of despair. The beginning of term is so near and yet still so very far away.

In the Dashwood home, it's just us now. There is always a point in the summer holidays when the population drops below critical mass. Everybody is away. There can be no relief. Friends, grandparents (Mum and Dad are striding around Scotland, refusing to carry mobile phones because they wouldn't want to inconvenience anyone who might be able to save them when they break their ankles halfway across a heather-hummocked moor), even untrustworthy teenagers next door who would still do in a late-summer pinch are all gone. So there are no playdates (half the WhatsApp group is typing from foreign parts, those of us left are running on empty). No whisking off of children for an hour or two in a café with Grandma ('I've found somewhere that just hands them cups of sugar with marsh-mallows on top!'). Every indoor and outdoor activity has been exhausted, and so have the family coffers. No more painting, no more football, and no more afternoon science, dance, Lego or any other kind of club whose few hours of respite (by which I mean 'furnishing of the ability to do paid vital work') require fees reckoned in gold bullion.

And it's too hot to dig. Sometimes I can persuade the children to sit inside and draw plans of their dream den-hole once excavations are complete, but it essentially fails to thrill.

I feel as if I'm looking straight down the barrel of a gun, but without the ability to pull the trigger and embrace the sweet release of death.

Wednesday, 23 August

I am a phoenix, reduced to my barest essence and then reborn. We have been saved, my friends, saved! And the name of our salvation is – papier mâché.

Under normal circumstances, I revile arts and crafts. I simply have not the words to tell you how much I hate any and all creative activities. Fucking about with coloured sand. Cutting out paper dolls. Constructing cardboard forts or overseeing painting jags. Hand me a pipe cleaner and I spit venom. Give me a stencil and my vitriol will burn a hole through your floor. Show me a decoupage kit and I will show you a Liz-shaped hole through the nearest wall. Maybe it's different for parents who have artistic leanings or a practical bent. I have nothing. All of it makes me want to smash things. I prayed nightly through both pregnancies that my children would be bookworms so that I could be freed of this terrible depredation against my soul. As they grew up and it became clear I was not to be granted this boon and they kept whining about how *booooooored* they were, I turned in desperation to my husband. I always feel that Richard being born a country boy should give him more insight into the unformed, primitive world of childhood. 'What would you do as a child when you were bored?' I asked.

'Fight,' he replied, turning another page of his book *More Naval Battles Than You Know What To Do With*. 'Builds character. And either leadership or survival skills. Then we'd throw some jacks at the wall and start dancing with a powerful yet graceful animal energy. No, wait – that was *West Side Story*.'

I was reminded why I only ever turn to my husband in desperation. 'What else?' I said helplessly.

'I talked to old people. But today's old people are rubbish. Baby boomers instead of war veterans. What are they going to do – tell stories about their final salary pension schemes? I took things apart – but now everything's modular and designed so that nobody can get in to repair it and you have to buy a new one every time. So they won't be able to do that. I climbed trees, but we live in an urban wasteland.'

Today I scour my own memories for inspiration once again, but they remain mainly of television and being left so long in front of one that it would eventually induce a sicky headache for the rest of the day. Even though the crunchy, screentime-equals-serial-killers brigade are not my people, deliberately reproducing that experience for the next generation feels off. Eventually I remember a brief period of French knitting. I imagine Evie's face if I propose weaving a purposeless woollen string on a miniature loom as a fun activity, and shudder.

But then Thomas points out that, these days, there's the internet to show you new things. And while most of them seem even worse than French knitting, a YouTube video of papier-mâché-ing snags our attention. Now, I do not resile from my anti-crafting stance. And I admit that the heat and the fury and the dust of the last month or so may have weakened me and addled my brain. But! What separates papier mâché from the vile herd of the activities customarily grouped under that dread heading is that there is no craft to it, let alone any art. It is not fiddly. It is not painstaking. It requires no special trips to special shops. It involves no glue. It leaves no fluff, glitter or stray googly eyes in its wake. It is a joy.

The very first time out, we make a bowl.

All you do is: get a newspaper. Make some runny flour and water paste. Cover a bowl with foil. Tear the newspaper into strips (a very soothing activity in itself, once you learn to do it with the grain). Dip it into the paste. That's quite soothing, too, because you simply cannot go wrong. Lay them over the foil until the foil is covered. Do it again, for as many layers as you like. Each person can do all the steps or you can form a conveyor-belt type arrangement. Either way, again – and I really cannot impress this upon you enough – you cannot go wrong.

The three of us just layer and chat, layer and chat, layer and chat. We discuss whether there is enough water on the earth to put the sun out and whether any living thing can see air and whether you would be scared if you were falling through the air if the ground didn't exist and so you knew you could never hit it.

Evie and Thomas carry on tearing and pasting quite happily while I get tea ready. I rejoin them for the last few strips. Then we place our creation reverently on the windowsill to dry out (because that's all you have to do – let it dry out!), and they rinse their hands (you don't even need soap! Just cold water will do!)

while I sweep all the leftover bits of paper into the recycling bin, give the table a quick wipe (no unexpectedly indelible pen or paint marks! No picking bits of glue off everything!). Then we sit down, eat and deliberate upon what colours we will paint Our Bowl. Blue and coloured dots on the inside, white and coloured flowers on the outside, we decide. The motion is passed without rancour.

It is an altogether blissful afternoon.

Thursday, 24 August

The kids painted the bowl today while I tidied the house. Both look great.

Friday, 25 August

David comes round and they form a bowl production line. I do two hours' extra uninterrupted work at my laptop, then call up our charity's Who We Are page of the website so that I can literally laugh in Temporary Child Boss's face.

Saturday, 26 August

They paint the bowls and branch out into papier-mâché plate-making. I make interested noises, do more work and can face my return to the office the week after next with a confidence I haven't felt since I first disappeared into the second-floor loo with morning sickness nine years ago.

Papier mâché is magic. Pass it on.

Thursday, 31 August

I hear Richard come out of our bedroom and onto the landing, from where he proceeds to shout down to me. 'Is there any reason your clothes are in my wardrobe?'

I pause in my ironing-cum-*Law & Order: SVU*-watching. I think back. On very rare occasions, when all my clothes are clean, I do temporarily borrow a little hanging space in the right-hand wardrobe (as I think of it, to my mind, the couple who has children together has no exclusive rights per wardrobe). But ... I look at the pile of remaining ironing to my right and the pile of unwashed clothes to my left and sigh ... that has not been necessary for a while. So ... Wait.

'Do you mean there's a bra or a pair of socks or something on top of your trousers?' I shout back.

'Yes!'

'They must be from when I was putting everyone's laundry away. Something fell, I didn't see what, couldn't see where and I forgot to check when I'd finished.'

There is a definite huffing sound as he returns to the bedroom.

A huffing sound.

A. Huffing. Sound.

A huffing sound because the person who was putting all the clean laundry she had done for him, herself and their jointly produced children had accidentally left a stray pair of socks on top of his trousers.

Pause to note that Richard refuses to hang his trousers up in the traditional manner. He folds them in half and lays them on top of each other on the bottom of his wardrobe. He contends that the vertical hanging method deployed unproblematically by 99 per cent of the population throughout human history destroys trousers. He cleaves to this as an article of faith, yielding neither to rational thought nor empirical evidence that the weight of several pairs of trousers pressing down on several other pairs of trousers does absolutely none of the trousers

216

any good at all. Sometimes when I want to remind myself of the inutility of argument with unreason, or the futility of life generally, I go down and look at them for a moment, before reclosing the doors, returning downstairs and pouring myself a wardrobe-sized gin.

Press play and continue. These stray socks that are concerning us at the moment. Are they an immovable or insuperable barrier to the operation of getting dressed? Are they an egregious incursion into his right to freedom of trouser? Have his plans to insert his legs into their traditional coverings been fatally thwarted? Or should he perhaps simply look down, register the small foreign object, recognise its nature and relocate it to its proper goddamn place – three feet to the left, in my wardrobe – without feeling a flicker of anything, let alone a huff-worthy degree of outrage or resentment? What would that be like? I wonder.

Breaking this down and parsing the thought further – how much of his and my resources are uselessly expended on his unwillingness/inability to navigate and ameliorate even the very smallest, sock-sized, cottonweight bumps in the route without requiring blame to be apportioned beforehand and penance and/or help to be solicited thereafter? If you did the sums, how much has been sapped from wives, mothers and any other women in the line of fire over this kind of thing down the ages? What it must be like to come from an unbroken lineage of people for whom life is so rarely not arranged in a manner purely advantageous to them that the intrusion of a strange sock registers as a barbarity distracts me so much that I am delighted to find that I have reached the end of the ironing before I know it. Which is, I guess, ironic.

Monday, 4 September

Mid-morning, I notice a message on my voicemail. 'It's from the school office,' I say, puzzled, to Richard. He and the children look up with vague interest from the toast they are crunching at the table.

'It says ... it says the children have been marked absent.'

'We're right here,' says Evie.

In the Douglas Adams/John Lloyd book *The Meaning of Liff*, the authors had the merry conceit of using place names to give labels to feelings and things that had not yet evolved their own. In *The Meaning of Liff*, 'Ely' means 'that first tiny inkling you get that something, somewhere has gone terribly wrong.'

I can feel the blood drain from my face as I listen to the rest of the message and an Ely air settles over the room. 'Kids,' says Richard warily, 'go and play in your room.'

'Can I get the Brio out?'

'Can I stick my pictures up?'

'You can do anything you want short of arson.'

Off they go.

'What,' says Richard, 'has happened?'

'In short,' I say, putting the phone down on the table with elaborate care, '*we* have happened. This is quintessential us. Which is to say, the worst us. I now have to die or move. I think I'll die.'

'What. Has. Happened?'

'Term starts today. Started today. All the other children are back at school. Ours are not. Because we thought it was next Monday.'

'It's on the wall planner as next Monday,' says Richard.

'Yes. But we did that. You see? We did that. We put it on the calendar. And we did it wrongly. We were a week out. We failed to translate a date from one piece of paper accurately to another piece of paper and then we went on holiday. And didn't talk or text or WhatsApp or email anyone from school in such a way that it became clear that *our* start-of-term was not *their* start-of-term.'

'This can't have happened,' says Richard.

'But it has,' say I.

'We simply cannot be that fucking stupid. It's the stupidest fucking thing I ever heard.'

'Yes,' I agree. 'And we did it.'

We spend ten minutes attempting first to apportion blame for this administrative error of administrative errors (our handwriting is too similar to help, though it doesn't stop us examining the planner and trying), then fighting over who has to ring the office and explain. I threaten to launch into one of my graphic descriptions of the fourth-degree tear I suffered during delivery, and Richard gives in.

He disappears into the study to make the call. I hear only a few muffled words, a penitent tone and a mirthless bark of laughter at the end.

'Well,' he says, coming back into the kitchen, 'that was painful.'

'As painful as a perineum coming apart?' I say, because I will not let an opportunity pass, not now, not ever.

'I'm sure not,' says Richard, because he has learned over the years.

There is suddenly so much to do. Uniform to iron, books to find, lunches to Tupperware, a summer's worth of sodding homework to do. And we have to tell the children, who are for once – but of course! – playing happily together. They have laid out a goodly amount of track and are happily chuffing things round it. We explain the situation to them. Evie smashes her steam engine into Thomas's string of passenger carriages. A gigantic trainwreck. Richard sighs.

'Everywhere is metaphor.'

Tuesday, 5 September

It occurred to me as I lay in bed last night contemplating our cock-up instead of sleeping (which is better than my normal method of waking suddenly at 4 a.m. to gibber in humiliation and writhe with regret at whatever misstep I have made over the previous twenty-four hours – maybe this is the beginning of the wisdom people keep telling me comes with age?) that there is an upside to our idiocy: I now have nearly a week off work *while the children are back at school*. I had some extra days to use up and I thought there was actually more benefit to taking them during the summer holidays and not having to juggle work and home than there was to going away at half-term.

Now, of course – well, we needn't go back over what happened, but as a result, I now have four days to myself from eight thirty to three thirty coming up. 'It is time,' I think I actually murmur to myself as I lie there, 'to look at the Long-term List.' It lies deep in the mental vault – I may not even be able to find the key – because it is so rarely needed. When you fall knackered into bed every night with the daily list of chores barely touched, anything that requires greater investment is going to have to wait a long time for its turn.

But now I drag it out of the depths and hold the brittle parchment up to the light of memory to see what it says:

1. Have meals. One each, morning, middle and end of day.
2. Batch cook (see above).
3. Watch all the films I've missed since giving birth (see Appendix I).
4. Inspect moles.
5. Research energy tariffs.
6. Get eye test.
7. Get smear.
8. Check penalties for late tax filing. If choice between financial or prison, see if you can bump it up to solitary confinement.

9. Write thank-you letters dating back to 2009.
10. Meet up with friends who live more than 200 metres away.
11. Get haircut. It doesn't matter when you retrieve this list. I guarantee you need a haircut.
12. Unblock pores.
13. And drains. Bound to be a drain blocked somewhere.
14. Establish skincare regime.
15. Stop buying comfortable trousers.

Later

Moles inspected and cleared for duty. Facemask applied, pores emptied. Feel like my face has lost weight.

Made massive fish pie – white sauce from jar, and children have been brainwashed over the years into thinking mashed potatoes *should* be lumpy, so edible – gave some to them for tea, froze remaining eight portions with sense of contentment I do not expect to feel again this side of the grave.

Wednesday, 6 September

Have eye test in the morning. Optician tells me I will probably need varifocals 'next time'. My mother is seventy-six and doesn't need glasses for anything. Maybe she will outlive us all. That would be great.

Have a smear test in the afternoon. I used to dread these when I was young. Now I can lie there compiling an Ocado order on my phone or firing off emails while medical professionals whack speculums up me, invite their students to watch – 'It's a vagina, dear doctors still in the first flush of fully elasticated young adulthood and white coats, but not as you know it' – and for all I know rent the place out for storage.

Thursday, 7 September

Research energy tariffs. Run out of energy. Am just making myself a cup of tea to refuel when my phone rings. Not pings – rings. Nobody rings with good news, these days, if they ever did. It's Fiona. 'Ding dong,' she says, when I pick up. 'The witch is dead.'

'Iain's mum?' I gasp. 'How? When? *How?*'

I am genuinely stunned. She was one we really did think would outlive us all, preserved for ever by gin and evil.

'Like herpes,' Fiona once said. 'There's no shifting her.'

'About forty minutes ago,' says Fiona. 'She was just in the middle of arguing with someone over her right to park in a handicapped space because she sprained her ankle in 1984, when she had a massive heart attack and just dropped down dead. Didn't even suffer.'

'Well,' I say doubtfully, 'condolences to you. Or condolences to Iain, definitely.'

'Yes,' says Fiona. 'He's a bit shocked, obviously. He's getting ready to go over to the hospital now but I don't want him doing the driving, so could you pick up David for me and give him his tea? And maybe keep him for a bit after that till we get ourselves together and work out how we're going to break the news.'

'Of course, of course,' I say. 'We'll keep him till you want to come for him.'

Fiona thanks me and hangs up. I sit for a minute with the news. Death – any death – reminds you of its ungraspable size and strangeness. And even if it's unaccompanied by personal devastation and grief – and I can't say I feel the loss of Mrs Slater in any significant way – it reminds you of all the times it was. Someone was there. And now they are not. No middle ground. No way to hedge or soften the stark fact. If you want to see them again – you can't. If you want to ask them something – you can't. If you want to kiss them once more, hug them once more, laugh with them once more, have one single moment more with them – you can't. How are you ever meant to get used to that as an idea, let alone a reality?

I realise I am perilously close to tears and to missing pick-up, so I give myself a good shake, check we have enough fish fingers to sustain an unexpected guest and head down to school. The children all look especially and gloriously alive and well as they pour out into the playground. The loss of one of them, of course, is impossible to contemplate. In bad times or the bleakest hours of a restless night you can find yourself circling the thought – a glance and away, a glance and away. And yet it happens. How people bear such a thing I hope beyond the telling of it never to know.

Friday, 8 September

Fiona and Iain have told David about Grandma.

'He asked if Iain was all right, which made Iain cry,' she sighs over coffee at mine. 'Then he asked if there would be a funeral and we explained what a cremation was. He said it sounded a bit drastic. I said it was actually quite usual and he seemed to accept that. Then he asked if he would be coming with us. And we said we thought he was a bit too young and that it was probably best if he stayed behind and just remembered Grandma as she was. And then there was a bit of a silence as we all remembered Grandma as she was, and David said, "Are you sure?" and that made Iain laugh. Then he told David that Grandma had been nicer when Iain was little. "Not nice. But nicer." And that made him cry again. So then we all had a cuddle and some ice cream and went to bed.'

'I think you did very well,' I say.

'Thank you,' Fiona says. 'David's been very quiet since but that's allowed, isn't it?'

'Of course it is,' I say. 'He's never one to act up. He goes away, digests things in his own time. He'll be okay. You'll be okay.'

'New territory,' says Fiona. 'There's always a new territory, isn't there? Just when you think you've got a handle on this whole childrearing, mothering business a whole new world of shite'll open up in front of you every time.'

'Do you want some whisky in your coffee?' I say.

'I think so,' says Fiona. 'Don't you?'

Monday, 11 September

Back to work. Feel relieved and happy – money! Appreciation, of a sort! Tangible goals to meet! – and resentful and mulish – work! Adulthood! Tangible ways to fail! – at the same time.

Unshackled to school holidays and peak pricing, Sofia and Amrit have just left for three weeks somewhere hot. They told Richard where, but he can't remember what they said. 'I was distracted by my piles,' he says. 'And trying not to hope that one day they would be by theirs too.'

Tuesday, 12 September

We must face the dread fact that Evie is about to turn a year older. The law of under-eights stipulates that she is still entitled to a party. After that, you can get away with taking a couple of them to Pizza Express, thank the occasionally benevolent gods. Kate rings with her traditional blessed offer of basically running the entire operation. 'I've got three themes she can choose from,' she says.

'Military coup?' suggests Richard. 'Blood feud? Post-apocalyptic hellscape and the rise to power?'

'Pirate, space or circus,' says Kate.

Evie plumps for circus and wants Richard to dress as a strongman. 'We'll see,' I tell her. She disappears upstairs for an hour and comes back down with a piece of paper gripped in a sweaty fist. We smooth it out to reveal two lists of names. 'Gudd pipl' reads one heading. 'Badd pipl' reads the other.

Between them they cover everyone in her class. The entries are cross-referenced with invites and star ratings that, she tells us, indicate how happy she will be to have them there. 'Except for the red ones – that's how happy I will be that they're not allowed to come.' There is one Badd person on the list of invitees. When questioned, she explains, 'You've got to have one bad person at a party. Otherwise it's just boring.'

She is eventually persuaded that everyone must be invited. This is an immutable part of the law – the expensive, exhausting law. Two more seasons of carnage to go and then it's simple Meat Feasts all round. She will argue till she's literally blue in the face, rage burning up her oxygen faster than she can gulp it in, but I will have Thomas, precedent and fairness on my side, and I. Will. Win.

Wednesday, 13 September

David has continued to be quiet. Then last night Fiona woke up to find him standing motionless by her bedside. 'I nearly had a frigging heart attack myself,' she tells us at the coven meeting, brought forward by a day because it's her mother-in-law's funeral tomorrow. '"Sorry," he says. "I couldn't decide whether to wake you, so I was just waiting."

'"That's okay," I say, still trying not to scream the place down. "What's wrong, sweetheart?"

'"I'm just … worried," he says eventually. Which is not like David. Nothing bothers him. So I asked him what about, obviously, and he says Grandma. So I ask why and he says, "Because … she wasn't nice. Dad said she was nicer before but she wasn't nice when we knew her, was she?"'

'Did you agree?' says Céline.

'I had to, didn't I?' says Fiona. 'I checked Iain was still asleep and then I said, "No, not really. No." And David says, "So she wasn't nice for quite a long time." And I just make encouraging noises because I still don't actually know where he's going with this. And eventually he says, "So, will she get into Heaven? Because I don't think she was nice enough to go there. But I don't want her to go to Hell because she wasn't bad enough for that. So where's she going to go?" Two o'clock in the pigging morning, this is.'

'Christ, what did you say?' says Nadia.

'I pulled him into bed with me and told him that nobody really knows if there's a Heaven or a Hell, but if they exist, only really bad people will go to Hell, and in Heaven there are probably different sections depending on how good you've been on earth. And by then, thank fuck, and before God could strike me down, he was asleep.'

'It's nice that she's still making life difficult for you from beyond the grave, isn't it?' I say, pouring Fiona more wine.

'Sure does help me not to miss her in the slightest,' Fiona says, knocking it back.

'At least he hasn't asked if you're going to die,' says Céline. 'When my grandmother died I was ten and that obsessed me. But I think when they are a little younger it is okay. They think death is just a piece of bad luck some people have. It is too much to know your parents are mortal at this age. Their brains protect them.'

'Here's to self-defence mechanisms,' says Fiona, and we can all raise our glasses to that.

Thursday, 14 September

It is the day of Mrs Slater's funeral. I've picked David up and he and my two play relatively quietly together in the children's bedroom, as they usually do, but after a while David drifts downstairs.

'Are you okay, darling?' I say.

'I'm just not in the mood for playing,' he says. 'I know it's not five o'clock yet,' David knows our house rules as well as he knows his own, 'but could I just watch telly?'

'Of course you can,' I say, giving him a quick hug. 'It's a weird day, a funeral day. Normal rules don't apply. Would you like some milk and a chocolate biscuit too?'

'Yes, please,' he says, his eyes widening. 'I didn't know it was *that* weird.'

'What do you mean?'

'Evie always says you're the meanest mummy with chocolate biscuits 'n' that,' he says.

My face must have given something away because he pats my arm and adds, 'Don't take it badly. She's young. And anyway,' he says, carefully gathering up his plate and cup in preparation for his removal to the sitting room, 'your house – your rules.'

Why, even on a funeral day, do I always end up being strangely comforted by this child?

Half an hour or so later – a bit surprised my two haven't come down to investigate David's whereabouts – I call up the stairs that their pizza-and-carrot-sticks-and-cherry-tomatoes-that-must-be-eaten-too is ready. Evie and Thomas come down with odd, uncertain expressions on their faces and clutching sheets of paper.

'What have you got there?' I say, as David comes through and they all sit up at the table.

'Just … some pictures,' mumbles Evie.

'For David,' says Thomas, pushing them all across the table to him.

'For me?' says David, as bemused and curious as I am.

'Yeah,' grunts Evie. 'Because … urgh.'

'Because we're sorry about your grandma,' says Thomas in a rush. 'I drew you some flowers because' – he shoots a defiant look at Evie – 'that's what people give you at funerals. I'm older and I *know*.'

'And I drew you a Superzing,' says Evie equally defiantly. 'Because that's what you like best. Not flowers. Flowers make no *sense*.'

'They're both dead good,' says David. 'Thanks. A lot.'

'Y'welcome,' mutters Thomas, scarlet.

'No problem,' says Evie, clearly relieved the gift-giving is over and ready to turn her attention to the pressing matter of equitable pizza division and wholesale vegetable avoidance.

I say nothing because I'll cry for ever if I do. I shovel extra chocolate biscuits onto a plate for afters instead, in mute acknowledgement of the infinite capacity for kindness that resides in the human heart. Not that I won't enjoy it messing with that little madam's head too.

Monday, 18 September

I read an article once – when I used to read articles, over coffee, or in the bath or on a leisurely trip into town or some other archaic pastime I now look on as something that exists only in legend – that said, 'Never make the mistake of comparing your inner life to others' outer lives.' And I get that this is very good advice, generally speaking. Everyone is more anxious, insecure, needy and sad than they look to the outside world and so you go through life thinking that your various mental states are much more abnormal than they are.

But I no longer have the time or energy to maintain an inner life, let alone compare it to others' (or their shiny carapaces). I only compare outer lives. And on that like-for-like comparison, I realise, as I hurtle round the house trying to get it into some semblance of order before Dee's children come round for a playdate, I am failing dismally. Dee is Savannah's third in command, behind Susannah. She hungers for the top spot but will never make it as her hair is simply not good enough. It is the only flaw in her otherwise immaculate life.

It is not enough to lessen my fury or dread. No one else's outer life, I note, as I slam the dishwasher shut for example, seems to include a kitchen that has been missing eight rows of tiles for the last five years. Inner lives may be invisible but I can see kitchens, so I know this. Unless everyone I've ever visited has a show kitchen and is keeping another half-finished one secretly somewhere. But they all seem to be using their fully tiled kitchens on a daily basis, the smug bastards, so I doubt it.

No one else's outer life, it occurs to me, as I grab the trowel from the shed, seems to include redigging the whirligig hole every time they put the thing up because they can't find the one they made last time.

No one else, I reckon, as I stare into my fridge for at least the third time this week, wondering why there is nothing to eat in there, seems to stare into their fridge at least three times a week and wonder why there is nothing to eat in there. People go to the supermarket regularly instead – like, on an actual specific, known day each week – or have an Ocado order set up for the basics and tweak it thereafter for the fancy stuff. Like meat. Or eggs. *Why have we no eggs?*

(Once, when I was late-pregnant with Evie, and Richard was away on a last-minute work thing in Durham, I gave Thomas canned tomatoes for breakfast and tomato soup for tea. I told him it was International Tomato Day. He just looked at me with the kind of unmediated, infinitely bleak reproach only a toddler can manage.)

No one else spends twenty minutes looking for her cash – or credit, or store or any other bastarding kind would do – card before going out. They just reach for their handbags and go. Just knowing, somehow, that all the necessary accoutrements for living lie therein. Again, I know. I've seen it happen.

No one else seems to count it a cause for celebration if they manage to get their children into a bath before bed more than three times a week.

No one else, I mutter as I whirl like a dervish round the sitting room collecting Evie's Lego, Henry's fur (normal-sized deposits but I doubt Dee will see this as a triumph) and Richard's legal papers as I go, has stained sofas. They just don't. I've never seen one.

I do my best. The children arrive. They play. Dee arrives.

Dee judges. Dee leaves. I close the front door and lean against it, weak with shame, fury and relief.

The dishwasher beeps. I open the door and water floods out.

'More water than a single dishwasher can possibly hold. It seemed less malfunctioning home appliance than malevolent Tardis,' I tell the coven, later that night. (We called an emergency Monday meeting. What with Dee, the witch's funeral and assorted other life malarkey we felt justified.) 'It was like it was pissing on every hope of peace and dream of civilisation I've ever had. I screamed at the children to grab towels and we spent the next forty minutes mopping up. Then I sent them to their iPads, sat down on the floor and cried for half an hour, like a fool.'

'Well, of course you did!' says Nadia, pouring me another large glass of prosecco (which we have instead of wine whenever anyone survives a particularly stressful playdate or domestic catastrophe, on the triumph/disaster/tastes the same, you need it more principle). 'It's very upsetting.'

'I take it very, very personally when inanimate objects that have one job – *one job* – let me down,' says Fiona, darkly. 'I always want to drag them out behind some bushes and punish them.'

'Totally,' I say. 'And then I spent four hundred pounds ordering a brand fucking new one like I should have done six months ago.'

'Tell me you're paying for installation and having the old one taken away and all that jazz,' says Fiona, 'Not fannying about trying to do it yourself or get some cheaper third party in?'

'God, no,' I say. 'If anyone has me over a barrel these days, it's synergised companies. I just take the beating and am quietly grateful for being given my life back. But, honestly, why do these things never happen to Dee? I bet she's never had a flooded kitchen – or a late plumber, or a raspberry seed stuck in her back teeth for three days *like I still have* in her whole entire life. No stains on her sofas either.'

'That's bollocks,' says Fiona. 'We're all running to stand still. It's normal. Though you could get the sofas cleaned.'

'But *no!*' I wail, because, truth be told, I started drinking as I was scrolling through dishwashers. 'Dee. Dee. Her house is *pristine. Always.* You've seen it! We've all seen it! It's like a show house! Fresh flowers in every alcove – oh, and alcoves, she's got *alcoves* – an actual playroom for the kids, where the toys are in *labelled boxes*, perfectly plumped cushions that tone with everything bloody everywhere …'

'I know,' says Nadia, nodding sympathetically. 'And when you go round for coffee she brews it in a cafetière and serves it to you in tiny bone china cups instead of throwing Nescafé into random tea-stained mugs.'

'And she brings them through on a tray,' I say weepily. 'And it's not melamine from Ikea, it's like a grown-up tray. With biscuits so beautiful you almost can't bring yourself to eat them. Almost. Last time, I ate seven.'

'And you want to hate her for it all – I mean, I do hate her for it all, but only afterwards when I'm home because suddenly "home" looks like a medieval pigpen, but I can't while I'm there because it's all so lovely and *soothing*.'

'But how does she do it? Is she a witch?'

'No,' says Céline, returning from the loo. 'She is a liar.'

'What?'

'I thought you knew?' says Céline, draining and refilling her glass in one smooth, practised motion. 'She has a housekeeper.'

'She hasn't! She never said!'

'No,' says Céline. 'We are supposed not to know. She only invites people round when the housekeeper's not there. Very unsisterly of her. But the housekeeper is married to one of the people who came round to give me a ridiculous estimate for my bathroom. He said my address was easy to find because his wife worked nearby, *et voilà*.'

'I can't believe you didn't tell us.'

Céline shrugs. 'I forgot. Getting a new bathroom is a very difficult time. But she comes in every day, morning or afternoon.'

'Even weekends?'

'*Non*. They have to manage without her for those cruel forty-eight hours.'

I have never even heard of anyone having a housekeeper before, unless that was the technical title of one of the below-stairs cast of *Downton Abbey*. We all, as one, sit back in our chairs the better to absorb the stunning fact of this woman's existence. I roll it around in my head for a minute. 'So – that's twenty or so hours a week. We're saying that for twenty hours a week, every week, Dee has someone looking after the house, the washing, the garden, the car, the bills, the admin, the cooking—'

'The fresh fucking flowers,' adds Fiona.

'The fresh fucking flowers,' I say. 'All that crap?'

'*Oui.*'

'But,' says Fiona, leaning forward the better to convey the intensity of her words 'but ... she *herself* doesn't work. She's a stay-at-home mum, isn't she? Okay, yes, yes, staying at home with children is work blah-blah-blah, but you know what I mean. She doesn't go out to work, right?'

'*Oui, encore une fois*,' says Céline, refilling all our glasses as it becomes clear we are all struggling with the implications of this news.

I gulp mine as my mind races. 'But that's like having ... two and a half extra working days in the week. Or ... or it's like having a three-parent household: one to work, one to do all the domestic stuff and one to raise the children.'

'Four parents if you count the fact that her husband earns as much as two people put together,' says Fiona.

'Five if you count the fact that she sends *les enfants* to every possible club and class after school and at the weekends,' says Céline.

'I keep trying to do that with David,' says Fiona. 'But he won't go to any. I ask him why and he just says, "Full of children." I can't argue with that.'

I pour another glass of prosecco – my God, but this stuff slips down easily – and think about Céline's revelation a bit more. I start to feel a great weight lifting off me. 'That's what it takes, then,' I say. 'Five. Five people to get you up to fresh-flowers-cafetière-coffee-clean-house-all-your-insurances-and-MOTs-up-to-date level. Five people paddling away like demons to keep a single family grandly afloat. And – apart from Céline, who sometimes has an au pair – we've all got two.'

'And none of us is being paid,' says Fiona. 'So naturally we're going to half-arse it quite a lot.'

We raise a glass and toast Dee. As Fiona says, for a lying bugger she's made us all feel really great.

I feel oddly floaty – even controlling for the prosecco input over the evening – and realise it is because I am unburdened momentarily by guilt. It is the oddest sensation. It feels almost as good as having a housekeeper for twenty hours a week. I imagine.

I imagine.

Tuesday, 19 September

'I couldn't remember Carol Vorderman's name yesterday,' announces Richard.

'Did you need to remember Carol Vorderman's name yesterday?' I say.

'No,' he replies. 'But I would like to be sure I could if I did.'

Wednesday, 20 September

I ask Evie why she hasn't tidied her room like I asked her to.

'I a slippery fellow,' she replies.

I'm sure some day soon my family will start saying things to me again that actually admit of a response. Until then, I shall just accept my lot.

Thursday, 21 September

After drop-off this morning, Fiona and I go for coffee round at Siobhan's – she's a mother from Evie's class whom we only really know well enough to smile at and occasionally small-talk with as we wait at the gates. We are giddy because Fiona has time to kill since her carpet fitter arrived early but she's booked time off work to stay in till ten. 'Come on,' says she. 'Let's take forty minutes out of our day and really live a little. There'll be different cups! Different sofas!'

'You're such a bad influence,' I say, shaking my head.

'We might pick up some valuable housekeeping tips that will make us better wives and mothers!' she says, putting on a glassy smile, going cross-eyed and pretending to walk into traffic.

'Well, I can't pass up that kind of opportunity!' I say, going cross-eyed back, and we head on over.

The doorbell rings when we – and Rachel, who has joined us on the way – are halfway through our decadent hot drinks, served by Siobhan's lovely husband George, who is putting the finishing touches to the kitchen he has installed. 'See,' says Fiona, nudging me. 'Tip one – marry George.'

At the door is Rachel's friend Hafsa. She is, it turns out, upset. She has an eighteen-month-old son and three days ago her husband took him to the hairdresser for his first haircut. Without telling her. Without consulting her. And, when he came back, without remotely understanding why his life was now in danger.

'He just kept saying he'd noticed Suleiman's hair was getting a bit long and so he thought, I'll get it cut!' she says, shaking her head in disbelief as she perches on the edge of the sofa and loads sugar frantically into her cup. 'Like – like – like it was nothing!'

We all shake our heads too. George, looking intrigued, leaves his grouting and moves slowly but definitely a little closer, inexorably drawn in as if by a magnetic field.

'That's unbelievable,' says Fiona.

'Appalling,' murmurs Siobhan.

'I'm really sorry,' says George, cautiously, edging a little closer, 'but what exactly is the problem here? Was his hair not too long?'

'It was far too long!' says Hafsa.

George's slight bafflement deepens to bewilderment. 'Then didn't he do a good thing – almost, maybe, a helpful thing – in taking him for a haircut?'

'I wasn't ready!' Hafsa cries.

'You have to get ready for a haircut?'

'Of course!' says Fiona.

'Just the first one?' says George, his face clearing slightly. 'Because it's a marker of them growing up?'

'No,' I say. 'All of them for the first five years or so.'

Everyone nods. Apart from George, whose expression starts to fog again.

'Why?'

'Because his hair is mine!' says Hafsa. 'I made it! I made all of him. He's all mine really.'

'I think it's because we don't really distinguish between parts of our children,' offers Fiona. 'Especially when they're younger. So you might as well be cutting their fingers off, in a way. In a sort of way,' she adds, when she sees George's face.

'Richard used to have to start warning me about three weeks beforehand that Thomas needed a haircut,' I say. 'So that I could prepare myself. I love his hair. It's my favourite thing about him, apart from his bum.'

'Mine too,' says Fiona. 'Hair, I mean. Of David, I mean. I think it's because it reminds me of how clever I was – managing to finish the job off properly. "Look – I even made something that covers the top of his head like it should!" It really impresses me, that.'

'Once, when Thomas was about three,' I say, 'Richard found me crying after his latest haircut. I told him it was because it was like a little death. I hadn't had much sleep, to be fair. Evie had been awake for a year.'

A slight trace of fear has been added to George's expression of bewilderment.

'But this is not right,' he says. 'This is not ... normal.'

'But it is,' says Fiona, gesturing at the group. 'We all feel the same. So it is normal. Sheer weight of numbers tells you that.'

'So – you want them never to have haircuts?'

'Oh, no,' says Rachel. 'They've got to be neat and tidy. Got to have haircuts. I just wish their hair didn't grow, so that everything could stay the same and never change.'

George gazes in disbelief around the room. I see us, for a moment, through his eyes – a collection of glittering-eyed women, including his wife, in the throes of a common emotion that runs too deeply, widely and madly to be wrestled into words. How much simpler kitchens must seem. We've just told him that we feel we own our children outright, that fingers are the same as hair, that we would like to arrest time, and that subjecting our offspring to wholly unremarkable, simple, painless grooming practices that have been with us since the dawn of time makes us hysterical.

'But it's how we keep them safe,' I say, in answer to the unasked questions I can feel emanating from George. 'These overreactions are the margin of error. If we did less than this, danger could creep in.' We nod, as one, again.

He nods back, carefully, while backing away towards the grouting and his own place of safety. He does not understand. He will never understand. That's okay. We understand each other. Mothers are mental, yes. But in an insane world, we are the sanest choice. A very restorative forty minutes, all in all.

Fiona and I walk home with Rachel and ask how things are going.

'It's okay,' she says. 'There are bits of the day – when I'm at work – when I sort of forget what's happened. And then I remember and ... I dunno. I suppose I'll just have to see if the forgetting bits get longer and start to join up. And if they don't ... I dunno.'

'That's what Iain's like about his mother,' says Fiona. 'Forgets she's gone, then gets thumped by the realisation again.'

'Poor Iain,' says Rachel. 'His mum died. My normal died. We've just got to get used to the new life and hope it's manageable in the end.'

'At least Iain doesn't have any happy memories of their relationship to haunt him,' Fiona says, and we're hysterical all the way home.

Friday, 22 September

Today Evie showed me the eighth revision of her guest list. Categories now include 'Foreva enemees', 'Tempry enemees' and 'Real Badd Pipl'). The gleam in her eye as she takes me through them is ... disconcerting.

Saturday, 23 September

Within the 500-acre grounds of Microsoft's headquarters in Washington State lie 125 buildings. Deep within one, Building 87, is a cubic construction designed to cut out every scintilla of sound. It comprises six layers of concrete, each twelve inches thick. And within them lies an anechoic chamber lined with clusters of four-feet-long wedges made of noise-absorbing foam and floating on top of sixty-eight vibration-dampening springs mounted on a separate foundation slab. It is used to test speakers and microphones for sound distortions and to rearrange the capacitors on circuit boards so that their hums cancel each other out and don't disturb the end user. When you're in it, you can hear not just your heartbeat but your blood moving through your veins, your joints softly crunching and your eyeballs moving moistly in their sockets. It is literally, certifiably, the quietest place on earth.

I am concentrating hard on this beautiful thought because I am in the soft-play centre and cannot remember a time when I was not.

Thomas's classmate Anil is having his birthday party here and guests' siblings have been invited too, which means there are about fifty children in a state of fibrillating hysteria as they clamber all over the thick, hairy, violently orange nylon netting that looks like the vector of every disease that the ball pit doesn't yet have covered, fling themselves into the primary-coloured ball pits that will doubtless function as the mixing vessel, allowing cross-species viral leaps, and hurl themselves down bright green wavy slides with screams that could shatter plate armour, never mind glass. Add the sickly odour of rubberised safety coatings and even more rubberised chicken nuggets and every one of my senses is being assaulted. It is like living inside the headache that it's also given you.

Actually, make that forty-eight children. While his sister screeches with the best of them and scrambles up, through and round every obstacle on every webby storey, like a monkey on acid, Thomas is picking his way round so cautiously he has yet to complete a full circuit. David has done two – stolidly, efficiently, missing nothing (he did two rounds because the paths diverge at one point and you have to choose between slide and zip wire) – and is now sitting by my side at the table, me sipping coffee, him cold milk. I am in loco parentis, because Fiona and I have a pact that never shall both of us suffer soft-play hell when one adult sacrifice will do, and it is my turn to sacrifice. I assume we will each get a reward in Heaven.

Loco parentisly, I try to encourage him to join in again. David sighs. 'I don't really,' he says patiently, 'see the point.'

'It's ... fun,' I say feebly.

'It's not,' he says, firmly and to my mind inarguably.

'I think your mum would like you to have another go,' I say.

'She wouldn't,' he says. 'She understands.'

We contemplate the vision of everyone else's idea of fun that is before us.

'What exactly is it you don't like?' I ask, genuinely curious.

'The noise,' he says, after a moment. 'The people.'

I nod. We sip our drinks. We do not speak again. We do not need to.

Tuesday, 26 September

Tonight's father–daughter conversation overheard on the monitor:

> EVIE: Who do you love more, me or Mummy?
> RICHARD: Mummy – I've known her longer.

Didn't really know where to start, so didn't. Anyway, if anyone's ego can take it – possibly even needs it – it's Evie's.

Sunday, 1 October

The phone rings. 'Fiona's mother-in-law dying made us think,' says the voice at the other end, only partly obscured by the sound of towels snapping and Ewbanks being run over carpet. 'Your father and I can't have long left either, all things considered. Especially your father. He's in a terrible state, really.'

'Mum?' I say, with exaggerated bafflement. 'Is that you?'

'Don't be clever,' she says. 'We need to talk about the Future. We can do it at the weekend. I've already checked your sister can come. We'll make sure we don't die before then. Don't cry.' She rings off.

I stare at the phone for a moment. Then I have a good cry, getting it out of my system before the weekend.

I have a cup of tea and a biscuit.

I cry again, only a small one.

I decide to cheer myself up by going to Jo Malone to buy a candle. I've heard it's a thing people do. The shop is beautiful, immaculate, peaceful – more temple than retailer. I breathe in the gorgeously perfumed air and relax. Then I see the prices. I think I've misread them – maybe I need those varifocals already

– but no. Suddenly I feel like I'm stealing just by breathing the heavily scented air, or – worse – they're going to charge me for the lungfuls I've already taken in. My inner everything is in a panic. I see a shop assistant – they're probably not called that, they're probably Aroma and Conflagration Consultants – coming towards me, so I fake a phone call, surprised expression and back quickly out of the shop. I cannot imagine the amount of money I would need to be earning before I could spend fifty pounds – that's half a hundred pounds! – on a candle. I suspect there is no such amount – I suspect a moral rather than fiscal responsibility switch has been flicked, and I wish I were different. But it's too late now. And at least I've saved myself fifty pounds. And the adrenalin rush has perked me right up. Bargain.

Monday, 2 October

I get up this morning to find that Evie has written a sign on a piece of yellow A4 card and stuck it on the fridge. It reads, in its entirety: 'Macke my life convinyant.'

When she gets up, I point to it and ask what prompted this action.

She shrugs. 'I just thought it would save us all time in the end.'

Friday, 6 October

When Richard gets home from work I go straight to my parents' so we – and Kate, who arrived last night – can Discuss the Future. I am ready. I am braced. I am not going to cry.

'Here,' says Mum, thrusting a page of sticky labels at me as soon as she opens the door. 'Yours are blue. Kate's are red. Put them on anything you want after we die.'

'Where's your money?' Kate yells from the sitting room.

'Don't be cheeky!' Mum yells back.

We join her in the sitting room and, like clockwork, Dad comes through with three large glasses of white and one of red wine on a tray. Like clockwork, my sister and I each lift a white off and Mum takes the other two. She waits till Dad has put the tray on the coffee-table, taken his glasses out of his cardigan pocket and lowered himself into his chair, then hands him the red as soon as he's put his glasses on and she considers him settled for the evening. Forty-three years of marriage distilled into one fluid sequence.

'What's going on?' I say, after a deep preparatory draught of Pinot Grigio.

'What does it look like?' says Mum. 'You pair – go round the house and put your stickers on whatever you want to have after we're gone. Save you a job later. Couldn't be simpler.'

Kate and I look round the sitting room and then – after we've taken in the high-backed, aggressively floral three-piece suite from 1985, the coffee-table and lamps of similar vintage from the Allders department-store sale, thought about the three divan beds upstairs set upon rugs so ugly that we would have trained our pets to ruin them if we had been allowed pets – at each other.

'No, seriously,' my sister says, 'where do you keep the money?'

In the end, as we were lovingly frogmarched round the house by our mother ('Look! Perfectly good antimacassars! And a Ewbank!'), we did find a few things. I chose a lovely water-colour that Dad bought early in their marriage ('It was twenty-three pounds,' he says. 'I had to sell my hair'). Kate stickered a beautiful antique vase he'd bought Mum for her fiftieth birthday ('She told me it would be hell to wash out and to take it back,' he recalls fondly. 'But I'd lost the receipt'). And we tossed a coin for who got the sewing cabinet. It was handmade by Mum's first boyfriend. He wanted it back when she wouldn't marry him. She refused.

'Hundreds of hours I spent making that for our home!' he said.

'Well,' said his former paramour, 'you should have had more sense.' Kate won the toss and I wasn't entirely sorry.

As Kate and I left to go to the pub – to the sound of Dad making his way to bed ('Is that me creaking or the stairs?'), and Mum dragging everything portable and unstickered out to the back garden and torching it with lighter fuel ('No point in it taking up space!'), I thought about how well our choices reflected our parents' natures and relationship. 'Really something to remember them by,' I said, as the flames behind us reached ever higher towards the sky.

'Should we wish to,' said my sister.

Monday, 9 October

At last I have an explanation for that day a few weeks ago when I dropped the kids off at school to find every other child in an inexplicably pristine state. Girls had ponytails or fancy clips in their hair. The boys were walking stiffly around in fresh sweatshirts and polished shoes, clearly under threat – I see now – of dire punishment if either were dirtied too early. I was running even later than usual, so didn't have time to wonder or question – I just threw my two into their respective classrooms and headed for the train.

Now, via the medium of email links to overpriced 6 × 4-inch colour prints, all is revealed. It was school photo day.

In the evening we crank up the ancient iPad and go through them. We have a quick look at Evie's first. Very quick. Her enraged glare would put Medusa to shame. Despite what I suspect were increasingly desperate entreaties from the photographer to smile – or perhaps just look slightly less fixedly contemptuous of humanity – she looks exactly the same in all of them. We tick one at random.

Thomas's take longer, as he has at least changed expression. 'Moron, sunny, sunny moron,' says Richard, as I swipe through. 'Wait, that one's quite nice. And I like the way it captures the felt-tip marks on his face. He looks industrious.'

I swipe again. 'This one really highlights the stains on his sweatshirt,' I note. 'I like the way it says, "Not only does Mummy not mark school dates on the calendar, she will also send me in in any old shit rather than manage a wash before the weekend."' We go back and tick 'sunny moron'.

Then I scrutinise Thomas's whole-class photo – just as I know everyone else will be, for the sado-masochist is strong in all of us – for telltale signs that everyone else is doing better than I am and praying for at least one figure out of thirty that shows me I am not The Worst.

'Those shoes are more scuffed than Thomas's,' I say with satisfaction.

'That's because your mother cannot rest until she has polished his and Evie's every time she sees them. I think it's so she can see their faces in them. Reflect their glory. You really must ask your sister to step up and produce a new grandchild. It's unhealthy.'

'This one's got food round his mouth. But look how clean everyone's hair is! And brushed. And cut within living memory. And they all look as though they can read at red-dot level. And could spell "Thomas" with the s the right pigging way round.'

'Also,' says Richard, rapidly expanding and contracting thumbnails of each of our offspring in turn, 'they're just not very photogenic, our two. Are they?'

This is tricky. Obviously when I look at them I see the most beautiful children who have ever lived. I love their little lips. Their ears are perfection. I think the tiny mole on the edge of Thomas's left nostril is the most endearing, perfectly placed melanin deposit that has ever existed. I love every single one of their eyelashes individually, and I could gaze for hours upon the slight purple tint to Evie's impossibly delicate five-year-old eyelids, if she'd just stay still for long enough. Imagine having eyelids that are just five years old! Amazing! And the identical way their hair whorls out of their crowns means I can be reduced, in weak moments at least, to tears of delight just by staring at the backs of their heads.

But.

There is no denying that (a) I am biased and (b) whatever beauty they do actually have in reality signally fails to make it across the lens. It must be genetic. I look like a fifty-year-old meth addict (which I am not, incidentally) in all photos, and Richard doesn't fare much better. David, meanwhile (Fiona and I always swap links and confer on choices), is a nice-looking boy in real life, but in pictures looks like a Greco-Roman statue: all noble mien, square jaw and a look in his eyes that suggests he is staring out over adoring multitudes, preparing to lead them to better days, a better world. 'How does he do it?' I asked Fiona once.

'I don't know. David?' she called. 'Come here. What were you thinking about when the man took this picture?'

'Teatime,' he said.

'Are you sure?' she asked.

'Yes,' he said simply. 'I'm always thinking about teatime.'

'I read somewhere,' says Richard, 'that they'll Photoshop school photos now.'

'I think you can only Photoshop stuff out – spots, wonky ears, that kind of thing. I don't think you can shop things like health, vitality, an alert and inquisitive air in.'

We buy, for the better part of fifty quid, the necessary for us, Grandma, godparents, and aunt regardless. The records of our children's school careers must be complete. It's just a pity they record my failings in quite such detail too.

Tuesday, 10 October

I'm watching *Friends* for the eighteen billionth time (it's The One Where I Lose Myself In Regret For Not Having Moved to Manhattan For My Twenties) and trying to marvel without envy at how very young and lithe they look, while Richard scrolls through the news on his phone. 'It says in a study here that ladies seeking a male partner are put off by men who are exceptionally handsome. I'm glad you had the courage not to be as other women.'

'I wasn't seeking a partner,' I remind him. 'You just sort of … arrived.'

'Ah, yes,' he said. 'Fiendishly clever of me.'

The next episode up is The One Where I Wonder What Would Have Happened If I Hadn't Taken My Eye Off the Ball.

Saturday, 14 October

Evie's birthday party. Sofia and Amrit are away and we have apologised to Mrs Bradley in advance. She nodded acknowledgement but with the air of someone not unwilling to invoke a formidable curse if pushed much further. As ever, I wish I did not feel as if I were failing her – and somehow her entire generation – at every turn.

We invited twenty-eight children. Twenty-two acceptances were received – mostly yesterday. Thirty-five children turned up. 'So sorry!' say various harried mothers, as they drag uninvited siblings (wildly overexcited if younger, surly and humiliated if older), citing various cancelled sports fixtures, other playdates, errant ex-husbands failing to turn up for handovers, across the threshold. 'I didn't know what else to do.'

'Christ,' says Kate, as we watch a stream of three- to twelve-year-olds rush past us. 'It seems even worse than last time.'

'Everything's always worse than last time,' I say. 'I've made my peace with that now.'

We don't say a lot more for the next two hours. I make up extra party bags, wondering if I can just put cans of lager and some cigarettes in the ones for older kids. Richard (not dressed as a strongman – Evie decided he was 'Too weak. It would be embarrassing') does the bulk of the crowd control, kettling the most determined to break into the room containing the food and corralling the rest towards the Big Top (the sitting room with miles of red and yellow bunting hanging in surprisingly tent-evoking swoops and hanks from the central ceiling light to the edges of the room). It is somewhere between galling and wondrous to watch how much authority he has simply by virtue of being an adult male in the room. He raises his voice a notch and absolute stillness falls. If it were me or any other mother, we would be roundly ignored until the point of nuclear meltdown. Not for the first time I am glad that there is no time to dwell on the millefeuille of injustices before me.

Kate leads the juvenile population through a treasure hunt, a circus-act obstacle course and Pin-the-Tails-on-the-Ringmaster while I deal with the parents. All of whom stay for the full two hours and most of whom have turned up in pairs. 'Why? For the love of God, *why*?' I mutter, as I open prosecco (if they're all staying, it's better that we're all drunk). You only need one and he/she only needs to stay twenty minutes to get the child settled. Then you can go off and have a lovely ninety minutes to yourself! That's coffee-the-paper-and-maybe-a-second-coffee-if-you-fancy-it kind of time! Who gives that up? ('Couples who love each other,' suggests Richard later. 'And/or their children.' He does come out with some shite sometimes.)

Even Savannah is there. 'Oh!' she says, catching sight of all the children clustered round my sister in a top hat in the garden. 'When you said it was a home party, I thought you meant bouncy castles and ball pools and entertainers and things. This is so ... quaint!'

'Shaddup, ya bitch!' I say gaily. No, I don't. But I do say a cheery 'Nope! Far too expensive for a bunch of six-year-olds! The world's gone mad, don't you think?' She looks distinctly – and in my experience unprecedentedly – taken aback. Then I peg it to the kitchen and open more prosecco to cover the sound of my hyperventilation. Nadia, who has witnessed our exchange from afar, wordlessly high-fives me.

The one person I want to be here (apart from my sister, obviously, though I have lost sight of her for a moment and wonder briefly if she's hiding behind the shed attempting to remove her ovaries with a rusty pair of secateurs. If so, I cannot blame her) is not. Fiona's mother is ill so she just dropped off David, threw me a look of deep sympathy and dashed to the hospital.

At one point, when I'm taking a breather, David comes and sits on the decking when he is 'out' at Musical Not Chairs But Those Giant Drum-like Things That Elephants Used to Stand on in Days of Yore. My sister knocked them up out of red crêpe paper and some old cabling reels she had left over after rewiring her village or something. He and I gaze out over the melee. 'It's mayhem, in't it?' he says. 'Mayhem.'

'It is,' I agree. 'But it will be over soon.'

'Let's 'ope,' he says, getting to his feet with a weary sigh. 'Let's 'ope.' His hand on my shoulder as he goes down the decking steps may be just for balance, but there is an ineffable comfort in it nevertheless.

Not soon, it is over. The children eat their stipulated quota of badly cut sandwiches and cheap crisps (I was in charge of savouries) and fall upon the billion cupcakes Kate has made and arranged in a red-and-yellow simulacrum of the simulacrum of the Big Top in the sitting room until there is nothing left but the sound of sugar buzzes and soft weeping and it is time for their mildly pissed parents to take them home. 'Don't thank me!' I say brightly, as they get their coats. 'Just fuck off!' No, I don't. I'm about half a glass of prosecco too short, and I high-five myself for my excellent time–alcohol management.

Afterwards, Kate, Richard and I clear up and collapse. We don't move again until bedtime. Thomas and Evie forage their tea from whatever fell on the floor during lunch. When eventually I can muster the energy, I text Fiona to apologise for not expressing my condolences for her own situation. 'Oh, God, don't worry about it,' she texts back. 'I sat in an armchair for two hours while she slept. She's not dying. It was great. I wouldn't have swapped places with you for a million pounds.'

'Thank you for a brilliant party, Mummy,' says Evie at

bedtime, when we eventually staple her still-buzzing frame to the mattress with croquet hoops. 'I had the *best* time. Did you *see* all the cakes?' Which, of course, makes it all worthwhile.

No, it doesn't. Next year I sell a kidney and we book Laser Quest – *for thirty-five* – or whatever other activity cannot possibly be carried out in a domestic setting with the proceeds. I shall be post-operative and unable to attend. Now that's a happy birthday.

Sunday, 15 October

We were about to start our obligatory evening episode of *The Sopranos*, because Richard says he cannot take me seriously as a person until I have watched it, when a wave of extreme tiredness washes over me. As Richard is yawning fit to beat the band, I suggest we abandon our viewing plans and go to bed early instead.

'Not for sex?' he says, horrified.

'God, no.'

'Okay, then.'

Half an hour later, when we are in bed with the lights out, he says, 'Can I change my mind about the sex?'

'No, I'm sorry. That vagina's sailed.'

'Are you sure?'

'God almighty – all right. As long as I don't have to do anything.'

'No, no, not at all. I'll just empty the pipes, I promise. Thanks.'

'No problem.'

To think there are some who say romance is dead.

Monday, 16 October

Temporary Toddler-Boss is leaving at the end of the week. Proper Boss returns next Monday. The relief all round the office is palpable, at least until we all receive an assessment sheet asking us to 'feed back' on TT-B's strengths, weaknesses, 'potentialities', something called 'actualisation' and, for all I know somewhere in the list of boxes to tick and comments solicited that went on long after I had lost the will to carry on reading, her bra size and preferred method of contraception. I thought for a moment and scrolled down to the final 'Any other comments' section, wrote, 'You're young. But you will learn' and pressed send. Someone else can teach her.

Tuesday, 17 October

'*Yeeeessss!*' I shout, shooting practically vertically up from my seat and punching the air.

The whole family is startled. I am not given to displays of emotion. Positive emotion, anyway.

Three faces look enquiringly at me.

'Claire's had her baby!' I explain, reading the rest of the text that has just come through from her husband, Al. 'Bit early, bit early but a boy, Daniel – good name, good name – seven and a half pounds – that's a good weight, a good weight, at half past five this morning – normal delivery, all's well. Home tomorrow. Yes!'

'That's good,' says Richard. 'Always a relief when everything goes sensibly. Then you've only got the next twenty years to worry about.'

'Can we go and see it?' says Thomas.

'Not right away,' I say. 'But soon.'

'When a lady has a boy,' says Evie, slowly, 'does that mean she's been growing a dinkle inside her?'

'Well, yes,' I say. 'I suppose it does.'

'So you grew a dinkle inside you when you made Thomas?'

'Yes, I suppose I did.'

'That's weird.'

'Yes,' I say. 'I've never thought about it before but I suppose it is.'

'Quite clever, though,' says Richard.

'You're just trying to make her feel better about doing something weird,' says Evie.

On the whole, I wish I'd kept the news to myself for a few minutes' private exultation over the miracle of life, rather than exposing myself to the decidedly non-miraculous world of life after those little bundles of newborn wonder have grown up and learned to speak.

But never mind. Daniel is here. Seven and a half pounds of pure miracle. Home tomorrow.

Friday, 20 October

The doorbell rings. It's Al, standing in the drive, in some disarray, looking lost. It transpires that Claire has sent him out for sushi – after nine months of being deprived of her favourite food she is now craving it more than she ever craved anything during her actual pregnancy – and the nearest place is two streets away from us.

'But I forgot to look up its opening times, because time in our house has no meaning any more,' he explains as he sits, cup of tea in hand, poised on the edge of an armchair to leap up as soon as he must, 'and I'm half an hour early.'

Three days after the birth he still has the glazed, disbelieving look of someone who has witnessed horrors and glories beyond imagination. Which, of course, he has.

He tells us – he has to tell us – about the birth. He tells us about Claire's contractions. 'She was in so much pain she couldn't even speak!' he says, shaking his head.

'I remember,' I say. 'I remember.'

'And then it just gets worse and worse,' he says, shuddering slightly. 'First there's water everywhere. Then blood. Then people start shouting about a head and you think, A head? A head? A head's actually going to come out of – of – of there?'

'You did know where babies come from, right?'

'Yes, yes – but until you're in the middle of it, who really believes that's true? I mean, it's not possible, is it? It's not sensible. It's not feasible.'

I think back and try to summon up the mental position of my dim and distant pre-partum days. It's true. I don't think I ever truly – not truly – believed it actually happened that way either. Though the knowledge has walked beside me, crabbed and dark, every day since. 'You're right.' I sigh. 'You're so right.'

'And then she started pushing. Like – really pushing. Like – we need a new word for "pushing", you know?'

'I do,' I say. 'I do.'

'And then she pushes even more and you think, How are you doing that even more? and then suddenly you're thinking, God – a head! And then you realise, Jesus Christ – shoulders!'

'Yes,' I say. 'Shoulders.'

'And *then*,' he says, eyes widening with remembered shock, 'they cut her! They cut her! With scissors! This is a thing! Did you know this was a thing?'

I nod. I did. I do. I know what an episiotomy is, which is why I can no longer bring myself to say the word.

'And then,' says Al – normally an eloquent and voluble man – struggling for expression, 'and then the baby comes. I mean, it just comes! It was inside, now it's outside. It's like – one minute it's not there and the next minute it's there. Do you know what I mean?'

'I do,' I say. 'I do.'

'And they cut the cord – that's not just something you see in films, they actually cut an actual cord – wipe him off a bit and give him to Claire, and he's outside, just looking at her. And he's about the size of a cat. But he's a child. We've got a child. It makes no sense. And then they wrap him up and give him to me and *it makes no sense.*'

'Nothing will again,' I assure him, lifting my coffee mug in a toast as he drains his tea. 'Nothing will again.'

'And then the next day,' he says, lowering his voice as if he's a KGB operative about to impart state secrets, 'they sent us home! And Claire just walked out. Like a normal person. But she'd just had a baby! I offered to carry her but she looked at me as if I was insane. As if *I* was insane! As if what she'd just done wasn't the most insane thing anyone could ever do! They should carry you all out on golden sedan chairs through streets lined with cheering crowds.'

'And cushions,' I say. 'We want cushions on the sedan chair. We want it to be mostly cushions.'

'Whatever you say,' he says earnestly.

Sunday, 22 October

Half-term begins tomorrow. Determined to keep disruption to a minimum, I made a fish pie to last us two days. I tasted the fish pie. I threw the fish pie in the bin. What is *wrong* with me?

Monday, 23 October

What is the point of half-term? Just nasty, brutish and too short to establish any new routine. Just gums up the works.

Tuesday, 24 October

Does this count as nearly halfway through half-term? Can we say that yet?

Wednesday, 25 October

Halfway. Through. Half-term.

Friday, 27 October

It's over. It is evening. I am nine parts alcohol.

Saturday, 28 October

Richard took the the children off to a museum – Science? Transport? History? Not my business – for the afternoon so I went and got my hair cut. No one has noticed. This is good. I never know why people want others to notice when they've had a haircut. The point of a haircut is unobtrusive improvement and/or restoration to acceptable aesthetic standards. Do other people have better standards? Or better haircuts? I remember the time Savannah bumped into me coming out of the hairdresser and said, 'Oh! Hello! I didn't expect to see you here. I didn't think it was your kind of thing.' So.

Tuesday, 31 October

Everything in me rebels against Halloween and its apparently unstoppable metastasising of this utter crapfest over the last few years. How much do I hate it? With the heat of a thousand burning crêpe-paper pumpkins. Let me count the ways:

1. The oceans of plastic tat to be used once and then discarded – into, ultimately, the bloody oceans themselves. That's one of my favourite things about motherhood, or possibly just modern life, incidentally – the number of overwhelmingly intractable, global anxieties

that wait to rush in to fill the void, should you ever find yourself with a spare second between mere domestic worries. Really terrific, that.

2. The artwork. Specifically, the size of the artwork. Spiders with pipe-cleaner legs, dangling skeletons, witches' hats – the children have come home with all of them and more, and each takes up at least a cubic foot of space plus an extended safety zone to avoid knocking the sodding things to bits. If either of them brings home a broomstick, like Thomas did last year, I'm taking it straight back to school and beating his art teacher to death with it.

3. The hanging of the effing artwork. Spiders and skeletons from the bedroom ceiling, a black sock cat at the end of the bed, pictures of black cats with green tissue-paper eyes on the windows ... I don't have enough time to change a tampon when I need to, but I'm supposed to curate a boutique exhibition every October.

4. Trick-or-treating. Eat sweets! Chat to strangers! We'll deal with the ramifications of the glimmering under-standing this induces that all rules are ultimately manmade and mutable later!

5. The making or buying of costumes for trick-or-treating. Expend time or money, a binary choice that never fails to endear me to any activity.

6. The standing around all evening while trick-or-treating. Because, of course, we don't just let the children go out and chat to strangers. We go with them and stand far enough back to give the kids the illusion of freedom and close enough to pull them away from anyone holding a bucket of sweets too close to his crotch. At least it's too dark for them to see your expression as you mourn the loss of innocence – mostly your own – from the world. Or to catch you eating all the fun-size Mars Bars from their haul.

'You're a joyless freak,' says Richard, as he vigorously revamps last year's ghost costume for Thomas by plastering it with creepy-crawly stickers and some weird fleecy stuff that he and his son are delighting in calling 'ectoplasm'. (Evie's already well-documented animus towards such proceedings having lessened not a whit in the intervening year, she will be accruing her share of trick-or-treat treats in the traditional manner: via basilisk stare in jeans and jumper.)

'I'm not,' I say. 'I just get my joy from seeing them tucked up in bed at night and knowing there's a glass of wine the size of my head waiting for me downstairs. Halloween delays both these things.'

'But the kids love it!' he says, draping more ectoplasm over the white cloth and standing back to admire the effect.

'That annoys me too,' I say. 'It's such a stupid, money-gouging, manufactured festival that I think even a child should be able to see through it.'

'You want to be the mother of an eight-year-old Communist?' he says.

'No, but it wouldn't be all bad.'

'Well, at least I'm around to do the trick-or-treating this year,' Richard says. 'Being married finally begins to pay off, eh?'

'As long as you save me the Mars Bars,' I say.

'But you are sweet enough!' he says.

'Just do it,' I say.

Wednesday, 1 November

As the children eat tea, I try to explain to Evie why it's not a good idea to call Maria, the new girl in their class, Maria Diarrhoea. 'But it rhymes!' she says furiously.

'Maybe so,' I say. 'But it's not kind and it will make her feel bad.'

'Not maybe!' she says. 'Definitely! It definitely rhymes!'

'That doesn't matter,' I say.

'It's a waste not to call her Maria Diarrhoea,' Evie insists.

Richard arrives home in time to gather the gist of what is going on. 'Evie,' he says. 'Do not call her by this name. It is not funny.' I look relieved.

'It is not funny,' he says, 'because – correct me, of course, if I'm wrong – she has not actually done any diarrhoea. To your, to public, knowledge – thereby linking herself inextricably with said substance or misfortune. Has she?'

'No,' says Evie, transfixed by her father's evolving argument.

'Therefore, you are simply noting that her name rhymes with another word. And any fool, Evie,' he says, lowering his voice and inclining his head confidingly towards hers, 'can do that. You – *you* – must wait. In case the glorious day comes, my child, when Maria *does* do diarrhoea.'

He sits back in satisfaction, Evie likewise in awe as the splendour of the vision opens up before her. 'So really,' she says slowly, 'it *would* be a waste to call her Maria Diarrhoea now.'

'Exactly,' he says. They nod at each other, two souls in perfect communion.

I don't know what to say. I just make a mental note to check Evie's bag for laxatives every morning for the rest of the year.

Thursday, 2 November

Nearly upended a table in a café this afternoon when I discovered there were nuts in the brownies and bits – I don't know what of, dates and ginger and other bloody nonsense, I suppose – in their sticky toffee pudding. Why do people fuck about with stuff? And while we're at it, why is everybody putting hamburgers in brioche buns these days? Who the fuck gave them permission to do that? Why not do a steak cupcake? A Barnsley-chop cheesecake? Useless fucks.

Writing this down, it occurs to me that it's possible I have PMT.

Friday, 3 November

This afternoon, Evie had a playdate ('Are you sure it's not a covert meeting to plan the retaking of Stalingrad?' said Richard) so Thomas and I went to the shopping centre to buy him some new trainers, because we can put men on the moon and access all of human knowledge in history through tiny handheld devices that hold more raw technology than the rockets that got them there but we cannot figure out how to make children's shoes that last longer than a fart. Then, as is our tradition, we headed up the escalators to the ersatz American diner that serves what I am assured is the best ice cream with sprinkles in the whole world – 'Mummy, I eshoor you.'

And, as is also traditional whenever the children and I go to the shopping centre, I let him (Evie too if she's there – it is, unfathomably but pleasingly, a delight to them both) go up the stairs that run between the up and down escalators while I kept pace with him on the former (occasionally stepping down sufficiently to allow him to 'win' at the top).

What was not traditional was that on this particular afternoon – one of the literal hundreds I have spent in this shopping centre, on these escalators, with one or other or both of my children over the last eight years – a man (fiftyish, neat, in a suit) drew up on my left-hand side as I watched Thomas to my right, who was pretending to be Howard Carter on his way to discover Tutankhamun's tomb because they are still doing the Egyptians at school. And he started berating me.

'Outrageous!' he said, nodding towards Thomas. 'Outrageous! Across there on his own! What are you thinking? What if he falls? You should think about these things, as a mother!'

As a mother. Only my favourite phrase in the whole world! It's the one that tells you, without fear of doubt, mitigation or redemption, that the person uttering it is a weapons-grade twunt.

He carried on with this as we made what began to feel like very slow progress indeed up towards the diner.

Normally, my instinct when confronted in such – or indeed any – manner, especially in public, is to cower. Apologise. Explain. Normally, a babbling stream of justification and clarification of his misunderstanding of the situation would have poured forth. Normally I would have scrambled to placate this stranger. It doesn't matter how rude or inappropriate you are, I am well trained: I will rush to conciliate. I will probably end up buying you coffee. Richard thinks I'm an idiot. My female friends think I am a product of a culture that teaches us that the best way to survive life is to defuse every potential threat as you go, because they are moulded in the same factory and they behave in exactly the same way. I think probably both are true.

But not today. No explaining to this stranger today that Thomas is the most cautious, sensible child I've ever met and is no more likely to put himself recklessly in danger of falling than a sixty-year-old stalwart of the WI is. No explaining today that my heart is still in my mouth every time he does it because, yes, accidents can happen and because whenever he reaches the little landings that break up the huge run of stairs the top of his little blond head, whose every hair I can identify individually, momentarily disappears from view and even though I know – I KNOW – that no one can have spirited him away, because – and I am ever aware and checking this – there is no one coming in either direction, and I don't believe in ghosts (although they, along with sudden earthquakes and intra-escalator sinkholes do insinuate their way into the rush of torturous imaginings that flood my mind during the half-second I cannot see him, I will admit). No explaining that nevertheless, I have decided that on balance my fears are unreasonable, restrictive and that indulging them would be more detrimental to our lives, his liberty and general happiness than resisting them and so I grant him this boon while I get a grip on myself and prepare for the day when he will want to do something more truly unendurable. Like go on a sleepover (paedophiles, housefire, burglars, sudden-onset fatal allergies), walk to the shops on his own (paedophiles, car accident, sudden-onset fatal allergies, meteor strike, nuclear war) or not let me kiss him while he cleans his teeth (End of Days).

No. I am a woman who has been through a Norfolk café fire and cannot be burned again. I am a woman who has swum in the sea. I am elemental and, crucially, also pre-menstrual. Today he has fucked with the wrong me. I turn on him, intending to deliver a diatribe. One about how the presence of my child on those stairs is the result of one of the eight million conscious and subconscious calculations in seven dimensions I make *as a mother* every single minute of every single day. About how my life *as a mother* is basically a ceaseless parsing of his needs, Evie's, Richard's and mine now, in the future (short, medium and long term even unto death), endlessly and minutely adjusted for impact on others (family, friends and – hey! Strangers), shortness of time, weather, location and an uncountable miscellany of other factors, depending on what that particular day has thrown at me and them thus far. About how my brain *as a mother* makes Deep Blue look like a baby's abacus. I am the *fons et origo* of my family's health and safety, the alpha and omega of everything that has ever and will ever touch them. AS A MOTHER.

Then I looked into his eyes and they weren't angry. They were glittering. With excitement. And I realised that, like most people who unilaterally insert themselves into your life instead of minding their own goddamn business, he wasn't concerned about anyone or anything outside himself: he was just a bully. So I just started shouting. Well, not actually shouting because *as a mother* I didn't want to upset Howard Carter, who was now labouring up the last few steps to King Tut – as my interrogator and I reached the top. But I snarled. I'm pretty sure I bared my teeth, but I definitely snarled in glorious, heartfelt fury, 'Who do you think you are? What gives you the right to say anything, *anything at all*, to me? How dare you? Who are you to me? WHO ARE YOU?' He actually backed down. Literally, he backed down the steps and stared gobsmacked at me as I rose above him, glared down and, with an inward convulsion and the outward confidence of a Wimbledon champion about to deliver match point, told him, 'Just FECK OFF.'

I gathered Thomas and we went off to the diner. And, let me tell you, ice cream never tasted sweeter.

Saturday, 4 November

Period has arrived. Normal service has resumed. Passengers, please have a pleasant flight. For the next twenty-three to thirty-five days, at least.

That said, the warm glow of backing that man TF down has not left me. Normally I'd try to dampen those embers, but I think this time I'll let them smoulder. Who knows when I might need them to ignite into righteous fury again? Quite a useful resource, really.

Sunday, 5 November

'Come on!' I cry, as I check everyone has their hat, coat, scarf, gloves and wellies on. 'Let's *go*!' I rush to the door and throw it open, fibrillating with excitement.

'What's wrong with Mummy?' Thomas whispers to Richard, a concerned look on the fraction of his face I have left uncovered.

'Nothing,' murmurs Richard. 'She's just happy, that's all.'

'Why?' asks Evie.

'I love Bonfire Night, that's why! Now, let's *go*!'

It's true. I do. It speaks to my very soul. Autumn is the best season anyway. Mists, mellow fruitfulness, all that. A chill in the air, jumpers on, 60-denier tights from M&S's Varicosal range, proper food – it has everything wonderful. It's a warmly welcoming embrace and I sink increasingly gratefully into its soft bosom after the unforgiving brutality of summer, season of sweat, children too hot to sleep, endless inner-thigh chafing and foot-shredding sandals. I literally don't make it to the end in one piece. And you're expected to think salad is a legitimate meal. I never understand that. The days are still the same length – no, longer! – yet people look askance if you still want to eat more than lettuce and tomatoes. GTFO.

Autumn looks after me. And at the very point when it might occasionally begin to drag, it gives me Bonfire Night: the primal pleasure of fire, the deep joy of reaching back through history to a pivotal (if anti-Catholic, sorry, Mum, sorry, Dad) moment, and the iridescent, ephemeral, unspeakable beauty of fireworks. And then home for BAKED POTATOES. Of all these delights, the last shall always be first in my heart.

'I'm boiling,' says Evie, as we stomp up the hill towards the firework display in the park. Grandma and Granddad are meeting us there. They used to come to the house first and walk with us, but Dad has not been up to it for the past couple of years. I banish this thought, along with all the others about what the future holds for my parents, to the outer reaches of my mind and ignore the crinkling path of anxiety it leaves in its wake. Fire may be a primal pleasure but this is not the night for giving in to primal fears.

'You're not boiling,' I say to Evie.

'I am,' she says.

She's quite right. We are all boiling. Dress for the Bonfire Night you want, is my motto, not the Bonfire Night you've got, and the Bonfire Night I want is one from the 1950s, before global warming got its claws in and ruined everything.

'Don't spoil Mummy's night,' says Richard. 'Boil quietly.'

'No, it's all right,' I say, looking at the three red faces in front of me. 'You can take stuff off. Just the minimum, though. I want to keep the dream alive.'

The children fling various woollen items at me and run ahead to the park entrance, where they have spotted Grandma and Granddad, Fiona, Iain and David waiting. The nine of us – three children and six adults! Luxurious ratio! – enter the maelstrom of people, burger vans, hot cider and rum toddy dispensaries, toddlers gazing from buggies in bewilderment at being up this late, children waving glow-sticks and assorted other modern aberrations that cause Richard to squeeze my hand in silent sympathy. 'Look!' he says, a few minutes later, bending down and stretching his arm along my eyeline to point in the desired direction, as you would with a particularly young or dim-witted child. 'There's a cinder toffee stand! Concentrate on that. No. No, no one has ever known what "cinder toffee" actually means.' The sound of excited chatter, overtired screaming, fairground tunes from the assortment of miniature rides around the perimeter of the park and pop music from the speakers everywhere else engulfs us.

Over the course of the evening we bump into just about everyone from school – Savannah greets us in so many layers of fine-knit autumn chic that she looks like a pile of cashmere leaves – but fortunately it's too noisy to engage in conversation, and then the fireworks start.

They just blast cynicism away, don't they? So incredible, so beautiful. Thomas and David are entranced from the off, Evie succumbs after a minute and even the teenagers lining the display area gradually shut off their phones and turn their faces to this ineffable joy.

On the way home, Granddad tells the children about the old days and how he and his friends would spend all week before Bonfire Night making a guy. 'That sounds very boring,' says Evie.

'It was,' says Granddad. 'But then we used to take it out in a cart round different streets and ask for a penny for the guy. "Penny for the guy?" we'd say.'

'A penny's not very much,' says Thomas.

'It was then,' says Granddad. 'You used to be able to buy a portion of chips for a penny and still have change for your TB medicine.'

'Was it begging?' Evie says.

'In a way I suppose it was, yes.'

'I'm going to do it next year,' says Evie, decisively. 'I like chips. But I'm going to ask for ten pounds. Otherwise it's a waste of time.'

I open my mouth to protest about seventeen different issues raised by the last few minutes' conversation. But I close it again. Next year is a long way off and with any luck she will have forgotten all about it without me needing to play the heavy. If Guy Fawkes teaches us nothing else, it's the importance of keeping your powder dry.

Monday, 6 November

Oh, my *God*. It's started. I knew we were living on borrowed time, but it hadn't made me any better prepared. Yesterday Thomas came home and said, 'Mummy – Bailey doesn't want to be my friend any more.'

The world started whirling round me. My own childhood memories came rushing back to me, warping time and space until all collapsed in upon itself. By the time the sentence ended my eyes saw not the chubby, ruddy face of my own offspring, but a hollow-cheeked, wide-eyed mask of infinite sorrow. He appeared to me like a Manga Oliver Twist, with a hefty dose of recently orphaned Bambi thrown in.

My mind started frantically paging through the snapshot images of Thomas's classmates. Which one was Bailey? Which was the face of pure evil? And what kind of a bloody name was 'Bailey' anyway? Ah, yes, the blond one who always has the proper crested sweatshirt on. Ha! What price your fully organised wardrobe and robust laundry system now, Mrs ... Mrs ... Mrs Bailey's Mother, when you have birthed a monster?

But motherhood is defined by controlled schizophrenia, so I outwardly betrayed nothing. My voice stayed as neutral as my enquiries while the maternal hell-beast within paced and roared and whetted its primal tusks for battle.

'Oh, really?' said Outer Mummy. 'What did Bailey say?' I WILL RAZE HIS HOME TO THE GROUND.

'That he doesn't want to be my friend any more.'

I WILL EAT HIS HEART.

'Oh,' said Outer Mummy. 'Did he say why?' DOES HE HAVE ANY PETS? I WILL KILL ALL HIS PETS.

'No. I think Andrew or Evan made him say it. He's friends with them now.'

Andrew, I remember Andrew. I should have hunted him down and staked him out in the broiling sun then. Consider his card doubly marked. But Evan. Evan. I don't know an Evan. He probably wears a disguise every day the better to carry out his foul play.

IT DOESN'T MATTER WHO HE IS. WE WILL FIND HIM AND WE WILL DISEMBOWEL HIM. MY FOCUS AND THE BURNING HEAT THAT WILL BE SLAKED BY VENGEANCE ONLY DOES NOT SPLIT BUT DOUBLES. AND I KNOW WHO ANDREW IS. HE IS THE ONE WHO CALLED YOU TOMMYMAS AND I BRUTALLY, CALLOUSLY, UNFORGIV-ABLY DISMISSED YOUR PLIGHT, AND THE GUILT WILL MAKE ME PUNISH HIM TENFOLD.

'Did he' – hey, look at me folding this washing so calmly and neatly! – 'or they do anything else?' BECAUSE IF THEY DID IT WILL BE THE LAST THING. IT WILL BE THE VERY LAST THING.

'When I tried to play with them at playtime, Andrew went backwards and pushed me away with his bum, like this.'

MY HEART IS BREAKING AND THE LOVE FOR YOU THAT POURS OUT BURNS LIKE ACID THROUGH MY INSIDES. I'M GOING TO HOLD YOU IN MY ARMS FOR EVER. WE WILL NEVER LEAVE THIS HOUSE AND THE BAD, BAD WORLD WILL NOT TOUCH YOUR TENDER FLESH NOR MARK YOUR TENDER SOUL.

'I see. Well, I think perhaps the best thing to do is to ignore those silly boys' – WHILE MUMMY FINDS OUT WHERE THEY LIVE AND WHERE SHE CAN BUY CHEESEWIRE – 'and play with someone else for a bit.'

SHE MAY NEED TO DIG A BIG PIT TOO.

'But why does he not want to be my friend any more?'

BECAUSE THE WORLD IS DARK AND INFINITELY CRUEL, A VALE OF MONSTROUS DEPREDATIONS AGAINST INNOCENCE AND RIGHT.

'Well, because Bailey maybe thinks that you're only supposed to have one friend at a time and he hasn't learned that he can have two, or three, or even more' – hey, listen to this light, tinkling new laugh I've got! Ignore the blood coming from my ears! – 'friends and that that's great.'

HE DIES TONIGHT.

'Can I have a biscuit?'

YOU CAN HAVE ANYTHING. I WOULD RAID THE SUN FOR YOU.

'No, it's nearly teatime.'

BUT I'M NOT GOING TO MAKE YOU EAT THE PEAS! I'M NOT GOING TO MAKE YOU EAT THE PEAS!

'Hmmpf. Going to do a poo now. You will have to check my poo-hole afterwards.'

'I will. Listen, does Bailey have a pet, d'you know? No? Okay. Well, probably best. Probably best.'

I report everything to Richard in the evening and, after he's checked me for grappling irons and blueprints of the boys' houses ('No balaclava or plastic gloves either, good') and calmed me down, he says it sounds like kids being kids but that he will quiz ('Gently,' he promised. 'Casually. With no more force or intrusion than the grass feels when the sunshine falls upon it on a fresh spring morn') Thomas next time they are alone together. Which I have arranged to be over tea tonight.

Quiztime is over. Thomas told Richard nothing more than he'd already told me and seems to be quite recovered, so I have agreed to leave it for now.

'But if it happens again ...' I warn.

'I will hand you the gloves and balaclava myself,' he promises.

Okay, then.

Thursday, 9 November

I have watched Thomas like a hawk (but cleverly, covertly – obviously I don't want him alerted to my concern or feel the death-wishes pulsing from me whenever I think of Andrew, Bailey or Evan) but there are no further signs of distress, so I have renewed my vow to Richard to say nothing as yet. I have been doing a lot of swimming. I find myself front-crawling at unprecedented speed through my lengths, so I will at least be fitter if I have to go to prison for murder.

Friday, 10 November

I cannot face any of the 687 things on my to-do list, so I decide that I have restrained myself long enough and, after ringing her with the proposal, set off to visit Claire and baby Daniel. Tom is back at work, her parents have left, and Claire says the house is ready for visitors and she is desperate for company. I remember those first brutal weeks of enforced solitude well.

I shudder to remember the see-the-newborn visits I made before I had kids of my own. I used to sit there politely, admiring the baby, having a little hold and studiously ignoring the disastrous state of the house. I didn't know that all the rules change when you have a baby – even and especially the ones about a woman's home being her castle. In the usual run of things you don't – ever – comment on the state of another person's house. Even noting that it looks really clean and tidy only throws up the unspoken fear that every other time you have come round you have secretly been thinking it should be the subject of a Channel 4 documentary. But once the domestic overseer is pinioned beneath maternal cares and woe, judgements spoken and unspoken are as naught. If you smile and wordlessly go about simply making things look, smell, work, simply be in any way better, she will love you for ever.

I used to take champagne, posh chocolates, flowers. Now

I take posh ready meals (and make sure I put some in the fridge and some in the freezer as soon as I arrive) and large slabs of Dairy Milk. And no flowers. Flowers require you to find a vase and arrange them at a time when you can't find your own face or a moment to go to the loo. I used to ask if there was anything I could do to help. Now I know just to get on with whatever needs doing. Baby asleep? Tell mother to go upstairs and nap. Tidy, wash up while she's gone. Baby awake but happy? Tell mother to go and have a shower. Keep baby entertained, ideally by your joviality as you wipe down surfaces sticky with substances long past easy recognition, empty the dishwasher, put a wash on or tackle some ironing (babies are so stupid – they'll watch any new activity as enthralled as if it were a new episode of *Fleabag*! Press this advantage. Along with some shirts). Baby breastfeeding? Position pint glass of water by mother's freest hand and get on with tidying, washing-up (vacuuming too if given the nod – some babies enjoy the white noise, some react as if you've just detonated a nuclear bomb beside them. And they bite down hard when affrighted). Mother and baby keen to go out for a walk? Help her pack the house into the changing bag, re-certificate yourself in pram engineering and get it ready, take the keys yourself, make sure she's got both boobs in her bra and the majority of any buttons anywhere done up, and go. Mother unable to let go of precious babe? Admire from afar while cleaning, tidying and washing-up. Mother desperate to let go of precious but life-draining babe? Pack house into the changing bag, put baby in pram, promise you will be back in not less than half an hour. Do not come back in less than half an hour.

The friends who do any of this are the ones you love and swear to cherish all the days of your life – and to repay the favour as soon as your life gets back to normal or they need help in their nursing homes, whichever comes first. In the meantime, until you can reciprocate directly, you have the simple duty to pass it on.

On my way to Claire's I think back to my babies' early weeks. Those weeks of feeding them every ten minutes, changing them every five and wondering when I would get the chance to do likewise. It was somewhere between war and penal servitude. Full reconstruction is difficult, though I do remember insisting on continuing to read the thousand-page novel (I'd like to claim it was Proust or one of the Russians but it was Edward Rutherfurd's *London*) that I'd foolishly started in my eighth month of pregnancy. It felt like my last link with the old, normal me and I wouldn't even let Richard download me an e-version onto the Kindle so I could at least have held it easily while breastfeeding. My brain must have been as broken as my vagina.

With Thomas, my mother kept saying how lucky I was to have such an easy baby. I, leaking from at least three different parts of my body at all times and well on the way to postnatal depression, did not agree entirely with this claim, but later I realised she was right. He fed well. There were no endless nights of inexplicable crying. No extensive, soul-destroying bouts of colic. He only cried if he was hungry ('What, again?') or if I had left him sitting in his own wee and poo for eight hours because – it turns out – nappies are by far the easiest thing to forget about. Even if, for the first few weeks at least, you've had to wear them yourself.

Evie was an entirely different story, but she had been such a comparatively easy birth that I forgave her everything.

I get to Claire's and ring the doorbell. She answers within five minutes, which is a good sign. When she sees me, she thrusts the baby at me, bursts into tears and slides down the wall until she is sitting, legs straight out in front of her, in the hall. This is a bad sign. Though at least she can sit.

I shut the door and join her on the floor, baby safely tucked in the crook of my arm. You forget how light and small they are ('Like oversized gerbils,' Richard once said, gazing adoringly at his infant daughter, which made me laugh, then cry, then laugh, as most things then did). I put the other arm round her and she cries on my shoulder.

'Is it anything in particular?' I say.

'No,' she sobs.

'Okay,' I say, and wait. I start to rock the three of us slightly from side to side. The baby's eyes close.

'It's just I'm very tired!' she wails.

'Yes,' I say.

'So tired!'

'Mm-hmm.'

'And I love him *so* much that I keep wanting someone to shoot at us so I can take a bullet for him and prove it.'

'Mm-hmm.'

'And at the same time I could leave him in a skip and just go to bed.'

'That's okay,' I say. 'That's normal.'

'It's not, though,' she cries, sobbing harder than ever.

'It totally, totally is, I promise you.'

I tell her all the things I used to fantasise about when I was sleep-deprived, stressed, hormonal and had just had my entire personality reconstituted round the two poles of undying love and grinding misery. I used to dream that the baby would be taken away for anything from twenty-four hours by a parade of Norland Nannies (muttering calculations under my breath to try to work out how we could afford it if we really, really had to) to a lifetime by a pack of kindly wolves. 'I didn't really see how they'd do a worse job than I was,' I explain. 'I was quite philosophical about it.'

Gradually Claire calms down. 'Thanks,' she says. 'Sorry. Thanks. Sorry.'

'*De rien*,' I say. 'Shall we try getting off the floor now? Or is that still a bit much to ask? I don't mind. It's quite comfortable down here.'

'Let's try it,' says Claire. 'See how we get on.'

We help each other up. The baby doesn't wake. 'Ooh,' winces Claire, after a few moments on her feet. I know that face. It's the face you pull when blood is rushing back into your recently battered nethers. We look at each other, knowing there is no need to explain why we have to wait a few moments more before she can start to walk.

'Okay,' she says eventually. 'Ready. As I'll ever be.'

Saturday, 11 November

I consult my lists and maps. I check the weather. I carb-load. I put an isotonic drink in my bag, a rucksack on my back and trainers on my feet. The family wave me off at the front door, with cries of 'Good luck!' and – from Evie – 'Don't come back soon!'

This is my Christmas shopping weekend. It just gets done. I literally plot a route through London that takes in all the shops I need according to that year's requests and requirements in the shortest time possible. I have one for Saturday and one for Sunday and I get it done. It is my one and only dependable feat of organisation and it happens because the alternative – rushing around buying the wrong and more expensive stuff in desperation at the last minute – is so very, very, very much worse.

Of course there are still better ways of doing it. Céline buys everything online. I do that with the big specific stuff, like Evie's bike this year or Thomas's Transformers. But for anything else, you can only get away with it if, like Céline, you have an innate sense of style and know instinctively from the most cursory glance at a thumbnail picture on screen that that particular pink jumper, that specific scarf or purse or tie or pair of earrings will transform its recipient's life. If I tried it, all I would be doing would be adding to someone's Boxing Day returns bundle. Céline also culls her present list each year, cutting out anyone who failed to thank her properly the previous December and thus keeps her purchasing duties lighter and more pleasurable than anyone else's. She is so thrillingly ruthless. Fiona buys things that catch her eye all year round and then divvies up whatever she finds in her present box according to what comes closest to suiting each person. 'If everyone's eighty per cent happy without having given me a nervous breakdown in the process,' she reasons, 'my job is done. Do you want soap again this year or a nice picture frame?'

Nadia, God love her, makes things. 'But I enjoy it!' she says, when we open our hand-tied parcels containing exquisitely knitted this or embroidered that or bags containing bottles of handmade sloe gin and weep over the love and effort that has gone into everything. 'And it's not hard! I do it while I'm watching the telly. It's relaxing!' I suppose you have to believe people when they tell you these things, however hard it is.

Sunday, 12 November

I retire, still undefeated, from the Christmas fray. I am a champion.

Tuesday, 14 November

Halfway through tea, Thomas gets up and announces he's off to do a poo to make room to finish the rest of his pizza. In both these endeavours, he succeeds.

Thursday, 16 November

Just a shit day. Drowning in emails, laundry, unmade beds, felt-tip-pen marks that need to be cleaned off inappropriate surfaces, meals that need to be thought of, bought for and made, juvenile nails that have to be cut, baths that need to be run and squirming bodies to be washed.

I remember – I cling to the memory of – the first time Thomas ever got himself a drink. He found a plastic cup, took it to the tap, turned it on, filled the cup and drank as I, mesmerised, watched. It was as if the clouds parted and the sun shone down, lighting an unsuspected expanse of broad, verdant uplands across which a tiny, distant figure ran free of the burden of petty maternal duties.

They closed again when he spilled the water on the floor and onto Henry, who shot up and onto the windowsill, dashing two plant pots and seventeen cubic metres of soil across the kitchen. But I had seen a glimpse of the Promised Land. I know it's there. And it will come again.

Saturday, 18 November

It's happening. Richard and I are going out. 'Out-out?' asked Fiona.

'Out-out,' I confirmed.

'Why?'

'It's our wedding anniversary, apparently.' He remembered at the last minute and started shouting in a panicked fashion about how it was *appalling* that neither of us had realised, and we *must* do something otherwise *decay* would set in and we would be divorced within the decade. I'm still on a bit of a sticky wicket, marital ceremony-wise, because of my whole 'hated my wedding day' slip, so I agreed without too much of a fight.

He is now ready to leave. Which is to say, he has put his shoes on, run a hand through his hair, glanced in the mirror and pronounced himself ready to leave.

I am still standing in front of my wardrobe trying to decide what to wear. The image in the full-length mirror and I eye each other in silent mutual reproach. An old joke always starts to play itself on a loop at this point in my efforts, the one about a traveller in Ireland asking directions of an old man about how to get to the village of Ballybegorrah. 'Well,' says the old fellow. 'I wouldn't start from here.'

To the untutored eye, I actually have quite a large collection of nice dresses – classic pieces from pre-children days (they no longer fit), plus a variety of others bought for around three to five years from now, depending on how ragged the kids have run me. That is, I calculate, when I will have the time and inclination to climb out of jeans and sweatshirts and into garb that doesn't throw a pall of depression over everything within a five-foot radius, including its wearer.

But that day is not yet here. Instead, the overstuffed rail is effectively empty. I rifle through it, mentally discarding outfits as I go, on grounds including but not limited to:

1. Stains
2. Too big (me)
3. Too small (it)
4. Need bigger boobs (me)
5. Just not in the mood
6. Needs heels
7. Needs the bra I can't find
8. Right for summer, wrong for coverage of toneless, ageing, pallid flesh
9. Right for winter, right for coverage. Basically a Slanket and wrong for outdoor consumption
10. Would look better on someone else

I am dog-tired, but have managed to have a shower and blow-dry my hair so I am determined to see this through and realise my investment. The thought of a meal I haven't cooked myself spurs me on too.

In the end I settle on black maternity jeans that manage to be both sturdy yet forgiving and a drapy top that reveals a bit of skin (safe collarbone area) and will fool Richard into thinking we're having a good time.

'Jeans and a nice top,' I murmur to my reflection in the mirror. 'Kill me now.'

I put flat shoes on and heels in my bag. I look again at my reflection, trying to imagine what I would think if I saw someone else looking like this. 'Drily witty best friend to cougar protagonist in Netflix Original comedy? Or the cover star of a clinic pamphlet about the perimenopause?' I look presentable and feel like crying.

Fortunately, the voice of my mother comes echoing down from my teenage years to help me. 'Who,' resounds the voice of yore, 'is going to be looking at you?' I am bolstered. I put on makeup. It, too, makes me feel better. People call it warpaint for a reason, I guess, and it works best when the war is with yourself.

I am so flushed with success – and Boots No7's Flushed Success – that I even put my flats in my bag and change into my heels so that I can greet Richard in the living room in full regalia.

I go arse over tit as I step across the threshold. 'Oh, for fuck's sake,' I snarl, as I grab my ankle tightly and rock against the pain. My flats have spilled out of my bag and lie before me in mute reproach.

'Ready to go?' enquires Richard, as he helps me up and keeps hold of my arm as I test my weight on my stupid ankle. 'Maybe in the shoes you can stay upright in? You always look like a newborn fawn trying to stagger across a restaurant in those anyway. I always worry someone's going to try to shoot you or put you in a nature documentary. And filming hours are awful. You look smashing, by the way. I like that top. And your face. But I always like your face.'

'Let's go,' I say. 'Get this over with.'

'That's the spirit,' says Richard, gathering up my bag while I test my ankle. 'Onward, Bambi! Let's get some drink in you.'

Sunday, 19 November

We had, actually, a nice night. Mrs Bradley nodded approvingly at us as we left. We found out what each other was doing at work. We planned a family trip to the Tower of London, where he will tell the children all about its history and architecture, and I will wander round pretending I am a princess imprisoned there but treated with every courtesy, given all my books and served three unassuming but decent meals a day. We talked about the children and how he is not sure that Evie's new propensity for calling him 'Brah' ('I think it's some kind of street salute') is not affording him the relief he thought her moving on from his previous title of 'Fat Dad' would.

Home by ten, only tipsy, in bed by half past, no sex, asleep by eleven, no hangover this morning. Brilliant. Almost worth doing again next year.

Tuesday, 21 November

I ask Thomas if Andrew and his henchmen (I don't say henchmen) are behaving themselves better now. Yes, he tells me. All is well.

Evie's head whips round and her mouth opens. Then her eyes narrow and she closes it again. She returns to colouring more viciously than before.

I send Thomas to get a clean tea-towel from the airing cupboard and turn purposefully towards his sister. 'What do you know about those boys and Thomas?' I say.

'Nothing,' she says. I wait, with an expression on my face that I can only muster when I am really Not Messing About Here.

Evie exhales exasperatedly. 'Fine! They keep teasing him and shoving him around because Thomas took one of the pink throwing beanbags in PE.'

Seeing my bafflement, Evie appends an explanation. 'Only girls take the pink ones.'

'But that's ridiculous!' I say.

'I know,' says Evie. 'But they were the only ones left. What was he supposed to do?'

'No, I meant—'

Thomas returns with the tea-towel. Our discussion for now is at an end.

I send an email to Thomas's teacher, asking if I can have a word with her tomorrow.

Wednesday, 22 November

His teacher says she will keep an eye on things but 'Boys will be boys!' Not filled with confidence, I say, 'Thomas is a boy. He doesn't pick on others or think pink things are for girls.' She smiles distractedly and says she has after-school homework club to go and supervise, reiterates that she'll keep an eye, and leaves.

I let out a strangulated cry of frustration this evening when Netflix failed to work ('Error: Nothing demonstrably wrong. I'm just not working. Please try again later. No, that's all. Just try again later').

> EVIE (conversationally, looking up from arc-welding a 1:250 scale replica of the Forth Bridge): Who peed in your tea?
> ME AND RICHARD: What?/Where did you hear that?
> EVIE (shrugging): Nowhere.
> ME: You mean you just made it up?
> EVIE: Yup.
> RICHARD: Well, don't say it again.
> EVIE: Why not?
> ME: It's a bit rude.
> EVIE: No, it's excellent. And I will say it again.
> RICHARD: No, you won't.
> EVIE: I will, though.
> RICHARD: Not if I say you won't, you won't.
> EVIE (gently, as if dispelling an unfortunate misunderstanding): Yes, I will.
> RICHARD (brokenly): Only in this house, to family.
> EVIE (considering): And to Grandma and Granddad, here or at their house.

RICHARD: Okay. But nowhere and no one else.

EVIE: Okay.

RICHARD: Promise me?

EVIE (rolling her eyes): I promise. Tch – who peed in *your* tea?

Thursday, 23 November

I am sitting in front of the PTA Christmas questionnaire, trying not to cry. 'The season is upon us!' it begins, joyfully. 'How can YOU best help your little one(s) enjoy the festivities at school? Please tick the relevant boxes below.'

I know what follows. There will be a section on the Christmas fete/fair/possibly fayre:

1. How many of the following can you provide?
   a) Pre-loved toys in a good state of repair. Really good. Remember, the PTA largely comprises stay-at-home mothers of a certain tax bracket and we will be judging. You might want to consider buying some new ones and just taking the tags off.
   b) Books – see above. This is not an opportunity for decluttering. You can get that idea out of your head. We're not here to help.
   c) Raffle and class hamper gifts. Suggestions: beauty products, Christmas delicacies, bottles of wine (champagne also welcome, prosecco acceptable – we'll drink it at the committee meetings. Waitrose Extra Dry preferred).
   d) Blood.
   e) Sweat.
   f) Tears.
   g) Bunting.
   h) Homemade cakes, biscuits, brownies, meringues, muffins, macaroons, *macarons* and traybakes,

including gluten-free, nut-free, dairy-free, flour-free, egg-free and sugar-free varieties. The days of adding a tin of Golden Syrup to a box of own-brand cornflakes are over, you lazy dog.

2. Can you help set up beforehand?
3. Clear up afterwards?
4. Man a stall?
5. You haven't ticked anything yet. Did you know?
6. Don't you feel you should be trying a bit harder at this whole mothering thing?
7. Hmm?

There will be a section on the school nativity play:

1. Can you spare 87 hours to come and make costumes with us at whoever's got the most recently decorated house she wants to show off? Or can you paint sets in the hall next weekend? Mr Handsome will be there, though not to help.
2. Can you help set up on the day?
3. Can you help clear up afterwards?
4. Free will is an illusion, you know.
5. Are you aware you still haven't ticked anything?
6. Shouldn't you be better organised than this?
7. Why not just take a day off work? We are SAHMs of a certain tax bracket and have no idea what this means.

To quote the baby Jesus a little later on in life: Oh, God, oh, God, why hast thou forsaken me?

I tick nothing. I will dig out all the pre-loved items that I can, help out if I'm free, and buy some stuff for hampers and raffles and the other shit, but I do not live a life that admits advance box-ticking. I shove the form into the bin on my way to bed. Like my ideal children at teatime, they will get what they're given and like it.

At teatime Evie and Thomas object vociferously to the chicken nuggets and mash they have eaten nine thousand times before and I end up making macaroni cheese.

I lie awake for two hours. I get up. I dig the form out of the bin. I scribble 'Whatever you need – let me know!' across the bottom and ram it into Thomas's backpack. I go back to bed. What else, really, can you do?

Friday, 24 November

'We've got the bloody monkey,' says my husband, throwing himself down on the sofa in despair.

'No!'

'Yes.'

It is Friday. My husband has just brought Thomas home from school and Chunky the bloody Monkey is in tow. This is the soft toy one child a week, of those who have succeeded in remaining on the Happy Face from Monday to Friday, is allowed to bring home and co-habit with for a week. For the child, he is the nonpareil of rewards. Forget stickers, certificates, merit badges, Golden Tickets and whatever the hell else school is currently using to shore up the wall between basic discipline and all-out anarchy. Chunky Monkey is the only prize they truly covet.

For parents, Chunky Monkey is the very devil. For Chunky Monkey has to keep a diary – a minimum of two pages of writing, artistic decoration and photographic proof – of all that he does on his five days with you, and competition to produce the best entry is stiff.

The pressure is on to make your child write more than the last, to outdo the last page of drawings and to paste in photos of you all having terrifically fun-yet-educational trips all effing weekend. If you have a glamorous or high-powered job, you bring him into work with you and take shots of you both at glamorous events or in meetings full of cowed underlings clearly at your command.

For a pair of congenitally unglamorous shut-ins like me and my husband, the prospect is unspeakable.

'Look at this,' says my husband, paging through the book. 'This child's written six paragraphs! That's *Moby-Dick* for an eight-year-old! This child's written *Moby-Dick*! In copperplate! And look at this! A watercolour of Hampton Court!'

'It's not. You're exagg— Oh.'

'We'll be lucky if he slaps a few Transformers stickers on the right way up.'

Parents in PR generally manage to snap Chunky with a Z-list celeb or two. Lawyers and the like prefer to take them on the train, with Chunky leaning over the paperwork they're already doing because they're so busy and efficient. Richard can do this if he can stay awake. His ability to sleep anywhere at any time extends easily to packed mass-transit systems.

To be honest, I'm more intimidated by the domestic ones. Here's Chunky 'n' child eating healthy snacks together. There's the pair of them reading ('Where's the telly? Search the other photos') or sitting together at a family mealtime round a table ('This one's got a cloth and napkins and everything! And look at the time on the oven – five o'clock! Why do we never manage tea at five o'clock? Why are we always screaming at them to get their chicken nuggets down their necks because it's bedtime?' 'I don't know! Why are you screaming at me, now?'). Savannah has managed to get one of the family all adorably in bed together one morning, but with a pair of black heels and lingerie just edging blurrily into shot. Nice.

'It comes down to this,' says my husband, after some thought. 'We either play the game and go all in – day trips, book him into after-school cor anglais and artisanal baking classes, do pictures of a Sunday roast with Latin worksheets and bank statements with extra zeroes Photoshopped in casually scattered in the background, me sneaking him into some shiny office and pretending its mine, you faking whatever the charity sector's version of a TED talk is, finding some oblique way to suggest we have regular intercourse—'

'I could write "I'm permanently aroused by the way he never calls it 'regular intercourse'," on the doctored bank statements?'

'—and paying Thomas in iPad minutes to write it up until his fingers drip blood. OR we can stand firm, opt out of the whole crazy business, and just record the simple truth: we do shit-all and even that not well.'

We look at each other and sigh. It's going to be a long week.

Saturday, 25 November

While I am busy cleaning the loo and mentally resolving once again to destroy the myth of the Toilet Fairy once and for all, possibly via a terse email that can be reverted to when reminders are needed thereafter that it is indeed a human woman who has to chip actual shit off an actual toilet pan if shitters don't scrub it as soon as they've shat – wait, where was I? Oh, yes – while I am busy cleaning the loo, Thomas and Evie take it upon themselves to ask Mrs Bradley if they can take a photograph of Chunky Monkey 'relaxing' in her garden. '"Because," I said, "you've got flowers and things that are alive in yours,"' Evie tells me, when asked how she went about this feat of persuasion. 'If he was in ours he wouldn't be relaxed, he'd be depressed.'

By the time I'd finished playing stonemason with my family's faecal deposits, they had been over there Lord Snow-doning it up with my phone for a good half-hour.

'I'm so sorry,' I say, hurrying over to the fence and preparing to yank them back over by the scruffs of their necks. 'I just turned my back for five minutes and ...'

Mrs Bradley pauses in her pruning and looks at me sternly. 'They have been No Trouble At All,' she says. 'They are,' she points her secateurs at me, 'Good Children. I wouldn't have allowed them over here otherwise.'

I literally cannot speak. I gape.

'When I was wee,' she says, still pointing the secateurs, 'my mother had a whole street of friends and family, all looking after each other. You girls, these days, you've nothing compared to that. And you do very well.'

'Th-thank you,' I manage. She nods and returns to her roses.

I retreat to the kitchen and collapse into a chair, reeling at the shock of this unexpected benediction. I don't really know what to do with myself. How often do you get compliments about your children from people who not only have no reason to lie – or even sugar-coat things for you – but who also give every impression of being constitutionally incapable of doing so?

'I think,' I say out loud, some minutes later, the better to try to make it real, 'that I might have to believe it.'

I stay in the chair until a very long spell of dizziness passes.

Sunday, 26 November

Email from Savannah saying Fiona and I are to manage one of the mince pie and mulled wine stations at the Christmas fete (which is now the Winter Snowflake A-Fayre, for reasons that passeth understanding). *Great!* Fiona texts me. *We can shove a tenner in the box and eat mince pies and drink mulled wine all morning.* Suspect Savannah will have installed surveillance to prevent this kind of dereliction of duty, but you never know. Hope springs eternal in the human breast.

Monday, 27 November

Fiona and I have been taken off mulled wine and given jumble again. We are at peace with this, even though Savannah has texted us to request that we not refer to it as such. It is to be called 'bric-à-brac' from now on instead. 'Imagine leading the kind of life that leaves you free to care about such a thing,' marvels Fiona. 'Do you think we should be envious? Or really, really not?'

Tuesday, 28 November

Sofia and Amrit have been coming and going much less and looking even more loved-up than usual. I wonder if she's pregnant. Now that I've thought it, I'm desperate to know – if only so I can start searching for a replacement couple through whom to live vicariously.

Thursday, 30 November

It has been a long week. I have secured photos of Chunky Monkey playing children's Scrabble (round which board the children sat for roughly three seconds), practising on a toy violin while Thomas did his (three seconds of) music practice, in the park (for the three seconds we were there before it pissed down), being read to in bed with Thomas and Evie by me (that one's real. I read to them every night. It's the one thing I don't fail at, even if I am almost felled by my longing for alcohol before the end), and at a stately home we dragged ourselves to at the weekend. The ones of him relaxing in Mrs Bradley's garden look great (she nodded when we showed them to her). And I managed to squeeze four sentences out of Thomas to accompany them. 'I hav lovd haveing Chuncky Monckey to stay. He is my best freind. I alredy miss him and he has not gon yet. It wil be hard to sai gudbiy.'

'Jesus Christ,' says Richard, when I show him. 'Jesus Christ.'

I ask Thomas how the week's gone with Andrew and his gimps. I don't say gimps. 'Fine,' he says.

I collar Evie as she heads to the loo and via the medium of fierce glare repeat the question. 'No better,' she says.

Richard agrees it would be 'within the bounds of non-neurotic propriety' for me to bring up the subject again with Miss Anderson when I deliver the monkey and his diary at pick-up tomorrow.

Friday, 1 December

She has seen nothing, she says. I suggest that teachers don't necessarily see everything. Are they calling him any discriminatory names? Not that I'm aware. Well, then – she says.

And maybe she's right – I am aware, after all, that it is very much at the lighter end of the bullying spectrum. But that's where you want to intervene, isn't it? Before they go full Flashman on you. I tried, in a roundabout way, to suggest that, without appearing to be telling her her job. Evidently I did not succeed because she stiffened, started focusing on a point somewhere behind my left shoulder and assured me in cool, detached tones that she will monitor the situation even though she is sure there is absolutely nothing to worry about. We were too far down the wrong road to try to hack our way back, so I just handed over Chunky Monkey and left. Why does every single little thing have to get worse before it gets better?

Monday, 4 December

'The nativity play's been casted!' cries Thomas, as he falls through the door with David and Evie, Fiona bringing up the rear.

'Has it?' I say, shutting my laptop and stifling a sigh as I put away the remaining stacks of work on each side that, despite my best efforts, have gone untouched. Something to do with twenty hours' worth of labour stoutly refusing to be crammed into six, I think.

My preternaturally sanguine child is rarely this excited about anything. He must have been given a part.

'What are you?' I ask. 'Joseph?'

'No,' says Evie, witheringly. 'Joseph's Joseph.'

This makes sense, though not quite for the reasons madam thinks. Joseph's mother, Alys, is the Savannah of Year Six and the young teacher – Mr Ames, essentially a toddler in a suit

– upon whose stripling shoulders lies responsibility for all music and drama, has evidently decided to take the easy way out. I cannot say I blame him.

'So?' I say. 'What are you, then?'

'A fence!' he says exuberantly.

'A fence?'

'Well, part of a fence. All the boys are. Except the ones who are something else.'

'I see. And what are the girls?'

'A host of angels.'

Feel sure there is legislation somewhere against this but in the absence of an intern to do the research for me I decide to let it slide. At least I'll only have to dress him in brown instead of fanny about with wings and a halo.

'Are you an angel, Evie?'

'No,' she says. 'I'm doing tickets. Collecting them at the door. Stop all the people who haven't paid getting in.'

'Very wise,' I say. 'The school nativity play *is* a destination event.'

'Did you not get a part, David?' says Fiona to her son, who has remained silent throughout.

'I'm the innkeeper,' he says.

'The innkeeper – why didn't you say?!'

'Not much to it.' He shrugs. 'Just gorra chuck 'em out. No room. No argument.'

We watch the three of them disappear to the bedroom.

'How do I have a forty-year-old child?' says Fiona.

'I don't know,' I say. 'But,' I add, looking ahead to the weeks of fervent discussion about ticket collection and fence portrayal that are my inescapable future now, 'I envy you.'

Wednesday, 6 December

Christmas fairy lights have started going up outside people's houses and the children are as usual in awe. It takes us half an hour to get home after school because we have to stop and discuss each display's peerless beauty, technical merits, and all-round impact before we can move on to the next. It is an endless source of fascination – how do they do it? Can we do it? Where are they plugged in? If it rains, will Santa get electrocuted and die? (Answers: no idea, no, inside, and, hmm, maybe.)

They are taking it in turns to eat the tiny chocolate the advent calendar yields every morning. Grandma thinks I am Cruella de Vil for not letting them have a calendar each. This from a woman who forbade them altogether in my youth ('Modern nonsense!'). And who didn't allow sweets on any day except Saturday (when we were allowed a quarter of whatever we liked least from the local shop) or her children to eat butter rather than margarine under her roof till they were twenty-five. Not because we were poor but because ... well, just because. Because we were children? Because life should never be furnished beyond necessity? I don't know. I do know that the first time I had a taste of Anchor I was at university and my senses lit up like I was Renton trying his first syringeful of heroin.

Thursday, 7 December

Tried again to broach the subject of Andrew and his hench-gimps with Miss Anderson. Failed again. Maybe things will be better after the holidays. Surely no one can remain exercised over contraventions of beanbag codes for that long. I know that's not the point. But no one seems to be interested in the point.

Friday, 8 December

'We were holding the line!' I say, horrified. 'We were holding the line!'

'I'm sorry,' says Richard helplessly. 'They worked together and they caught me at a weak moment. There was nothing I could do.'

This is what happens when you let fathers do pick-up. They are not prepared. They do not have their defences up, their answers ready, their arsenal of distractions primed. And so the three of them have come home with two packs of thirty tiny Christmas cards for Thomas and Evie to write to their class-mates. Well, for them to write three each and someone else – guess who? – to write the remaining fifty-four.

It is too late to save ourselves. As a couple we send about eight cards a year, to my beloved godmother, an aged aunt and the handful of friends whom I genuinely miss and never see enough of in the year. The remaining mass is sent out as a result of panic, politics and peer pressure – but we had hoped to do better with the children. But, thanks to one man's weakness, we join sixty other sets of parents doing the same ridiculous thing. The maths is terrifying, especially if I've done it right. It's 60 × 60, isn't it? 3,600. Can it be? Really? 3,600 meaningless cards out there, from our two kids' classes alone? Cluttering up houses for weeks, representing hours of precious time, pounds of precious money and tonnes of precious tree wasted? Unless, of course, you're one of those parents whose child does actually write all thirty, showing the world that it has mastered copper-plate, and whose accompanying renditions of robins look like something Bewick would have produced if he'd been working in felt-tip instead of woodblock. It's an unseasonally pass-agg move (or thirty) but at least you're getting something for your smug buck.

'And we've already bought two packs of the school ones!' I add. The PTA did its usual snatching of our children's abysmal artwork, sent it off to the printers and put a 1000 per cent

mark-up on the price knowing that beleaguered parents and/
or enraptured grandparents will pay. 'They cost more than my
first car!'

Then beautiful realisation dawns. The light turns golden,
the sound of heavenly voices singing seems to fill the air – 'tis
as if the glory of the very first Christmas morn has descended
once more. 'This is on you,' I say, beaming. 'You bought them.
You're off work for two days. You do them!'

Richard hangs his head. He knows the depth of his sin and
the righteousness of his punishment and silently accepts both.

After tea, the children do three each. I am so long and fast
asleep by the time Richard finishes the rest and comes to bed
that I do not even stir when he gets in.

It's called self-gifting, I believe, and I intend to do much
more of it from now on. Next year, I firmly resolve, I am going
to be brave and send a mass text message on 1 December that
says, *I am saving myself and you the bother of cards this year and have
made a donation to charity instead. Maybe you think this is selfish,
maybe you think it is virtue-signally. I don't know, I'm too tired. If
you care, by all means strike my name from the record. I already feel
so wildly free. Top o' the season to ye!* Yes, that will work perfectly.
SEND.

Saturday, 9 December

The tree is up. *The World of Interiors* is yet to call, but we are very
happy with it. Evie has hung her favourite toy gun front and
centre. 'It's the season of goodwill,' I say feebly.

'What does that even mean?' she replies.

Sunday, 10 December

Thomas doesn't want to go to school tomorrow 'because of
everything Andrew does. Even Evan doesn't join in now.'

I go downstairs and take Andrew's card and a handful of others out of his bag. Enough's enough.

Monday, 11 December

I arrive early at drop-off, bundle Thomas into school, note who is still outside, exclaim loudly and make a big show of handing out the cards that 'fell out of his bag'. I march quickly, smiling broadly, over to Andrew's mother just as she is sending him in. I hand Andrew the card, so he knows he hasn't been overlooked, and once he's safely on his way inside I turn to her and say, 'Merry Christmas! I've been meaning to catch you, actually! Could you ask Andrew to stop teasing Thomas? And getting others to gang up on him? It's really starting to get to him and I can't have him being upset like this. I know they're all so excited about Christmas! Thank you so much!'

'And if that doesn't work,' I mutter under my breath as I march equally quickly away, 'I'll boil the pair of you in oil and chuck your carcasses in the sea.'

Round the corner my legs go wobbly as my body acknowledges that I have just contravened every social rule in the parental book. You don't ever – ever, ever, ever, ever, ever – mention a child's bad behaviour to its mother. It's not A Thing you do. I don't know when it stopped being A Thing you did – I'm sure I remember friends of my mother who had 'lively' children for ever fielding complaints from other parents and exhortations to keep their kids in line, like Mrs Bradley's streetful of *de facto* parents in a minor key – but it sure isn't one now. Oh, well. I guess maybe they can fuck off too if they don't like it.

Tuesday, 12 December

Andrew, Bailey – still a stupid name – and Evan behaved themselves today, apparently.

Wednesday, 13 December

And again today. Their mothers have cold-shouldered me since Monday pick-up, but this is a trade-off I could not be happier to make. It could almost be considered a bonus .

The round robins have started arriving. I am old enough to remember when these were first unleashed upon an unsuspecting world. It was about thirty-five years ago, when people first looked at the new dot matrix printer standing on their desks and thought, How best can I use this groundbreaking technology to increase the sum total of human happiness? A self-aggrandising newsletter, you say? Okay! Let's get to work!

It was bad enough when you just had to read a page of minutiae about a friend's building works, pregnancy or labrador's hip dysplasia but now it's a laser-printed booklet with full photographic illustrations of the conservatory, bump and tortured joint in all their various stages of development. And the humble-bragging has reached pathological proportions. 'We were so sorry that Angus had to leave his many, many sweet friends at St Asinine's in order to take up his place at the Nonpareil Institute for the Preternaturally Gifted. We promise to be in touch just as soon as we have settled in to our beautiful – if slightly overlarge for a family of three! – new home in the gorgeous little village of Much Equity. We do feel we are RATTLING round the eight bedrooms somewhat, but it's good for George to have somewhere to store his sex dolls. Just the lower paddock and the water meadows to sort out now, and so lovely to have so many familiar faces from TV as our neighbours! I keep telling Nigella she must come round for my famous roast turd in pomegranate couscous.'

Or whatever.

On this at least we have successfully held the line. No round robin from us. The relentless recalcitrance of our printer sees to that but, anyway, what would I put? That we're all still here and healthy and I live every moment in dread that that must one day change? That we have successfully got away with pretending to be functioning adults at home and at work for another year? That after nearly twenty years of earning a living I am still astonished that a monthly wedge of recompense lands in my account because I still haven't been unmasked as an imposter? That I now start dreaming of a glass of wine at 2 p.m. instead of 5 p.m. and give in at 6 p.m. instead of eight? That in a moment of high seasonal cheer last week I decided to make cracker-shaped biscuits to ice beautifully and give as gifts in little coloured cellophane bags, and the kindest thing my family could say about them was that crackers are made of cardboard and I had paid that due homage? 'Let's set up a stall at a hipster market and call them Meta-Snax!' Richard suggested, as I lobbed them into the bin.

Better, on the whole, that no one unbounded by blood ties ever knows any of it.

Thursday, 14 December

Thomas, Evie and David are busy demolishing a vat of spag bol and I deem the moment propitious for asking if Andrew *et al* are still behaving themselves.

'Oh,' he says, hardly looking up from his bowl. 'Everything's fine. They sorted it all out.'

'What do you mean?' I say, startled. 'Who's they?'

'Me and him,' says Evie, nodding at David opposite her.

'What do you mean?' I say again.

'Well, no offence,' says Evie, 'but first you weren't doing anything about it ...'

'I spoke to Miss Anderson!' I say indignantly. 'Multiple times!'

'Her!' snorts Evie, contemptuously. 'She never does anything. Ashok stole Chloë's sister's special pencil once and Miss Anderson just told her to get another one because all pencils do the same thing. She's an idiot.'

'You mustn't call people idiots,' I say.

'I must when they are,' says Evie. 'And she is. And I hate her.'

'Anyway,' David breaks in, always keen not to let a conversation be derailed, 'Andrew was still being a right pain, and then you spoke to Andrew's mum and Thomas said at Tuesday playtime that everything was worse so me and Evie told Andrew to stop it.'

'You and Evie?'

'Yup. Well, Evie told him and I just stood behind her and made myself look big. Bigger. I'm already quite big.'

'I told him he was an idiot,' says Evie, with satisfaction. 'Because he *is*. And I told him David would beat him up if him and the others kept being stupid with Thomas.'

'I wouldn't have,' David assures me. 'But I really do look like I can. That's the important thing.'

'Yes,' says Thomas, cheerfully. 'And it worked! Better than teachers. They just make things worse even if they try to help. So do most grown-ups.'

'I see,' I say faintly. There is much to unpack here but I am not equal to the task. The important thing is that Andrew and the other little tykes have been shown the error of their ways and that Thomas is no longer being harassed. I think that's the important thing. But I'm just a grown-up, so what the hell do I know?

Friday, 15 December

The great day dawns. This afternoon the pupils of St Holding-Pen give us their version of the Christmas with Due Homage Paid to the Existence and Equality of All Other Faiths Incorporated Story. I see the ticket collector and the fence segment off in states of heightened excitement and manage a couple of hours' work before Richard comes home early to accompany me and Fiona to this for-one-afternoon-only extravaganza.

We are greeted on the door by Evie. Greeted is possibly putting it too strongly. No flicker of recognition crosses her face as we descend on her, smiling, with tickets outstretched. 'Fill up from the front,' she barks, as she grabs them.

'No,' says the teacher, standing with her. 'Remember what we talked about, Evie? A pleasant manner, to encourage everyone to relax and enjoy themselves.'

'I don't have to this time,' our daughter explains. 'They're my mum and dad. And Fiona.'

'Remind me what he is in this?' says Richard, as we settle as unobtrusively as possible in seats near the back of the hall.

'A sexist fence,' I reply.

Savannah and her gang and their au pairs (I hope they're being paid for this) arrive together and take up the second row. Alys and her gang and their au pairs arrive a few minutes later and take up the first. The lights dim – well, are switched off in two-thirds of the hall so the stage is the only bit left illuminated – and the curtain opens. Well, starts to open. Then stops. Then closes. Then opens again. Then stops. Then an adult voice is heard whispering violently, 'Just let *me* do it, Harley!' and they open again, properly.

All goes smoothly for a while. Alys leans tensely forward in her seat every time Joseph appears, mouthing the words fiercely along with him, but he doesn't make a mistake.

Then Joseph and Mary (Savannah's older daughter – of course) find themselves refused entry at every decent hostelry ('WE'RE ALL FULL!' yells a row of Reception midgets in grey tabards, delirious with the joy of being allowed to shout in school) and have to knock at the door of the final inn. David stomps solidly across the stage towards it but pauses halfway and turns to face the audience. 'I wanted,' he says, with profound regret, 'to be an ox. But I'm the innkeeper.' He sighs.

'I'll be a good innkeeper,' he says, turning to resume his journey. 'But I would have been a better ox. There's nowt here either!' he shouts suddenly at Mary and Joseph. 'Burrav got a stable you can have. If you don't want it, suit yourselves.' And he stomps back whence he came. Fiona puts her head in her hands, but I think she should be proud.

Gabriel delivers his messages to the three wise men and the shepherds. The Messiah is safely born. 'Away in a Manger' is sung. The audience collapses in tears. Mary holds Jesus upside down throughout. We've all been there, girl, I think.

'Why did you stop and talk to the audience like that?' Fiona says to David, as we stand around – *sans* Evie, who has insisted on accompanying Mrs Hunt to put the takings in the office safe ('Trust yet verify,' Richard tells her approvingly) – eating the mince pies and drinking the squash the Year Sixes are carefully handing round.

'I thought it'd make Miss Anderson happy,' says David, through a mouthful of pastry. 'She's always going on about talking about your feelings, isn't she? I thought it'd be sort of like a Christmas present for her. Because I really wanted to be an ox. Who looks more like an ox than me?'

'Did you see me, Mummy?' asks Thomas. 'Was I good?'

'Wonderful!' I say. 'None stiller. Or browner. Or altogether more fencelike.' And I mean it. I've never seen such a fence. Not Benedict Cumberbatch, not Mark Rylance, not Olivier himself could have given us a better agrarian enclosure. Magnificent.

I should perhaps mention that Fiona had smuggled in a Thermos full of amaretto for the three of us to enjoy. It was a large Thermos and we were just drinking the last of it in our squash.

'Well,' says Fiona, clinking plastic cups. 'Here's to fences and to feelings. Merry Christmas, everyone.'

'Yeah!' says Evie, suddenly skidding in from nowhere. 'We made two hundred and twenty-three pounds! Merry Christmas!'

Saturday, 16 December

Winter A-Fayre Thingy went well. Fiona and I were absolutely sloshed by the end. Savannah furious. Especially when I shouted, 'Never mind!' at her when she told us how cross she was and we went off laughing hysterically. To the pub.

Wednesday, 20 December

Last day of term. The children charge out of school carrying a term's worth of work, a thousand terrible handmade Christmas decorations with which we will later festoon our uncomplaining tree, and high on the mini Mars Bars they've been given during final storytime.

'Christmas starts here!' roars Evie. 'No sleep till Santa!'

'"Tis the season to take Val-ium,"' sings Fiona. '"Fa-la-la-la-la, la-la-la-laaah!"'

Friday, 22 December

Sofia and Amrit called round last night. 'We've got some news,' said Sofia, face aglow, as Amrit beamed behind her. 'And we thought we'd better tell you because there might be a bit of noise and things ...'

'Oh, yes?' I said, trying to look curious while smiling knowingly.

'We're getting a puppy!' burst out Amrit.

'Oh!' I said, trying not to laugh. 'I see! That's great news – congratulations!'

'Our jobs have calmed down,' explained Sofia. 'And we just felt ready.'

'It's time,' agreed Amrit, earnestly. 'Definitely.'

The kids clamour for permission to visit as soon as it arrives.

'When's your due— I mean, when's the puppy coming?'

'January the sixth,' says Amrit. 'It's a King Charles spaniel. We're just getting everything ready before we bring him home.'

We have a glass of wine together while they show pictures of the puppy and his mother to the children, who are beside themselves with excitement. Visits, they are promised, will be allowed as soon as the new arrival has settled in.

Honestly, I can't wait either. I've had two babies but was never allowed a puppy. And they'll have to go away occasionally and I'll look after it. Like a godmother. Yes. Godmother to a puppy. This is a new station in life I will happily accept.

Saturday, 23 December

We spend three hours packing presents, decanting food from the fridge into cool bags, getting Henry into his carrier and the whole lot, plus two children who are jittering with seasonal fervour and absolutely unbearable, into the car. 'God,' I mutter, as I slide into the front seat with a distraught, caged Henry on my lap and hope nothing vital is crushed as Richard slams the overfilled boot shut, 'can't we just cancel Christmas?'

'Oh, come on,' says Richard, as he puts the key into the ignition. 'What parent would really want to miss being woken at five, or the way a child's eyes roll back in its head with over-excitement, or the traditional series of increasingly severe admonishments delivered as the day wears on to try to quell the greed and atavism you have been entirely responsible for creating?'

He'll change his tune when he finds out he's got to put stabilisers on Evie's new bike.

Sunday, 24 December, Christmas Eve

As tradition dictates, the last thing we all do before the children go to bed is lay the Big Table for Christmas dinner tomorrow. ('What are these?' says Evie, as we ferry accoutrements in. 'They're napkins,' I say. 'Pretend to Grandma that you've seen one before.') Candles and their holders must be chosen, with childish whim prioritised beyond aesthetic harmony ('Will they set fire to the decorations?' both Thomas and Evie ask me, the former anxiously, the latter with undisguised longing). The glittery runner must be lovingly spread down it and, of course, crackers (real crackers, not sad fucking biscuits) set by every plate. Long after our own interest in the subject is exhausted, Thomas is still there choosing which colour he thinks best suits each person. Gold for Grandma and Granddad ('Because they're the best'), silver for me and Kate, red for Evie ('For danger') and 'Whatever's left over for Daddy. It's a shame, but it can't be helped.'

Eventually the children settle in bed and, despite even Evie's best efforts (last year she took a fork to bed with her, intending to jab herself awake and see Father Christmas – we pat her down now), go to sleep.

Richard sets to work fitting stabilisers to Evie's bike while Grandma and I – Dad having, as is customary these days, gone to bed slightly before he got up – sneak upstairs and place the stockings carefully at the ends of Evie and Thomas's beds. My eyes fill with tears when I see how small my children are. Their feet barely reach halfway to the stockings! But one day they will and what will we do about stockings then? What will I do about everything then? Fortunately my mother sees my face about to crumple and punches me in the kidneys to distract me. Not really. She just has the face on that tells me she will if she must.

Downstairs, we find Richard sweating profusely and swearing more generously still. Grandma silently holds out her hands for the tools. Equally silently he hands them over. She has the stabilisers on before he has finished mopping his brow.

Time for bed.

Monday, 25 December, Christmas Day

I know I was up at six with the children, but after that it's a blur. Of stockings, squeals of delight, hasty breakfasts, Richard and Thomas hunching over the wooden castle and reconstructing the Middle Ages with Superzings, and Evie zooming round the garden on her bike, showing as fine a disregard for her own safety as she does for that of Grandma's herbaceous borders. 'Oh, leave her alone!' cries Grandma, as I attempt to remonstrate with my child before she razes forty years' work to the ground. 'It's Christmas!'

Tuesday, 26 December, Boxing Day

A true sign of adulthood – Boxing Day is better than Christmas Day. The high excitement has abated. Evie is still in the garden with her bike, which she has pimped out with all the shiny metallic paper and bits that Christmas and Grandma can provide. Thomas is playing happily with his Stormtrooper and the slotted-together castle while wearing his new fancy dress costume from Fiona and the large plastic diamond ring ('I'm Princess Batman!') that has been fervently adored since the moment it fell out of his cracker. I am settled with tea and my new hardback novel, Richard and Granddad are asleep, like snoring bookends, at opposite ends of the sofa, and Grandma is contentedly buzzing around. 'Another twenty minutes,' she says happily, as she folds the last of the reusable wrapping paper and lays it away in the green units for next year and lobs the rest into the recycling. 'And it'll be like nothing ever happened!'

Wednesday, 27 December

It's like nothing ever happened.

Thursday, 28 December

Apart from the leftovers and general sense of wellbeing as the children play uninterruptedly with their new toys and Dad continues to insist that I drink Baileys all evening every evening 'because nobody else will finish it if you don't'.

Mum is as busy as ever. Think she may have converted the loft.

Friday, 29 December

Still plenty of Baileys left. Love the Merryneum. Though not whoever called it the Merryneum. Which was a man, betcha. No woman jokes about the perineum. We know what can happen to it.

Saturday, 30 December

The Baileys is finished. Time to go home.

Sunday, 31 December, New Year's Eve

Mrs Bradley is in the front garden when we pull up outside the house. We wish her a happy new year. 'Hmm,' she replies. Sofia and Amrit are away – one last trip before the puppy arrives. When we get in, the children rush upstairs to get reacquainted with all their old toys, and Richard and I park ourselves on the sofa, glorying in the knowledge that we are not going out on New Year's Eve. More than that – we never even entertained the idea of going out on New Year's Eve. More, even, than that, we haven't entertained the idea of going out for at least six years, and this year we didn't even entertain the idea of having people round. And nary a fleeting touch of compunction has it visited upon either of us. There is Netflix on the telly, a bottle of prosecco at our feet and not an ounce of FOMO in our souls. Richard and I are united instead in the untrammelled joy of missing out.

As midnight looms, we turn over to BBC One and watch the fireworks and crowds by the Thames.

'Imagine,' says Richard, in incredulous tones. 'Imagine *going* there. Imagine *being* there.'

I cannot. Even though I was, several times, in my twenties. But it feels like a lifetime ago. It was, I suppose. Thomas's lifetime, Evie's lifetime. It feels as though it happened in a dream. E. B. White once referred to his childhood self as 'a boy I knew'. I feel similarly towards any pre-thirty-year-old version of myself. I remember and am fond of her, but she exists, somehow, somewhere outside me now. Draining my glass, I don't know whether to be happy or sad about that. Christ, maybe I should go out if all I'm going to do is sit here and overthink things.

Midnight chimes. Richard leans over and kisses me. 'Happy new year!' he says. 'Though I always think it's fascinating how much stock we all put in what's essentially an arbitrary mark on a calendar that already represents a futile gesture to impose meaning and narrative on an unconnected series of events we constantly insist are significant, don't you?'

'Sure,' I say, regretting draining my glass.

'I mean,' he says cheerfully, 'as if anything will change just because a clock ticks forward another minute!'

My forty-year-old self – forty-one this year, of course – thinks about this for a moment. If nothing changed from last year, what would that mean? We would all stay healthy. We would all remain loved. We would stay safe. We would have enough food, clothes, shelter and money to add to those basics. We'd stay luckier than most and far luckier than we need to be in order to be happy. And we'd still have David to help us out when we got stuck, practically, philosophically and all points in between.

Forty-year-old me is happy. Especially with a puppy on the way too.

Richard opens his mouth to speak again. But if my previous four decades have taught me nothing else, it's that moments of peace and contentment are rare, fragile and worth stretching out for as long as possible. So – 'Shut up, my love,' I say. 'And maybe we'll make it through the next twelve months too.' He raises his glass in wordless salute.

Happy new year.

Acknowledgements

Obviously, before anything, I'd like to thank the coronavirus for giving the gift of the pandemic and such perfect conditions to work and write in. It's been really, really great. I shall remember lockdown, homeschooling, two parents WFH and all the merry rest of it fondly for years and years to come.

Rather less sarcastically, I would like to thank the whole team at Profile and Souvenir Press – Rebecca Gray, Lottie Fyfe, Anna-Marie Fitzgerald, Niamh Murray, Calah Singleton, Sinem Erkas, Pete Dyer – for bringing all their powers of improvement to bear on every aspect of Liz's domestic perils and adventures, and Sam Baker for hosting her first appearance in The Pool.

Thank you too to my ever-wonderful agents, Juliet Pickering and Louise Lamont, who went even further above and beyond their duties with this book than they usually do.

More than ever too, over this year-and-counting of madness and increasingly grinding stress and strain, my friends were a lifeline. Thank you all, but especially Sali Hughes, Michael Hogan, Caitlin Moran, Sarah Perry, Sarah Moule, Jason Hazeley and – for first-reader duties – Tim Sutton for your kindness, support, Zoom drinks, rude messages and everything else.

Lastly, of course, I must thank my husband Christopher, even though I really think he could have done much better, and my son Alexander, who really couldn't and must teach his father a thing or two before the next book and/or lockdown. I love you both very, very much. You may now start interrupting me in the study again.

The Unexpected Guest

Agatha Christie is known throughout the world as the Queen
of Crime. Her books have sold over a billion copies in English
with another billion in 44 foreign languages. She is the most
widely published author of all time and in any language,
outsold only by the Bible and Shakespeare. She is the author
of 80 crime novels and short story collections, 19 plays, and
six novels written under the name of Mary Westmacott.

Agatha Christie's first novel, *The Mysterious Affair at Styles*,
was written towards the end of the First World War, in which
she served as a VAD. In it she created Hercule Poirot, the
little Belgian detective who was destined to become the most
popular detective in crime fiction since Sherlock Holmes. It
was eventually published by The Bodley Head in 1920.

In 1926, after averaging a book a year, Agatha Christie wrote
her masterpiece. *The Murder of Roger Ackroyd* was the first
of her books to be published by Collins and marked the
beginning of an author-publisher relationship which lasted for
50 years and well over 70 books. *The Murder of Roger Ackroyd*
was also the first of Agatha Christie's books to be dramatised
– under the name *Alibi* – and to have a successful run in
London's West End. *The Mousetrap*, her most famous play of
all, opened in 1952 and is the longest-running play in history.

Agatha Christie was made a Dame in 1971. She died in 1976,
since when a number of books have been published posthum-
ously: the bestselling novel *Sleeping Murder* appeared later that
year, followed by her autobiography and the short story collections *Miss Marple's Final Cases*, *Problem at Pollensa Bay* and
While the Light Lasts. In 1998 *Black Coffee* was the first of her
plays to be novelised by another author, Charles Osborne.

Charles Osborne was born in Brisbane in 1927. He is known internationally as an authority on opera, and has written a number of books on musical and literary subjects, among them *The Complete Operas of Verdi* (1969), *Wagner and his World* (1977), *W.H. Auden: The Life of a Poet* (1980) and *The Life and Crimes of Agatha Christie* (1982).

The Unexpected Guest

BY THE SAME AUTHOR

AGATHA CHRISTIE

THE UNEXPECTED GUEST

Adapted as a Novel by
Charles Osborne

HarperCollinsPublishers

HarperCollins*Publishers*
77–85 Fulham-Palace Road,
Hammersmith, London W6 8JB
www.**fire**and**water**.com

This paperback edition 2000

1 3 5 7 9 8 6 4 2

First published in Great Britain by
HarperCollins*Publishers* 1999

A catalogue record for this book
is available from the British Library

ISBN 0 00 651368 9

Typeset by Palimpsest Book Production Limited,
Polmont, Stirlingshire
Printed in Great Britain by
Omnia Books Ltd, Glasgow

CHAPTER ONE

It was shortly before midnight on a chilly November evening, and swirls of mist obscured parts of the dark, narrow, tree-lined country road in South Wales, not far from the Bristol Channel whence a foghorn sounded its melancholy boom automatically every few moments. Occasionally, the distant barking of a dog could be heard, and the melancholy call of a night-bird. What few houses there were along the road, which was little better than a lane, were about a half-mile apart. On one of its darkest stretches the road turned, passing a handsome, three-storey house standing well back from its spacious garden, and it was at this spot that a car sat, its front wheels caught in the ditch at the side of the road. After two or three attempts to accelerate out of the ditch, the driver of the car must have decided it was no use persevering, and the engine fell silent.

A minute or two passed before the driver emerged from the vehicle, slamming the door behind him. He was a somewhat thick-set, sandy-haired man of about thirty-five, with an outdoor look about him, dressed in a rough tweed suit and dark overcoat and wearing a hat. Using a torch to find his way, he began to walk cautiously across the lawn towards the house, stopping halfway to survey the eighteenth-century building's elegant façade. The house appeared to be in total darkness as he approached the french windows on that side of the edifice which faced him. After turning to look back at the lawn he had crossed, and the road beyond it, he walked right up to the french windows, ran his hands over the glass, and peered in. Unable to discern any movement within, he knocked on the window. There was no response, and after a pause he knocked again much louder. When he realized that his knocking was not having any effect, he tried the handle. Immediately, the window opened and he stumbled into a room that was in darkness.

Inside the room, he paused again, as though attempting to discern any sound or movement. Then, 'Hello,' he called. 'Is anyone there?' Flashing his torch around the room which revealed itself to be a well-furnished study, its walls lined with books, he saw in the centre of the room a handsome middle-aged man sitting in a wheelchair facing the french windows, with a rug over his knees. The man appeared to have fallen asleep in his chair. 'Oh, hello,' said the intruder. 'I didn't mean to startle you. So sorry. It's this confounded fog. I've just run my car off the road into a ditch, and I haven't the faintest idea where I am. Oh, and I've left the window open. I'm so sorry.' Continuing to speak apologetically as he moved, he turned back to the french windows, shut them, and closed the curtains. 'Must have run off the main road somewhere,' he explained. 'I've been

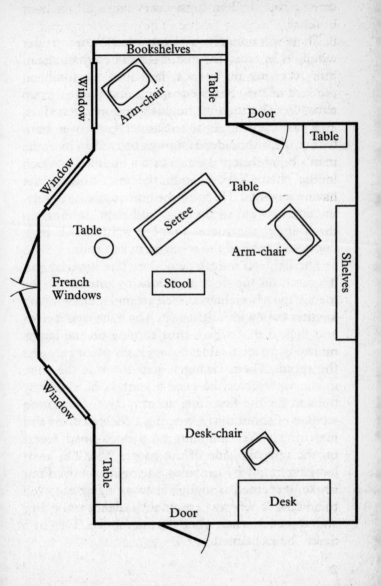

driving round these topsy-turvy lanes for an hour or more.'

There was no reply. 'Are you asleep?' the intruder asked, as he faced the man in the wheelchair again. Still receiving no answer, he shone his torch on the face of the chair's occupant, and then stopped abruptly. The man in the chair neither opened his eyes nor moved. As the intruder bent over him, touching his shoulder as though to awaken him, the man's body slumped down into a huddled position in the chair. 'Good God!' the man holding the torch exclaimed. He paused momentarily, as though undecided what to do next, and then, shining his torch about the room, found a light switch by a door, and crossed the room to switch it on.

The light on a desk came on. The intruder put his torch on the desk and, looking intently at the man in the wheelchair, circled around him. Noticing another door with a light switch by it, he went across and flicked the switch, thus turning on the lamps on two occasional tables strategically placed around the room. Then, taking a step towards the man in the wheelchair, he gave a start as he suddenly noticed for the first time an attractive, fair-haired woman of about thirty, wearing a cocktail dress and matching jacket, standing by a book-lined recess on the opposite side of the room. With her arms hanging limply by her sides, she neither moved nor spoke. It seemed as though she was trying not even to breathe. There was a moment's silence while they stared at each other. Then the man spoke. 'He – he's dead!' he exclaimed.

4

Completely without expression, the woman answered him. 'Yes.'

'You already knew?' asked the man.

'Yes.'

Cautiously approaching the body in the wheelchair, the man said, 'He's been shot. Through the head. Who – ?'

He paused as the woman slowly brought her right hand up from where it had been hidden by the folds of her dress. In her hand was a revolver. The man drew in his breath sharply. When it seemed that she was not threatening him with it, he approached her, and gently took the gun from her. 'You shot him?' he asked.

'Yes,' the woman replied, after a pause.

The man moved away from her, and put the gun on a table by the wheelchair. For a moment he stood looking at the dead body, and then gazed uncertainly around the room.

'The telephone is over there,' said the woman, nodding towards the desk.

'Telephone?' the man echoed. He sounded startled.

'If you want to ring up the police,' the woman continued, still speaking in the same detached, expressionless manner.

The stranger stared at her as though unable to make her out. Then, 'A few minutes one way or the other won't make any difference,' he said. 'They'll have a bit of a job getting here in this fog anyway. I'd like to know a little more –' He broke off and looked at the body. 'Who is he?'

5

'My husband,' replied the woman. She paused, and then continued, 'His name is Richard Warwick. I am Laura Warwick.'

The man continued to stare at her. 'I see,' he murmured finally. 'Hadn't you better – sit down?'

Laura Warwick moved slowly and somewhat unsteadily to a sofa. Looking around the room, the man asked, 'Can I get you a – drink – or something? It must have been a shock.'

'Shooting my husband?' Her tone was drily ironic.

Appearing to regain his poise somewhat, the man attempted to match her expression. 'I should imagine so, yes. Or was it just fun and games?'

'It was fun and games,' replied Laura Warwick inscrutably as she sat down on the sofa. The man frowned, looking puzzled. 'But I would like – that drink,' she continued.

The man took off his hat and threw it onto an armchair, then poured brandy from a decanter on the table close to the wheelchair and handed her the glass. She drank and, after a pause, the man said, 'Now, suppose you tell me all about it.'

Laura Warwick looked up at him. 'Hadn't you better ring the police?' she asked.

'All in good time. Nothing wrong with having a cosy little chat first, is there?' He took off his gloves, stuffed them into his overcoat pocket, and started unbuttoning his coat.

Laura Warwick's poise began to break. 'I don't –' she began. She paused and then continued, 'Who are you? How did you happen to come here tonight?'

Without giving him time to answer, she went on, her voice now almost a shout, 'For God's sake, tell me who you are!'

CHAPTER TWO

'By all means,' the man replied. He ran a hand through his hair, looked around the room for a moment as though wondering where or how to begin, and then continued, 'My name's Michael Starkwedder. I know it's an unusual name.' He spelt it out for her. 'I'm an engineer. I work for Anglo-Iranian, and I'm just back in this country from a term in the Persian Gulf.' He paused, seeming briefly to be remembering the Middle East, or perhaps trying to decide how much detail to go into, then shrugged his shoulders. 'I've been down here in Wales for a couple of days, looking up old landmarks. My mother's family came from this part of the world and I thought I might buy a little house.'

He shook his head, smiling. 'The last two hours – more like three, I should think – I've been hopelessly lost. Driving round all the twisting lanes in South Wales, and ending up in a ditch! Thick fog everywhere. I found a gate, groped my way to this house, hoping to get hold of a telephone or perhaps, if I was lucky, get put up for the night. I tried the handle of the french window there, found it wasn't locked, so I walked in. Whereupon I find –' He gestured towards the wheelchair, indicating the body slumped in it.

Laura Warwick looked up at him, her eyes expressionless. 'You knocked on the window first – several times,' she murmured.

'Yes, I did. Nobody answered.'

Laura caught her breath. 'No, I didn't answer.' Her voice was now almost a whisper.

Starkwedder looked at her, as though trying to make her out. He took a step towards the body in the wheelchair, then turned back to the woman on the sofa. To encourage her into speaking again, he repeated, 'As I say, I tried the handle, the window wasn't locked, so I came in.'

Laura stared down into her brandy glass. She spoke as though she were quoting. '"The door opens and the unexpected guest comes in."' She shivered slightly. 'That saying always frightened me when I was a child. "The unexpected guest".' Throwing her head back she stared up at her unexpected visitor, and exclaimed with sudden intensity, 'Oh, why don't you ring up the police and get it over?'

Starkwedder walked over to the body in the chair. 'Not yet,' he said. 'In a moment, perhaps. Can you tell me why you shot him?'

The note of irony returned to Laura's voice as she answered him. 'I can give you some excellent reasons. For one thing, he drank. He drank excessively. For another, he was cruel. Unbearably cruel. I've hated him for years.' Catching the sharp look Starkwedder gave her at this, she continued angrily, 'Oh, what do you expect me to say?'

'You've hated him for years?', Starkwedder murmured as though to himself. He looked thoughtfully at the body. 'But something – something special – happened tonight, didn't it?' he asked.

'You're quite right,' Laura replied emphatically. 'Something special indeed happened tonight. And so – I took the gun off the table from where it was lying beside him, and – and I shot him. It was as simple as that.' She threw an impatient glance at Starkwedder as she continued, 'Oh, what's the good of talking about it? You'll only have to ring up the police in the end. There's no way out.' Her voice dropped as she repeated, 'No way out!'

Starkwedder looked at her from across the room. 'It's not quite as simple as you think,' he observed.

'Why isn't it simple?' asked Laura. Her voice sounded weary.

Approaching her, Starkwedder spoke slowly and deliberately. 'It isn't so easy to do what you're urging me to do,' he said. 'You're a woman. A very attractive woman.'

Laura looked up at him sharply. 'Does that make a difference?' she asked.

Starkwedder's voice sounded almost cheerful as he replied, 'Theoretically, certainly not. But in practical terms, yes.' He took his overcoat over to the recess, put it on the armchair, and returned to stand looking down at the body of Richard Warwick.

'Oh, you're talking about chivalry,' Laura observed listlessly.

'Well, call it curiosity if you prefer,' said Starkwedder. 'I'd like to know what this is all about.'

Laura paused before replying. Then, 'I've told you,' was all she said.

11

Starkwedder walked slowly around the wheel-chair containing the body of Laura's husband, as though fascinated by it. 'You've told me the bare facts, perhaps,' he admitted. 'But nothing *more* than the bare facts.'

'And I've given you my excellent motive,' Laura replied. 'There's nothing more to tell. In any case, why should you believe what I tell you? I could make up any story I liked. You've only got my word for it that Richard was a cruel beast and that he drank and that he made life miserable for me – and that I hated him.'

'I can accept the last statement without question, I think,' said Starkwedder. 'After all, there's a certain amount of evidence to support it.' Approaching the sofa again, he looked down at Laura. 'All the same, it's a bit drastic, don't you think? You say you've hated him for years. Why didn't you leave him? Surely that would have been much simpler.'

Laura's voice was hesitant as she replied, 'I've – I've no money of my own.'

'My dear girl,' said Starkwedder, 'if you could have proved cruelty and habitual drunkenness and all the rest of it, you could have got a divorce – or separation – and then you'd get alimony or whatever it is they call it.' He paused, waiting for an answer.

Finding it difficult to reply, Laura rose and, keeping her back to him, went across to the table to put her glass down.

'Have you got children?' Starkwedder asked her.

12

'No – no, thank God,' Laura replied.

'Well, then, why didn't you leave him?'

Confused, Laura turned to face her questioner. 'Well –' she said finally, 'well – you see – now I shall inherit all his money.'

'Oh, no, you won't,' Starkwedder informed her. 'The law won't allow you to profit as the result of a crime.' Taking a step towards Laura, he asked, 'Or did you think that – ?' He hesitated, and then continued, 'What *did* you think?'

'I don't know what you mean,' Laura told him.

'You're not a stupid woman,' Starkwedder said, looking at her. 'Even if you did inherit his money, it wouldn't be much good to you if you were going to be imprisoned for life.' Settling himself comfortably in the armchair, he added, 'Supposing that I hadn't come knocking at the window just now? What were you going to do?'

'Does it matter?'

'Perhaps not – but I'm interested. What was your story going to be, if I hadn't come barging in and caught you here red-handed? Were you going to say it was an accident? Or suicide?'

'I don't *know*,' Laura exclaimed. She sounded distraught. Crossing to the sofa, she sat facing away from Starkwedder. 'I've no idea,' she added. 'I tell you I – I haven't had time to think.'

'No,' he agreed. 'No, perhaps not – I don't think it was a premeditated affair. I think it was an impulse. In fact, I think it was probably something your husband said. Was that it?'

'It doesn't matter, I tell you,' Laura replied.

'What *did* he say?' Starkwedder insisted. 'What was it?'

Laura gazed at him steadily. 'That is something I shall never tell anybody,' she exclaimed.

Starkwedder went over to the sofa and stood behind her. 'You'll be asked it in court,' he informed her.

Her expression was grim as she replied, 'I shan't answer. They can't make me answer.'

'But your counsel will have to know,' said Starkwedder. Leaning over the sofa and looking at her earnestly, he continued, 'It might make all the difference.'

Laura turned to face him. 'Oh, don't you see?' she exclaimed. 'Don't you understand? I've no hope. I'm prepared for the worst.'

'What, just because I came in through that window? If I hadn't –'

'But you did!' Laura interrupted him.

'Yes, I did,' he agreed. 'And consequently you're for it. Is that what you think?'

She made no reply. 'Here,' he said as he handed her a cigarette and took one himself. 'Now, let's go back a little. You've hated your husband for a long time, and tonight he said something that just pushed you over the edge. You snatched up the gun that was lying beside –' He stopped suddenly, staring at the gun on the table. 'Why was he sitting here with a gun beside him, anyway? It's hardly usual.'

'Oh, that,' said Laura. 'He used to shoot at cats.'

14

Starkwedder looked at her, surprised. 'Cats?' he asked.

'Oh, I suppose I shall have to do some explaining,' said Laura resignedly.

CHAPTER THREE

Starkwedder looked at her with a somewhat bemused expression. 'Well?' he prompted.

Laura took a deep breath. Then, staring straight ahead of her, she began to speak. 'Richard used to be a big-game hunter,' she said. 'That was where we first met – in Kenya. He was a different sort of person then. Or perhaps his good qualities showed, and not his bad ones. He did have good qualities, you know. Generosity and courage. Supreme courage. He was a very attractive man to women.'

She looked up suddenly, seeming to be aware of Starkwedder for the first time. Returning her gaze, he lit her cigarette with his lighter, and then his own. 'Go on,' he urged her.

'We married soon after we met,' Laura continued. 'Then, two years later, he had a terrible accident – he was mauled by a lion. He was lucky to escape alive, but he's been a semi-cripple ever since, unable to walk properly.' She leaned back, apparently more relaxed, and Starkwedder moved to a footstool, facing her.

Laura took a puff at her cigarette and then exhaled the smoke. 'They say misfortune improves your character,' she said. 'It didn't improve his. Instead, it developed all his bad points. Vindictiveness, a streak of sadism, drinking too much. He made life pretty impossible for everyone in this house, and we all put up with it because – oh, you know what one says. "So sad for poor Richard being an invalid." We shouldn't have put up with it, of course. I see that, now. It simply encouraged him to feel that he was different from other people, and that he could do as he chose without being called to account for it.'

She rose and went across to the table by the armchair to flick ash in the ashtray. 'All his life,' she continued, 'shooting had been the thing Richard liked doing best. So, when we came to live in this house, every night after everyone else had gone to bed, he'd sit here' – she gestured towards the wheel-chair – 'and Angell, his – well, valet and general factotum I suppose you'd call him – Angell would bring the brandy and one of Richard's guns, and put them beside him. Then he'd have the french windows wide open, and he'd sit in here looking out, watching for the gleam of a cat's eyes, or a stray rabbit, or a dog for that matter. Of course, there haven't been so many rabbits lately. That disease – what d'you call it? – mixymatosis or whatever – has been killing them off. But he shot quite a lot of cats.' She took a drag on her cigarette. 'He shot them in the daytime, too. And birds.'

'Didn't the neighbours ever complain?' Stark-wedder asked her.

'Oh, of couse they did,' Laura replied as she returned to sit on the sofa. 'We've only lived here for a couple of years, you know. Before that, we lived on the east coast, in Norfolk. One or two household pets were victims of Richard's there, and we had a lot of complaints. That's really why we came to live here. It's very isolated, this house. We've only got one neighbour for miles around. But there are plenty of squirrels and birds and stray cats.'

She paused for a moment, and then continued. 'The main trouble in Norfolk was really because a woman came to call at the house one day, collecting subscriptions for the village fête. Richard sent shots to the right and left of her as she was going away, walking down the drive. She bolted like a hare, he said. He roared with laughter when he told us about it. I remember him saying her fat backside was quivering like a jelly. But she went to the police about it, and there was a terrible row.'

'I can well imagine that,' was Starkwedder's dry comment.

'But Richard got away with it all right,' Laura told him. 'He had a permit for all his firearms, of course, and he assured the police that he only used them to shoot rabbits. He explained away poor Miss Butterfield by claiming that she was just a nervous old maid who imagined he was shooting at her, which he swore he would never have done. Richard was always plausible. He had no trouble making the police believe him.'

Starkwedder got up from his footstool and went across to Richard Warwick's body. 'Your husband seems to have had a rather perverted sense of humour,' he observed tartly. He looked down at the table beside the wheelchair. 'I see what you mean,' he continued. 'So a gun by his side was a nightly routine. But surely

19

he couldn't have expected to shoot anything tonight. Not in this fog.'

'Oh, he always had a gun put there,' replied Laura. 'Every night. It was like a child's toy. Sometimes he used to shoot into the wall, making patterns. Over there, if you look.' She indicated the french windows. 'Down there to the left, behind the curtain.'

Starkwedder went across and lifted the curtain on the left-hand side, revealing a pattern of bullet holes in the panelling. 'Good heavens, he's picked out his own initials in the wall. "R.W", done in bullet holes. Remarkable.' He replaced the curtain, and turned back to Laura. 'I must admit that's damned good shooting. Hm, yes. He must have been pretty frightening to live with.'

'He was,' Laura replied emphatically. With almost hysterical vehemence, she rose from the sofa and approached her uninvited guest. 'Must we go on talking and talking about all this?' she asked in exasperation. 'It's only putting off what's got to happen in the end. Can't you realize that you've *got* to ring up the police? You've no option. Don't you see it would be far kinder to just do it now? Or is it that you want me to do it? Is that it? All right, I will.'

She moved quickly to the phone, but Starkwedder came up to her as she was lifting the receiver, and put his hand over hers. 'We've got to talk first,' he told her.

'We've been talking,' said Laura. 'And anyway, there's nothing to talk about.'

20

'Yes, there is,' he insisted. 'I'm a fool, I dare say. But we've got to find some way out.'

'Some way out? For me?' asked Laura. She sounded incredulous.

'Yes. For you.' He took a few steps away from her, and then turned back to face her. 'How much courage have you got?' he asked. 'Can you lie if necessary – and lie convincingly?'

Laura stared at him. 'You're crazy,' was all she said.

'Probably,' Starkwedder agreed.

She shook her head in perplexity. 'You don't know what you're doing,' she told him.

'I know very well what I'm doing,' he answered. 'I'm making myself an accessory after the fact.'

'But why?' asked Laura. 'Why?'

Starkwedder looked at her for a moment before replying. Then, 'Yes, why?' he repeated. Speaking slowly and deliberately, he said, 'For the simple reason, I suppose, that you're a very attractive woman, and I don't like to think of you being shut up in prison for all the best years of your life. Just as horrible as being hanged by the neck until you are dead, in my view. And the situation looks far from promising for you. Your husband was an invalid and a cripple. Any evidence there might be of provocation would rest entirely on your word, a word which you seem extremely unwilling to give. Therefore it seems highly unlikely that a jury would acquit you.'

Laura looked steadily at him. 'You don't know me,' she said. 'Everything I've told you may have been lies.'

'It may,' Starkwedder agreed cheerfully. 'And perhaps I'm a sucker. But I'm believing you.'

Laura looked away, then sank down on the footstool with her back to him. For a few moments nothing was said. Then, turning to face him, her eyes suddenly alight with hope, she looked at him questioningly, and then nodded almost imperceptibly. 'Yes,' she told him, 'I can lie if I have to.'

'Good,' Starkwedder exclaimed with determination. 'Now, talk and talk fast.' He walked over to the table by the wheelchair, flicking ash in the ashtray. 'In the first place, who exactly is there in this house? Who lives here?'

After a moment's hesitation, Laura began to speak, almost mechanically. 'There's Richard's mother,' she told him. 'And there's Benny – Miss Bennett, but we call her Benny – she's a sort of combined housekeeper and secretary. An ex-hospital nurse. She's been here for ages, and she's devoted to Richard. And then there's Angell. I mentioned him, I think. He's a male nurse-attendant, and – well, valet, I suppose. He looks after Richard generally.'

'Are there servants who live in the house as well?'

'No, there are no live-in servants, only dailies who come in.' She paused. 'Oh – and I almost forgot,' she continued. 'There's Jan, of course.'

'Jan?' Starkwedder asked, sharply. 'Who's Jan?'

Laura gave him an embarrassed look before replying. Then, with an air of reluctance, she said, 'He's Richard's young half-brother. He – he lives with us.'

Starkwedder moved over to the stool where she

still sat. 'Come clean, now,' he insisted. 'What is there about Jan that you don't want to tell me?'

After a moment's hesitation, Laura spoke, though she still sounded guarded. 'Jan is a dear,' she said. 'Very affectionate and sweet. But – but he isn't quite like other people. I mean he's – he's what they call retarded.'

'I see,' Starkwedder murmured sympathetically. 'But you're fond of him, aren't you?'

'Yes,' Laura admitted. 'Yes – I'm very fond of him. That's – that's really why I couldn't just go away and leave Richard. Because of Jan. You see, if Richard had had his own way, he would have sent Jan to an institution. A place for the mentally retarded.'

Starkwedder slowly circled the wheelchair, looking down at Richard Warwick's body, and pondering. Then, 'I see,' he murmured. 'Is that the threat he held over you? That, if you left him, he'd send the boy to an institution?'

'Yes,' replied Laura. 'If I – if I believed that I could have earned enough to keep Jan and myself – but I don't know that I could. And anyway, Richard was the boy's legal guardian of course.'

'Was Richard kind to him?' Starkwedder asked.

'Sometimes,' she replied.

'And at other times?'

'He'd – he'd quite frequently talk about sending Jan away,' Laura told him. 'He'd say to Jan, "They'll be quite kind to you, boy. You'll be well looked after. And Laura, I'm sure, would come and see you once or twice a year." He'd get Jan all worked up, terrified, begging, pleading, stammering. And then Richard would lean back in his chair and roar with laughter. Throw back his head and laugh, laugh, laugh.'

'I see,' said Starkwedder, watching her carefully. After a pause, he repeated thoughtfully, 'I see.'

Laura rose quickly, and went to the table by the armchair to stub out her cigarette. 'You needn't believe me,' she exclaimed. 'You needn't believe a word I say. For all you know, I might be making it all up.'

'I've told you I'll risk it,' Starkwedder replied. 'Now then,' he continued, 'what's this, what's-her-name, Bennett – Benny – like? Is she sharp? Bright?'

'She's very efficient and capable,' Laura assured him.

Starkwedder snapped his fingers. 'Something's just occurred to me,' he said. 'How is it that nobody in the house heard the shot tonight?'

'Well, Richard's mother is quite old, and she's rather deaf,' Laura replied. 'Benny's room is over on the other side of the house, and Angell's quarters are quite separate, shut off by a baize door. There's young Jan, of course. He sleeps in the room over this. But he goes to bed early, and he sleeps very heavily.'

'That all seems extremely fortunate,' Starkwedder observed.

Laura looked puzzled. 'But what are you suggesting?' she asked him. 'That we could make it look like suicide?'

He turned to look at the body again. 'No,' he

said, shaking his head. 'There's no hope of suicide, I'm afraid.' He walked over to the wheelchair and looked down at the corpse of Richard Warwick for a moment, before asking, 'He was right-handed, I assume?'

'Yes,' replied Laura.

'Yes, I was afraid so. In which case he couldn't possibly have shot himself at that angle,' he declared, pointing to Warwick's left temple. 'Besides, there's no mark of scorching.' He considered for a few seconds and then added, 'No, the gun must have been fired from a certain distance away. Suicide is certainly out.' He paused again before continuing. 'But there's accident, of course. After all, it could have been an accident.'

After a longer pause, he began to act out what he had in mind. 'Now, say for instance that I came here this evening. Just as I did, in fact. Blundered in through this window.' He went to the french windows, and mimed the act of stumbling into the room. 'Richard thought I was a burglar, and took a pot shot at me. Well, that's quite likely, from all you've been telling me about his exploits. Well, then, I come up to him' – and Starkwedder hastened to the body in the wheelchair – 'I get the gun away from him –'

Laura interrupted eagerly. 'And it went off in the struggle – yes?'

'Yes,' Starkwedder agreed, but immediately corrected himself. 'No, that won't do. As I say, the police would spot at once that the gun wasn't fired at such close quarters.' He took a few more moments to reconsider, and then continued. 'Well now, say I got the gun right away from him.' He shook his head, and waved his arms in a gesture of frustration. 'No, that's no good. Once I'd done that, why the hell should I shoot him? No, I'm afraid it's tricky.'

He sighed. 'All right,' he decided, 'let's leave it at murder. Murder pure and simple. But murder by someone from outside. Murder by person or persons unknown.' He crossed to the french windows, held back a curtain, and peered out as though seeking inspiration.

'A real burglar, perhaps?' Laura suggested helpfully.

Starkwedder thought for a moment, and then said, 'Well, I suppose it *could* be a burglar, but it seems a bit bogus.' He paused, then added, 'What about an enemy? That sounds melodramatic perhaps, but from what you've told me about your husband it seems he was the sort who might have had enemies. Am I right?'

'Well, yes,' Laura replied, speaking slowly and uncertainly, 'I suppose Richard had enemies, but –'

'Never mind the buts for the time being,' Starkwedder interrupted her, stubbing out his cigarette at the table by the wheelchair, and moving to stand over her as she sat on the sofa. 'Tell me all you can about Richard's enemies. Number One, I suppose, would be Miss – you know, Miss quivering backside – the woman he took pot shots at. But I don't suppose she's a likely murderer. Anyway, I imagine she still lives in Norfolk, and it would be a bit far-fetched to imagine her taking a cheap day return to Wales to bump him off. Who else?' he urged. 'Who else is there who had a grudge against him?'

Laura looked doubtful. She got up, moved about, and began to unbutton her jacket. 'Well,' she began cautiously, 'there was a gardener, about a year ago. Richard sacked him and wouldn't give him a reference. The man was very abusive about it and made a lot of threats.'

'Who was he?' Starkwedder asked. 'A local chap?'

'Yes,' Laura replied. 'He came from Llanfechan, about four miles away.' She took off her jacket and laid it across an arm of the sofa.

Starkwedder frowned. 'I don't think much of your gardener,' he told her. 'You can bet he's got a nice, stay-at-home alibi. And if he hasn't got an alibi, or it's an alibi that only his wife can confirm or support, we might end up getting the poor chap convicted for something he hasn't done. No, that's no good. What we want is some enemy out of the past, who wouldn't be so easy to track down.'

Laura moved slowly around the room, trying to think, as Starkwedder continued, 'How about someone from Richard's tiger- and lion-shooting days? Someone in Kenya, or South Africa, or India? Some place where the police can't check up on him very easily.'

'If I could only think,' said Laura, despairingly. 'If I could only remember. If I could remember some of the stories about those days that Richard told us at one time or another.'

'It isn't even as though we'd got any nice props handy,' Starkwedder muttered. 'You know, a Sikh turban carelessly draped over the decanter, or a Mau Mau knife, or a poisoned arrow.' He pressed his hands to his forehead in concentration. 'Damn it all,' he went on, 'what we want is someone with a grudge, someone who'd been kicked around by Richard.' Approaching Laura, he urged her, 'Think, woman. Think. Think!'

'I – I *can't* think,' replied Laura, her voice almost breaking with frustration.

'You've told me the kind of man your husband was. There must have been incidents, people. Heavens above, there must have been *something*,' he exclaimed.

Laura paced about the room, trying desperately to remember.

'Someone who made threats. Justifiable threats, perhaps,' Starkwedder encouraged her.

Laura stopped her pacing, and turned to face him. 'There was – I've just remembered,' she said. She spoke slowly. 'There was a man whose child Richard ran over.'

CHAPTER FOUR

Starkwedder stared at Laura. 'Richard ran over a child?' he asked excitedly. 'When was this?'

'It was about two years ago,' Laura told him. 'When we were living in Norfolk. The child's father certainly made threats at the time.'

Starkwedder sat down on the footstool. 'Now, that sounds like a possibility,' he said. 'Anyway, tell me all you can remember about him.'

Laura thought for a moment, and then began to speak. 'Richard was driving back from Cromer,' she said. 'He'd had far too much to drink, which was by no means unusual. He drove through a little village at about sixty miles an hour, apparently zig-zagging quite a bit. The child – a little boy – ran out into the road from the inn there – Richard knocked him down and he was killed instantly.'

'Do you mean,' Starkwedder asked her, 'that your husband could drive a car, despite his disability?'

'Yes, he could. Oh, it had to be specially built, with special controls that he could manage, but, yes, he was able to drive that vehicle.'

'I see,' said Starkwedder. 'What happened about the child? Surely the police could have got Richard for manslaughter?'

'There was an inquest, of course,' Laura explained.

A bitter note crept into her voice as she added, 'Richard was exonerated completely.'

'Were there any witnesses?' Starkwedder asked her.

'Well,' Laura replied, 'there was the child's father. He saw it happen. But there was also a hospital nurse – Nurse Warburton – who was in the car with Richard. She gave evidence, of course. And according to her, the car was going under thirty miles an hour and Richard had had only one glass of sherry. She said that the accident was quite unavoidable – the little boy just suddenly rushed out, straight in front of the car. They believed *her*, and not the child's father who said that the car was being driven erratically and at a very high speed. I understand the poor man was – rather over-violent in expressing his feelings.' Laura moved to the armchair, adding, 'You see, anyone *would* believe Nurse Warburton. She seemed the very essence of honesty and reliability and accuracy and careful understatement and all that.'

'You weren't in the car yourself?' Starkwedder asked.

'No, I wasn't,' Laura replied. 'I was at home.'

'Then how do you know that what Nurse what's-her-name said mightn't have been the truth?'

'Oh, the whole thing was very freely discussed by Richard,' she said bitterly. 'After they came back from the inquest, I remember very clearly. He said, "Bravo, Warby, jolly good show. You've probably got me off quite a stiff jail sentence." And she said, "You don't deserve to have got off, Mr Warwick.

30

You know you were driving much too fast. It's a shame about that poor child." And then Richard said, "Oh, forget it! I've made it worth your while. Anyway, what's one brat more or less in this overcrowded world? He's just as well out of it all. It's not going to spoil *my* sleep, I assure you."'

Starkwedder rose from the stool and, glancing over his shoulder at Richard Warwick's body, said grimly, 'The more I hear about your husband, the more I'm willing to believe that what happened tonight was justifiable homicide rather than murder.' Approaching Laura, he continued, 'Now then. This man whose child was run over. The boy's father. What's his name?'

'A Scottish name, I think,' Laura replied. 'Mac – Mac something – MacLeod? MacCrae? – I can't remember.'

'But you've got to try to remember,' Starkwedder insisted. 'Come on, you must. Is he still living in Norfolk?'

'No, no,' said Laura. 'He was only over here for a visit. To his wife's relations, I think. I seem to remember he came from Canada.'

'Canada – that's a nice long way away,' Starkwedder observed. 'It would take time to chase up. Yes,' he continued, moving to behind the sofa, 'yes, I think there are possibilities there. But for God's sake try to remember the man's name.' He went across to his overcoat on the armchair in the recess, took his gloves from a pocket, and put them on. Then, looking searchingly around the room, he asked, 'Got any newspapers about?'

'Newspapers?' Laura asked, surprised.

'Not today's,' he explained. 'Yesterday's or the day before would do better.'

Rising from the sofa, Laura went to a cupboard behind the armchair. 'There are some old ones in the cupboard here. We keep them for lighting fires,' she told him.

Starkwedder joined her, opened the cupboard door, and took out a newspaper. After checking the date, he announced, 'This is fine. Just what we want.' He closed the cupboard door, took the newspaper to the desk, and from a pigeon-hole on the desk extracted a pair of scissors.

'What are you going to do?' asked Laura.

'We're going to manufacture some evidence.' He clicked the scissors as though to demonstrate.

Laura stared at him, perplexed. 'But suppose the police succeed in finding this man,' she asked. 'What happens then?'

Starkwedder beamed at her. 'If he still lives in Canada, it'll take a bit of doing,' he announced with an air of smugness. 'And by the time they do find him, he'll no doubt have an alibi for tonight. Being a few thousand miles away ought to be satisfactory enough. And by then it will be a bit late for them to check up on things here. Anyway, it's the best we can do. It'll give us breathing space at all events.'

Laura looked worried. 'I don't like it,' she complained.

Starkwedder gave her a somewhat exasperated look. 'My dear girl,' he admonished her, 'you can't afford to be choosy. But you must try to remember that man's name.'

'I can't, I tell you, I can't,' Laura insisted.

'Was it MacDougall, perhaps? Or Mackintosh?' he suggested helpfully.

Laura took a few steps away from him, putting her hands to her ears. 'Do stop,' she cried. 'You're only making it worse. I'm not sure now that it was Mac anything.'

'Well, if you can't remember, you can't,' Starkwedder conceded. 'We shall have to manage without. You don't remember the date, by any chance, or anything useful like that?'

'Oh, I can tell you the date, all right,' said Laura. 'It was May the fifteenth.'

Surprised, Starkwedder asked, 'Now, how on earth can you remember that?'

There was bitterness in Laura's voice as she replied, 'Because it happened on my birthday.'

'Ah, I see – yes – well, that solves one little problem,' observed Starkwedder. 'And we've also got one little piece of luck. This paper is dated the fifteenth.' He cut the date out carefully from the newspaper.

Joining him at the desk and looking over his shoulder, Laura pointed out that the date on the newspaper was November the fifteenth, not May. 'Yes,' he admitted, 'but it's the numbers that are the more awkward. Now, May. May's a short word – ah, yes, here's an M. Now an A, and a Y.'

'What in heaven's name are you doing?' Laura asked.

Starkwedder's only response, as he seated himself in the desk chair, was, 'Got any paste?'

Laura was about to take a pot of paste from a pigeon-hole, but he stopped her. 'No, don't touch,' he instructed. 'We don't want your fingerprints on it.' He took the pot of paste in his gloved hands, and removed the lid. 'How to be a criminal in one easy lesson,' he continued. 'And, yes, here's a plain block of writing paper – the kind sold all over the British Isles.' Taking a notepad from the pigeon-hole, he proceeded to paste words and letters onto a sheet of notepaper. 'Now, watch this, one – two – three – a bit tricky with gloves. But there we are. "May fifteen. Paid in full." Oh, the "in" has come off.' He pasted it back on again. 'There, now. How do you like that?'

He tore the sheet off the pad and showed it to her, then went across to Richard Warwick's body in its wheelchair. 'We'll tuck it neatly into his jacket pocket, like that.' As he did so, he dislodged a pocket lighter, which fell to the floor. 'Hello, what's this?'

Laura gave a sharp exclamation and tried to snatch the lighter up, but Starkwedder had already done so, and was examining it. 'Give it to me,' cried Laura breathlessly. 'Give it to me!'

Looking faintly surprised, Starkwedder handed it to her. 'It's – it's my lighter,' she explained, unnecessarily.

'All right, so it's your lighter,' he agreed. 'That's nothing to get upset about.' He looked at her curiously. 'You're not losing your nerve, are you?'

She walked away from him to the sofa. As she did

so, she rubbed the lighter on her skirt as though to remove possible fingerprints, taking care to ensure that Starkwedder did not observe her doing so. 'No, of course I'm not losing my nerve,' she assured him.

Having made certain that the pasted-up message from the newspaper in Richard Warwick's breast pocket was tucked securely under the lapel, Starkwedder went over to the desk, replaced the lid of the paste-pot, removed his gloves, took out a handkerchief, and looked at Laura. 'There we are!' he announced. 'All ready for the next step. Where's that glass you were drinking out of just now?'

Laura retrieved the glass from the table where she had deposited it. Leaving her lighter on the table, she returned with the glass to Starkwedder. He took it from her, and was about to wipe off her fingerprints, but then stopped. 'No,' he murmured. 'No, that would be stupid.'

'Why?' asked Laura.

'Well, there ought to be fingerprints,' he explained, 'both on the glass and on the decanter. This valet fellow's, for one, and probably your husband's as well. No fingerprints at all would look very fishy to the police.' He took a sip from the glass he was holding. 'Now I must think of a way to explain mine,' he added. 'Crime isn't easy, is it?'

With sudden passion, Laura exclaimed, 'Oh, don't! Don't get mixed up in this. They might suspect *you*.'

Amused, Starkwedder replied, 'Oh, I'm a very respectable chap – quite above suspicion. But, in a sense I *am* mixed up in it already. After all, my car's out there, stuck fast in the ditch. But don't worry, just a spot of perjury and a little tinkering with the time element – that's the worst they'd be able to bring against me. And they won't, if you play your part properly.'

Frightened, Laura sat on the footstool, with her back to him. He came round to face her. 'Now then,' he said, 'are you ready?'

'Ready – for what?' asked Laura.

'Come on, you must pull yourself together,' he urged her.

Sounding dazed, she murmured, 'I feel – stupid – I – I can't think.'

'You don't have to think,' Starkwedder told her. 'You've just got to obey orders. Now then, here's the blueprint. First, have you got a furnace of any kind in the house?'

'A furnace?' Laura thought, and then replied, 'Well, there's the water boiler.'

'Good.' He went to the desk, took the newspaper, and rolled up the scraps of paper in it. Returning to Laura, he handed her the bundle. 'Now then,' he instructed her, 'the first thing you do is to go into the kitchen and put this in the boiler. Then you go upstairs, get out of your clothes and into a dressing-gown – or negligée, or what-have-you.' He paused. 'Have you got any aspirin?'

Puzzled, Laura replied, 'Yes.'

As though thinking and planning as he spoke, Starkwedder continued, 'Well – empty the bottle down the loo. Then go along to someone – your mother-in-law, or Miss – what is it – Bennett? – and say you've got a headache and want some aspirin. Then, while you're with whoever it is – leave the door open, by the way – you'll hear the shot.'

'What shot?' asked Laura, staring at him.

Without replying, Starkwedder crossed to the table by the wheelchair and picked up the gun. 'Yes, yes,' he murmured absently, 'I'll attend to that.' He examined the gun. 'Hm. Looks foreign to me – war souvenir, is it?'

Laura rose from the stool. 'I don't know,' she told him. 'Richard had several foreign makes of pistol.'

'I wonder if it's registered,' Starkwedder said, almost to himself, still holding the gun.

Laura sat on the sofa. 'Richard had a licence – if that's what you call it – a permit for his collection,' she said.

'Yes, I suppose he would have. But that doesn't mean that they would all be registered in his name. In practice, people are often rather careless about that kind of thing. Is there anyone who'd be likely to know definitely?'

'Angell might,' said Laura. 'Does it matter?'

Starkwedder moved about the room as he replied. 'Well, the way we're building this up, old MacThing – the father of the child Richard ran over – is more likely to come bursting in, breathing blood and thunder and revenge, with his own weapon at the ready. But one could, after all, make out quite a plausible case the other way. This man – whoever he is – bursts in. Richard, only half awake, snatches up his gun. The other fellow wrenches it away from

37

him, and shoots. I admit it sounds a bit far-fetched, but it'll have to do. We've got to take some risks, it just can't be avoided.'

He placed the gun on the table by the wheelchair, and approached her. 'Now then,' he continued, 'have we thought of everything? I hope so. The fact that he was shot a quarter of an hour or twenty minutes earlier won't be apparent by the time the police get here. Driving along these roads in this fog won't be easy for them.' He went over to the curtain by the french windows, lifted it, and looked at the bullet holes in the wall. ' "R.W". Very nice. I'll try to add a full stop.'

Replacing the curtain, he came back to her. 'When you hear the shot,' he instructed Laura, ' what you do is register alarm, and bring Miss Bennett – or anyone else you can collect – down here. Your story is that you don't know anything. You went to bed, you woke up with a violent headache, you went along to look for aspirin – and that's *all* you know. Understand?'

Laura nodded.

'Good,' said Starkwedder. 'All the rest you leave to me. Are you feeling all right now?'

'Yes, I think so,' Laura whispered.

'Then go along and do your stuff,' he ordered her.

Laura hesitated. 'You – you oughtn't to do this,' she urged him again. 'You oughtn't. You shouldn't get involved.'

'Now, don't let's have any more of that,' Starkwedder insisted. 'Everyone has their own form of –

what did we call it just now? – fun and games. You had your fun and games shooting your husband. I'm having my fun and games now. Let's just say I've always had a secret longing to see how I could get on with a detective story in real life.' He gave her a quick, reassuring smile. 'Now, can you do what I've told you?'

Laura nodded. 'Yes.'

'Right. Oh, I see you've got a watch. Good. What time do you make it?'

Laura showed him her wristwatch, and he set his accordingly. 'Just after ten minutes to,' he observed. 'I'll allow you three – no, four – minutes. Four minutes to go along to the kitchen, pop that paper in the boiler, go upstairs, get out of your things and into a dressing-gown, and along to Miss Bennett or whoever. Do you think you can do that, Laura?' He smiled at her reassuringly.

Laura nodded.

'Now then,' he continued, 'at five minutes to midnight exactly, you'll hear the shot. Off you go.'

Moving to the door, she turned and looked at him, uncertain of herself. Starkwedder went across to open the door for her. 'You're not going to let me down, are you?' he asked.

'No,' replied Laura faintly.

'Good.'

Laura was about to leave the room when Starkwedder noticed her jacket lying on the arm of the sofa. Calling her back, he gave it to her, smiling. She went out, and he closed the door behind her.

CHAPTER FIVE

After closing the door behind Laura, Starkwedder paused, working out in his mind what was to be done. After a moment, he glanced at his watch, then took out a cigarette. He moved to the table by the armchair and was about to pick up the lighter when he noticed a photograph of Laura on one of the bookshelves. He picked it up, looked at it, smiled, replaced it, and lit a cigarette, leaving the lighter on the table. Taking out his handkerchief, he rubbed any fingerprints off the arms of the armchair and the photograph, and then pushed the chair back to its original position. He took Laura's cigarette from the ashtray, then went to the table by the wheelchair and took his own stub from the ashtray. Crossing to the desk, he next rubbed any fingerprints from it, replaced the scissors and notepad, and adjusted the blotter. He looked around him on the floor for any scrap of paper that might have been missed, found one near the desk, screwed it up and put it in his trousers pocket. He rubbed fingerprints off the light switch by the door and off the desk chair, picked up his torch from the desk, went over to the french windows, drew the curtain back slightly, and shone the torch through the window onto the path outside.

'Too hard for footprints,' he murmured to himself. He put the torch on the table by the wheelchair and picked up the gun. Making sure that it was sufficiently loaded, he polished it for fingerprints, then went to the stool and put the gun down on it. After glancing again at his watch, he went to the armchair in the recess and put on his hat, scarf and gloves. With his overcoat on his arm, he crossed to the door. He was about to switch off the lights when he remembered to remove the fingerprints from the door-plate and handle. He then switched off the lights, and came back to the stool, putting his coat on. He picked up the gun, and was about to fire it at the initials on the wall when he realized that they were hidden by the curtain.

'Damn!' he muttered. Quickly taking the desk chair, he used it to hold the curtain back. He returned to his position by the stool, fired the gun, and then quickly went back to the wall to examine the result. 'Not bad!' he congratulated himself.

As he replaced the desk chair in its proper position, Starkwedder could hear voices in the hall. He rushed off through the french windows, taking the gun with him. A moment later he reappeared, snatched up the torch, and dashed out again.

From various parts of the house, four people hurried towards the study. Richard Warwick's mother, a tall, commanding old lady, was in her dressing-gown. She looked pallid and walked with the aid of a stick. 'What is it, Jan?' she asked the teenage boy in pyjamas with the strange, rather innocent,

42

faun-like face, who was close behind her on the landing. 'Why is everybody wandering about in the middle of the night?' she exclaimed as they were joined by a grey-haired, middle-aged woman, wearing a sensible flannel dressing-gown. 'Benny,' she ordered the woman, 'tell me what's going on.'

Laura was close behind, and Mrs Warwick continued, 'Have you all taken leave of your senses? Laura, what's happened? Jan – Jan – will someone tell me what is going on in this house?'

'I'll bet it's Richard,' said the boy, who looked about nineteen, though his voice and manner were those of a younger child. 'He's shooting at the fog again.' There was a note of petulance in his voice as he added, 'Tell him he's not to shoot and wake us all up out of our beauty sleep. I was deep asleep, and so was Benny. Weren't you, Benny? Be careful, Laura, Richard's dangerous. He's dangerous, Benny, be careful.'

'There's thick fog outside,' said Laura, looking through the landing window. 'You can barely make out the path. I can't imagine what he can be shooting at in this mist. It's absurd. Besides, I thought I heard a cry.'

Miss Bennett – Benny – an alert, brisk woman who looked like the ex-hospital nurse that she was, spoke somewhat officiously. 'I really can't see why you're so upset, Laura. It's just Richard amusing himself as usual. But I didn't hear any shooting. I'm sure there's nothing wrong. I think you're imagining things. But he's certainly very selfish and I shall tell him so. Richard,' she called as she entered the study, 'really, Richard, it's too bad at this time of night. You frightened us – Richard!'

Laura, wearing her dressing-gown, followed Miss Bennett into the room. As she switched on the lights and moved to the sofa, the boy Jan followed her. He looked at Miss Bennett who stood staring at Richard Warwick in his wheelchair. 'What is it, Benny?' asked Jan. 'What's the matter?'

'It's Richard,' said Miss Bennett, her voice strangely calm. 'He's killed himself.'

'Look,' cried young Jan excitedly, pointing at the table. 'Richard's revolver's gone.'

A voice from outside in the garden called, 'What's going on in there? Is anything wrong?' Looking through the small window in the recess, Jan shouted, 'Listen! There's someone outside!'

'Outside?' said Miss Bennett. 'Who?' She turned to the french windows and was about to draw back the curtain when Starkwedder suddenly appeared. Miss Bennett stepped back in alarm as Starkwedder came forward, asking urgently, 'What's happened here? What's the matter?' His glance fell on Richard Warwick in the wheelchair. 'This man's dead!' he exclaimed. 'Shot.' He looked around the room suspiciously, taking them all in.

'Who are you?' asked Miss Bennett. 'Where do you come from?'

'Just run my car into a ditch,' replied Starkwedder. 'I've been lost for hours. Found some gates and came up to the house to try to get some help and telephone. Heard a shot, and someone came rushing out of the windows and collided with me.'

44

Holding out the gun, Starkwedder added, 'He dropped this.'

'Where did this man go?' Miss Bennett asked him.

'How the hell should I know in this fog?' Starkwedder replied.

Jan stood in front of Richard's body, staring excitedly at it. 'Somebody's shot Richard,' he shouted.

'Looks like it,' Starkwedder agreed. 'You'd better get in touch with the police.' He placed the gun on the table by the wheelchair, picked up the decanter, and poured brandy into a glass. 'Who is he?'

'My husband,' said Laura, expressionlessly, as she went to sit on the sofa.

With what sounded a slightly forced concern, Starkwedder said to her, 'Here – drink this.' Laura looked up at him. 'You've had a shock,' he added emphatically. As she took the glass, with his back turned to the others Starkwedder gave her a conspiratorial grin, to call her attention to his solution of the fingerprint problem. Turning away, he threw his hat on the armchair, and then, suddenly noticing that Miss Bennett was about to bend over Richard Warwick's body, he swung quickly round. 'No, don't touch anything, madam,' he implored her. 'This looks like murder, and if it is then nothing must be touched.'

Straightening up, Miss Bennett backed away from the body in the chair, looking appalled. 'Murder?' she exclaimed. 'It can't be murder!'

Mrs Warwick, the mother of the dead man, had

stopped just inside the door of the study. She came forward now, asking, 'What has happened?'

'Richard's been shot! Richard's been shot!' Jan told her. He sounded more excited than concerned.

'Quiet, Jan,' ordered Miss Bennett.

'What did I hear you say?' asked Mrs Warwick, quietly.

'*He* said – murder,' Benny told her, indicating Starkwedder.

'Richard,' Mrs Warwick whispered, as Jan leaned over the body, calling, 'Look – look – there's something on his chest – a paper – with writing on it.' His hand went out to it, but he was stopped by Starkwedder's command: 'Don't touch – whatever you do, don't touch.' Then he read aloud, slowly, '"May – fifteen – paid in full".'

'Good Lord! MacGregor,' Miss Bennett exclaimed, moving behind the sofa.

Laura rose. Mrs Warwick frowned. 'You mean,' she said, '– that man – the father – the child that was run over – ?'

'Of course, MacGregor,' Laura murmured to herself as she sat in the armchair.

Jan went up to the body. 'Look – it's all newspaper – cut up,' he said in excitement. Starkwedder again restrained him. 'No, don't touch it,' he ordered. 'It's got to be left for the police.' He stepped towards the telephone. 'Shall I – ?'

'No,' said Mrs Warwick firmly. 'I will.' Taking charge of the situation, and summoning her courage, she went to the desk and started to dial. Jan moved excitedly to the stool and knelt upon it. 'The

46

man that ran away,' he asked Miss Bennett. 'Do you think he – ?'

'Ssh, Jan,' Miss Bennett said to him firmly, while Mrs Warwick spoke quietly but in a clear, authoritative voice on the telephone. 'Is that the police station? This is Llangelert House. Mr Richard Warwick's house. Mr Warwick has just been found – shot dead.'

She went on speaking into the phone. Her voice remained low, but the others in the room listened intently. 'No, he was found by a stranger,' they heard her say. 'A man whose car had broken down near the house, I believe . . . Yes, I'll tell him. I'll phone the inn. Will one of your cars be able to take him there when you've finished here? . . . Very well.'

Turning to face the company, Mrs Warwick announced, 'The police will be here as soon as they can in this fog. They'll have two cars, one of which will return right away to take this gentleman' – she gestured at Starkwedder – 'to the inn in the village. They want him to stay overnight and be available to talk to them tomorrow.'

'Well, since I can't leave with my car still in the ditch, that's fine with me,' Starkwedder exclaimed. As he spoke, the door to the corridor opened, and a dark-haired man of medium height in his mid-forties entered the room, tying the cord of his dressing-gown. He suddenly stopped short just inside the door. 'Is something the matter, madam?' he asked, addressing Mrs Warwick. Then, glancing past her, he saw the body of Richard Warwick. 'Oh, my God,' he exclaimed.

47

'I'm afraid there's been a terrible tragedy, Angell,' Mrs Warwick replied. 'Mr Richard has been shot, and the police are on their way here.' Turning to Starkwedder, she said, 'This is Angell. He's – he was Richard's valet.'

The valet acknowledged Starkwedder's presence wth a slight, absent-minded bow. 'Oh, my God,' he repeated, as he continued to stare at the body of his late employer.

CHAPTER SIX

At eleven the following morning, Richard Warwick's study looked somewhat more inviting than it had on the previous foggy evening. For one thing, the sun was shining on a cold, clear, bright day, and the french windows were wide open. The body had been removed overnight, and the wheelchair had been pushed into the recess, its former central place in the room now occupied by the armchair. The small table had been cleared of everything except decanter and ashtray. A good-looking young man in his twenties with short dark hair, dressed in a tweed sports jacket and navy-blue trousers, was sitting in the wheelchair, reading a book of poems. After a few moments, he got up. 'Beautiful,' he said to himself. 'Apposite and beautiful.' His voice was soft and musical, with a pronounced Welsh accent.

The young man closed the book he had been reading, and replaced it on the bookshelves in the recess. Then, after surveying the room for a minute or two, he walked across to the open french windows, and went out onto the terrace. Almost immediately, a middle-aged, thick-set, somewhat poker-faced man carrying a briefcase entered the room from the hallway. Going to the armchair which faced out onto the terrace, he put his briefcase on it, and looked out of the windows. 'Sergeant Cadwallader!' he called sharply.

The younger man turned back into the room. 'Good morning, Inspector Thomas,' he said, and then continued, with a lilt in his voice, '"Season of mists and mellow fruitfulness, close bosom friend of the maturing sun".'

The inspector, who had begun to unbutton his overcoat, stopped and looked intently at the young sergeant. 'I beg your pardon?' he asked, with a distinct note of sarcasm in his voice.

'That's Keats,' the sergeant informed him, sounding quite pleased with himself. The inspector responded with a baleful look at him, then shrugged, took off his coat, placed it on the wheelchair in the recess, and came back for his briefcase.

'You'd hardly credit the fine day it is,' Sergeant Cadwallader went on. 'When you think of the terrible time we had getting here last night. The worst fog I've known in years. "The yellow fog that rubs its back upon the window-panes". That's T.S. Eliot.' He waited for a reaction to his quotation from the inspector, but got none, so continued, 'It's no wonder the accidents piled up the way they did on the Cardiff road.'

'Might have been worse,' was his inspector's uninterested comment.

'I don't know about that,' said the sergeant, warming to his subject. 'At Porthcawl, that was a nasty smash. One killed and two children badly injured. And the mother crying her heart out there on the road. "The pretty wretch left crying" –'

The inspector interrupted him. 'Have the finger-print boys finished their job yet?' he asked.

Suddenly realizing that he had better get back to the business in hand, Sergeant Cadwallader replied, 'Yes, sir. I've got them all ready here for you.' He picked up a folder from the desk and opened it. The inspector sat in the desk chair and started to examine the first sheet of fingerprints in the folder. 'No trouble from the household about taking their prints?' he asked the sergeant casually.

'No trouble whatever,' the sergeant told him. 'Most obliging they were – anxious to help, as you might say. And that is only to be expected.'

'I don't know about that,' the inspector observed. 'I've usually found most people kick up no end of a fuss. Seem to think their prints are going to be filed in the Rogues' Gallery.' He took a deep breath, stretching his arms, and continued to study the prints. 'Now, let's see. Mr Warwick – that's the deceased. Mrs Laura Warwick, his wife. Mrs Warwick senior, that's his mother. Young Jan Warwick, Miss Bennett and – who's this? Angle? Oh, Angell. Ah yes, that's his nurse-attendant, isn't it? And two other sets of prints. Let's see now – Hm. On outside of win-dow, on decanter, on brandy glass overlaying prints of Richard Warwick and Angell and Mrs Laura Warwick, on cigarette lighter – and on the revolver. That will be that chap Michael Starkwedder. He gave Mrs Warwick brandy, and of course it was he who carried the gun in from the garden.'

Sergeant Cadwallader nodded slowly. 'Mr Stark-wedder,' he growled, in a voice of deep suspicion.

The inspector, sounding amused, asked, 'You don't like him?'

'What's he doing here? That's what I'd like to know,' the sergeant replied. 'Running his car into a ditch and coming up to a house where there's been a murder done?'

The inspector turned in his chair to face his young colleague. 'You nearly ran *our* car into the ditch last night, coming up to a house where there'd been a murder done. And as to what he's doing here, he's been here – in this vicinity – for the last week, looking around for a small house or cottage.'

The sergeant looked unconvinced, and the inspector turned back to the desk, adding wryly, 'It seems he had a Welsh grandmother and he used to come here for holidays when he was a boy.'

Mollified, the sergeant conceded, 'Ah, well now, if he had a Welsh grandmother, that's a different matter, isn't it?' He raised his right arm and declaimed, '"One road leads to London, One road leads to Wales. My road leads me seawards, To the white dipping sails." He was a fine poet, John Masefield. Very underrated.'

The inspector opened his mouth to complain, but then thought better of it and grinned instead. 'We ought to get the report on Starkwedder from Abadan any moment now,' he told the young sergeant. 'Have you got his prints for comparison?'

'I sent Jones round to the inn where he stayed last night,' Cadwallader informed his superior, 'but he'd gone out to the garage to see about getting his car salvaged. Jones rang the garage and spoke to him while he was there. He's been told to report at the station as soon as possible.'

'Right. Now, about this second set of unidentified prints. The print of a man's hand flat on the table by the body, and blurred impressions on both the outside and the inside of the french windows.'

'I'll bet that's MacGregor,' the sergeant exclaimed, snapping his fingers.

'Ye-es. Could be,' the inspector admitted reluctantly. 'But they weren't on the revolver. And you would think any man using a revolver to kill someone would have the sense enough to wear gloves, surely.'

'I don't know,' the sergeant observed. 'An unbalanced fellow like this MacGregor, deranged after the death of his child, he wouldn't think of that.'

'Well, we ought to get a description of MacGregor through from Norwich soon,' the inspector said.

The sergeant settled himself on the footstool. 'It's sad story, whichever way you look at it,' he suggested. 'A man, his wife but lately dead, and his only child killed by furious driving.'

'If there'd been what you call furious driving,' the inspector corrected him impatiently, 'Richard Warwick would have got a sentence for manslaughter, or at any rate for the driving offence. In point of fact, his licence wasn't even endorsed.' He reached down to his briefcase, and took out the murder weapon.

'There is some fearful lying goes on sometimes,' Sergeant Cadwallader muttered darkly. '"Lord, Lord, how this world is given to lying." That's Shakespeare.'

His superior officer merely rose from the desk and

looked at him. After a moment, the sergeant pulled himself together and rose to his feet. 'A man's hand flat on the table,' murmured the inspector as he went across to the table, taking the gun with him, and looking down at the table-top. 'I wonder.'

'Perhaps that could have been a guest in the house,' Sergeant Cadwallader suggested helpfully.

'Perhaps,' the inspector agreed. 'But I understand from Mrs Warwick that there were no visitors to the house yesterday. That manservant – Angell – might be able to tell us more. Go and fetch him, would you?'

'Yes, sir,' said Cadwallader as he went out. Left alone, the inspector spread out his own left hand on the table, and bent over the chair as if looking down at an invisible occupant. Then he went to the window and stepped outside, glancing both to left and right. He examined the lock of the french windows, and was turning back into the room when the sergeant returned, bringing with him Richard Warwick's valet-attendant, Angell, who was wearing a grey alpaca jacket, white shirt, dark tie and striped trousers.

'You're Henry Angell?' the inspector asked him.

'Yes, sir,' Angell replied.

'Sit down there, will you?' said the inspector.

Angell moved to sit on the sofa. 'Now then,' the inspector continued, 'you've been nurse-attendant and valet to Mr Richard Warwick – for how long?'

'For three and a half years, sir,' replied Angell. His manner was correct, but there was a shifty look in his eyes.

'Did you like the job?'

'I found it quite satisfactory, sir,' was Angell's reply.

'What was Mr Warwick like to work for?' the inspector asked him.

'Well, he was difficult.'

'But there were advantages, were there?'

'Yes, sir,' Angell admitted. 'I was extremely well paid.'

'And that made up for the other disadvantages, did it?' the inspector persisted.

'Yes, sir. I am trying to accumulate a little nest-egg.'

The inspector seated himself in the armchair, placing the gun on the table beside him. 'What were you doing before you came to Mr Warwick?' he asked Angell.

'The same sort of job, sir. I can show you my references,' the valet replied. 'I've always given satisfaction, I hope. I've had some rather difficult employers – or patients, really. Sir James Walliston, for example. He is now a voluntary patient in a mental home. A *very* difficult person, sir.' He lowered his voice slightly before adding, 'Drugs!'

'Quite,' said the inspector. 'There was no question of drugs with Mr Warwick, I suppose?'

'No, sir. Brandy was what Mr Warwick liked to resort to.'

'Drank a lot of it, did he?' the inspector asked.

'Yes, sir,' Angell replied. 'He was a heavy drinker, but not an alcoholic, if you understand me. He never showed any ill-effects.'

The inspector paused before asking, 'Now, what's all this about guns and revolvers and – shooting at animals?'

'Well, it was his hobby, sir,' Angell told him. 'What we call in the profession a compensation. He'd been a big-game hunter in his day, I understand. Quite a little arsenal he's got in his bedroom there.' He nodded over his shoulder to indicate a room elsewhere in the house. 'Rifles, shotguns, air-guns, pistols and revolvers.'

'I see,' said the inspector. 'Well, now, just take a look at this gun here.'

Angell rose and stepped towards the table, then hesitated. 'It's all right,' the inspector told him, 'you needn't mind handling it.'

Angell picked up the gun, gingerly. 'Do you recognize it?' the inspector asked him.

'It's difficult to say, sir,' the valet replied. 'It looks like one of Mr Warwick's, but I don't really know very much about firearms. I can't say for certain which gun he had on the table beside him last night.'

'Didn't he have the same one every night?' asked the inspector.

'Oh, no, he had his fancies, sir,' said Angell. 'He kept using different ones.' The valet offered the gun back to the inspector, who took it.

'What was the good of his having a gun last night with all that fog?' queried the inspector.

'It was just a habit, sir,' Angell replied. 'He was used to it, as you might say.'

'All right, sit down again, would you?'

Angell sat again at one end of the sofa. The

56

inspector examined the barrel of the gun before asking, 'When did you see Mr Warwick last?'

'About a quarter to ten last night, sir,' Angell told him. 'He had a bottle of brandy and a glass by his side, and the pistol he'd chosen. I arranged his rug for him, and wished him good-night.'

'Didn't he ever go to bed?' the inspector asked.

'No, sir,' replied the valet. 'At least, not in the usual sense of the term. He always slept in his chair. At six in the morning I would bring him tea, then I would wheel him into his bedroom, which had its own bathroom, where he'd bath and shave and so on, and then he'd usually sleep until lunch-time. I understand that he suffered from insomnia at night, and so he preferred to remain in his chair then. He was rather an eccentric gentleman.'

'And the window was shut when you left him?'

'Yes, sir,' Angell replied. 'There was a lot of fog about last night, and he didn't want it seeping into the house.'

'All right. The window was shut. Was it locked?'

'No, sir. That window was never locked.'

'So he could open it if he wanted to?'

'Oh, yes, sir. He had his wheelchair, you see. He could wheel himself over to the window and open it if the night should clear up.'

'I see.' The inspector thought for a moment, and then asked, 'You didn't hear a shot last night?'

'No, sir,' Angell replied.

The inspector walked across to the sofa and looked down at Angell. 'Isn't that rather remarkable?' he asked.

'No, not really, sir,' was the reply. 'You see, my room is some distance away. Along a passage and through a baize door on the other side of the house.'

'Wasn't that rather awkward, in case your master wanted to summon you?'

'Oh no, sir,' said Angell. 'He had a bell that rang in my room.'

'But he didn't press that bell last night at all?'

'Oh no, sir,' Angell repeated. 'If he had done so, I would have woken up at once. It is, if I may say so, a very loud bell, sir.'

Inspector Thomas leaned forward on the arm of the sofa to approach Angell in another way.

'Did you –' he began in a voice of controlled impatience, only to be interrupted by the shrill ring of the telephone. He waited for Sergeant Cadwallader to answer it, but the sergeant appeared to be dreaming with his eyes open and his lips moving soundlessly, perhaps immersed in some poetic reflection. After a moment, he realized that the inspector was staring at him, and that the phone was ringing. 'Sorry, sir, but a poem is on the way,' he explained as he went to the desk to answer the phone. 'Sergeant Cadwallader speaking,' he said. There was a pause, and then he added, 'Ah yes, indeed.' After another pause, he turned to the inspector. 'It's the police at Norwich, sir.'

Inspector Thomas took the phone from Cadwallader, and sat at the desk. 'Is that you, Edmundson?' he asked. 'Thomas here . . . Got it, right . . . Yes . . . Calgary, yes . . . Yes . . . Yes, the aunt, when did she die? . . . Oh, two months ago . . . Yes, I see . . .

Eighteen, Thirty-fourth Street, Calgary.' He looked up impatiently at Cadwallader, and gestured to him to take a note of the address. 'Yes . . . Oh, it was, was it? . . . Yes, slowly please.' He looked meaningfully again at his sergeant. 'Medium height,' he repeated. 'Blue eyes, dark hair and beard . . . Yes, as you say, you remember the case . . . Ah, he did, did he? . . . Violent sort of fellow? . . . Yes . . . You're sending it along? Yes . . . Well, thank you, Edmundson. Tell me, what do you think, yourself? . . . Yes, yes, I know what the findings were, but what did *you* think yourself? . . . Ah, he had, had he? . . . Once or twice before . . . Yes, of course, you'd make some allowances . . . All right. Thanks.'

He replaced the receiver and said to the sergeant, 'Well, we've got some of the dope on MacGregor. It seems that, when his wife died, he travelled back to England from Canada to leave the child with an aunt of his wife's who lived in North Walsham, because he had just got himself a job in Alaska and couldn't take the boy with him. Apparently he was terribly cut up at the child's death, and went about swearing revenge on Warwick. That's not uncommon after one of these accidents. Anyway, he went off back to Canada. They've got his address, and they'll send a cable off to Calgary. The aunt he was going to leave the child with died about two months ago.' He turned suddenly to Angell. 'You were there at the time, I suppose, Angell? Motor accident in North Walsham, running over a boy.'

'Oh yes, sir,' Angell replied. 'I remember it quite well.'

The inspector got up from the desk and went across to the valet. Seeing the desk chair empty, Sergeant Cadwallader promptly took the opportunity to sit down. 'What happened?' the inspector asked Angell. 'Tell me about the accident.'

'Mr Warwick was driving along the main street, and a little boy ran out of a house there,' Angell told him. 'Or it might have been the inn. I think it was. There was no chance of stopping. Mr Warwick ran over him before he could do a thing about it.'

'He was speeding, was he?' asked the inspector.

'Oh no, sir. That was brought out very clearly at the inquest. Mr Warwick was well within the speed limit.'

'I know that's what he said,' the inspector commented.

'It was quite true, sir,' Angell insisted. 'Nurse Warburton – a nurse Mr Warwick employed at the time – she was in the car, too, and she agreed.'

The inspector walked across to one end of the sofa. 'Did she happen to look at the speedometer at the time?' he queried.

'I believe Nurse Warburton did happen to see the speedometer,' Angell replied smoothly. 'She estimated that they were going at between twenty and twenty-five miles an hour. Mr Warwick was completely exonerated.'

'But the boy's father didn't agree?' the inspector asked.

'Perhaps that's only natural, sir,' was Angell's comment.

'Had Mr Warwick been drinking?'

Angell's reply was evasive. 'I believe he had had a glass of sherry, sir.' He and Inspector Thomas exchanged glances. Then the inspector crossed to the french windows, taking out his handkerchief and blowing his nose. 'Well, I think that'll do for now,' he told the valet.

Angell rose and went to the door. After a moment's hesitation, he turned back into the room. 'Excuse me, sir,' he said. 'But was Mr Warwick shot with his own gun?'

The inspector turned to him. 'That remains to be seen,' he observed. 'Whoever it was who shot him collided with Mr Starkwedder, who was coming up to the house to try to get help for his stranded vehicle. In the collision, the man dropped a gun. Mr Starkwedder picked it up – this gun.' He pointed to the gun on the table.

'I see, sir. Thank you, sir,' said Angell as he turned to the door again.

'By the way,' added the inspector, 'were there any visitors to the house yesterday? Yesterday evening in particular?'

Angell paused for just a moment, then eyed the inspector shiftily. 'Not that I can recall, sir – at present,' he replied. He left the room, closing the door behind him.

Inspector Thomas went back to the desk. 'If you ask me,' he said quietly to the sergeant, 'that fellow's a nasty bit of goods. Nothing you can put your finger on, but I don't like him.'

'I'm of the same opinion as you, regarding that,' Cadwallader replied. 'He's not a man I would trust, and what's more, I'd say there may have been something fishy about that accident.' Suddenly realizing that the inspector was standing over him, he got up quickly from his chair. The inspector took the notes Cadwallader had been making, and began to peruse them. 'Now I wonder if Angell knows something he hasn't told us about last night,' he began, and then broke off. 'Hello, what's this? "'Tis misty in November, But seldom in December." That's not Keats, I hope?'

'No,' said Sergeant Cadwallader proudly. 'That's Cadwallader.'

CHAPTER SEVEN

The inspector thrust Cadwallader's notebook back at him roughly, as the door opened and Miss Bennett came in, closing the door carefully behind her. 'Inspector,' she said, 'Mrs Warwick is very anxious to see you. She is fussing a little.' She added quickly, 'I mean Mrs Warwick senior, Richard's mother. She doesn't admit it, but I don't think she's in the best of health, so please be gentle with her. Will you see her now?'

'Oh, certainly,' replied the inspector. 'Ask her to come in.'

Miss Bennett opened the door, beckoning, and Mrs Warwick came in. 'It's all right, Mrs Warwick,' the housekeeper assured her, leaving the room and shutting the door behind her.

'Good morning, madam,' the inspector said. Mrs Warwick did not return his greeting, but came directly to the point. 'Tell me, Inspector,' she ordered, 'what progress are you making?'

'It's rather early to say that, madam,' he replied, 'but you can rest assured that we're doing everything we can.'

Mrs Warwick sat on the sofa, placing her stick against the arm. 'This man MacGregor,' she asked. 'Has he been seen hanging about locally? Has anyone noticed him?'

'Enquiries have gone out about that,' the inspector informed her. 'But so far there's been no record of a stranger being seen in the locality.'

'That poor little boy,' Mrs Warwick continued. 'The one Richard ran over, I mean. I suppose it must have unhinged the father's brain. I know they told me he was very violent and abusive at the time. Perhaps that was only natural. But after two years! It seems incredible.'

'Yes,' the inspector agreed, 'it seems a long time to wait.'

'But he was a Scot, of course,' Mrs Warwick recalled. 'A MacGregor. A patient, dogged people, the Scots.'

'Indeed they are,' exclaimed Sergeant Cadwallader, forgetting himself and thinking out loud. '"There are few more impressive sights in the world than a Scotsman on the make,"' he continued, but the inspector immediately gave him a sharp look of disapproval, which quietened him.

'Your son had no preliminary warning?' Inspector Thomas asked Mrs Warwick. 'No threatening letter? Anything of that kind?'

'No, I'm sure he hadn't,' she replied quite firmly. 'Richard would have said so. He would have laughed about it.'

'He wouldn't have taken it seriously at all?' the inspector suggested.

'Richard always laughed at danger,' said Mrs Warwick. She sounded proud of her son.

'After the accident,' the inspector continued, 'did your son offer any compensation to the child's father?'

'Naturally,' Mrs Warwick replied. 'Richard was not a mean man. But it was refused. Indignantly refused, I may say.'

'Quite so,' murmured the inspector.

'I understand MacGregor's wife was dead,' Mrs Warwick recalled. 'The boy was all he had in the world. It was a tragedy, really.'

'But in your opinion it was not your son's fault?' the inspector asked. When Mrs Warwick did not answer, he repeated his question. 'I said – it was not your son's fault?'

She remained silent a moment longer before replying, 'I heard you.'

'Perhaps you don't agree?' the inspector persisted.

Mrs Warwick turned away on the sofa, embarrassed, fingering a cushion. 'Richard drank too much,' she said finally. 'And of course he'd been drinking that day.'

'A glass of sherry?' the inspector prompted her.

'A glass of sherry!' Mrs Warwick repeated with a bitter laugh. 'He'd been drinking pretty heavily. He did drink – very heavily. That decanter there –' She indicated the decanter on the table near the armchair in the french windows. 'That decanter was filled every evening, and it was always practically empty in the morning.'

Sitting on the stool and facing Mrs Warwick, the inspector said to her, quietly, 'So you think that your son was to blame for the accident?'

'Of course he was to blame,' she replied. 'I've never had the least doubt of it.'

'But he was exonerated,' the inspector reminded her.

Mrs Warwick laughed. 'That nurse who was in the car with him? That Warburton woman?' she snorted. 'She was a fool, and she was devoted to Richard. I expect he paid her pretty handsomely for her evidence, too.'

'Do you actually know that?' the inspector asked, sharply.

Mrs Warwick's tone was equally sharp as she replied, 'I don't know anything, but I arrive at my own conclusions.'

The inspector went across to Sergeant Cadwallader and took his notes from him, while Mrs Warwick continued. 'I'm telling you all this now,' she said, 'because what you want is the truth, isn't it? You want to be sure there's sufficient incentive for murder on the part of that little boy's father. Well, in my opinion, there was. Only, I didn't think that after all this time –' Her voice trailed away into silence.

The inspector looked up from the notes he had been consulting. 'You didn't hear anything last night?' he asked her.

'I'm a little deaf, you know,' Mrs Warwick replied quickly. 'I didn't know anything was wrong until I heard people talking and passing my door. I came down, and young Jan said, "Richard's been shot. Richard's been shot." I thought at first –' She passed her hand over her eyes. 'I thought it was a joke of some kind.'

'Jan is your younger son?' the inspector asked her.

'He's not *my* son,' Mrs Warwick replied. The

66

inspector looked at her quickly as she went on, 'I divorced my husband many years ago. He remarried. Jan is the son of the second marriage.' She paused, then continued. 'It sounds more complicated than it is, really. When both his parents died, the boy came here. Richard and Laura had just been married then. Laura has always been very kind to Richard's half-brother. She's been like an elder sister to him, really.'

She paused, and the inspector took the opportunity to lead her back to talking about Richard Warwick. 'Yes, I see,' he said, 'but now, about your son Richard –'

'I loved my son, Inspector,' Mrs Warwick said, 'but I was not blind to his faults, and they were very largely due to the accident that made him a cripple. He was a proud man, an outdoor man, and to have to live the life of an invalid and a semi-cripple was very galling to him. It did not, shall we say, improve his character.'

'Yes, I see,' observed the inspector. 'Would you say his married life was happy?'

'I haven't the least idea.' Mrs Warwick clearly had no intention of saying any more on the subject. 'Is there anything else you wish to know, Inspector?' she asked.

'No thank you, Mrs Warwick,' Inspector Thomas replied. 'But I should like to talk to Miss Bennett now, if I may.'

Mrs Warwick rose, and Sergeant Cadwallader went to open the door for her. 'Yes, of course,' she said. 'Miss Bennett. Benny, we call her. She's the person who can help you most. She's so practical and efficient.'

'She's been with you for a long time?' the inspector asked.

'Oh yes, for years and years. She looked after Jan when he was little, and before that she helped with Richard, too. Oh, yes, she's looked after all of us. A very faithful person, Benny.' Acknowledging the sergeant at the door with a nod, she left the room.

CHAPTER EIGHT

Sergeant Cadwallader closed the door and stood with his back against it, looking at the inspector. 'So Richard Warwick was a drinking man, eh?' he commented. 'You know, I've heard that said of him before. And all those pistols and air-guns and rifles. A little queer in the head, if you ask me.'

'Could be,' Inspector Thomas replied laconically.

The telephone rang. Expecting his sergeant to answer it, the inspector looked meaningfully at him, but Cadwallader had become immersed in his notes as he strolled across to the armchair and sat, completely oblivious of the phone. After a while, realizing that the sergeant's mind was elsewhere, no doubt in the process of composing a poem, the inspector sighed, crossed to the desk, and picked up the receiver.

'Hello,' he said. 'Yes, speaking . . . Starkwedder, he came in? He gave you his prints? . . . Good . . . yes – well, ask him to wait . . . yes, I shall be back in half an hour or so . . . yes, I want to ask him some more questions . . . Yes, goodbye.'

Towards the end of this conversation, Miss Bennett had entered the room, and was standing by the door. Noticing her, Sergeant Cadwallader rose from his armchair and took up a position behind it. 'Yes?'

said Miss Bennett with an interrogative inflection. She addressed the inspector. 'You want to ask me some questions? I've got a good deal to do this morning.'

'Yes, Miss Bennett,' the inspector replied. 'I want to hear your account of the car accident with the child in Norfolk.'

'The MacGregor child?'

'Yes, the MacGregor child. You remembered his name very quickly last night, I hear.'

Miss Bennett turned to close the door behind her. 'Yes,' she agreed. 'I have a very good memory for names.'

'And no doubt,' the inspector continued, 'the occurrence made some impression on you. But you weren't in the car yourself, were you?'

Miss Bennett seated herself on the sofa. 'No, no, I wasn't in the car,' she told him. 'It was the hospital nurse Mr Warwick had at the time. A Nurse Warburton.'

'Did you go to the inquest?' the inspector asked.

'No,' she replied. 'But Richard told us about it when he came back. He said the boy's father had threatened him, had said he'd get even with him. We didn't take it seriously, of course.'

Inspector Thomas came closer to her. 'Had you formed any particular impression about the accident?' he asked.

'I don't know what you mean.'

The inspector regarded Miss Bennett for a moment, and then said, 'I mean do you think it happened because Mr Warwick had been drinking?'

She made a dismissive gesture. 'Oh, I suppose his mother told you that,' she snorted. 'Well, you mustn't go by all she says. She's got a prejudice against drink. Her husband – Richard's father – drank.'

'You think, then,' the inspector suggested to her, 'that Richard Warwick's account was true, that he was driving well within the speed limit, and that the accident could not have been avoided?'

'I don't see why it shouldn't have been the truth,' Miss Bennett insisted. 'Nurse Warburton corroborated his evidence.'

'And her word was to be relied upon?'

Clearly taking exception to what she seemed to regard as an aspersion on her profession, Miss Bennett said with some asperity, 'I should hope so. After all, people don't go around telling lies – not about that sort of thing. Do they?'

Sergeant Cadwallader, who had been following the questioning, now broke in. 'Oh, do they not, indeed!' he exclaimed. 'The way they talk sometimes, you'd think that not only were they within the speed limit, but that they'd managed to get into reverse at the same time!'

Annoyed at this latest interruption, the inspector turned slowly and looked at the sergeant. Miss Bennett also regarded the young man in some surprise. Embarrassed, Sergeant Cadwallader looked down at his notes, and the inspector turned again to Miss Bennett. 'What I'm getting at is this,' he told her. 'In the grief and stress of the moment, a man might easily threaten revenge for an accident that had killed his child. But on reflection, if things were as stated, he would surely have realized that the accident was not Richard Warwick's fault.'

'Oh,' said Miss Bennett. 'Yes, I see what you mean.'

The inspector paced slowly about the room as he continued, 'If, on the other hand, the car had been driven erratically and at excessive speed – if the car had been, shall we say, out of control –'

'Did Laura tell you that?' Miss Bennett interrupted him.

The inspector turned to look at her, surprised at her mention of the murdered man's wife. 'What makes you think she told me?' he asked.

'I don't know,' Miss Bennett replied. 'I just wondered.' Looking confused, she glanced at her watch. 'Is that all?' she asked. 'I'm very busy this morning.' She walked to the door, opened it, and was about to leave when the inspector said, 'I'd like to have a word with young Jan next, if I may.'

Miss Bennett turned in the doorway. 'Oh, he's rather excited this morning,' she said, sounding somewhat truculent. 'I'd really be much obliged if you wouldn't talk to him – raking it all up. I've just got him calmed down.'

'I'm sorry, but I'm afraid we must ask him a few questions,' the inspector insisted.

Miss Bennett closed the door firmly and came back into the room. 'Why can't you just find this man MacGregor, and question him?' she suggested. 'He can't have got far away.'

'We'll find him. Don't you worry,' the inspector assured her.

72

'I hope you will,' Miss Bennett retorted. 'Revenge, indeed! Why, it's not Christian.'

'Of course,' the inspector agreed, adding meaningfully, 'especially when the accident was not Mr Warwick's fault and could not have been avoided.'

Miss Bennett gave him a sharp look. There was a pause, and then the inspector repeated, 'I'd like to speak to Jan, please.'

'I don't know if I can find him,' said Miss Bennett. 'He may have gone out.' She left the room quickly. The inspector looked at Sergeant Cadwallader, nodding his head towards the door, and the sergeant followed her out. In the corridor, Miss Bennett admonished Cadwallader. 'You're not to worry him,' she said. She came back into the room. 'You're not to worry the boy,' she ordered the inspector. 'He's very easily – unsettled. He gets excited, temperamental.'

The inspector regarded her silently for a moment, and then asked, 'Is he ever violent?'

'No, of course not. He's a very sweet boy, very gentle. Docile, really. I simply meant that you might upset him. It's not good for children, things like murder. And that's all he is, really. A child.'

The inspector sat in the chair at the desk. 'You needn't worry, Miss Bennett, I assure you,' he told her. 'We quite understand the position.'

CHAPTER NINE

Just then, Sergeant Cadwallader ushered in Jan, who rushed up to the inspector. 'Do you want me?' he cried excitedly. 'Have you caught him yet? Will there be blood on his clothes?'

'Now, Jan,' Miss Bennett cautioned him, 'you must behave yourself. Just answer any questions the gentleman asks you.'

Jan turned happily to Miss Bennett, and then back to the inspector. 'Oh, yes, I will,' he promised. 'But can't I ask any questions?'

'Of course you can ask questions,' the inspector assured him kindly.

Miss Bennett sat on the sofa. 'I'll wait while you're talking to him,' she said.

The inspector got up quickly, went to the door and opened it invitingly. 'No thank you, Miss Bennett,' he said firmly. 'We shan't need you. And didn't you say you're rather busy this morning?'

'I'd rather stay,' she insisted.

'I'm sorry.' The inspector's voice was sharp. 'We always like to talk to people one at a time.'

Miss Bennett looked at the inspector and then at Sergeant Cadwallader. Realizing that she was defeated, she gave a snort of annoyance and swept out of the room, the inspector closing the door after her. The sergeant moved to the alcove, preparing to take more notes, while Inspector Thomas sat on the sofa. 'I don't suppose,' he said amiably to Jan, 'that you've ever been in close contact with a murder before, have you?'

'No, no, I haven't,' Jan replied eagerly. 'It's very exciting, isn't it?' He knelt on the footstool. 'Have you got any clues – fingerprints or bloodstains or anything?'

'You seem very interested in blood,' the inspector observed with a friendly smile.

'Oh, I am,' Jan replied, quietly and seriously. 'I like blood. It's a beautiful colour, isn't it? That nice clear red.' He too sat down on the sofa, laughing nervously. 'Richard shot things, you know, and then they used to bleed. It's really very funny, isn't it? I mean it's funny that Richard, who was always shooting things, should have been shot himself. Don't you think that's funny?'

The inspector's voice was quiet, his inflection rather dry, as he replied, 'I suppose it has its humorous side.' He paused. 'Are you very upset that your brother – your half-brother, I mean – is dead?'

'Upset?' Jan sounded surprised. 'That Richard is dead? No, why should I be?'

'Well, I thought perhaps you were – very fond of him,' the inspector suggested.

'Fond of him!' exclaimed Jan in what sounded like genuine astonishment. 'Fond of Richard? Oh, no, nobody could be *fond* of Richard.'

'I suppose his wife was fond of him, though,' the inspector urged.

A look of surprise passed across Jan's face. 'Laura?' he exclaimed. 'No, I don't think so. She was always on *my* side.'

'On your side?' the inspector asked. 'What does that mean, exactly?'

Jan suddenly looked scared. 'Yes. Yes,' he almost shouted, hurriedly. 'When Richard wanted to have me sent away.'

'Sent away?' the inspector prompted him gently.

'To one of those places,' the youngster explained. 'You know, where they send you, and you're locked up, and you can't get out. He said Laura would come and see me, perhaps, sometimes.' Jan shook a little, then rose, backed away from the inspector, and looked across at Sergeant Cadwallader. 'I wouldn't like to be locked up,' he continued, his voice now tremulous. 'I'd hate to be locked up.'

He stood at the french windows, looking out onto the terrace. 'I like things open, always,' he called out to them. 'I like my window open, and my door, so that I can be sure I can get out.' He turned back into the room. 'But nobody can lock me up *now*, can they?'

'No, lad,' the inspector assured him. 'I shouldn't think so.'

'Not now that Richard's dead,' Jan added. Momentarily, he sounded almost smug.

The inspector got up and moved round the sofa. 'So Richard wanted you locked up?' he asked.

'Laura says he only said it to tease me,' Jan told him. 'She said that was all it was, and she said it was all right, and that as long as she was

77

here she'd make quite sure that I would never be locked up.' He went to perch on one arm of the armchair. 'I love Laura,' he continued, speaking with a nervous excitement. 'I love Laura a terrible lot. We have wonderful times together, you know. We look for butterflies and birds' eggs, and we play games together. Bezique. Do you know that game? It's a clever one. And Beggar-my-neighbour. Oh, it's great fun doing things with Laura.'

The inspector went across to lean on the other arm of the chair. His voice had a kindly tone to it as he asked, 'I don't suppose you remember anything about this accident that happened when you were living in Norfolk, do you? When a little boy got run over?'

'Oh, yes, I remember that,' Jan replied quite cheerfully. 'Richard went to the inquest.'

'Yes, that's right. What else do you remember?' the inspector encouraged him.

'We had salmon for lunch that day,' Jan said immediately. 'Richard and Warby came back together. Warby was a bit flustered, but Richard was laughing.'

'Warby?' the inspector queried. 'Is that Nurse Warburton?'

'Yes, Warby. I didn't like her much. But Richard was so pleased with her that day that he kept saying, "Jolly good show, Warby."'

The door suddenly opened, and Laura Warwick appeared. Sergeant Cadwallader went across to her, and Jan called out, 'Hello, Laura.'

'Am I interrupting?' Laura asked the inspector.

78

'No, of course not, Mrs Warwick,' he replied. 'Do sit down, won't you?'

Laura came further into the room, and the sergeant shut the door behind her. 'Is – is Jan – ?' Laura began. She paused.

'I'm just asking him,' the inspector explained, 'if he remembers anything about that accident to the boy in Norfolk. The MacGregor boy.'

Laura sat at the end of the sofa. 'Do you remember, Jan?' she asked him.

'Of course I remember,' the lad replied, eagerly. 'I remember everything.' He turned to the inspector. 'I've told you, haven't I?' he asked.

The inspector did not reply to him directly. Instead, he moved slowly to the sofa and, addressing Laura Warwick, asked, 'What do you know about the accident, Mrs Warwick? Was it discussed at luncheon that day, when your husband came back from the inquest?'

'I don't remember,' Laura replied immediately.

Jan rose quickly and moved towards her. 'Oh, yes, you do, Laura, surely,' he reminded her. 'Don't you remember Richard saying that one brat more or less in the world didn't make any difference?'

Laura rose. 'Please –' she implored the inspector.

'It's quite all right, Mrs Warwick,' Inspector Thomas assured her gently. 'It's important, you know, that we get at the truth of that accident. After all, presumably it's the motive for what happened here last night.'

'Oh yes,' she sighed. 'I know. I know.'

'According to your mother-in-law,' the inspector continued, 'your husband had been drinking that day.'

'I expect he had,' Laura admitted. 'It – it wouldn't surprise me.'

The inspector moved to sit at the end of the sofa. 'Did you actually see or meet this man, MacGregor?' he asked her.

'No,' said Laura. 'No, I didn't go to the inquest.'

'He seems to have felt very revengeful,' the inspector commented.

Laura gave a sad smile. 'It must have affected his brain, I think,' she agreed.

Jan, who had gradually been getting very excited, came up to them. 'If I had an enemy,' he exclaimed aggressively, 'that's what I'd do. I'd wait a long time, and then I'd come creeping along in the dark with my gun. Then –' He shot at the armchair with an imaginary gun. 'Bang, bang, bang.'

'Be quiet, Jan,' Laura ordered him, sharply.

Jan suddenly looked upset. 'Are you angry with me, Laura?' he asked her, childishly.

'No, darling,' Laura reassured him, 'I'm not angry. But try not to get too excited.'

'I'm not excited,' Jan insisted.

CHAPTER TEN

Crossing the front hall, Miss Bennett paused to admit Starkwedder and a police constable who seemed to have arrived on the doorstep together.

'Good morning, Miss Bennett,' Starkwedder greeted her. 'I'm here to see Inspector Thomas.'

Miss Bennett nodded. 'Good morning – oh, good morning, Constable. They're in the study, both of them – I don't know what's going on.'

'Good morning, madam,' the police constable replied. 'I've brought these for the inspector. Perhaps Sergeant Cadwallader could take them.'

'What's this?' Laura asked, over the rumble of voices outside.

The inspector rose and moved towards the door. 'It sounds as if Mr Starkwedder is back.'

As Starkwedder entered the room, Sergeant Cadwallader went out into the hall to deal with the constable. Meanwhile, young Jan sank into the armchair, and observed the proceedings eagerly.

'Look here,' exclaimed Starkwedder as he came into the room. 'I can't spend all day kicking my heels at the police station. I've given you my fingerprints, and then I insisted that they bring me along here. I've got things to do. I've got two appointments with a house agent today.' He suddenly noticed

Laura. 'Oh – good morning, Mrs Warwick,' he greeted her. 'I'm terribly sorry about what has happened.'

'Good morning,' Laura replied, distantly.

The inspector went across to the table by the armchair. 'Last night, Mr Starkwedder,' he asked, 'did you by any chance lay your hand on this table, and subsequently push the window open?'

Starkwedder joined him at the table. 'I don't know,' he admitted. 'I could have done. Is it important? I can't remember.'

Sergeant Cadwallader came back into the room, carrying a file. After shutting the door behind him, he walked across to the inspector. 'Here are Mr Starkwedder's prints, sir,' he reported. 'The constable brought them. And the ballistics report.'

'Ah, let's see,' said the inspector. 'The bullet that killed Richard Warwick definitely came from this gun. As for the fingerprints, well, we'll soon see.' He went to the chair by the desk, sat, and began to study the documents, while the sergeant moved into the alcove.

After a pause, Jan, who had been staring intently at Starkwedder, asked him, 'You've just come back from Abadan, haven't you? What's Abadan like?'

'It's hot,' was the only response he got from Starkwedder, who then turned to Laura. 'How are you today, Mrs Warwick?' he asked. ' Are you feeling better?'

'Oh yes, thank you,' Laura replied. 'I've got over the shock now.'

'Good,' said Starkwedder.

The inspector had risen, and now approached Starkwedder on the sofa. 'Your prints,' he announced, 'are on the window, decanter, glass and cigarette lighter. The prints on the table are not yours. They're a completely unidentified set of prints.' He looked around the room. 'That settles it, then,' he continued. 'Since there were no visitors here –' he paused and looked at Laura – 'last night – ?'

'No,' Laura assured him.

'Then they must be MacGregor's,' continued the inspector.

'MacGregor's?' asked Starkwedder, looking at Laura.

'You sound surprised,' said the inspector.

'Yes – I am, rather,' Starkwedder admitted. 'I mean, I should have expected him to have worn gloves.'

The inspector nodded. 'You're right,' he agreed. 'He handled the revolver with gloves.'

'Was there any quarrel?' Starkwedder asked, addressing his question to Laura Warwick. 'Or was nothing heard but the shot?'

It was with an effort that Laura replied, 'I – we – Benny and I, that is – we just heard the shot. But then, we wouldn't have heard anything from upstairs.'

Sergeant Cadwallader had been gazing out at the garden through the small window in the alcove. Now, seeing someone approaching across the lawn, he moved to one side of the french windows. In through the windows there entered a handsome man in his mid-thirties, above medium height, with fair hair, blue eyes and a somewhat military aspect. He paused at the entrance, looking very worried. Jan, the first of the others in the room to notice him, squealed excitedly, 'Julian! Julian!'

The newcomer looked at Jan and then turned to Laura Warwick. 'Laura!' he exclaimed. 'I've just heard. I'm – I'm most terribly sorry.'

'Good morning, Major Farrar,' Inspector Thomas greeted him.

Julian Farrar turned to the inspector. 'This is an extraordinary business.' he said. 'Poor Richard.'

'He was lying here in his wheelchair,' Jan told Farrar excitedly. 'He was all crumpled up. And there was a piece of paper on his chest. Do you know what it said? It said "Paid in full".'

'Yes. There, there, Jan,' Julian Farrar murmured, patting the boy's shoulder.

'It *is* exciting, isn't it?' Jan continued, looking eagerly at him.

Farrar moved past him. 'Yes. Yes, of course it's exciting,' he assured Jan, looking enquiringly towards Starkwedder as he spoke.

The inspector introduced the two men to each other. 'This is Mr Starkwedder – Major Farrar, who may be our next Member of Parliament. He's contesting the by-election.'

Starkwedder and Julian Farrar shook hands, politely murmuring, 'How do you do?' The inspector moved away, beckoning to the sergeant who joined him. They conferred, as Starkwedder explained to Major Farrar, 'I'd run my car into a ditch, and I was coming up to the house to see if I could telephone and get some help. A man dashed out of the house, almost knocking me over.'

'But which way did this man go?' Farrar asked.

'No idea,' Starkwedder replied. 'He vanished into the mist like a conjuring trick.' He turned away, while Jan, kneeling in the armchair and looking expectantly at Farrar, said, 'You told Richard someone would shoot him one day, didn't you, Julian?'

There was a pause. Everyone in the room looked at Julian Farrar.

Farrar thought for a moment. Then, 'Did I? I don't remember,' he said brusquely.

'Oh, yes, you did,' Jan insisted. 'At dinner one night. You know, you and Richard were having a sort of argument, and you said, "One of these days, Richard, somebody'll put a bullet through your head."'

'A remarkable prophecy,' the inspector commented.

Julian Farrar moved to sit on one end of the footstool. 'Oh well,' he said, 'Richard and his guns were pretty fair nuisance value, you know. People didn't like it. Why, there was that fellow – you remember, Laura? Your gardener, Griffiths. You know – the one Richard sacked. Griffiths certainly said to me – and on more than one occasion – "One of these days, look you, I shall come with my gun and I shall shoot Mr Warwick."'

'Oh, Griffiths wouldn't do a thing like that,' Laura exclaimed quickly.

Farrar looked contrite. 'No, no, of course not,'

he admitted. 'I – I didn't mean that. I mean that it was the sort of thing that – er – people said about Richard.'

To cover his embarrassment, he took out his cigarette-case and extracted a cigarette.

The inspector sat in the desk chair, looking thoughtful. Starkwedder stood in a corner near the alcove, close to Jan who gazed at him with interest.

'I wish I'd come over here last night,' Julian Farrar announced, addressing no one in particular. 'I meant to.'

'But that awful fog,' Laura said quietly. 'You couldn't come out in that.'

'No,' Farrar replied. 'I had my committee members over to dine with me. When they found the fog coming on, they went home rather early. I thought then of coming along to see you, but I decided against it.' Searching in his pockets, he asked, 'Has anyone got a match? I seem to have mislaid my lighter.'

He looked around, and suddenly noticed the lighter on the table where Laura had left it the night before. Rising, he went across to pick it up, observed by Starkwedder. 'Oh, here it is,' said Farrar. 'Couldn't imagine where I'd left it.'

'Julian –' Laura began.

'Yes?' Farrar offered her a cigarette, and she took one. 'I'm most awfully sorry about all this, Laura,' he said. 'If there's anything I can do –' His voice trailed off indecisively.

'Yes. Yes, I know,' Laura replied, as Farrar lit their cigarettes.

86

Jan suddenly spoke, addressing Starkwedder. 'Can you shoot, Mr Starkwedder?' he asked. 'I can, you know. Richard used to let me try, sometimes. Of course, I wasn't as good as he was.'

'Did he, indeed?' said Starkwedder, turning to Jan. 'What sort of gun did he let you use?'

As Jan engaged Starkwedder's attention, Laura took the opportunity of speaking quickly to Julian Farrar.

'Julian, I must talk to you. I must,' she murmured softly.

Farrar's voice was equally low. 'Careful,' he warned her.

'It was a .22,' Jan was telling Starkwedder. 'I'm quite good at shooting, aren't I, Julian?' He went across to Julian Farrar. 'Do you remember the time you took me to the fair? I knocked two of the bottles down, didn't I?'

'You did indeed, my lad,' Farrar assured him. 'You've got a good eye, that's what counts. Good eye for a cricket ball, too. That was quite a sensational game, that match we had last summer,' he added.

Jan smiled at him happily, and then sat on the footstool, looking across at the inspector who was now examining documents on the desk. There was a pause. Then Starkwedder, as he took out a cigarette, asked Laura, 'Do you mind if I smoke?'

'Of course not,' replied Laura.

Starkwedder turned to Julian Farrar. 'May I borrow your lighter?'

'Of course,' said Farrar. 'Here it is.'

'Ah, a nice lighter, this,' Starkwedder commented, lighting his cigarette.

Laura made a sudden movement, and then stopped herself. 'Yes,' Farrar said carelessly. 'It works better than most.'

'Rather – distinctive,' Starkwedder observed. He gave a quick glance at Laura, and then returned the lighter to Julian Farrar with a murmured word of thanks.

Jan left his footstool, and stood behind the inspector's chair. 'Richard has lots of guns,' he confided. 'Air-guns, too. And he's got one gun that he used to use in Africa to shoot elephants. Would you like to see them? They're in Richard's bedroom through there.' He pointed the way.

'All right,' said the inspector, rising. 'You show them to us.' He smiled at Jan, adding genially, 'You know, you're being very helpful to us. Helping us quite a lot. We ought to take you into the police force.'

Putting a hand on the boy's shoulder, he steered him towards the door, which the sergeant opened for them. 'We don't need to keep you, Mr Starkwedder,' the inspector called from the door. 'You can go about your business now. Just keep in touch with us, that's all.'

'All right,' replied Starkwedder, as Jan, the inspector and the sergeant left the room, the sergeant closing the door behind them.

CHAPTER ELEVEN

There was an awkward pause after the police officers had left the room with Jan. Then Starkwedder remarked, 'Well, I suppose I'd better go and see whether they've managed to get my car out of the ditch yet. We didn't seem to pass it on the way here.'

'No,' Laura explained. 'The drive comes up from the other road.'

'Yes, I see,' Starkwedder answered, as he walked across to the french windows. He turned. 'How different things look in the daylight,' he observed as he stepped out onto the terrace.

As soon as he had gone, Laura and Julian Farrar turned to each other. 'Julian!' Laura exclaimed. 'That lighter! I said it was *mine*.'

'You said it was yours? To the inspector?' Farrar asked.

'No. To *him*.'

'To – to this fellow –' Farrar began, and then stopped as they both noticed Starkwedder walking along the terrace outside the windows. 'Laura –' he began again.

'Be careful,' said Laura, going across to the little window in the alcove and looking out. 'He may be listening to us.'

'Who is he?' asked Farrar. 'Do you know him?'

Laura came back to the centre of the room. 'No. No, I don't know him,' she told Farrar. 'He – he had an accident with his car, and he came here last night. Just after –'

Julian Farrar touched her hand which rested on the back of the sofa. 'It's all right, Laura. You know that I'll do everything I can.'

'Julian – *fingerprints*,' Laura gasped.

'What fingerprints?'

'On that table. On that table there, and on the pane of glass. Are they – yours?'

Farrar removed his hand from hers, indicating that Starkwedder was again walking along the terrace outside. Without turning to the window, Laura moved away from him, saying loudly, 'It's very kind of you, Julian, and I'm sure there will be a lot of business things you can help us with.'

Starkwedder was pacing about, outside on the terrace. When he had moved out of sight, Laura turned to face Julian Farrar again. 'Are those fingerprints yours, Julian? Think.'

Farrar considered for a moment. Then, 'On the table – yes – they might have been.'

'Oh God!' Laura cried. 'What shall we do?'

Starkwedder could now be glimpsed again, walking back and forth along the terrace just outside the windows. Laura puffed at her cigarette. 'The police think it's a man called MacGregor –' she told Julian. She gave him a desperate look, pausing to allow him an opportunity to make some comment.

'Well, that's all right, then,' he replied. 'They'll probably go on thinking so.'

'But suppose –' Laura began.

Farrar interrupted her. 'I must go,' he said. 'I've got an appointment.' He rose. 'It's all right, Laura,' he said, patting her shoulder. 'Don't worry. I'll see that you're all right.'

The look on Laura's face was one of an incomprehension verging on desperation. Apparently oblivious of it, Farrar walked across to the french windows. As he pushed a window open, Starkwedder was approaching with the obvious intention of entering the room. Farrar politely moved aside, to avoid colliding with him.

'Oh, are you off now?' Starkwedder asked him.

'Yes,' said Farrar. 'Things are rather busy these days. Election coming on, you know, in a week's time.'

'Oh, I see,' Starkwedder replied. 'Excuse my ignorance, but what are you? Tory?'

'I'm a Liberal,' said Farrar. He sounded slightly indignant.

'Oh, are they still at it?' Starkwedder asked, brightly.

Julian Farrar drew a sharp breath, and left the room without another word. When he had gone, not quite slamming the door behind him, Starkwedder looked at Laura almost fiercely. Then, 'I see,' he said, his anger rising. 'Or at least I'm beginning to see.'

'What do you mean?' Laura asked him.

'That's the boyfriend, isn't it?' He came closer to her. 'Well, come on now, is it?'

'Since you ask,' Laura replied, defiantly, 'yes, it is!'

Starkwedder looked at her for a moment without speaking. Then, 'There are quite a few things you didn't tell me last night, aren't there?' he said angrily. 'That's why you snatched up his lighter in such a hurry and said it was yours.' He walked away a few paces and then turned to face her again. 'And how long has this been going on between you and him?'

'For quite some time now,' Laura said quietly.

'But you didn't ever decide to leave Warwick and go away together?'

'No,' Laura answered. 'There's Julian's career, for one thing. It might ruin him politically.'

Starkwedder sat himself down ill-temperedly at one end of the sofa. 'Oh, surely not, these days,' he snapped. 'Don't they all take adultery in their stride?'

'These would have been special circumstances,' Laura tried to explain. 'He was a friend of Richard's, and with Richard being a cripple –'

'Oh yes, I see. It certainly wouldn't have been good publicity!' Starkwedder retorted.

Laura came over to the sofa and stood looking down at him. 'I suppose you think I ought to have told you this last night?' she observed, icily.

Starkwedder looked away from her. 'You were under no obligation,' he muttered.

Laura seemed to relent. 'I didn't think it mattered –' she began. 'I mean – all I could think of was my having shot Richard.'

Starkwedder seemed to warm to her again, as he murmured, 'Yes, yes, I see.' After a pause, he added,

92

'*I* couldn't think of anything else, either.' He paused again, and then looked up at her. 'Do you want to try a little experiment?' he asked. 'Where were you standing when you shot Richard?'

'Where was I standing?' Laura echoed. She sounded perplexed.

'That's what I said.'

After a moment's thought, Laura replied, 'Oh – over there.' She nodded vaguely towards the french windows.

'Go and stand where you were standing,' Starkwedder instructed her.

Laura rose and began to move nervously about the room. ' I – I can't remember,' she told him. 'Don't ask me to remember.' She sounded scared now. 'I – I was upset. I –'

Starkwedder interrupted her. 'Your husband said something to you,' he reminded her. 'Something that made you snatch up the gun.'

Rising from the sofa, he went to the table by the armchair and put his cigarette out. 'Well, come on, let's act it out,' he continued. 'There's the table, there's the gun.' He took Laura's cigarette from her, and put it in the ashtray. 'Now then, you were quarrelling. You picked up the gun – pick it up –'

'I don't want to!' Laura cried.

'Don't be a little fool,' Starkwedder growled. 'It's not loaded. Come on, pick it up. Pick it up.'

Laura picked up the gun, hesitantly.

'You snatched it up,' he reminded her. 'You didn't pick it up gingerly like that. You snatched it up, and you shot him. Show me how you did it.'

93

Holding the gun awkwardly, Laura backed away from him. ' I – I –' she began.

'Go on. Show me,' Starkwedder shouted at her.

Laura tried to aim the gun. 'Go on, shoot!' he repeated, still shouting. 'It isn't loaded.'

When she still hesitated, he snatched the gun from her in triumph. 'I thought so,' he exclaimed. 'You've never fired a revolver in your life. You don't know how to do it.' Looking at the gun, he continued, 'You don't even know enough to release the safety catch.'

He dropped the gun on the footstool, then walked to the back of the sofa, and turned to face her. After a pause, he said quietly, 'You didn't shoot your husband.'

'I did,' Laura insisted.

'Oh no, you didn't,' Starkwedder repeated with conviction.

Sounding frightened, Laura asked, 'Then why should I say I did?'

Starkwedder took a deep breath and then exhaled. Coming round the sofa, he threw himself down on it heavily. 'The answer to that seems pretty obvious to me. Because it was Julian Farrar who shot him,' he retorted.

'No!' Laura exclaimed, almost shouting.

'Yes!'

'No!' she repeated.

'I say yes,' he insisted.

'If it was Julian,' Laura asked him, 'why on earth should I say *I* did it?'

Starkwedder looked at her levelly. 'Because,' he

said, 'you thought – and thought quite rightly – that I'd cover up for *you*. Oh yes, you were certainly right about that.' He lounged back into the sofa before continuing, 'Yes, you played me along very prettily. But I'm through, do you hear? I'm through. I'm damned if I'm going to tell a pack of lies to save Major Julian Farrar's skin.'

There was a pause. For a few moments Laura said nothing. Then she smiled and calmly walked over to the table by the armchair to pick up her cigarette. Turning back to Starkwedder, she said, 'Oh yes, you are! You'll have to! You can't back out now! You've told your story to the police. You can't change it.'

'What?' Starkwedder gasped, taken aback.

Laura sat in the armchair. 'Whatever you know, or think you know,' she pointed out to him, 'you've got to stick to your story. You're an accessory after the fact – you said so yourself.' She drew on her cigarette.

Starkwedder rose and faced her. Dumbfounded, he exclaimed, 'Well, I'm damned! You little bitch!' He glared at her for a few moments without saying anything further, then suddenly turned on his heel, went swiftly to the french windows, and left. Laura watched him striding across the garden. She made a movement as though to follow and call him back, but then apparently thought better of it. With a troubled look on her face, she slowly turned away from the windows.

CHAPTER TWELVE

Later that day, towards the end of the afternoon, Julian Farrar paced nervously up and down in the study. The french windows to the terrace were open, and the sun was about to set, throwing a golden light onto the lawn outside. Farrar had been summoned by Laura Warwick, who apparently needed to see him urgently. He kept glancing at his watch as he awaited her.

Farrar seemed very upset and distraught. He looked out onto the terrace, turned back into the room again, and glanced at his watch. Then, noticing a newspaper on the table by the armchair, he picked it up. It was a local paper, *The Western Echo*, with a news story on the front page reporting Richard Warwick's death. 'PROMINENT LOCAL RESIDENT MURDERED BY MYSTERIOUS ASSAILANT,' the headline announced. Farrar sat in the armchair and began nervously to read the report. After a moment, he flung the paper aside, and strode over to the french windows. With a final glance back into the room, he set off across the lawn. He was halfway across the garden, when he heard a sound behind him. Turning, he called, 'Laura, I'm sorry I –' and then stopped, disappointed, as he saw that the person coming towards him was not Laura Warwick, but Angell, the late Richard Warwick's valet and attendant.

'Mrs Warwick asked me to say she will be down in a moment, sir,' said Angell as he approached Farrar. 'But I wondered if I might have a brief word with you?'

'Yes, yes. What is it?'

Angell came up to Julian Farrar, and walked on for a pace or two further away from the house, as if anxious that their talk should not be overheard. 'Well?' said Farrar, following him.

'I am rather worried, sir,' Angell began, 'about my own position in the house, and I felt I would like to consult you on the matter.'

His mind full of his own affairs, Julian Farrar was not really interested. 'Well, what's the trouble?' he asked.

Angell thought for a moment before replying. Then, 'Mr Warwick's death, sir,' he said, 'it puts me out of a job.'

'Yes. Yes, I suppose it does,' Farrar responded. 'But I imagine you will easily get another, won't you?'

'I hope so, sir,' Angell replied.

'You're a qualified man, aren't you?' Farrar asked him.

'Oh, yes, sir. I'm qualified,' Angell replied, 'and there is always either hospital work or private work to be obtained. I know that.'

'Then what's troubling you?'

'Well, sir,' Angell told him, 'the circumstances in which this job came to an end are very distasteful to me.'

98

'In plain English,' Farrar remarked, 'you don't like having been mixed up with murder. Is that it?'

'You could put it that way, sir,' the valet confirmed.

'Well,' said Farrar, 'I'm afraid there is nothing anyone can do about that. Presumably you'll get a satisfactory reference from Mrs Warwick.' He took out his cigarette-case and opened it.

'I don't think there will be any difficulty about that, sir,' Angell responded. 'Mrs Warwick is a very nice lady – a very charming lady, if I may say so.' There was a faint insinuation in his tone.

Julian Farrar, having decided to await Laura after all, was about to go back into the house. However, he turned, struck by something in the valet's manner. 'What do you mean?' he asked quietly.

'I shouldn't like to inconvenience Mrs Warwick in any way,' Angell replied, unctuously.

Before speaking, Farrar took a cigarette from his case, and then returned the case to his pocket. 'You mean,' he said, 'you're – stopping on a bit to oblige her?'

'That is quite true, sir,' Angell affirmed. 'I am helping out in the house. But that is not exactly what I meant.' He paused, and then continued, 'It's a matter, really – of my conscience, sir.'

'What in hell do you mean – your conscience?' Farrar asked sharply.

Angell looked uncomfortable, but his voice was quite confident as he continued, 'I don't think you quite appreciate my difficulties, sir. In the matter of giving my evidence to the police, that is. It is my

99

duty as a citizen to assist the police in any manner possible. At the same time, I wish to remain loyal to my employers.'

Julian Farrar turned away to light his cigarette. 'You speak as though there was a conflict,' he said quietly.

'If you think about it, sir,' Angell remarked, 'you will realize that there is bound to be a conflict – a conflict of loyalties if I may so put it.'

Farrar looked directly at the valet. 'Just exactly what are you getting at, Angell?' he asked.

'The police, sir, are not in a position to appreciate the background,' Angell replied. 'The background might – I just say *might* – be very important in a case like this. Also, of late I have been suffering rather severely from insomnia.'

'Do your ailments have to come into this?' Farrar asked him sharply.

'Unfortunately they do, sir,' was the valet's smooth reply. 'I retired early last night, but I was unable to get to sleep.'

'I'm sorry about that,' Farrar commiserated drily, 'but really –'

'You see, sir,' Angell continued, ignoring the interruption, 'owing to the position of my bedroom in this house, I have become aware of certain matters of which perhaps the police are not fully cognizant.'

'Just what are you trying to say?' Farrar asked, coldly.

'The late Mr Warwick, sir,' Angell replied, 'was a sick man and a cripple. It's really only to be expected under those sad circumstances that an attractive lady like Mrs Warwick might – how shall I put it? – form an attachment elsewhere.'

'So that's it, is it?' said Farrar. 'I don't think I like your tone, Angell.'

'No, sir,' Angell murmured. 'But please don't be too precipitate in your judgement. Just think it over, sir. You will perhaps realize my difficulty. Here I am, in possession of knowledge which I have not, so far, communicated to the police – but knowledge which, perhaps, it is my duty to communicate to them.'

Julian Farrar stared at Angell coldly. 'I think,' he said, 'that this story of going to the police with your information is all ballyhoo. What you're really doing is suggesting that you're in a position to stir up dirt unless –' he paused, and then completed his sentence: '– unless what?'

Angell shrugged his shoulders. 'I am, of course, as you have just pointed out,' he observed, 'a fully qualified nurse-attendant. But there are times, Major Farrar, when I feel I would like to set up on my own. A small – not a nursing-home, exactly – but an establishment where I could take on perhaps five or six patients. With an assistant, of course. The patients would probably include gentlemen who are alcoholically difficult to manage at home. That sort of thing. Unfortunately, although I have accumulated a certain amount of savings, they are not enough. I wondered –' His voice trailed off suggestively.

Julian Farrar completed his thought for him. 'You wondered,' he said, 'if I – or I and Mrs Warwick together – could come to your assistance in this project, no doubt.'

'I just wondered, sir,' Angell replied meekly. 'It would be a great kindness on your part.'

'Yes, it would, wouldn't it?' Farrar observed sarcastically.

'You suggested rather harshly,' Angell went on, 'that I'm threatening to stir up dirt. Meaning, I take it, scandal. But it's not that at all, sir. I wouldn't dream of doing such a thing.'

'What exactly is it you are driving at, Angell?' Farrar sounded as though he were beginning to lose his patience. 'You're certainly driving at something.'

Angell gave a self-deprecating smile before replying. Then he spoke quietly but with emphasis. 'As I say, sir, last night I couldn't sleep very well. I was lying awake, listening to the booming of the foghorn. An extremely depressing sound I always find it, sir. Then it seemed to me that I heard a shutter banging. A very irritating noise when you're trying to get to sleep. I got up and leaned out of my window. It seemed to be the shutter of the pantry window, almost immediately below me.'

'Well?' asked Farrar, sharply.

'I decided, sir, to go down and attend to the shutter,' Angell continued. 'As I was on my way downstairs, I heard a shot.' He paused briefly. 'I didn't think anything of it at the time. "Mr Warwick at it again," I thought. "But surely he can't see what he's shooting at in a mist like this." I went to the pantry, sir, and fastened back the shutter securely.

But, as I was standing there, feeling a bit uneasy for some reason, I heard footsteps coming along the path outside the window –'

'You mean,' Farrar interrupted, 'the path that –' His eyes went towards it.

'Yes, sir,' Angell agreed. 'The path that leads from the terrace, around the corner of the house, that way – past the domestic offices. A path that's not used very much, except of course by you, sir, when you come over here, seeing as it's a short cut from your house to this one.'

He stopped speaking, and looked intently at Julian Farrar, who merely said icily, 'Go on.'

'I was feeling, as I said, a bit uneasy,' Angell continued, 'thinking there might be a prowler about. I can't tell you how relieved I was, sir, to see *you* pass the pantry window, walking quickly – hurrying on your way back home.'

After a pause, Farrar said, 'I can't really see any point in what you're telling me. Is there supposed to be one?'

With an apologetic cough, Angell answered him. 'I just wondered, sir, whether you have mentioned to the police that you came over here last night to see Mr Warwick. In case you have not done so, and supposing that they should question me further as to the events of last night –'

Farrar interrupted him. 'You do realize, don't you,' he asked tersely, 'that the penalty for blackmail is severe?'

'Blackmail, sir?' responded Angell, sounding shocked. 'I don't know what you mean. It's just

103

a question, as I said, of deciding where my duty lies. The police –'

'The police,' Farrar interrupted him sharply, 'are perfectly satisfied as to who killed Mr Warwick. The fellow practically signed his name to the crime. They're not likely to come asking you any more questions.'

'I assure you, sir,' Angell interjected, with alarm in his voice, 'I only meant –'

'You know perfectly well,' Farrar interrupted again, 'that you couldn't have recognized anybody in that thick fog last night. You've simply invented this story in order to –' He broke off, as he saw Laura Warwick emerging from the house into the garden.

CHAPTER THIRTEEN

'I'm sorry I've kept you waiting, Julian,' Laura called as she approached them. She looked surprised to see Angell and Julian Farrar apparently in conversation.

'Perhaps I may speak to you later, sir, about this little matter,' the valet murmured to Farrar. He moved away, half bowing to Laura, then walked quickly across the garden and around a corner of the house.

Laura watched him go, and then spoke urgently. 'Julian,' she said, 'I must –'

Farrar interrupted her. 'Why did you send for me, Laura?' he asked, sounding annoyed.

'I've been expecting you all day,' Laura replied, surprised.

'Well, I've been up to my ears ever since this morning,' Farrar exclaimed. 'Committees, and more meetings this afternoon. I can't just drop any of these things so soon before the election. And in any case, don't you see, Laura, that it's much better that we shouldn't meet at present?'

'But there are things we've got to discuss,' Laura told him.

Taking her arm briefly, Farrar led her further away from the house. 'Do you know that Angell is setting out to blackmail me?' he asked her.

'Angell?' cried Laura, incredulously. 'Angell is?'

'Yes. He obviously knows about us – and he also knows, or at any rate pretends to know, that I was here last night.'

Laura gasped. 'Do you mean he saw you?'

'He *says* he saw me,' Farrar retorted.

'But he couldn't have seen you in that fog,' Laura insisted.

'He's got some story,' Farrar told her, 'about coming down to the pantry and doing something to the shutter outside the window, and seeing me pass on my way home. He also says he heard a shot, not long before that, but didn't think anything of it.'

'Oh my God!' Laura gasped. 'How awful! What are we going to do?'

Farrar made an involuntary gesture as though he were about to comfort Laura with an embrace, but then, glancing towards the house, thought better of it. He gazed at her steadily. 'I don't know yet what we're going to do,' he told her. 'We'll have to think.'

'You're not going to pay him, surely?'

'No, no,' Farrar assured her. 'If one starts doing that, it's the beginning of the end. And yet, what is one to do?' He passed a hand across his brow. 'I didn't think anyone knew I came over yesterday evening,' he continued. 'I'm certain my housekeeper didn't. The point is, did Angell really see me, or is he pretending he did?'

'Supposing he does go to the police?' Laura asked, tremulously.

'I know,' murmured Farrar. Again, he ran his hand across his brow. 'One's got to think – think carefully.' He began to walk to and fro. 'Either bluff it out – say he's lying, that I never left home yesterday evening –'

'But there are the fingerprints,' Laura told him.

'What fingerprints?' asked Farrar, startled.

'You've forgotten,' Laura reminded him. 'The fingerprints on the table. The police have been thinking that they're MacGregor's, but if Angell goes to them with this story, then they'll ask to take your fingerprints, and then –'

She broke off. Julian Farrar now looked very worried. 'Yes, yes, I see,' he muttered. 'All right, then. I'll have to admit that I came over here and – tell some story. I came over to see Richard about something, and we talked –'

'You can say he was perfectly all right when you left him,' Laura suggested, speaking quickly.

There was little trace of affection in Farrar's eyes as he looked at her. 'How easy you make it sound!' he retorted, hotly. 'Can I really say that?' he added sarcastically.

'One has to say something!' she told him, sounding defensive.

'Yes, I must have put my hand there as I bent over to see –' He swallowed, as the scene came back to him.

'So long as they believe the prints are Mac-Gregor's,' said Laura, eagerly.

'MacGregor! MacGregor!' Farrar exclaimed

angrily. He was almost shouting now. 'What on earth made you think of cooking up that message from the newspaper and putting it on Richard's body? Weren't you taking a terrific chance?'

'Yes – no – I don't know,' Laura cried in confusion.

Farrar looked at her with silent revulsion. 'So damned cold-blooded,' he muttered.

'We had to think of something,' Laura sighed. 'I – I just couldn't think. It was really Michael's idea.'

'Michael?'

'Michael – Starkwedder,' Laura told him.

'You mean he helped you?' Farrar asked. He sounded incredulous.

'Yes, yes, yes!' Laura cried impatiently. 'That's why I wanted to see you – to explain to you –'

Farrar came up close to her. His tone was icily jealous as he asked, firmly, 'What's *Michael*' – he emphasized Starkwedder's Christian name with a cold anger – 'what's Michael Starkwedder doing in all this?'

'He came in and – and found me there,' Laura told him. 'I'd – I'd got the gun in my hand and –'

'Good God!' Farrar exclaimed with distaste, moving away from her. 'And somehow you persuaded him –'

'I think he persuaded me,' Laura murmured sadly. She moved closer to him. 'Oh, Julian –' she began.

Her arms were about to go around his neck, but he pushed her away slightly. 'I've told you, I'll do anything I can,' he assured her. 'Don't think I won't – but –'

Laura looked at him steadily. 'You've changed,' she said quietly.

'I'm sorry, but I can't feel the same,' Farrar admitted desperately. 'After what's happened – I just can't feel the same.'

'I can,' Laura assured him. 'At least, I think I can. No matter what you'd done, Julian, I'd always feel the same.'

'Never mind our feelings for the moment,' said Farrar. 'We've got to get down to facts.'

Laura looked at him. 'I know,' she said. 'I – I told Starkwedder that *I'd* – you know, that I'd done it.'

Farrar looked at her incredulously. 'You told Starkwedder that?'

'Yes.'

'And he agreed to help you? He – a stranger? The man must be mad!'

Stung, Laura retorted, 'I think perhaps he *is* a little mad. But he was very comforting.'

'So! No man can resist you,' Farrar exclaimed angrily. 'Is that it?' He took a step away from her, and then turned to face her again. 'All the same, Laura, murder –' His voice died away and he shook his head.

'I shall try never to think of it,' Laura answered. 'And it wasn't premeditated, Julian. It *was* just an impulse.' She spoke almost pleadingly.

'There's no need to go back over it all,' Farrar told her. 'We've got to think now what we're going to do.'

'I know,' she replied. 'There are the fingerprints and your lighter.'

'Yes,' he recalled. 'I must have dropped it as I leaned over his body.'

'Starkwedder knows it's yours,' Laura told him. 'But he can't do anything about it. He's committed himself. He can't change his story now.'

Julian Farrar looked at her for a moment. When he spoke, his voice had a slightly heroic tone. 'If it comes to it, Laura, I'll take the blame,' he assured her.

'No, I don't want you to,' Laura cried. She clasped his arm, and then released him quickly with a nervous glance towards the house. 'I don't want you to!' she repeated urgently.

'You mustn't think that I don't understand – how it happened,' said Farrar, speaking with an effort. 'You picked up the gun, shot him without really knowing what you were doing, and –'

Laura gave a gasp of surprise. 'What? Are you trying to make me say *I* killed him?' she cried.

'Not at all,' Farrar responded. He sounded embarrassed. 'I've told you I'm perfectly prepared to take the blame if it comes to it.'

Laura shook her head in confusion. 'But – you said –' she began. 'You said you knew how it happened.'

He looked at her steadily. 'Listen, Laura,' he said. 'I don't think you did it deliberately. I don't think it was premeditated. I know it wasn't. I know quite well that you only shot him because –'

Laura interrupted quickly. '*I* shot him?' she gasped.

110

'Are you really pretending to believe that *I* shot him?'

Turning his back on her, Farrar exclaimed angrily, 'For God's sake, this is impossible if we're not going to be honest with each other!'

Laura sounded desperate as, trying not to shout, she announced clearly and emphatically, 'I didn't shoot him, and you know it!'

There was a pause. Julian Farrar slowly turned to face her. 'Then who did?' he asked. Suddenly realizing, he added, 'Laura! Are you trying to say that *I* shot him?'

They stood facing each other, neither of them speaking for a moment. Then Laura said, 'I heard the shot, Julian.' She took a deep breath before continuing. 'I heard the shot, and your footsteps on the path going away. I came down, and there he was – dead.'

After a pause Farrar said quietly, 'Laura, I didn't shoot him.' He gazed up at the sky as though seeking help or inspiration, and then looked at her intently. 'I came over here to see Richard,' he explained, 'to tell him that after the election we'd got to come to some arrangement about a divorce. I heard a shot just before I got here. I just thought it was Richard up to his tricks as usual. I came in here, and there he was. Dead. He was still warm.'

Laura was now very perplexed. 'Warm?' she echoed.

'He hadn't been dead more than a minute or two,' said Farrar. 'Of course I believed you'd shot him. Who else could have shot him?'

'I don't understand,' Laura murmured.

'I suppose – I suppose it could have been suicide,' Farrar began, but Laura interrupted him. 'No, it couldn't, because –'

She broke off, as they both heard Jan's voice inside the house, shouting excitedly.

CHAPTER FOURTEEN

Julian Farrar and Laura ran towards the house, almost colliding with Jan as he emerged through the french windows. 'Laura,' Jan cried as she gently but firmly propelled him back into the study. 'Laura, now that Richard's dead, all of his pistols and guns and things belong to me, don't they? I mean, I'm his brother, I'm the next man in the family.'

Julian Farrar followed them into the room and wandered distractedly across to the armchair, sitting on an arm of it as Laura attempted to pacify Jan who was now complaining petulantly, 'Benny won't let me have his guns. She's locked them up in the cupboard in there.' He waved vaguely towards the door. 'But they're mine. I've got a right to them. Make her give me the key.'

'Now listen, Jan darling,' Laura began, but Jan would not be interrupted. He went quickly to the door, and then turned back to her, exclaiming, 'She treats me like a child. Benny, I mean. Everyone treats me like a child. But I'm not a child, I'm a man. I'm nineteen. I'm nearly of age.' He stretched his arms across the door as though protecting his guns. 'All of Richard's sporting things belong to me. I'm going to do what Richard did. I'm going to shoot squirrels and birds and cats.' He laughed hysterically. 'I might shoot people, too, if I don't like them.'

'You mustn't get too excited, Jan,' Laura warned him.

'I'm not excited,' Jan cried petulantly. 'But I'm not going to be – what's it called? – I'm not going to be victimized.' He came back into the centre of the room, and faced Laura squarely. 'I'm master here now. I'm the master of this house. Everybody's got to do as I say.' He paused, then turned and addressed Julian Farrar. 'I could be a JP if I wanted to, couldn't I, Julian?'

'I think you're a little young for that yet,' Farrar told him.

Jan shrugged, and turned back to Laura. 'You all treat me like a child,' he complained again. 'But you can't do it any longer – not now that Richard's dead.' He flung himself onto the sofa, legs sprawling. 'I expect I'm rich, too, aren't I?' he added. 'This house belongs to me. Nobody can push me around any longer. I can push *them* around. I'm not going to be dictated to by silly old Benny. If Benny tries ordering me about, I shall –' He paused, then added childishly, 'I know what I shall do!'

Laura approached him. 'Listen, Jan darling,' she murmured gently. 'It's a very worrying time for all of us, and Richard's things don't belong to anybody until the lawyers have come and read his will and granted what they call probate. That's what happens when anyone dies. Until then, we all have to wait and see. Do you understand?'

114

Laura's tone had a calming and quietening effect on Jan. He looked up at her, then put his arms around her waist, nestling close to her. 'I understand what you tell me, Laura,' he said. 'I love you, Laura. I love you very much.'

'Yes, darling,' Laura murmured soothingly. 'I love you, too.'

'You're glad Richard's dead, aren't you?' Jan asked her suddenly.

Slightly startled, Laura replied hurriedly, 'No, of course I'm not glad.'

'Oh yes, you are,' said Jan, slyly. 'Now you can marry Julian.'

Laura looked quickly at Julian Farrar, who rose to his feet as Jan continued, 'You've wanted to marry Julian for a long time, haven't you? *I* know. They think I don't notice or know things. But I do. And so it's all right for both of you now. It's been made all right for you, and you're both pleased. You're pleased, because –'

He broke off, hearing Miss Bennett out in the corridor calling, 'Jan!', and laughed. 'Silly old Benny!' he shouted, bouncing up and down on the sofa.

'Now, do be nice to Benny,' Laura cautioned Jan, as she pulled him to his feet. 'She's having such a lot of trouble and worry over all this.' Guiding Jan to the door, Laura continued gently, 'You must help Benny, Jan, because you're the man of the family now.'

Jan opened the door, then looked from Laura to Julian. 'All right, all right,' he promised, with a smile. 'I will.' He left the room, shutting the door behind him and calling 'Benny!' as he went.

Laura turned to Julian Farrar who had risen from his armchair and walked over to her. 'I'd no idea he knew about us,' she exclaimed.

'That's the trouble with people like Jan,' Farrar retorted. 'You never know how much or how little they do know. He's very – well, he gets rather easily out of hand, doesn't he?'

'Yes, he does get easily excited,' Laura admitted. 'But now that Richard isn't here to tease him, he'll calm down. He'll get to be more normal. I'm sure he will.'

Julian Farrar looked doubtful. 'Well, I don't know about that,' he began, but broke off as Starkwedder suddenly appeared at the french windows.

'Hello – good evening,' Starkwedder called, sounding quite happy.

'Oh – er – good evening,' Farrar replied, hesitantly.

'How's everything? Bright and cheerful?' Starkwedder enquired, looking from one to the other. He suddenly grinned. 'I see,' he observed. 'Two's company and three's none.' He stepped into the room. 'Shouldn't have come in by the window this way. A gentleman would have gone to the front door and rung the bell. Is that it? But then, you see, I'm no gentleman.'

'Oh, please –' Laura began, but Starkwedder interrupted her. 'As a matter of fact,' he explained, 'I've come for two reasons. First, to say goodbye. My character's been cleared. High-level cables from Abadan saying what a fine, upright fellow I am. So I'm free to depart.'

116

'I'm so sorry you're going – so soon,' Laura told him, with genuine feeling in her voice.

'That's nice of you,' Starkwedder responded with a touch of bitterness, 'considering the way I butted in on your family murder.' He looked at her for a moment, then moved across to the desk chair. 'But I came in by the window for another reason,' he went on. 'The police brought me up in their car. And, although they're being very tight-lipped about it, it's my belief there's something up!'

Dismayed, Laura gasped, 'The police have come back?'

'Yes,' Starkwedder affirmed, decisively.

'But I thought they'd finished this morning,' said Laura.

Starkwedder gave her a shrewd look. 'That's why I say – something's up!' he exclaimed.

There were voices in the corridor outside. Laura and Julian Farrar drew together as the door opened, and Richard Warwick's mother came in, looking very upright and self-possessed, though still walking with the aid of a cane.

'Benny!' Mrs Warwick called over her shoulder, and then addressed Laura. 'Oh, there you are, Laura. We've been looking for you.'

Julian Farrar went to Mrs Warwick and helped her into the armchair. 'How kind you are to come over again, Julian,' the old lady exclaimed, 'when we all know how busy you are.'

'I would have come before, Mrs Warwick,' Farrar told her, as he settled her in the chair, 'but it's been a particularly hectic day. Anything that I can possibly

117

do to help –' He stopped speaking as Miss Bennett entered followed by Inspector Thomas. Carrying a briefcase, the inspector moved to take up a central position. Starkwedder went to sit in the desk chair, and lit a cigarette as Sergeant Cadwallader came in with Angell, who closed the door and stood with his back to it.

'I can't find young Mr Warwick, sir,' the sergeant reported, crossing to the french windows.

'He's out somewhere. Gone for a walk,' Miss Bennett announced.

'It doesn't matter,' said the inspector. There was a momentary pause as he surveyed the occupants of the room. His manner had changed, for it now had a grimness it did not have before.

After waiting a moment for him to speak, Mrs Warwick asked coldly, 'Do I understand that you have further questions to ask us, Inspector Thomas?'

'Yes, Mrs Warwick,' he replied, 'I'm afraid I have.'

Mrs Warwick's voice sounded weary as she asked, 'You still have no news of this man MacGregor?'

'On the contrary.'

'He's been found?' Mrs Warwick asked, eagerly.

'Yes,' was the inspector's terse reply.

There was a definite reaction of excitement from the assembled company. Laura and Julian Farrar looked incredulous, and Starkwedder turned in his chair to face the inspector.

Miss Bennett's voice suddenly rang out sharply. 'You've arrested him, then?'

The inspector looked at her for a moment before

replying. Then, 'That, I'm afraid, would be impossible, Miss Bennett,' he informed her.

'Impossible?' Mrs Warwick interjected. 'But why?'

'Because he's dead,' the inspector replied, quietly.

CHAPTER FIFTEEN

A shocked silence greeted Inspector Thomas's announcement. Then, hesitantly and, it seemed, fearfully, Laura whispered, 'Wh– what did you say?'

'I said that this man MacGregor is dead,' the inspector affirmed.

There were gasps from everyone in the room, and the inspector expanded upon his terse announcement. 'John MacGregor,' he told them, 'died in Alaska over two years ago – not very long after he returned to Canada from England.'

'Dead!' Laura exclaimed, incredulously.

Unnoticed by anyone in the room, young Jan passed quickly along the terrace outside the french windows, and disappeared from view.

'That makes a difference, doesn't it?' the inspector continued. 'It wasn't John MacGregor who put that revenge note on the dead body of Mr Warwick. But it's clear, isn't it, that it was put there by someone who knew all about MacGregor and the accident in Norfolk. Which ties it in, very definitely, with someone in this house.'

'No,' Miss Bennett exclaimed sharply. 'No, it could have been – surely it could have been –' She broke off.

121

'Yes, Miss Bennett?' the inspector prompted her. He waited for a moment, but Miss Bennett could not continue. Suddenly looking completely broken, she moved away towards the french windows.

The inspector turned his attention to Richard Warwick's mother. 'You'll understand, madam,' he said, attempting to put a note of sympathy into his voice, 'that this alters things.'

'Yes, I see that,' Mrs Warwick replied. She rose. 'Do you need me any further, Inspector?' she asked.

'Not for the moment, Mrs Warwick,' the inspector told her.

'Thank you,' Mrs Warwick murmured as she went to the door, which Angell hastened to open for her. Julian Farrar helped the old lady to the door. As she left the room, he returned and stood behind the armchair, looking pensive. Meanwhile, Inspector Thomas had been opening his briefcase, and was now taking out a gun.

Angell was about to follow Mrs Warwick from the room when the inspector called, peremptorily, 'Angell!'

The valet gave a start, and turned back into the room, closing the door. 'Yes, sir?' he responded quietly.

The inspector approached him, carrying what was clearly the murder weapon. 'About this gun,' he asked the valet. 'You were uncertain this morning. Can you, or can you not, say definitely that it belonged to Mr Warwick?'

'I wouldn't like to be definite, Inspector,' Angell

replied. 'He had so many, you see.'

'This one is a continental weapon,' the inspector informed him, holding the gun out in front of him. 'It's a war souvenir of some kind, I'd say.'

As he was speaking, again apparently unnoticed by anyone in the room Jan passed along the terrace outside, going in the opposite direction, and carrying a gun which he seemed to be attempting to conceal.

Angell looked at the weapon. 'Mr Warwick did have some foreign guns, sir,' he stated. 'But he looked after all his shooting equipment himself. He wouldn't let me touch them.'

The inspector went over to Julian Farrar. 'Major Farrar,' he said, 'you probably have war souvenirs. Does this weapon mean anything to you?'

Farrar glanced at the gun casually. 'Not a thing, I'm afraid,' he answered.

Turning away from him, the inspector went to replace the gun in his briefcase. 'Sergeant Cadwallader and I,' he announced, turning to face the assembled company, 'will want to go over Mr Warwick's collection of weapons very carefully. He had permits for most of them, I understand.'

'Oh yes, sir,' Angell assured him. 'The permits are in one of the drawers in his bedroom. And all the guns and other weapons are in the gun cupboard.'

Sergeant Cadwallader went to the door, but was stopped by Miss Bennett before he could leave the room. 'Wait a minute,' she called to him. 'You'll want the key of the gun cupboard.' She took a key from her pocket.

'You locked it up?' the inspector queried, turning sharply to her. 'Why was that?'

Miss Bennett's retort was equally sharp. 'I should hardly think you'd need to ask that,' she snapped. 'All those guns, and ammunition as well. Highly dangerous. Everyone knows that.'

Concealing a grin, the sergeant took the key she offered him, and went to the door, pausing in the doorway to see whether the inspector wished to accompany him. Sounding distinctly annoyed at Miss Bennett's uncalled-for comment, Inspector Thomas remarked, 'I shall need to talk to you again, Angell,' as he picked up his briefcase and left the room. The sergeant followed him, leaving the door open for Angell.

However, the valet did not leave the room immediately. Instead, after a nervous glance at Laura who now sat staring at the floor, he went up to Julian Farrar, and murmured, 'About that little matter, sir. I am anxious to get something settled soon. If you could see your way, sir –'

Speaking with difficulty, Farrar answered, 'I think – something – could be managed.'

'Thank you, sir,' Angell responded with a faint smile on his face. 'Thank you very much, sir.' He went to the door and was about to leave the room when Farrar stopped him with a peremptory 'No! Wait a moment, Angell.'

As the valet turned to face him, Farrar called loudly, 'Inspector Thomas!'

There was a tense pause. Then, after a moment

or two, the inspector appeared in the doorway, with the sergeant behind him. 'Yes, Major Farrar?' the inspector asked, quietly.

Resuming a pleasant, natural manner, Julian Farrar strolled across to the armchair. 'Before you get busy with routine, Inspector,' he remarked, 'there is something I ought to have told you. Really, I suppose, I should have mentioned it this morning. But we were all so upset. Mrs Warwick has just informed me that there are some fingerprints that you are anxious to identify. On the table here, I think you said.' He paused, then added, easily, 'In all probability, Inspector, those are my fingerprints.'

There was a pause. The inspector slowly approached Farrar, and then asked quietly, but with an accusing note in his voice, 'You were over here last night, Major Farrar?'

'Yes,' Farrar replied. 'I came over, as I often do after dinner, to have a chat with Richard.'

'And you found him – ?' the inspector prompted.

'I found him very moody and depressed. So I didn't stay long.'

'At about what time was this, Major Farrar?'

Farrar thought for a moment, and then replied, 'I really can't remember. Perhaps ten o'clock, or ten-thirty. Thereabouts.'

The inspector regarded him steadily. 'Can you get a little closer than that?' he asked.

'I'm sorry. I'm afraid I can't,' was Farrar's immediate answer.

After a somewhat tense pause, the inspector asked,

trying to sound casual, 'I don't suppose there would have been any quarrel – or bad words of any kind?'

'No, certainly not,' Farrar retorted indignantly. He looked at his watch. 'I'm late,' he observed. 'I've got to take the chair at a meeting in the Town Hall. I can't keep them waiting.' He turned and walked towards the french windows. 'So, if you don't mind –' He paused on the terrace.

'Mustn't keep the Town Hall waiting,' the inspector agreed, following him. 'But I'm sure you'll understand, Major Farrar, that I should like a full statement from you of your movements last night. Perhaps we could do this tomorrow morning.' He paused, and then continued, 'You realize, of course, that there is no obligation on you to make a statement, that it is purely voluntary on your part – and that you are fully entitled to have your solicitor present, should you so wish.'

Mrs Warwick had re-entered the room. She stood in the doorway, leaving the door open, and listening to the inspector's last few words. Julian Farrar drew in his breath as he grasped the significance of what the inspector had said. 'I understand – perfectly,' he said. 'Shall we say ten o'clock tomorrow morning? And my solicitor will be present.'

Farrar made his exit along the terrace, and the inspector turned to Laura Warwick. 'Did you see Major Farrar when he came here last night?' he asked her.

'I – I –,' Laura began uncertainly, but was interrupted by Starkwedder who suddenly jumped up from his chair and went across to them, interposing himself between the inspector and Laura. 'I don't think Mrs Warwick feels like answering any questions just now,' he said.

CHAPTER SIXTEEN

Starkwedder and Inspector Thomas faced each other in silence for a moment. Then the inspector spoke. 'What did you say, Mr Starkwedder?' he asked, quietly.

'I said,' Starkwedder replied, 'that I don't think Mrs Warwick feels like any more questions just at the moment.'

'Indeed?' growled the inspector. 'And what business is it of yours, might I ask?'

Mrs Warwick senior joined in the confrontation. 'Mr Starkwedder is quite right,' she announced.

The inspector turned to Laura questioningly. After a pause, she murmured, 'No, I don't want to answer any more questions just now.'

Looking rather smug, Starkwedder smiled at the inspector who turned away angrily and swiftly left the room with the sergeant. Angell followed them, shutting the door behind him. As he did so, Laura burst out, 'But I should speak. I must – I must tell them –'

'Mr Starkwedder is quite right, Laura,' Mrs Warwick interjected forcefully. 'The less you say now, the better.' She took a few paces about the room, leaning heavily on her stick, and then continued. 'We must get in touch with Mr Adams at once.' Turning to Starkwedder, she explained, 'Mr Adams is our solicitor.' She glanced across at Miss Bennett. 'Ring him up now, Benny.'

Miss Bennett nodded and went towards the telephone, but Mrs Warwick stopped her. 'No, use the extension upstairs,' she instructed, adding, 'Laura, go with her.'

Laura rose, and then hesitated, looking confusedly at her mother-in-law, who merely added, 'I want to talk to Mr Starkwedder.'

'But –' Laura began, only to be immediately interrupted by Mrs Warwick. 'Now don't worry, my dear,' the old lady assured her. 'Just do as I say.'

Laura hesitated for a moment, then went out into the hall, followed by Miss Bennett who closed the door. Mrs Warwick immediately went up to Starkwedder. 'I don't know how much time we have,' she said, speaking rapidly and glancing towards the door. 'I want you to help me.'

Starkwedder looked surprised. 'How?' he asked.

After a pause, Mrs Warwick spoke again. 'You're an intelligent man – and you're a stranger. You've come into our lives from outside. We know nothing about you. You've nothing to do with any of us.'

Starkwedder nodded. 'The unexpected guest, eh?' he murmured. He perched on an arm of the sofa. 'That's been said to me already,' he remarked.

'Because you're a stranger,' Mrs Warwick continued, 'there is something I'm going to ask you to do for me.' She moved across to the french windows and stepped out onto the terrace, looking along it in both directions.

After a pause, Starkwedder spoke. 'Yes, Mrs Warwick?'

Coming back into the room, Mrs Warwick began to speak with some urgency. 'Up until this evening,' she told him, 'there was a reasonable explanation for this tragedy. A man whom my son had injured – by accidentally killing his child – came to take his revenge. I know it sounds melodramatic, but, after all, one does read of such things happening.'

'As you say,' Starkwedder remarked, wondering where this conversation was leading.

'But now, I'm afraid that explanation has gone,' Mrs Warwick continued. 'And it brings the murder of my son back into the family.' She took a few steps towards the armchair. 'Now, there are two people who definitely could not have shot my son. And they are his wife and Miss Bennett. They were actually together when the shot was fired.'

Starkwedder gave a quick look at her, but all he said was, 'Quite.'

'However,' Mrs Warwick continued, 'although Laura could not have shot her husband, she could have known who did.'

'That would make her an accessory before the fact,' Starkwedder remarked. 'She and this Julian Farrar chap in it together? Is that what you mean?'

A look of annoyance crossed Mrs Warwick's face. 'That is *not* what I mean,' she told him. She cast another quick glance at the door, and then continued, 'Julian Farrar did not shoot my son.'

Starkwedder rose from the arm of the sofa. 'How can you possibly know that?' he asked her.

'I do know it,' was Mrs Warwick's reply. She looked steadily at him. 'I am going to tell you, a stranger, something that none of my family know,' she stated calmly. 'It is this. I am a woman who has not very long to live.'

'I am sorry –' Starkwedder began, but Mrs Warwick raised her hand to stop him. 'I am not telling you this for sympathy,' she remarked. 'I am telling you in order to explain what otherwise might be difficult of explanation. There are times when you decide on a course of action which you would not decide upon if you had several years of life before you.'

'Such as?' asked Starkwedder quietly.

Mrs Warwick regarded him steadily. 'First, I must tell you something else, Mr Starkwedder,' she said. 'I must tell you something about my son.' She went to the sofa and sat. 'I loved my son very dearly. As a child, and in his young manhood, he had many fine qualities. He was successful, resourceful, brave, sunny-tempered, a delightful companion.' She paused, and seemed to be remembering. Then she continued. 'There were, I must admit, always the defects of those qualities in him. He was impatient of controls, of restraints. He had a cruel streak in him, and he had a kind of fatal arrogance. So long as he was successful, all was well. But he did not have the kind of nature that could deal with adversity, and for some time now I have watched him slowly go downhill.'

Starkwedder quietly seated himself on the stool, facing her.

'If I say that he had become a monster,' Richard

132

Warwick's mother continued, 'it would sound exaggerated. And yet, in some ways he *was* a monster – a monster of egoism, of pride, of cruelty. Because he had been hurt himself, he had an enormous desire to hurt others.' A hard note crept into her voice. 'So others began to suffer because of him. Do you understand me?'

'I think so – yes,' Starkwedder murmured softly.

Mrs Warwick's voice became gentle again as she went on. 'Now, I am very fond of my daughter-in-law. She has spirit, she is warm-hearted, and she has a very brave power of endurance. Richard swept her off her feet, but I don't know whether she was ever really in love with him. However, I will tell you this – she did everything a wife could do to make Richard's illness and inaction bearable.'

She thought for a moment, and her voice was sad as she continued, 'But he would have none of her help. He rejected it. I think at times he hated her, and perhaps that's more natural than one might suppose. So, when I tell you that the inevitable happened, I think you will understand what I mean. Laura fell in love with another man, and he with her.'

Starkwedder regarded Mrs Warwick thoughtfully. 'Why are you telling me all this?' he asked.

'Because you are a stranger,' she replied, firmly. 'These loves and hates and tribulations mean nothing to you, so you can hear about them unmoved.'

'Possibly.'

As though she had not heard him, Mrs Warwick went on speaking. 'So there came a time,' she said, 'when it seemed that only one thing would solve all the difficulties. Richard's death.'

Starkwedder continued to study her face. 'And so,' he murmured, 'conveniently, Richard died?'

'Yes,' Mrs Warwick answered.

There was a pause. Then Starkwedder rose, moved around the stool, and went to the table to stub out his cigarette. 'Excuse me putting this bluntly, Mrs Warwick,' he said, 'but are you confessing to murder?'

CHAPTER SEVENTEEN

Mrs Warwick was silent for a few moments. Then she said sharply, 'I will ask you a question, Mr Starkwedder. Can you understand that someone who has given life might also feel themselves entitled to take that life?'

Starkwedder paced around the room as he thought about this. Finally, 'Mothers have been known to kill their children, yes,' he admitted. 'But it's usually been for a sordid reason – insurance – or perhaps they have two or three children already and don't want to be bothered with another one.' Turning back suddenly to face her, he asked quickly, 'Does Richard's death benefit you financially?'

'No, it does not,' Mrs Warwick replied firmly.

Starkwedder made a deprecatory gesture. 'You must forgive my frankness –' he began, only to be interrupted by Mrs Warwick, who asked with more than a touch of asperity in her voice, 'Do you understand what I am trying to tell you?'

'Yes, I think I do,' he replied. 'You're telling me that it's possible for a mother to kill her son.' He walked over to the sofa and leaned across it as he continued. 'And you're telling me – specifically – that it's possible that *you* killed *your* son.' He paused, and looked at her steadily. 'Is that a theory,' he asked, 'or am I to understand it as a fact?'

'I am not confessing to *anything*,' Mrs Warwick answered. 'I am merely putting before you a certain point of view. An emergency might arise at a time when I was no longer here to deal with it. And in the event of such a thing happening, I want you to have this, and to make use of it.' She took an envelope from her pocket and handed it to him.

Starkwedder took the envelope, but remarked, 'That's all very well. However, I shan't be here. I'm going back to Abadan to carry on with my job.'

Mrs Warwick made a gesture of dismissal, clearly regarding the objection as insignificant. 'You won't be out of touch with civilization,' she reminded him. 'There are newspapers, radio and so on in Abadan, presumably.'

'Oh yes,' he agreed. 'We have all the civilized blessings.'

'Then please keep that envelope. You see whom it's addressed to?'

Starkwedder glanced at the envelope. 'The Chief Constable. Yes. But I'm not at all clear what's really in your mind,' he told Mrs Warwick. 'For a woman, you're really remarkably good at keeping a secret. Either you committed this murder yourself, or you know who did commit it. That's right, isn't it?'

She looked away from him as she replied, 'I don't propose to discuss the matter.'

Starkwedder sat in the armchair. 'And yet,' he

persisted, 'I'd like very much to know exactly what is in your mind.'

'Then I'm afraid I shan't tell you,' Mrs Warwick retorted. 'As you say, I am a woman who can keep her secrets well.'

Deciding to try a different tack, Starkwedder said, 'This valet fellow – the chap who looked after your son –' He paused as though trying to remember the valet's name.

'You mean Angell,' Mrs Warwick told him. 'Well, what about Angell?'

'Do you like him?' asked Starkwedder.

'No, I don't, as it happens,' she replied. 'But he was efficient at his job, and Richard was certainly not easy to work for.'

'I imagine not,' Starkwedder remarked. 'But Angell put up with these difficulties, did he?'

'It was made worth his while,' was Mrs Warwick's wry response.

Starkwedder again began to pace about the room. Then he turned to face Mrs Warwick and, trying to draw her out, asked, 'Did Richard have anything on him?'

The old lady looked puzzled for a moment. 'On him?' she repeated. 'What do you mean? Oh, I see. You mean, did Richard know something to Angell's discredit?'

'Yes, that's what I mean,' Starkwedder affirmed. 'Did he have a hold over Angell?'

Mrs Warwick thought for a moment before replying. Then, 'No, I don't think so,' she said.

'I was just wondering –' he began.

'You mean,' Mrs Warwick broke in, impatiently, 'did Angell shoot my son? I doubt it. I doubt that very much.'

'I see. You're not buying that one,' Starkwedder remarked. 'A pity, but there it is.'

Mrs Warwick suddenly got to her feet. 'Thank you, Mr Starkwedder,' she said. 'You have been very kind.'

She gave him her hand. Amused at her abruptness, he shook hands with her, then went to the door and opened it. After a moment she left the room. Starkwedder closed the door after her, smiling. 'Well, I'm damned!' he exclaimed to himself, as he looked again at the envelope. 'What a woman!'

Hurriedly, he put the envelope into his pocket, as Miss Bennett came into the room looking upset and preoccupied. 'What's she been saying to you?' she demanded.

Taken aback, Starkwedder played for time. 'Eh? What's that?' he responded.

'Mrs Warwick – what's she been saying?' Miss Bennett asked again.

Avoiding a direct reply, Starkwedder merely remarked, 'You seem upset.'

'Of course I'm upset,' she replied. 'I know what she's capable of.'

Starkwedder looked at the housekeeper steadily before asking, 'What *is* Mrs Warwick capable of? Murder?'

Miss Bennett took a step towards him. 'Is that what she's been trying to make you believe?' she asked. 'It isn't true, you know. You've got to realize that. It isn't true.'

'Well, one can't be sure. After all, it might be,' he observed judiciously.

'But I tell you it isn't,' she insisted.

'How can you possibly know that?' Starkwedder asked.

'I do know,' Miss Bennett replied. 'Do you think there's anything I don't know about the people in this house? I've been with them for years. Years, I tell you.' She sat in the armchair. 'I care for them very much, all of them.'

'Including the late Richard Warwick?' Starkwedder asked.

Miss Bennett seemed lost in thought for a moment. Then, 'I used to be fond of him – once,' she replied.

There was a pause. Starkwedder sat on the stool and regarded her steadily before murmuring, 'Go on.'

'He changed,' said Miss Bennett. 'He became – warped. His whole mentality became quite different. Sometimes he could be a devil.'

'Yes, everybody seems to agree on that,' Starkwedder observed.

'But if you'd known him as he used to be –' she began.

He interrupted her. 'I don't believe that, you know. I don't think people change.'

'Richard did,' Miss Bennett insisted.

'Oh, no, he didn't,' Starkwedder contradicted her. He resumed his prowling about the room. 'You've got things the wrong way round, I'll bet.

I'd say he was always a devil underneath. I'd say he was one of those people who have to be happy and successful – or else! They hide their real selves as long as it gets them what they want. But underneath, the bad streak's always there.'

He turned to face Miss Bennett. 'His cruelty, I bet, was always there. He was probably a bully at school. He was attractive to women, of course. Women are always attracted by bullies. And he took a lot of his sadism out in his big-game hunting, I dare say.' He indicated the hunting trophies on the walls.

'Richard Warwick must have been a monstrous egoist,' he continued. 'That's how he seems to me from the way all you people talk about him. He enjoyed building himself up as a good fellow, generous, successful, lovable and all the rest of it.' Starkwedder was still pacing restlessly. 'But the mean streak was there, all right. And when his accident came, it was just the façade that was torn away, and you all saw him as he really was.'

Miss Bennett rose. 'I don't see that you've got any business to talk,' she exclaimed indignantly. 'You're a stranger, and you know nothing about it.'

'Perhaps not, but I've heard a great deal about it,' Starkwedder retorted. 'Everyone seems to talk to me for some reason.'

'Yes, I suppose they do. Yes, I'm talking to you now, aren't I?' she admitted, as she sat down again. 'That's because we none of us here dare talk to one another.' She looked up at him, appealingly. 'I wish you weren't going away,' she told him.

Starkwedder shook his head. 'I've done nothing to

help at all, really,' he said. 'All I've done is blunder in and discover a dead body for you.'

'But it was Laura and I who discovered Richard's body,' Miss Bennett contradicted him. She paused and then suddenly added, 'Or did Laura – did you – ?' Her voice trailed off into silence.

CHAPTER EIGHTEEN

Starkwedder looked at Miss Bennett and smiled. 'You're pretty sharp, aren't you?' he observed.

Miss Bennett stared at him fixedly. 'You helped her, didn't you?' she asked, making it sound like an accusation.

He walked away from her. 'Now you're imagining things,' he told her.

'Oh, no, I'm not,' Miss Bennett retorted. 'I want Laura to be happy. Oh, I so very much want her to be happy!'

Starkwedder turned to her, exclaiming passionately, 'Damn it, so do I!'

Miss Bennett looked at him in surprise. Then she began to speak. 'In that case I – I've got to –' she began, but was interrupted. Gesturing to her to be silent, Starkwedder murmured, 'Just a minute.' He hastened to the french windows, opened a window and called, 'What are you doing?'

Miss Bennett now caught sight of Jan out on the lawn, brandishing a gun. Rising quickly, she too went across to the french windows and called urgently, 'Jan! Jan! Give me that gun.'

Jan, however, was too quick for her. He ran off laughing, and shouting, 'Come and get it,' as he ran. Miss Bennett followed him, with urgent cries of 'Jan! Jan!'

Starkwedder looked out across the lawn, trying to see what was happening. Then he turned back, and was about to go to the door, when Laura suddenly entered the room.

'Where's the inspector?' she asked him.

Starkwedder made an ineffectual gesture. Laura shut the door behind her, and came over to him. 'Michael, you must listen to me,' she implored him. 'Julian didn't kill Richard.'

'Indeed?' Starkwedder replied coldly. 'He told you so, did he?'

'You don't believe me, but it's true.' Laura sounded desperate.

'You mean you believe it's true,' Starkwedder pointed out to her.

'No, I know it's true,' Laura replied. 'You see, he thought *I'd* killed Richard.'

Starkwedder moved back into the room, away from the french windows. 'That's not exactly surprising,' he said with an acid smile. 'I thought so, too, didn't I?'

Laura's voice sounded even more desperate as she insisted, 'He thought I'd shot Richard. But he couldn't cope with it. It made him feel –' She stopped, embarrassed, then continued, 'It made him feel differently towards me.'

Starkwedder looked at her coldly. 'Whereas,' he pointed out, 'when you thought *he'd* killed Richard, you took it in your stride without turning a hair!' Suddenly relenting a little, he smiled. 'Women are wonderful!' he murmured. He perched on the sofa

144

arm. 'What made Farrar come out with the damaging fact that he was here last night? Don't tell me it was a pure and simple regard for the truth?'

'It was Angell,' Laura replied. 'Angell saw – or says he saw – Julian here.'

'Yes,' Starkwedder remarked with a somewhat bitter laugh. 'I thought I got a whiff of blackmail. Not a nice fellow, Angell.'

'He says he saw Julian just after the – after the shot was fired,' Laura told him. 'Oh, I'm frightened. It's all closing in. I'm so frightened.'

Starkwedder went over to her and took her by the shoulders. 'You needn't be,' he said, reassuringly. 'It's going to be all right.'

Laura shook her head. 'It can't be,' she cried.

'It will be all right, I tell you,' he insisted, shaking her gently.

She looked at him wonderingly. 'Shall we ever know who shot Richard?' she asked him.

Starkwedder looked at her for a moment without replying, and then went to the french windows and gazed out into the garden. 'Your Miss Bennett,' he said, 'seems very positive she knows all the answers.'

'She's always positive,' Laura replied. 'But she's sometimes wrong.'

Apparently glimpsing something outside, Starkwedder suddenly beckoned to Laura to join him. Running across to him, she took his outstretched hand. 'Yes, Laura,' he exclaimed excitedly, still looking out into the garden. 'I thought so!'

'What is it?' she asked.

'Ssh!' he cautioned. At almost the same moment, Miss Bennett came into the room from the hallway. 'Mr Starkwedder,' she said hurriedly. 'Go into the room next door – the inspector's already there. Quickly!'

Starkwedder and Laura crossed the study swiftly, and hurried into the corridor, closing the door behind them. As soon as they had gone, Miss Bennett looked out into the garden, where daylight was beginning to fade. 'Now come in, Jan,' she called to him. 'Don't tease me any more. Come in, come inside.'

CHAPTER NINETEEN

Miss Bennett beckoned to Jan, then stepped back into the room and stood to one side of the french windows. Jan suddenly appeared from the terrace, looking half mutinous and half flushed with triumph. He was carrying a gun.

'Now, Jan, how on earth did you get hold of that?' Miss Bennett asked him.

Jan came into the room. 'Thought you were so clever, didn't you, Benny?' he said, quite belligerently. 'Very clever, locking up all Richard's guns in there.' He nodded in the direction of the hallway. 'But I found a key that fitted the gun cupboard. I've got a gun now, just like Richard. I'm going to have lots of guns and pistols. I'm going to shoot things.' He suddenly raised the gun and pointed it at Miss Bennett, who flinched. 'Be careful, Benny,' he went on with a chuckle, 'I might shoot you.'

Miss Bennett tried not to look too alarmed as she said, in as soothing a tone as she could muster, 'Why, you wouldn't do a thing like that, Jan, I know you wouldn't.'

Jan continued to point the gun at Miss Bennett, but after a few moments he lowered it.

Miss Bennett relaxed slightly, and after a pause Jan exclaimed, sweetly and rather eagerly, 'No, I wouldn't. Of course I wouldn't.'

'After all, it's not as though you were just a careless boy,' Miss Bennett told him, reassuringly. 'You're a man now, aren't you?'

Jan beamed. He walked over to the desk and sat in the chair. 'Yes, I'm a man,' he agreed. 'Now that Richard's dead, I'm the only man in the house.'

'That's why I know you wouldn't shoot me,' Miss Bennett said. 'You'd only shoot an enemy.'

'That's right,' Jan exclaimed with delight.

Sounding as though she were choosing her words very carefully, Miss Bennett said, 'During the war, if you were in the Resistance, when you killed an enemy you put a notch on your gun.'

'Is that true?' Jan responded, examining his gun. 'Did they really?' He looked eagerly at Miss Bennett. 'Did some people have a lot of notches?'

'Yes,' she replied, 'some people had quite a lot of notches.'

Jan chortled with glee. 'What fun!' he exclaimed.

'Of course,' Miss Bennett continued, 'some people don't like killing anything – but other people do.'

'Richard did,' Jan reminded her.

'Yes, Richard liked killing things,' Miss Bennett admitted. She turned away from him casually, as she added, 'You like killing things, too, don't you, Jan?'

Unseen by her, Jan took a penknife from his pocket and began to make a notch on his gun. 'It's exciting to kill things,' he observed, a trifle petulantly.

Miss Bennett turned back to face him. 'You didn't

want Richard to have you sent away, did you, Jan?' she asked him quietly.

'He said he would,' Jan retorted with feeling. 'He was a beast!'

Miss Bennett walked around behind the desk chair in which Jan was still sitting. 'You said to Richard once,' she reminded him, 'that you'd kill him if he was going to send you away.'

'Did I?' Jan responded. He sounded nonchalantly offhand.

'But you didn't kill him?' Miss Bennett asked, her intonation making her words into only a half-question.

'Oh, no, I didn't kill him.' Again, Jan sounded unconcerned.

'That was rather weak of you,' Miss Bennett observed.

There was a crafty look in Jan's eyes as he responded, 'Was it?'

'Yes, I think so. To say you'd kill him, and then not to do it.' Miss Bennett moved around the desk, but looked towards the door. 'If anyone was threatening to shut *me* up, I'd want to kill him, and I'd do it, too.'

'Who says someone else did?' Jan retorted swiftly. 'Perhaps it *was* me.'

'Oh, no, it wouldn't be you,' Miss Bennett said, dismissively. 'You were only a boy. You wouldn't have dared.'

Jan jumped up and backed away from her. 'You think I wouldn't have dared?' His voice was almost a squeal. 'Is that what you think?'

149

'Of course it's what I think.' She seemed now deliberately to be taunting him. 'Of course you wouldn't have dared to kill Richard. You'd have to be very brave and grown-up to do that.'

Jan turned his back on her, and walked away. 'You don't know everything, Benny,' he said, sounding hurt. 'Oh no, old Benny. You don't know everything.'

'Is there something I don't know?' Miss Bennett asked him. 'Are you laughing at me, Jan?' Seizing her opportunity, she opened the door a little way. Jan stood near the french windows, whence a shaft of light from the setting sun shone across the room.

'Yes, yes, I'm laughing,' Jan suddenly shouted at her. 'I'm laughing because I'm so much cleverer than you are.'

He turned back into the room. Miss Bennett involuntarily gave a start and clutched the door frame. Jan took a step towards her. 'I know things you don't know,' Jan added, speaking more soberly.

'What do you know that I don't know?' Miss Bennett asked. She tried not to sound too anxious.

Jan made no reply, but merely smiled mysteriously. Miss Bennett approached him. 'Aren't you going to tell me?' she asked again, coaxingly. 'Won't you trust me with your secret?'

Jan drew away from her. 'I don't trust anybody,' he said, bitterly.

Miss Bennett changed her tone to one of puzzlement. 'I wonder, now,' she murmured. 'I wonder if perhaps you've been very clever.'

Jan giggled. 'You're beginning to see how clever I can be,' he told her.

150

She regarded him speculatively. 'Perhaps there are a lot of things I don't know about you,' she agreed.

'Oh, lots and lots,' Jan assured her. 'And I know a lot of things about everybody else, but I don't always tell. I get up sometimes in the night and I creep about the house. I see a lot of things, and I find out a lot of things, but I don't tell.'

Adopting a conspiratorial air, Miss Bennett asked, 'Have you got some big secret now?'

Jan swung one leg over the stool, sitting astride it. 'Big secret! Big secret!' he squealed delightedly. 'You'd be frightened if you knew,' he added, laughing almost hysterically.

Miss Bennett came closer to him. 'Would I? Would I be frightened?' she asked. 'Would I be frightened of *you*, Jan?' Placing herself squarely in front of Jan, she stared intently at him.

Jan looked up at her. The expression of delight left his face, and his voice was very serious as he replied, 'Yes, you'd be very frightened of me.'

She continued to regard him closely. 'I haven't known what you were really like,' she admitted. 'I'm just beginning to understand what you're like, Jan.'

Jan's mood changes were becoming more pronounced. Sounding more and more wild, he exclaimed, 'Nobody knows anything about me really, or the things I can do.' He swung round on the stool, and sat with his back to her. 'Silly old Richard, sitting there and shooting at silly old birds.' He turned back to Miss Bennett, adding intensely, 'He

151

didn't think anyone would shoot *him*, did he?'

'No,' she replied. 'No, that was his mistake.'

Jan rose. 'Yes, that was his mistake,' he agreed. 'He thought he could send me away, didn't he? *I* showed him.'

'Did you?' asked Miss Bennett quickly. 'How did you show him?'

Jan looked at her craftily. He paused, then finally said, 'Shan't tell you.'

'Oh, do tell me, Jan,' she pleaded.

'No,' he retorted, moving away from her. He went to the armchair and climbed into it, nestling the gun against his cheek. 'No, I shan't tell anyone.'

Miss Bennett went across to him. 'Perhaps you're right,' she told him. 'Perhaps I can guess what you did, but I won't say. It will be just your secret, won't it?'

'Yes, it's my secret,' Jan replied. He began to move restlessly about the room. 'Nobody knows what I'm like,' he exclaimed excitedly. 'I'm dangerous. They'd better be careful. Everybody had better be careful. I'm *dangerous*.'

Miss Bennett looked at him sadly. 'Richard didn't know how dangerous you were,' she said. 'He must have been surprised.'

Jan went back to the armchair, and looked into it. 'He was. He was surprised,' he agreed. 'His face went all silly. And then – and then his head dropped down when it was done, and there was blood, and he didn't move any more. I showed him. I showed him! Richard won't send me away now!'

He perched on one end of the sofa, waving the

gun at Miss Bennett who was trying to fight back her tears. 'Look,' Jan ordered her. 'Look. See? I've put a notch on my gun!' He tapped the gun with his knife.

'So you have!' Miss Bennett exclaimed, approaching him. 'Isn't that exciting?' She tried to grab the gun, but he was too quick for her.

'Oh, no, you don't,' he cried, as he danced away from her. 'Nobody's going to take my gun away from me. If the police come and try to arrest me, I shall shoot them.'

'There's no need to do that,' Miss Bennett assured him. 'No need at all. You're clever. You're so clever that they would never suspect you.'

'Silly old police! Silly old police!' Jan shouted jubilantly. 'And silly old Richard.' He brandished the gun at an imaginary Richard, then caught sight of the door opening. With a cry of alarm, he quickly ran off into the garden. Miss Bennett collapsed upon the sofa in tears, as Inspector Thomas hastened into the room followed by Sergeant Cadwallader.

CHAPTER TWENTY

'After him! Quickly!' the inspector shouted to Cadwallader as they ran into the room. The sergeant raced out onto the terrace through the french windows, as Starkwedder rushed into the room from the hallway. He was followed by Laura, who ran to the french windows and looked out. Angell was the next to appear. He, too, went across to the french windows. Mrs Warwick stood, an upright figure, in the doorway.

Inspector Thomas turned to Miss Bennett. 'There, there, dear lady,' he comforted her. 'You mustn't take on so. You did very well.'

In a broken voice, Miss Bennett replied. 'I've known all along,' she told the inspector. 'You see, I know better than anyone else what Jan is like. I knew that Richard was pushing him too far, and I knew – I've known for some time – that Jan was getting dangerous.'

'Jan!' Laura exclaimed. With a sigh of deep distress, she murmured, 'Oh, no, oh, no, not Jan.' She sank into the desk chair. 'I can't believe it,' she gasped.

Mrs Warwick glared at Miss Bennett. 'How could you, Benny?' she said, accusingly. 'How could you? I thought that at least you would be loyal.'

Miss Bennett's reply was defiant. 'There are times,' she told the old lady, 'when truth is more important than loyalty. You didn't see – any of you – that Jan was becoming dangerous. He's a dear boy – a sweet boy – but –' Overcome with grief, she was unable to continue.

Mrs Warwick moved slowly and sadly across to the armchair and sat, staring into space.

Speaking quietly, the inspector completed Miss Bennett's thought. 'But when they get above a certain age, then they get dangerous, because they don't understand what they're doing any more,' he observed. 'They haven't got a man's judgement or control.' He went across to Mrs Warwick. 'You mustn't grieve, madam. I think I can take it upon myself to say that he'll be treated with humanity and consideration. There's a clear case to be made, I think, for his not being responsible for his actions. It'll mean detention in comfortable surroundings. And that, you know, is what it would have come to soon, in any case.' He turned away, and walked across the room, closing the hall door as he passed it.

'Yes, yes, I know you're right,' Mrs Warwick admitted. Turning to Miss Bennett, she said, 'I'm sorry, Benny. You said that nobody else knew he was dangerous. That's not true. I knew – but I couldn't bring myself to do anything about it.'

'Somebody had to do something!' Benny replied strongly. The room fell silent, but tension mounted as they all waited for Sergeant Cadwallader's return with Jan in custody.

By the side of the road several hundred yards from the house, with a mist beginning to close in, the sergeant had got Jan cornered with a high wall behind him. Jan brandished his gun, shouting, 'Don't come any closer. No one's going to shut me away anywhere. I'll shoot you. I mean it. I'm not frightened of anyone!'

The sergeant stopped a good twenty feet away. 'Now come on, lad,' he called, coaxingly. 'No one's going to hurt you. But guns are dangerous things. Just give it to me, and come back to the house with me. You can talk to your family, and they'll help you.'

He advanced a few steps towards Jan, but stopped when the boy cried hysterically, 'I mean it. I'll shoot you. I don't care about policemen. I'm not frightened of you.'

'Of course you're not,' the sergeant replied. 'You've no reason to be frightened of me. I wouldn't hurt you. But come back into the house with me. Come on, now.' He stepped forward again, but Jan jerked the gun up and fired two shots in quick succession. The first went wide, but the second struck Cadwallader in the left hand. He gave a cry of pain, but rushed at Jan, knocking him to the ground, and attempting to get the gun away from him. As they struggled, the gun suddenly went off again. Jan gave a quick gasp, and lay silent.

Horrified, the sergeant knelt over him, staring at him in disbelief. 'No, oh no,' he murmured. 'Poor, silly boy. No! You can't be dead. Oh, please God –' He checked Jan's pulse, then shook his head slowly.

Rising to his feet, he backed slowly away for a few paces, and only then noticed that his hand was bleeding badly. Wrapping a handkerchief around it, he ran back to the house, holding his left arm in the air and gasping with pain.

By the time he got back to the french windows, he was staggering. 'Sir!' he called, as the inspector and the others ran out onto the terrace.

'What on earth's happened?' the inspector asked.

His breath coming with difficulty, the sergeant replied, 'It's terrible, what I've got to tell you.' Starkwedder helped him into the room and the sergeant staggered to the stool and sank onto it.

The inspector moved quickly to his side. 'Your hand!' he exclaimed.

'I'll see to it,' Starkwedder murmured. Holding Sergeant Cadwallader's arm, he discarded the now heavily bloodstained piece of cloth, took out a handkerchief from his own pocket, and began to tie it around the sergeant's hand.

'The mist coming on, you see,' Cadwallader began to explain. 'It was difficult to see clearly. He shot at me. Up there, along the road, near the edge of the spinney.'

With a look of horror on her face, Laura rose and went across to the french windows.

'He shot at me twice,' the sergeant was saying, 'and the second time he got me in the hand.'

Miss Bennett suddenly rose, and put her hand to her mouth. 'I tried to get the gun away from him,' the sergeant went on, 'but I was hampered with my hand, you see –'

'Yes. What happened?' the inspector prompted him.

'His finger was on the trigger,' the sergeant gasped, and it went off. He's shot through the heart. He's dead.'

CHAPTER TWENTY-ONE

Sergeant Cadwallader's announcement was greeted with a stunned silence. Laura put her hand to her mouth to stifle a cry, then slowly moved back to the desk chair and sat, staring at the floor. Mrs Warwick lowered her head and leaned on her stick. Starkwedder paced about the room, looking distracted.

'Are you sure he's dead?' the inspector asked.

'I am indeed,' the sergeant replied. 'Poor young lad, shouting defiance at me, loosing off his gun as though he loved the firing of it.'

The inspector walked across to the french windows. 'Where is he?'

'I'll come with you and show you,' the sergeant replied, struggling to his feet.

'No, you'd better stay here.'

'I'm all right now,' the sergeant insisted. 'I'll do all right until we get back to the station.' He walked out onto the terrace, swaying slightly. Looking back at the others, his face filled with misery, he murmured distractedly, '"One would not, sure, be frightful when one's dead." That's Pope. Alexander Pope.' He shook his head, and then walked slowly away.

The inspector turned back to face Mrs Warwick and the others. 'I'm more sorry than I can say, but

161

perhaps it's the best way out,' he said, then followed the sergeant out into the garden.

Mrs Warwick watched him go. 'The best way out!' she exclaimed, half angrily, half despairingly.

'Yes, yes,' Miss Bennett sighed. 'It is for the best. He's out of it now, poor boy.' She went to help Mrs Warwick up. 'Come, my dear, come, this has been too much for you.'

The old lady looked at her vaguely. 'I – I'll go and lie down,' she murmured, as Miss Bennett supported her to the door. Starkwedder opened it for them, and then took an envelope out of his pocket, holding it out to Mrs Warwick. 'I think you'd better have this back,' he suggested.

She turned in the doorway and took the envelope from him. 'Yes,' she replied. 'Yes, there's no need for that now.'

Mrs Warwick and Miss Bennett left the room. Starkwedder was about to close the door after them when he realized that Angell was moving across to Laura who was still sitting at the desk. She did not turn at his approach.

'May I say, madam,' Angell addressed her, 'how sorry I am. If there is anything I can do, you have only –'

Without looking up, Laura interrupted him. 'We shall need no more help from you, Angell,' she told him coldly. 'You shall have a cheque for your wages, and I should like you out of the house today.'

'Yes, madam. Thank you, madam,' Angell replied, apparently without feeling, then turned away and left the room. Starkwedder closed the door after him.

162

The room was now growing dark, the last rays of the sun throwing shadows on the walls.

Starkwedder looked across at Laura. 'You're not going to prosecute him for blackmail?' he asked.

'No,' Laura replied, listlessly.

'A pity.' He walked over to her. 'Well, I suppose I'd better be going. I'll say goodbye.' He paused. Laura still had not looked at him. 'Don't be too upset,' he added.

'I *am* upset,' Laura responded with feeling.

'Because you loved the boy?' Starkwedder asked.

She turned to him. 'Yes. And because it's my fault. You see, Richard was right. Poor Jan should have been sent away somewhere. He should have been shut up where he couldn't do any harm. It was I who wouldn't have that. So, really, it was my fault that Richard was killed.'

'Come now, Laura, don't let's sentimentalize,' Starkwedder retorted roughly. He came closer to her. 'Richard was killed because he asked for it. He could have shown some ordinary kindness to the boy, couldn't he? Don't you fret yourself. What you've got to do now is to be happy. Happy ever after, as the stories say.'

'Happy? With Julian?' Laura responded with bitterness in her voice. 'I wonder!' She frowned. 'You see, it isn't the same now.'

'You mean between Farrar and you?' he asked.

'Yes. You see, when I thought Julian had killed Richard, it made no difference to me. I loved him just the same.' Laura paused, then continued, 'I was even willing to say I'd done it myself.'

'I know you were,' said Starkwedder. 'More fool you. How women enjoy making martyrs of themselves!'

'But when Julian thought *I* had done it,' Laura continued passionately, 'he changed. He changed towards me completely. Oh, he was willing to try to do the decent thing and not incriminate me. But that was all.' She leaned her chin on her hand, dispirited. 'He didn't feel the same any more.'

Starkwedder shook his head. 'Look here, Laura,' he exclaimed, 'men and women don't react in the same way. What it comes down to is this. Men are really the sensitive sex. Women are tough. Men can't take murder in their stride. Women apparently can. The fact is, if a man's committed a murder for a woman, it probably enhances his value in her eyes. A man feels differently.'

She looked up at him. 'You didn't feel that way,' she observed. 'When *you* thought I had shot Richard, you helped me.'

'That was different,' Starkwedder replied quickly. He sounded slightly taken aback. 'I had to help you.'

'Why did you have to help me?' Laura asked him.

Starkwedder did not reply directly. Then, after a pause, he said quietly, 'I still want to help you.'

'Don't you see,' said Laura, turning away from him, 'we're back where we started. In a way it *was* I who killed Richard because – because I was being so obstinate about Jan.'

Starkwedder drew up the stool and sat down

beside her. 'That's what's eating you, really, isn't it?' he declared. 'Finding out that it was Jan who shot Richard. But it needn't be true, you know. You needn't think that unless you like.'

Laura stared at him intently. 'How can you say such a thing?' she asked. 'I heard – we all heard – he admitted it – he boasted of it.'

'Oh, yes,' Starkwedder admitted. 'Yes, I know that. But how much do you know about the power of suggestion? Your Miss Bennett played Jan very carefully, got him all worked up. And the boy was certainly suggestible. He liked the idea, as many adolescents do, of being thought to have power, of – yes, of being a killer, if you like. Your Benny dangled the bait in front of him, and he took it. He'd shot Richard, and he put a notch on his gun, and he was a hero!' He paused. 'But you don't know – none of us really know – whether what he said was true.'

'But, for heaven's sake, he shot at the sergeant!' Laura expostulated.

'Oh, yes, he was a potential killer all right!' Starkwedder admitted. 'It's quite likely he shot Richard. But you can't say for sure that he did. It might have been –' He hesitated. 'It might have been somebody else.'

Laura stared at him in disbelief. 'But who?' she asked, incredulously.

Starkwedder thought for a moment. Then, 'Miss Bennett, perhaps,' he suggested. 'After all, she's very fond of you all, and she might have thought it was all for the best. Or, for that matter, Mrs Warwick. Or

165

even your boyfriend Julian – afterwards pretending that he thought you'd done it. A clever move which took you in completely.'

Laura turned away. 'You don't believe what you're saying,' she accused him. 'You're only trying to console me.'

Starkwedder looked absolutely exasperated. 'My dear girl,' he expostulated, 'anyone might have shot Richard. Even MacGregor.'

'MacGregor?' she asked, staring at him. 'But MacGregor's dead.'

'Of course he's dead,' Starkwedder replied. 'He'd have to be.' He rose and moved to the sofa. 'Look here,' he continued, 'I can put up a very pretty case for MacGregor having been the killer. Say he decided to kill Richard as revenge for the accident in which his little boy was killed.' He sat on the sofa arm. 'What does he do? Well, first thing is he has to get rid of his own personality. It wouldn't be difficult to arrange for him to be reported dead in some remote part of Alaska. It would cost a little money and some fake testimony, of course, but these things can be managed. Then he changes his name, and he starts building up a new personality for himself in some other country, some other job.'

Laura stared at him for a moment, then left the desk and went to sit in the armchair. Closing her eyes, she took a deep breath, then opened her eyes and looked at him again.

Starkwedder continued with his speculative narrative. 'He keeps tabs on what's going on over here, and when he knows that you've left Norfolk and come to this part of the world, he makes his plans. He shaves his beard, and dyes his hair, and all that sort of thing, of course. Then, on a misty night, he comes here. Now, let's say it goes like this.' He went and stood by the french windows. 'Let's say MacGregor says to Richard, "I've got a gun, and so have you. I count three, and we both fire. I've come to get you for the death of my boy."'

Laura stared at him, appalled.

'You know,' Starkwedder went on, 'I don't think that your husband was quite the fine sporting fellow you think he was. I have an idea he mightn't have waited for a count of three. You say he was a damn good shot, but this time he missed, and the bullet went out here' – he gestured as he walked out onto the terrace – 'into the garden where there are a good many other bullets. But MacGregor doesn't miss. He shoots and kills.' Starkwedder came back into the room. 'He drops his gun by the body, takes Richard's gun, goes out of the window, and presently he comes back.'

'Comes back?' Laura asked. 'Why does he come back?'

Starkwedder looked at her for a few seconds without speaking. Then, taking a deep breath, he asked, 'Can't you guess?'

Laura looked at him wonderingly. She shook her head. 'No, I've no idea,' she replied.

He continued to regard her steadily. After a pause, he spoke slowly and with an effort. 'Well,' he said, 'suppose MacGregor has an accident with his car and can't get away from here. What else can he do?

Only one thing – come up to the house and discover the body!'

'You speak –' Laura gasped, 'you speak as though you know just what happened.'

Starkwedder could no longer restrain himself. 'Of course I know,' he burst out passionately. 'Don't you understand? *I'm* MacGregor!' He leaned back against the curtains, shaking his head desperately.

Laura rose, an incredulous look on her face. She stepped towards him, half raising her arm, unable to grasp the full meaning of his words. 'You –' she murmured. 'You –'

Starkwedder walked slowly towards Laura. 'I never meant any of this to happen,' he told her, his voice husky with emotion. 'I mean – finding you, and finding that I cared about you, and that – Oh, God, it's hopeless. Hopeless.' As she stared at him, dazed, Starkwedder took her hand and kissed the palm. 'Goodbye, Laura,' he said, gruffly.

He went quickly out through the french windows and disappeared into the mist. Laura ran out onto the terrace and called after him, 'Wait – wait. Come back!'

The mist swirled, and the Bristol fog signal began to boom. 'Come back, Michael, come back!' Laura cried. There was no reply. 'Come back, Michael,' she called again. 'Please come back! I care about you too.'

She listened intently, but heard only the sound of a car starting up and moving off. The fog signal continued to sound as she collapsed against the window and burst into a fit of uncontrollable sobbing.

POSTSCRIPT

The following chapter is taken from Charles Osborne's *The Life and Crimes of Agatha Christie*, a biographical companion to the works of the 'Queen of Crime'. First published in 1982 and fully revised in 1999, it examines chronologically each of Agatha Christie's books and plays in detail, together with the events in her life at the time, and this chapter offers a fascinating insight into the origins of *The Unexpected Guest*.

The Unexpected Guest
PLAY (1958)

On 12 April 1958, *The Mousetrap* reached its 2,239th
performance at the Ambassadors Theatre, thereby
breaking the record for the longest London run of
a play. To commemorate the breaking of the record, Agatha Christie presented to the Ambassadors
Theatre a specially designed mousetrap. She was, of
course, delighted that her *Mousetrap* had broken all
records, and she must have had great hopes for a
new play she had written, and of which she thought
very highly. This was *Verdict*, which Peter Saunders
presented at the Strand Theatre on 22 May. But
Verdict failed to please, and closed one month later,
on 21 June. The resilient Mrs Christie murmured,
'At least I am glad *The Times* liked it,' and set to work
to write another play, which she finished within four
weeks, and Peter Saunders immediately put it into
production. The new play, *The Unexpected Guest*,
played for a week at the Hippodrome in Bristol, and
then moved to the Duchess Theatre in the West End
of London, where it opened on 12 August. It played
604 performances there over the following eighteen
months.

The Unexpected Guest could perhaps be described as a murder mystery disguised as a murder
non-mystery, for it begins when a stranger, the

'unexpected guest' of the title, runs his car into a ditch in dense fog in South Wales, near the coast, and makes his way to a house where he finds a woman standing with a gun in her hand over the dead body of her husband, Richard Warwick, whom she admits she has killed. He decides to help her, and together they concoct a story and a plan of action.

The murdered man, a cripple in a wheelchair, appears to have been an unpleasant and sadistic character; apart from members of his own family, there are others who might have murdered him if they had been given the opportunity, among them the father of a child killed two years earlier by Richard Warwick's careless and perhaps drunken driving. As the play progresses, the possibility arises that Laura Warwick may not have killed her husband, but may be shielding someone else. Richard Warwick's young half-brother, mentally retarded and potentially dangerous? Laura's lover, Julian Farrar, who is about to stand for Parliament? Warwick's mother, a strong-minded old matriarch who knows she has not long to live? Or, of course, the father of the little boy who was killed?

The investigating policemen who turn up in Act I, Scene ii, are a shrewd and sarcastic inspector and a poetically inclined young sergeant who quotes Keats. Towards the end of the play's second and final act, they identify and apprehend the real murderer. Or do they? This being an Agatha Christie mystery, there is a further surprise in the play's last lines. Can it be that Mrs Christie allows a killer to escape punishment? If so, might this be because she thinks of the murder of Richard Warwick as a just retribution?

Through the character of Michael Starkwedder, 'the unexpected guest', Mrs Christie makes the interesting assertion that:

Men are really the sensitive sex. Women are tough. Men can't take murder in their stride. Women apparently can.

The character of the murdered man, as described by his wife, was based, at least in part, on someone whom Agatha Christie had known very well. Here is Laura Warwick, describing one of her late husband's nocturnal habits:

Then he'd have this window open and he'd sit here looking out, watching for the gleam of a cat's eyes, or a stray rabbit, or a dog. Of course, there haven't been so many rabbits lately. But he shot quite a lot of cats. He shot them in the daytime, too. And birds . . . a woman came to call one day for subscriptions for the vicarage fête. Richard sent shots to right and left of her as she was going away down the drive. She bolted like a hare, he said. He roared with laughter when he told us about it. Her fat backside was quivering like a jelly, he said. However, she went to the police about it and there was a terrible row.

And here is Agatha Christie, in her autobiography,

describing her brother Monty, as an invalid towards the end of his life:

> Monty's health was improving, and as a result he was much more difficult to control. He was bored, and for relaxation took to shooting out of his window with a revolver. Tradespeople and some of mother's visitors complained. Monty was unrepentant. 'Some silly old spinster going down the drive with her behind wobbling. Couldn't resist it – I sent a shot or two right and left of her. My word, how she ran' . . . Someone complained and we had a visit from the police.

The Unexpected Guest was an original Christie, not only in the sense that it was written by the author herself and not dramatized by someone else from a Christie novel or story, but also in being, like *Spider's Web* but unlike *The Mousetrap* or *Witness for the Prosecution*, completely new and not an adaptation by the author of an earlier work of hers. It is, in fact, one of the best of her plays, its dialogue taut and effective and its plot full of surprises despite being economical and not over-complex. It demonstrates, incidentally, the profound truth that seeing is not believing. The leading roles in 1958 were played by Renee Asherson (Laura Warwick), Nigel Stock (Michael Starkwedder) and Violet Farebrother (Mrs Warwick, senior), with Christopher Sandford (Jan Warwick), Paul Curran (Henry Angell), Roy Purcell (Julian Farrar), Winifred Oughton (Miss

Bennett), Michael Golden (Inspector Thomas), Tenniel Evans (Sergeant Cadwallader) and Philip Newman (the corpse). The play was directed by Hubert Gregg.

Reviews were uniformly enthusiastic, many of them contrasting the success of the new play with the recent failure of *Verdict*. 'After the failure of her last play, *Verdict*,' wrote the *Daily Telegraph* critic, 'it was suggested in some quarters that Scotland Yard ought to be called in to discover who killed Agatha Christie. But *The Unexpected Guest*, turning up last night at the Duchess before even the reverberations of her last failure have died away, indicates that the corpse is still very much alive. Burial of her thriller reputation is certainly premature.' The *Guardian* combined reportage and criticism: 'Only seven weeks after Agatha Christie's last play was booed off the stage, the old lady of 66 [sic] stumped defiantly back into a London theatre last night. She had a new whodunit ready. She watched from the back of the circle, white-faced and apprehensive . . . But no boos came this time. No rude interruptions. At the end she heard the kind of applause that has given her *Mousetrap* a record six-year run.'

ALSO BY AGATHA CHRISTIE
ADAPTED BY CHARLES OSBORNE

Black Coffee

Sir Claud Amory has discovered the formula for a new powerful explosive, which is stolen by one of the large household of relatives and friends. Locking everyone in the library, Sir Claud switches off the lights to allow the thief to replace the formula on the table, no questions asked. When the lights come on, he is dead, and Hercule Poirot – with assistance from Hastings and Inspector Japp – has to unravel a tangle of family feuds, old flames and suspicious foreigners to find the killer and prevent a global catastrophe.

Black Coffee was Agatha Christie's first playscript, originally performed in 1930 and made into a now rarely-seen film the following year. Now Charles Osborne, author of *The Life and Crimes of Agatha Christie*, has adapted the play into a full-length novel. Combining her typically beguiling plot and sparkling dialogue with his own faithful narrative, he has produced a novel that will endure for as long as any of Agatha Christie's books.

'A lively and light-hearted read which will give pleasure to all those who have long wished that there was just one more Christie to devour'

ANTONIA FRASER, *Sunday Telegraph*

ISBN: 0 00 651137 6

ALSO BY AGATHA CHRISTIE
ADAPTED BY CHARLES OSBORNE

Spider's Web

Clarissa, the wife of a Foreign Office diplomat, is given to daydreaming. 'Supposing I were to come down one morning and find a dead body in the library, what should I do?' she muses.

Clarissa has her chance to find out when she discovers a body in her drawing-room. Desperate to dispose of it before her husband comes home with an important foreign politician, Clarissa attempts to persuade her three house guests to become accessories and accomplices. As the search begins for the murderer in their midst, the house party is interrupted by the arrival of a police inspector, who needs convincing that there has been no murder at all . . .

Written in 1954 specifically for Margaret Lockwood, *Spider's Web* became one of three successful Agatha Christie plays running simultaneously in London that Christmas, alongside *The Mousetrap* and *Witness for the Prosecution*. Now, following his acclaimed *Black Coffee* and *The Unexpected Guest* play novelisations, Charles Osborne brings Agatha Christie's elusive mystery to a new legion of fans.

Published in hardback September 2000

ISBN: 0 00 226198 7

The Life and Crimes of Agatha Christie

Agatha Christie was the author of over 100 plays, short story collections and novels which have been translated into 103 languages; she is outsold only by the Bible and Shakespeare. Many have tried to copy her but none has succeeded. Attempts to capture her personality on paper, to discover her motivations or the reasons for her popularity, have usually failed. Charles Osborne, a lifelong student of Agatha Christie, has approached this most private of people above all through her books, and the result is a fascinating companion to her life and work.

This 'professional life' of Agatha Christie provides authoritative information on each book's provenance, on the work itself and on its contemporary critical reception set against the background of the major events in the author's life. Illustrated with many rare photographs, this comprehensive guide to the world of Agatha Christie has been fully updated to include details of all the publications, films and TV adaptations in the 25 years since her death.

ISBN: 0 00 257033 5 Hardback
ISBN: 0 00 653097 4 Paperback

ALSO BY AGATHA CHRISTIE

The Mousetrap
and Selected Plays

The first-ever publication in book form of The Mousetrap,
the longest-running play in the history of London's West
End, plus three other Christie thrillers.

The Mousetrap
A homicidal maniac terrorizes a group of snowbound
guests to the refrain of 'Three Blind Mice'. . .

And Then There Were None
Ten guilty people, brought together on an island in mysterious circumstances, await their sentence . . .

Appointment With Death
The suffocating heat of an exotic Middle-Eastern setting
provides a backdrop for murder . . .

The Hollow
A set of friends convene at a country home where their
convoluted relationships mean that any one of them could
be a murderer . . .

Christie's plays are as compulsive as her novels. Their
colourful characters and ingenious plots provide yet more
evidence of her mastery of the detective thriller.

ISBN: 0 00 649618 0

ALSO BY AGATHA CHRISTIE

Witness for the Prosecution and Selected Plays

The first-ever publication in book form of *Witness for the Prosecution*, Christie's highly successful stage thriller which won the New York Drama Critics Circle Award for best foreign play, plus three of her classic mysteries.

Witness for the Prosecution
A stunning courtroom drama in which a scheming wife testifies against her husband in a shocking murder trial . . .

Towards Zero
A psychopathic murderer homes in on unsuspecting victims in a seaside house, perched high on a cliff . . .

Go Back For Murder
When the young feity Carla, orphaned at the tender age of five, discovers 16 years later that her mother was imprisoned for murdering her father, she determines to prove her dead mother's innocence . . .

Verdict
Passion, murder and love are the deadly ingredients which combine to make this one of Christie's more unusual thrillers, which she described as 'the best play I have written with the exception of *Witness for the Prosecution*.'

ISBN: 0 00 649045 X

ALSO BY AGATHA CHRISTIE
WRITING AS 'MARY WESTMACOTT'

Absent in the Spring

'The one book that has satisfied me completely'

Agatha Christie

Returning from a visit to her daughter in Iraq, Joan Scudamore finds herself unexpectedly alone and stranded in an isolated rest house by flooding of the railway tracks. This sudden solitude compels Joan to assess her life for the first time ever and face up to many of the truths about herself. Looking back over the years, Joan painfully re-examines her attitudes, relationships and actions and becomes increasingly uneasy about the person who is revealed to her . . .

'I've not been so emotionally moved by a story since the memorable *Brief Encounter* . . . *Absent in the Spring* is a *tour de force* which should be recognized as a classic.'

New York Times

ISBN: 0 00 649947 3

ALSO BY AGATHA CHRISTIE

While the Light Lasts
and Other Stories

Like many of her contemporaries, Agatha Christie wrote
stories for magazines in the 1920s and '30s, and most
eventually found their way into her books of short stories.
Now detective work worthy of Christie herself has un-
earthed seven 'new' stories, plus early magazine versions
of two Poirot short stories which she later extended for
book publication.

The House of Dreams is the first story Agatha Christie
ever wrote and recounts the effects of a macabre recurring
dream on a man's life. **The Actress** tells of a woman who
turns the tables on her blackmailer, **The Edge** is a grip-
ping tale of jealousy and infidelity, and in **Christmas
Adventure** Poirot is caught up in some unseasonal
mayhem. **The Lonely God** is an unlikely love story about
two lost souls who meet in the British Museum, while
in **Manx Gold** two young heroes race against time to
discover buried treasure. **Within a Wall** tells of a tragic
love triangle between a portrait painter, his wife and his
daughter's godmother, and after **The Mystery of the
Baghdad Chest**, another early Poirot story which Agatha
Christie would later rework, the book concludes with
While the Light Lasts, where a Rhodesian tobacco plan-
tation is the setting for an unexpected visitor from beyond
the grave . . .

ISBN: 0 00 651018 3

For a full list of the Agatha Christie titles available in paperback, hardback or on audio, please write to *The Agatha Christie Collection*, HarperCollins*Publishers*, 77-85 Fulham Palace Road, Hammersmith, London W6 8JB.

All Agatha Christie titles are available from your local bookseller or can be ordered direct from the publishers. To order direct just list the titles you want and fill in this form:

Name: _____

Address: _____

_____ Postcode: _____

Send to HarperCollins Mail Order, Dept 8, HarperCollins *Publishers*, Westerhill Road, Bishopbriggs, Glasgow G64 2QT.
Please enclose a cheque or postal order or your authority to debit your Visa/Mastercard account –

Credit card no: _____

Expiry date: _____ Signature: _____

to the value of the cover price plus:
UK & BFPO: Add £1.00 for the first book and 25p for each additional book ordered.
Overseas orders including Eire: Please add £2.95 service charge.
Books will be sent by surface mail but quotes for airmail despatches will be given on request.

24 HOUR TELEPHONE ORDERING SERVICE FOR MASTERCARD/VISA CARDHOLDERS – 0870 900 2050

 Due to the many and varied queries from the loyal fans of Agatha Christie it was decided to form an *Agatha Christie Society* to open the channels of communication between those fans and the various media who strive to bring her works, in their various forms, to the public.

If you wish to apply for membership of the Society, please write to:
Agatha Christie Society, PO Box 2749, London W1A 5DS

www.fireandwater.com